WILL
THEY
or
WON'T
THEY

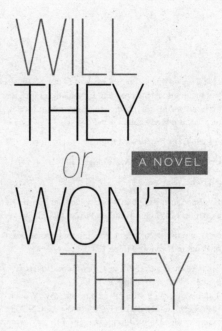

WILL
THEY
or WON'T
THEY

A NOVEL

Ava Wilder

DELL
New York

A Dell Trade Paperback Original

Copyright © 2023 by Ava Wilder, LLC

Published in the United States by Dell, an imprint of Random House, a division of Penguin Random House LLC, New York.

DELL and the D colophon are registered trademarks of Penguin Random House LLC.

LIBRARY OF CONGRESS CATALOGING-IN-PUBLICATION DATA
Names: Wilder, Ava, author.
Title: Will they or won't they: a novel / Ava Wilder.
Identifiers: LCCN 2022043769 (print) | LCCN 2022043770 (ebook) |
ISBN 9780593358979 (trade paperback) |
ISBN 9780593358986 (ebook)
Classification: LCC PS3623.I5376 W55 2023 (print) |
LCC PS3623.I5376 (ebook) | DDC 892.8—dc23/eng/20220912
LC record available at https://lccn.loc.gov/2022043769
LC ebook record available at https://lccn.loc.gov/2022043770

Printed in the United States of America on acid-free paper

randomhousebooks.com

9 8 7 6 5 4 3 2 1

Book design by Debbie Glasserman

FOR EVERYONE WHO HAD TO
PUT UP WITH ME WHILE I WAS
WORKING ON THIS.
THANK YOU, AND I'M SORRY.

WILL
THEY
or
WON'T
THEY

PROLOGUE

Eight years ago

Lilah Hunter knew better than to get her hopes up. The odds of booking something her first pilot season were slim, and even if she did, the odds of it getting picked up were even slimmer. The week before, she'd made it to the final round of callbacks for a sitcom about a group of hot young singles in some un-specified city, only to find out today she hadn't gotten it, while en route to the audition she was currently in the waiting room for.

This one seemed like even more of a long shot: co-lead of a network drama, not just a supporting character or part of an ensemble. Like most roles she was sent out for, she knew almost nothing about the show itself, other than the title (*Intangible*), her character's name (Kate), and the name of the other lead (Harrison). She'd read for it twice already, doing her best to piece together a coherent characterization out of the context-free scenes she'd been given. Whatever she'd done must've worked, though, since she'd made it all the way to the chemistry round.

There were six of them there: two other potential Kates and three Harrisons, all pretending they weren't sizing one another up. At this stage, they knew it wasn't about their individual performances anymore; it was about finding the right combination that was greater than the sum of its parts. Lilah had gotten this far on her own, but her future with *Intangible* hinged on her ability to find—or fake—an instant, palpable connection with at least one of the three random strangers sitting across from her.

But no pressure.

The other two Kates looked around her age, early to mid-twenties, but otherwise seemed superficially varied enough that it was obvious the creative team didn't have any particular type in mind. The prospective Harrisons were fairly different, too, other than checking all the basic boxes to qualify as TV handsome.

As soon as she'd walked in, her eye had immediately been drawn to one Harrison in particular. There was something less coiffed and groomed about him than the other two, less obviously telegraphing his aspirations to be a professional Beautiful Person.

He *was* beautiful, though. Long legs, long lashes, dark hair that fell over his forehead without reaching his eyes. Not just beautiful, but attractive, too—which weren't always the same thing. In her brief time in L.A., she'd already met more than her share of conventionally hot people with the charisma of a rock.

But there was something magnetic about this guy, something compulsively watchable, even as he sat there doing nothing. Maybe it was his aura of quiet confidence, out of place in a room full of people quivering with nerves.

He caught her staring at him and held her gaze before flicking his eyes over her in an appraising look that stayed just on the respectful side of leering. To her surprise, she felt her heart rate speed up slightly, her cheeks heating. She looked away so she wouldn't have to see him see her blush.

Maybe she didn't need to worry about faking the chemistry, after all.

Macy, the casting director, came out into the lobby with a clipboard. "Well, hel-*lo,* everyone," she said, beaming. "Thank you so much for coming back in today; we'll do our best to keep things moving."

She went on to explain how the six of them would be paired off and rotated so each Kate would get the chance to read with each Harrison, but all Lilah took away from it was that she'd be going last: both a blessing and a curse. Everyone would definitely be sick of hearing the scene by then, but at least she had the chance to leave the final impression.

As the first potential Kate and Harrison stood and followed Macy into the hallway, Lilah pulled the sides out of her purse. They'd already been folded and unfolded so many times that the paper had softened, in danger of slipping off the staple. She knew these lines backward and forward, but auditioning had never been her strong suit, so it was impossible to be overprepared.

Nerves crackled through her, the pages trembling slightly in her hands, and she closed her eyes, trying to breathe through it. When she was calm enough to open them again, that same Harrison was watching her. She felt her anxiety rush back, even more acutely than before. Was it possible chemistry could be a *bad* thing in this situation, if he was messing with her focus before they'd exchanged a single word?

While they waited, the two remaining auditioners struck up a conversation, quiet murmurs punctuated by skittish, too-loud laughter. Lilah let herself meet his eyes again. He looked right back, one side of his mouth curving up, revealing a dimple.

Before she could figure out what, if anything, she wanted to say, Macy came out and called him in to read with one of the other Kates. When he came back, though, he sat down in the chair next to her.

She shot him a sideways glance, but he was intently studying the script in his hands. She returned to her own sides, embarrassed. Out of the corner of her eye, she saw him fold up the pages, and when she looked back, he was looking straight at her, that dimple even more powerful up close.

"Hi," he said.

She already felt another blush creeping up her neck. "Hi."

"I'm Shane."

"Lilah."

She shook his hand, grateful he didn't mention how cold hers must feel, thanks to the combination of her nerves and the overly air-conditioned room—especially in comparison to his.

"Where are you from?" she asked. "Your accent, I mean. Texas?" The twang in his vowels was subtle enough that she might've missed it if she hadn't been taught to listen for it.

"Oklahoma." He winced. "Is it that bad?"

"No, no. Not bad at all." She bit her tongue before an *it's cute* could slip out.

"Where are *you* from?"

"Philadelphia. Right outside."

Shane's grin returned, wider than before. "Oh yeah? Say 'water.'"

She laughed. "Nice try. I just spent four years getting it trained out of me."

He laughed, too, and her stomach swooped like she'd missed a stair. "If you're trying to intimidate me with your experience, it's working."

She cast her eyes down at her script, needing a break from the tractor-beam focus of his gaze. "Is this your first pilot season?"

"My first audition, actually. Well, third, if you count the other rounds for this."

"Wow. Lucky you."

He laughed under his breath. "Tell me about it." He glanced around, then lowered his voice. "I'm not even an actor. I waited on Macy at The Vine last month, and she asked me to come in and read for it."

His devil-may-care energy suddenly made perfect sense. He wasn't like the rest of them, painfully aware they were inches away from achieving their dream but were far more likely to be smacked back down to earth. If he'd seemed at all smug or cocky about it, it probably would have killed her attraction to him right then and there. But he'd said it almost guiltily, like he knew he shouldn't be there. Like he was ashamed of even making it this far.

The fact that he *had* made it this far, though, said something.

Lilah raised an eyebrow. "So you *do* exist. I thought that kind of thing was an urban legend to get all our hopes up. Since the L.A. economy would probably collapse without the aspiring-actor-to-service-industry pipeline." She had her catering uniform stashed in her car so she could go straight from the audition to the party she was working later that night.

Shane shook his head, a self-deprecating smile creeping across his face. "I haven't given up the rest of my shifts yet, that's for damn sure."

"I'm sure this whole thing is just a formality before they cast a couple of industry kids instead. Your dad doesn't run the network, does he?"

"Not that I know of, but it's been a few weeks since we've talked." He jutted his chin at the script pages in her hand. "They tell you the twist at the end?"

"What? That you don't know you're a ghost?"

"And you don't know you're psychic."

Lilah flipped through the sides absentmindedly. "Pretty smart of them."

"What do you mean?"

"You know how these things go. I'm sure they're setting Kate and Harrison up for the long game, trying to draw out the unresolved sexual tension as long as possible. If the characters literally can't touch each other, they can coast on that for years."

"Years," he repeated, with a sardonic twitch of his eyebrows. "You really think they'll make us wait that long?"

His delivery was innocent, but when his eyes met hers, the suggestion in them made her breath hitch. She fought to keep her expression blank. "Well. It might not be us."

"Right." He nodded slowly. "Maybe that would be for the best, though. This is the kind of thing that changes the course of your whole life, right? I'm not sure I'm ready for that." Though his tone was still blasé, she sensed a hint of truth lurking beneath it.

"Not necessarily," she said. "We could shoot the pilot and then it never gets picked up. Or it gets canceled after three episodes. No matter what happens, there's, like, a ninety-nine percent chance you'll be back at The Vine by next pilot season."

He cocked his head, and she wondered if he was going to chastise her for being so cynical. Instead, his grin widened. "I like those odds. Sounds like we have nothing to worry about, then."

"No, there's always something to worry about," she said reflexively, half under her breath; but she was smiling, too, gratified when he chuckled in response.

His gaze caught on hers again, both their grins fading as their eye contact lingered, the easy rhythm of their conversation lurching to a standstill. It was a little unnerving, the way he was looking at her. Dark pupils swallowed amber irises, leaving her helpless as a trapped fly.

"We'll be okay," he said simply.

Something about the way his mouth wrapped around that "we" sparked a deeply unprofessional thrill in her lower belly—quickly overpowered by the rush of shame that followed. But that was why they were there, wasn't it? It was hard to avoid, in a situation that felt closer to speed dating than a job interview.

Feeling it was one thing. It would only be wrong to act on it.

He was close enough for her to notice he'd missed a spot shaving, a small, dark patch of stubble decorating the corner of his jaw. She found her mind drifting to what it might feel like against her lips, dragging over her skin, the thought sending a hot quiver through her.

All of a sudden she was grateful that, unlike in most chemistry reads, there would be no physical contact involved. She wouldn't have to fumble her way through touching him for the first time with a table full of strangers watching them.

For the first time? Where the fuck did that come from? Talk about getting ahead of herself. Even if they got cast, they wouldn't be touching—that was the whole point.

She realized belatedly that she'd gone way too long staring at him without saying anything. He was still watching her, the corner of his mouth quirking up in amusement. *Dimple,* she thought stupidly, involuntarily. She opened her mouth and inhaled sharply—like that would make the words come faster—then hesitated.

"Lilah? Shane?" Macy's voice came to Lilah's rescue, making her jolt. "They're ready for you."

1

As if she needed another reminder, the fact that Lilah Hunter was once again trapped alone in a room with Shane McCarthy was confirmation that her life had gone completely off the rails.

She should've prepared herself. It was only a matter of time. Luckily, he hadn't been on her flight to New York, and they hadn't run into each other at the hotel. She knew she'd be seeing him tonight, obviously. But she'd naïvely assumed that things would be hectic enough that there would always be some kind of buffer between them—that they wouldn't have to acknowledge each other, let alone interact. Not yet, anyway.

At first, she'd been correct. Just an hour ago, the backstage holding area for talent at Radio City Music Hall had been bustling with people, all assembled for the same purpose: the annual UBS upfronts, part of the most important television event of the year. Over the course of one week in May, every major network took turns revealing their fall schedules to potential sponsors, flying out their biggest stars to make their presentations as flashy as possible in an attempt to lure in advertising dollars.

She'd avoided Shane from the moment she'd entered the greenroom, but really, he'd avoided her first. When she'd walked through the door, their eyes had met immediately, and her spine had tingled with that familiar, involuntary frisson of disgust. She should've prepared herself for that, too.

If he'd seemed at all happy to see her, or even just neutral, she would've gone over and greeted him warmly like everything was fine. Really, she would have. Instead, he'd paused for a moment, face clouding, mouth tightening, before returning to his conversation, angling his back resolutely toward her. Fine. If that was how he wanted it. She'd squared her shoulders, sauntered into the room, and struck up some small talk with the first familiar face she saw.

Slowly, though, the crowd had dwindled, as people were escorted to the stage in small groups. *Intangible*'s slot was last on UBS's agenda that evening: the grand finale. They'd somehow successfully managed to keep Lilah's return to the show a secret ahead of the big reveal, which, even in a gathering of the network's best and brightest, had caused a stir when she'd first shown up backstage. She'd been a little embarrassed by the attention, but relieved for the distraction.

Now it was just the two of them, slouched on couches on opposite sides of the room, ignoring each other. Even though they'd been in the same room for more than an hour, it had still been nearly three years since they'd spoken. Since the night of her final wrap party.

Lilah felt heat rise to her face. That was the last thing she should be thinking about right now. She needed to focus. They would be called to the stage at any moment, and he was enough of a distraction as it was.

He had a beard now. His hair was longer, too, dark as ever but wavier than she'd thought it would be, the back of it almost brushing his collar. But she knew all that already. It had been impossible to avoid the ads for the last few seasons of *Intangible*. The ones without her. Shane's newly hairy face had been plastered, solo, over every billboard on Sunset.

Her throat tightened as a memory popped up, unbidden, of the first time they'd spotted an *Intangible* billboard with the two of them on it, back before the first season had even aired. They'd taken turns posing for pictures in front of it, laughing and giddy. Once they'd sent them off to their respective parents, Shane had slung one arm around her shoulders and stretched the other out as far as it could go, capturing a single blurry selfie of them together, the billboard barely in frame. That one had been just for them.

She let out an exhale that was louder than she intended, so loud it bordered on a sigh. Shane's eyes flicked over to her, just for a heartbeat, then away again. Lilah stared at her lap. This whole thing was a mistake, the latest in a long line of them. She couldn't unburn this bridge, no matter how much money they'd thrown at her to rebuild it.

"Nice hair."

Lilah whipped her head up to see Shane looking at her, almost bored, from under half-lidded eyes. Her hand flew above her shoulder, fingering the ends of her hair involuntarily. She'd cut it to her chin several months ago in a fit of acute emotional distress (as was the case with most drastic haircuts).

His tone was so bland that it was hard to tell whether he was being sincere or sarcastic. When it came to Shane, the least char-itable reading was usually the correct one. He wasn't wrong, though. This particular cut, still overly feathered and layered even after months of growing it out, wasn't doing her any favors. It looked okay tonight, after being professionally wrangled ahead of the event, but most days it felt like one more mistake staring back at her in the mirror.

She dropped her hand and crossed her arms, trying to match his sardonic inflection.

"Thanks. Nice beard."

Unfortunately, his beard *did* look good, but hopefully her delivery was ambiguous enough to plant those same seeds of self-doubt. If it worked, he showed no sign of it.

"Thanks."

He held her gaze for a long moment, inhaling sharply like he was about to say something else. But instead, he just shook his head slightly, smirked, and looked away.

"What?" she asked before she could help herself.

He met her eyes again. "Bet you never thought you'd end up back here again, huh?" The superficial friendliness only made the bitter undertone more stark.

There was no point in responding. It wasn't a real question. Of course she never thought she'd end up back here. He obvi-ously hadn't, either. Otherwise they wouldn't have spent her final weeks on the show adding a few last-minute items to their endless list of grievances against each other.

He shifted positions, leaning forward to rest his elbows loosely on his knees. From the way his neck craned toward the door, he was clearly as eager to get out of there as she was. He muttered something under his breath.

"Sorry? I didn't catch that," Lilah said crisply.

He turned back to her. "I said, *this is bullshit*." Every word was perfectly enunciated this time.

She forced herself to take a deep breath, but it didn't help; her tone was just as venomous as his. "Well, it wasn't my idea. *Believe* me."

A flicker of amusement crossed his face, relieving some of the tension pulsating between them. "Oh, I know. I saw your movie." He winced.

Lilah fought the blush rising to her cheeks as she glowered at him.

It had seemed like a no-brainer to leave the show at the time. She'd been there for five seasons, her contract was up, her star was on the rise, and things between her and Shane were as bad as they'd ever been. They barely said a word to each other that wasn't in the script. So, naturally, she'd jumped at the offer of what seemed like her dream role: a feature adaptation of an award-winning journalist's memoir about his relationship with his troubled mother, helmed by a legendary director she'd been dying to work with.

In retrospect, the fact that they were willing to cast a twenty-seven-year-old in a role that spanned the ages of thirty-five to seventy should've been her first hint that things were creatively awry behind the scenes. Still, Lilah had thrown everything she had into her performance, ignoring the misgivings that piled higher and higher as the shoot went on, writing them off as the standard insecurities that came from pushing herself as an actor for the first time in years.

She'd known for sure that she was in trouble before they'd even wrapped, when an unflattering candid picture of her on set in her old-age makeup had leaked and gone viral, instantly taking off as a humiliating meme. Her own sister had texted it to her with the caption "You after seeing this picture for the millionth time." That was the only one she'd laughed at.

The movie itself had fared even worse, hailed as a career low for everyone involved. Not just mediocre but laughably bad—an instant camp classic. When she'd first received the script, she'd been practicing her Oscar acceptance speech in the shower; by the time the movie was released, she was contemplating whether to go pick up her Razzie in person. For the next year, she couldn't get an offer for anything more substantial than a birth control commercial.

But, thankfully, *Intangible* had been just as desperate as she was. Despite their best efforts, the ratings had plummeted without her. Lilah didn't let it go to her head. They'd be in the same situation if Shane had left instead of her. No matter how the two of them felt about each other when the cameras were off, it was the chemistry between their characters, Kate and Harrison, that made the show worth watching. She knew it. He knew it. The whole fucking world knew it.

And so, mistake or not, she'd agreed to come back for one last season.

At first, it had seemed like a lifeline. A starring role in a hit TV show wasn't a worst-case scenario by any standard. But she'd gotten a taste of what was in store for her when she'd stepped backstage and every head in the room had turned practically in unison. Some people had seemed happy to see her, sure, but there'd been just as many that had raised their eyebrows and turned away, her former (and future) costar leading the charge.

She didn't blame them. She understood. She'd abandoned the people who'd given her her break, then come crawling back once her reach for bigger and better things had exceeded her grasp. Her stomach roiled at the thought of how the cast and crew of *Intangible* would treat her once she was back on set.

Based on the icy reception she was getting from the cast member sitting across from her, it wasn't promising. But that was par for the course with him.

Just then, the door cracked open, and a production assistant poked her head in.

"Lilah? Shane? Come along with me."

Lilah stood, smoothing her skirt, and quickened her pace to catch up with Shane, who was already halfway out the door. With the boost from her not-so-high heels, they were the same height—six-two, give or take a slouch. She'd always been grateful that she was allowed to wear comfortable shoes whenever they had to stand next to each other, since she'd be taller than him in anything above three inches (which would obviously confuse and distress the audience). She jutted her chin high, trying to elongate herself as much as possible as she walked beside him, matching him stride for stride. She wanted whatever edge on him she could get.

The PA led them to a spot in the wings and handed each of them a cordless mic. "Just wait here until he introduces you," she stage-whispered before disappearing again.

Lilah stood still, every muscle rigid, trying to ignore the sensation of Shane's eyes burning into her. Her stomach twisted when she caught a whiff of his soap—faint, but still painfully familiar. Only when he looked away again did she allow herself to sneak another glance at him.

Now that she was closer, she could see the light from the stage glinting off the handful of new grays threaded through his dark hair. Her gaze moved past the angular jawline she knew was hiding under his beard, drifting down to his suit—oxblood, expensive-looking, perfectly tailored to shoulders and biceps that were definitely broader than they used to be.

The first time they'd done this, he'd shown up way overdressed, wearing a cheap rented tuxedo that was somehow too big and too small at the same time—not that she had room to judge, in an obnoxiously trendy dress she'd maxed out her credit card to buy, carefully tucking the tags back inside after she'd zipped it up. She'd teased him about it anyway: *I didn't realize we were going to junior prom.*

What do you want me to do with your corsage, then? he'd replied with a grin.

With effort, she redirected her attention back to what she could see of the stage. Hal Kagan, the president of UBS, was presenting the Tuesday night lineup, sounding only moderately stilted as he read off the teleprompter.

"Almost a decade ago, I stood on this stage introducing you to a pilot that would go on to become one of our most popular shows: the one-hour supernatural drama *Intangible*." He paused for applause. "But, unfortunately, all good things must come to an end. *Intangible* will be wrapping up next year after nine incredible seasons, and you better believe we're sending it off with a bang. First, let's take a look back at some of Kate and Harrison's most memorable moments over the years."

Hal stepped off to the other side of the stage, and the lights dimmed. Though Lilah couldn't see the screen, her brain easily filled in the images from the pilot that accompanied the blaring audio. Kate and Harrison's first meeting had been her audition sides. By now, eight years on, most of the material was a blur—memorized, shot, then promptly forgotten—but she could still recite that scene by heart.

"What do you want?" She sounded so young, her voice higher and breathier than she ever remembered it being.

"Well, actually, I was hoping you could help me figure that out," Shane drawled in response. Even without seeing it, she knew he was giving her The Look, the one that had made her lines tum-

ble right out of her head at their chemistry read. She'd been sure her flub had cost her the role, only to find out later that it was the moment that convinced the network to cast them both.

The next five seasons flew by in a montage set to a high-octane cover of the theme song: the two of them bickering, bantering, solving supernatural mysteries (most of which conveniently took place in the L.A. metro area), and, of course, staring longingly at each other when they thought the other one wasn't looking.

The overarching storyline for the fifth season had centered around Kate and Harrison's mission to restore Harrison's corporeal form, bringing him back to life. In the season finale, it seemed like they'd accomplished it, falling into each other's arms at long last—only for Kate to go limp, her life force drained as an unexpected side effect.

Shane's overamplified sobs filled the theater.

"Kate . . . oh my god, please, no . . . please . . . you can't leave me, not now . . . Kate . . . KATE!"

Lilah swore she could hear scattered sniffles throughout the auditorium. Even she had to admit that she'd been impressed by Shane's performance; she hadn't thought he'd had it in him. She'd been less impressed by the garlic bagel with extra lox he'd eaten right before shooting it and had used every last scrap of her training to keep her face relaxed as he exhaled cured fish breath directly into it.

The video ended to applause, and the lights came back up as Hal returned to the stage.

"Though we couldn't be prouder of the last three seasons, the relationship between Kate and Harrison has always been the heart of the show." He paused for dramatic effect. "Ladies and gentlemen . . . I am *thrilled* to announce that Lilah Hunter will be returning for *Intangible's* ninth and final season."

The end of his sentence was swallowed by riotous cheers. Lilah could practically feel the annoyance radiating off Shane in waves. Hal continued, "Please welcome to the stage the stars of *Intangible*: Shane McCarthy and Lilah Hunter!"

At least Hal had said Shane's name first, she thought ruefully. That should pacify his ego a little.

Lilah slapped on a smile and angled herself out toward the blinding lights, walking a few steps behind Shane, both of them waving as the audience roared. Shane and Hal shook hands, and Lilah ducked down to kiss Hal on the cheek.

Shane turned toward the crowd and raised his microphone. "Thank you." He cleared his throat, glancing over at Lilah. "I think I speak for both of us when I say that we've been so grateful for this entire journey, especially the fact that we get to finish it the way we started: together."

He took a step toward her, and her stomach bottomed out. Before she knew what was happening, he'd reached down and taken her hand, drawing her closer—platonic, but undeniably intimate. All she could do was gape at him, and there it was: The Look, larger than life, his face inches from hers, without even giving her time to brace for impact. It was so fucking unfair that it still had this much of an effect on her after all these years, after everything they'd been through. Lilah struggled to regain her composure.

"Absolutely," she finally managed, beaming at him before turning her face back to the crowd. "I—*we*—are so excited to have the opportunity to give Kate and Harrison the ending they deserve."

"Thank you again for all the love you've shown them, and us, over the years. We wouldn't be here without you." Shane gave her hand one last squeeze before releasing her.

Numbly, she followed him offstage, unable to feel her legs,

the cheers echoing in her ears. Another PA escorted them down to the stage door, where a long line of town cars was waiting outside to ferry them back to their hotel.

Lilah glanced at the tense set of Shane's jaw, the hard line between his eyebrows. His face was already scrubbed clean of every last trace of the warmth and affection he'd oozed moments earlier. She wondered if he was thinking about the same thing she was: their first time at upfronts, exactly eight years ago, right after *Intangible* had been picked up.

The first time they'd slept together.

They'd closed down the hotel bar after UBS's presentation, the attraction that had been simmering between them since before they'd shot the pilot coming to a boil at last. The pseudo-innocent touches—accidental knee brushes, lips murmuring against cheeks, hands pressed to forearms or lower backs—becoming more intentional, more heated, until she'd returned from the bathroom and he'd slid his arm around her waist, pulling her into his lap like it was inevitable. Like she'd been there the whole time.

Being back here with him now, all those firsts and lasts and never agains were as sharp and vivid as they'd ever been, forming a knot of unease in her chest that made it difficult to breathe.

It wasn't until Shane met her eyes that she realized she was still staring at him. Lilah quickly redirected her gaze straight ahead.

"Would you like to ride together or separately?" the PA chirped.

"Separately," they replied in unison.

2

There were forty-four Lilah Hunter–less days between the UBS upfronts and the first table read of the season, and Shane enjoyed every last one of them. He'd had only one close call—when he'd gone in to shoot the first promotional images for season nine—but, as they'd done it since the second season, the two of them were photographed in separate sessions and composited together afterward.

On day forty-three, Shane pulled his car up to the valet at The Vine, where he was meeting his agent for lunch. He was early, but Renata was earlier, already perched against the floral throw pillows as the hostess led Shane through the packed back patio.

The Vine wouldn't have been his first choice, but he knew why Renata had picked it. One, it was the place to go when you wanted to be sure you'd be seen. And two, it was where he'd been, quote-unquote, "discovered." Ironically, he'd been one of the only staff members who wasn't actively trying to break into the business at the time—a fact that made him deeply unpopular once the news of his audition had gotten around. It was a good thing he'd gotten the part, since he probably would've had to find another job no matter what.

In a way, his career had started in reverse, his agent search only beginning after he had already booked the show. He'd signed with Renata because she was the only one who hadn't promised to make him the next Ethan Atkins in five years or less. It also didn't hurt that, with her loud ex-smoker rasp and shrewd eyes, she was a dead ringer for his favorite aunt, the one who'd been married five times (but to only three different husbands).

Eight years into their working relationship, he still had no idea whether he'd made the right call, since she'd never actually gotten him a single audition—but then, he hadn't wanted any. *Intangible* shot twelve to sixteen hours a day, nine months out of the year, and he preferred not to fill his time off with even more work. But now, for the first time in his career, he had choices to make.

It was still borderline surreal to him sometimes, the fact that he even had a career, that people thought of him as an actor at all. He knew Lilah didn't, at least. To Ms. Classically Trained Juilliard MFA, he would always be a waiter who got lucky.

"Hi, sweetheart." Renata rose to give him a hug, her perfume embracing him long before she did. They had barely settled into their seats before she started peppering him with questions.

"Are you an oyster guy? I can never remember who is and who isn't. You wouldn't be interested in splitting the cold seafood platter for two, would you? No? Well, never hurts to ask."

As soon as the hostess left the table, Renata planted her chin on her hands and smiled warmly at him.

"So. *Intangible*'s finally kicking the bucket."

"That's what they tell me."

Her brow creased. "How are you feeling about everything?" He knew what she was really asking: *How are you feeling about working with Lilah again?*

The fucked-up thing was, when they'd first told him Lilah was coming back, for a split second, he'd actually been happy about it.

Thankfully, that feeling had passed almost immediately. Then he'd tried to do everything in his power to stop it from happening.

Unfortunately, it turned out his power was not as far-reaching as he'd hoped. The producer credit Renata had negotiated for him before season six was nothing more than a salary bump and an empty title. Besides, as successful as *Intangible* had been in its prime, he knew it was running on borrowed time at this point—especially in a television landscape that had changed drastically over the past decade. He couldn't blame them for resorting to this kind of cheap stunt to keep all their jobs around for another year, give them the chance to go out on their own terms.

Shane shrugged, looking down at his menu. "Hopefully there's life after life after death."

Renata fixed him with a calculating stare, then clearly decided not to push it. She unfolded her napkin and placed it on her lap with a flourish. "Well, that's exactly why we're here.

You're in a very delicate position right now, and we want to make sure your next move is the right one."

"Isn't it a little early for this conversation? I won't be free again until next summer."

"I don't have any hard offers or anything. But it's a good time to think about what's important to you, what you want the next stage of your career to look like. This is a real turning point for you. There's a lot of buzz around the show right now, which is good, but it's a double-edged sword, because people only see you as Harrison. A lot of actors have trouble following up an iconic TV role like that. You don't want to go too similar and pigeonhole yourself, but you don't want to go too far in the other direction, either."

Shane nodded slowly. Tendrils of anxiety curled up his spine, threatening to wrap around him. Harrison was essentially a heightened version of himself—especially after eight seasons of the writers tailoring the role to him—and he'd never tried to do anything else. Any attempt to move in a different direction might end up being a short stroll with a long drop. There was no way to find out without risking total public humiliation, the kind he'd seen Lilah try her best to weather over the past few years. The kind that had sunk her career low enough that she needed to come back to the show for a hard reset. But now that it was ending, he wouldn't have that safety net anymore.

"I think stability is the most important thing to me right now. If I could get another regular gig like this one, I'd be flexible about what it was."

The waiter came by to refill Renata's sweet tea and take their orders. She took a long sip before setting the glass down with a satisfied exhale.

"How do you feel about superheroes? I don't know about an

offer, but I could definitely get you an audition. What about a villain? That might be fun for you."

Shane leaned back in his chair, considering it. "Would I have to get jacked?"

"Probably."

"Pass." He was in decent shape, but judging by how miserable he was every time he had to spend a few weeks cutting carbs for the occasional shirtless scene on *Intangible,* he probably wasn't cut out for sacrificing months (if not years) of his life to brutal workouts and strictly regimented meal plans. Plus, his other least-favorite shooting days were the ones in which he had to act against a green screen. He doubted he could pull off an entire movie of reacting to nothing.

Renata pursed her lips. "It's your call. But if you want my advice, I wouldn't rule it out entirely. You want stability, that's a good wagon to try to hitch on to."

"What are my other options?"

She sighed, plucking a roll out of the bread basket. "Okay. Opposite direction. I got a tip that Perry McAllister is developing an F. Scott Fitzgerald biopic, but they're still working on getting the script together. I think you'd be perfect for it, if you're interested. It's a bit of a gamble, but you'd have your pick of projects if you pull it off. Could really show your range, maybe even be an awards contender. Perry has a pretty good track record."

He had another jolt of nerves, so quick and strong that he physically shivered. *If I even have any range.*

"Maybe. What else?"

"*Anna Karenina?* There's a new miniseries in the works, and you've already got the beard."

"I'm not sure I have a Russian accent in me."

Renata waved her hand dismissively. "They'd want British. You've never seen a period piece?"

Shane grimaced. His accent work was limited to either toning down or amping up his own. "I don't know . . ."

Renata barked out a laugh. "So you don't want commercial, and you don't want prestige. You're about to lose your spot at the top of my Easiest Clients list."

Shane drained his water glass. "What about another show? Not just a miniseries. Anything there?"

They were interrupted by the waiter stopping by to deposit their entrees: shrimp tacos for him, Margherita pizza for her.

Renata delicately separated a slice from the rest of her pie. "Too early to tell on that front, but I'll keep an ear out as we get closer to pilot season." She took a bite, hesitating as she chewed. "Actually . . . there is one thing. But I already know you're not gonna like it."

Shane squeezed his lime wedge over his tacos. "What is it?"

Renata set down her pizza slice. "UBS approached me about a new prime-time game show for next season. They want you to host. Keeping things in the family, and all that."

Shane perked up. Hosting was definitely in his skill set. If nothing else, he was charming—at least, most people not named Lilah Hunter seemed to think so. And even she had, once upon a time. "Why wouldn't I like it? What's the show?"

She sighed. "It's called *I'm Not Swallowing That*. Contestants try to catch each other lying, and if they do, the one that gets caught has to eat something disgusting. Supposedly it's a huge hit in the UK."

"They have to eat it, or they have to swallow it?"

Renata rolled her eyes. "I don't know. I assume chewing's a personal choice."

"How much are they offering?"

"A fuckload." She raised her eyebrows. "You're actually considering it?"

He leaned back in his chair and ran his hand over his beard. "I mean . . . it would probably be a long-term job, right?"

"Could be. That kind of thing either gets canceled halfway through the first episode or runs for fifteen years. But it would be very hard—maybe impossible—for people to think of you as a serious actor again after doing something like that."

Shane was silent, holding the question on the tip of his tongue: *Am I a serious actor now?* He'd never admitted the extent of his insecurities to Renata, though he sensed she picked up on it somewhat. He wasn't sure what he was more afraid of: that she'd lie to him, or that she'd tell him the truth.

Renata gave him a sharp look, the corner of her mouth turning up sardonically. "Well, if you're open to that one, I got a script the other day you're gonna love. You're a struggling single dad who hires a new nanny, but there's a big mix-up, and you end up with—wait for it—a monkey."

Shane burst out laughing. Renata kept her expression stern, though he could tell she was struggling to maintain it as she continued. "The monkey would be CGI, if that's what you're worried about."

"*Renata.*"

Renata smiled, dabbing her lips with her napkin. "Good to know you still have some sense left." She put it down, the humor draining from her expression. "I don't want to pry. But is everything . . . okay with you? Moneywise?"

Shane shrugged. "Yeah, fine. I'd just like to keep making it, is all." His own lifestyle wasn't especially lavish, but he'd just bought his parents a new house and promised his sister college tuition for all three of her kids. Plus, even though Shane wasn't directly subsidizing him, his brother, Dean, had been working as his stand-in since season two. If Shane had an extended spell of unemployment, it would affect more than just him.

"Just checking. You have a money guy, right? I can give you some names, if you need them."

"I've mostly been sticking with gold bars under the mattress. Better safe than sorry."

"Sounds lumpy. My condolences to your overnight guests."

"You know I'm saving myself for marriage," he said innocently.

Renata grinned. "You're lucky you're so cute, so you can get away with being such a smart-ass." She stacked the crusts of her pizza neatly on the corner of her plate. "Which reminds me. I can tell you don't want to talk about it, but: you and Lilah. Anything I need to know about?"

Shane narrowly avoided choking on his taco. "What do you mean?" he managed between sips of water. "I've barely seen her. Production hasn't even started yet."

"Word at upfronts was the two of you were pretty frosty to each other backstage. I know you aren't thrilled to be working with her again. Do you need me to step in at all?"

He shook his head. "I don't think so. Me and Lilah . . . we'll figure it out."

Even as he said it, it seemed impossible—but they didn't have a choice. They were both adults, both professionals. Most important, their profession literally revolved around their ability to convincingly mask their true feelings. But nothing could've prepared him for the wave of anger and resentment, fresh as ever, that had crashed over him as soon as he'd spotted her in that greenroom, framed in the doorway, their eyes locking instantly.

Renata searched his face, brow furrowed. "Okay. Just let me know if there's anything I can do. I hope you do work it out, though. You two were adorable together."

"You mean Kate and Harrison were adorable together."

"Of course," she replied smoothly. He forced a smile.

"Well. That's why she's back, I guess."

"Exactly. Everyone's finally getting what they want." Renata jabbed a seafoam talon in his direction. "Now the next step is figuring out what *you* want."

He felt his smile falter. That was the million-dollar question. But right now, the only question on his mind was whether it was possible for both him and Lilah to exit this final season in one piece. And as the clock ran down on his last day of freedom, the lump of dread in his stomach growing larger by the hour, life after *Intangible* seemed further away than ever.

3

The production offices for *Intangible* were nestled in the Valley, on the same back lot where they shot the interiors. Even when the traffic was bad, it never took Lilah more than thirty minutes to get there from her house in Beachwood Canyon—the main reason she'd settled there in the first place.

The show had offered her a driver, of course, but she'd always been a nervous passenger—plus, she got carsick in the back seat. Ever since the first season, driving herself had been an essential part of her routine, a meditative buffer at the beginning and end of her workday. She'd driven down that same stretch of the 101 dozens of times since she'd quit without so much as a second thought. But now, en route to the table read, she was hounded by memory after memory that, up until this moment, she thought she'd successfully suppressed.

The first day, when she'd overestimated the amount of time it would take her to get there from her Los Feliz sublet, and arrived so early she'd sat in the parking lot for an hour.

The beginning of things with Shane. The pains they'd taken to hide it from everyone else. She'd roll out of his bed (or he out of hers) and they'd stagger their arrivals, each of them commuting alone, floating in on the fizzy high of good sex and secrets.

Then, when everything had blown up after the first season wrapped, her knuckles would clench white on her steering wheel every morning, her mind racing, and she'd try her best to put on a professional face and leave her irritation confined to the doors of her sedan. But once the sharpest edges had dulled, she'd spent most of the subsequent drives staring blankly out at the highway, arriving on set or back in her driveway with zero memory of how she got there.

This drive, though, felt interminable. It wasn't her performance she was nervous about—as expected, she wouldn't be appearing in the episode until the very last page, resurrected as a ghost without any memory of her former life. She could've predicted that they would want to drag out Kate and Harrison's final arc for as long as they could. That's why people were watching, after all.

But that was the irony. As much as the fans were dying for them to get together, it would've been the kiss of death for the show once it actually happened. That tension was the engine that kept it running. As soon as they consummated things, either the relationship would become bloodless and boring or the writers would have to resort to an endless cycle of breakups, makeups, and manufactured drama.

The promise of their relationship—the fantasy of what could

be—was what was appealing. Not the reality, after the honeymoon period was over and one heart or another had been broken, when they couldn't be in the same room without sniping at, undermining, or just plain ignoring each other.

And, as expected, without that engine, the well-oiled machine of *Intangible* had begun to falter. After some trial and error, it had shifted to a Shane-led ensemble cast, picking up some recurring characters from previous seasons and adding a few new ones.

Which meant that Lilah was about to walk into what felt like the first day at a new school, but worse. She wasn't coming in with a clean slate, the chance to reinvent herself. All she could do was keep her head down, do her job, and hope Shane hadn't turned too many people against her while she was gone.

On the passenger seat next to her was a box of vegan, gluten-free, refined-sugar-free donuts—her signature move when she wanted to win new people over with treats, without alienating them further by offering something most of them would refuse to eat. Mitzi's was a neighborhood favorite and one of L.A.'s best-kept secrets, since somehow, despite not containing any ingredients that would indicate it, the donuts were genuinely delicious.

Lilah balanced the box on her hip and slung her bag over her shoulder as she headed toward the entrance, breathing a sigh of relief when the door buzzed and clicked open without issue at the press of her key card. As she padded down the hallway toward the main bullpen, the uncanny feeling of déjà vu mixed with dread got stronger with every step.

She rounded the corner and yelped as she nearly collided with Walt London, *Intangible*'s showrunner. Walt looked stricken—but then, he kind of always looked like that. He was in his early forties, tall, pale, and sallow, with long black hair and three deeply etched lines on his forehead that reminded her of dragging the end of a paper clip through Silly Putty.

Walt had been running *Intangible* since the third season, after the show's creator, Ruth Edwards, had departed due to creative clashes with the network. Once he'd been hired, the tone had shifted drastically. *Intangible* had started as a quirky, somewhat philosophical exploration of grief, with the ghost characters filling a role that was as equal parts metaphorical as it was paranormal. Walt's main innovation had been to bring in every mythological creature under the sun, as well as open the show up to the world of larger supernatural conspiracies (government and otherwise).

Lilah had been less than thrilled about the turn things had taken, but she couldn't deny it got results. The show had been a breakout hit in its first season, but by the end of season two, the ratings had hit a slump. After Walt took over, they reclaimed their spot as the top show in their time slot. Until she left, that is.

When Walt realized it was her, he smiled, an expression that somehow only made him look more worried.

"Lilah, hey. Good to see you."

It was difficult to tell if he still had hard feelings about her departure, since hard feelings seemed to be the only kind he had. She'd already met with both him and the network months ago, ahead of her return, and he'd seemed just as distressed then as he did now.

She nodded at him. "You, too. Is everyone else here already?"

He shook his head. "They're still trickling in. You know how it is." That was one of his catchphrases, almost always delivered with a world-weary exhale. Whenever he deployed it, the only option was to nod contemplatively, even if she did not, in fact, know how it was.

She nodded contemplatively. "Cool. I'm just gonna put these down, then."

His gaze alighted on the box in her arms. "Oh. That's nice of you. I think Shane brought something, too."

Lilah felt her smile falter. Of course he had. The annoying thing was, Shane was so naturally goddamn likable, he didn't even *need* to bribe anyone with baked goods.

"Great," she said, resuscitating her smile so forcefully she thought she might pull a muscle. "See you in there." She moved to pass him, but Walt put his hand on her forearm, stopping her in her tracks.

"Listen." His expression was dire. "I just want you to know that I'm glad you're back. No matter what . . . whatever anyone else may think. You're an essential part of the show. You and Shane . . . you're our anchors. Our North Stars. Remember that."

Her mouth suddenly went dry. "I think there's only one North Star."

He inclined his head gruffly and shrugged. "Well. You know how it is." He released her arm and continued his journey down the hall. Lilah took a deep breath, heart hammering in her ears, and pushed open the door that led to the writers' floor.

The *Intangible* offices were drab and unpretentious: fluorescent lighting, nubby gray carpet, the lingering smell of stale coffee. It was only the framed promo posters from past seasons lining the walls—plus the shelf sporting a handful of Emmys and Golden Globes—that separated it from any run-of-the-mill accounting firm or insurance office. As far as Lilah could tell, nothing had changed since the last time she'd been there.

In the center of the room were four long folding tables arranged in a square shape, surrounded by molded plastic chairs. On the tables were lines of tented cards, one in front of each chair, each printed with a different name. Even though she couldn't see hers, she knew exactly where she'd be: right next to Shane.

He was already at the table, studying his script. She was a little surprised not to see him mingling; there were at least a dozen people in the room—actors, writers, producers, assorted coordinators and assistants—mostly gathered around the table by the wall where the coffee was laid out.

As she approached the group, her eyes instinctively glued on Shane, she considered Walt's comments. She and Shane did have a responsibility to lead the show. Could they put aside their history, their differences, their long-simmering resentments—at least for the next few months? After all, they'd gotten along once before, though that practically felt like a fever dream at this point. But wasn't it a little immature, after all these years, to still hate him as fervently as if he'd wronged her yesterday?

Maybe the tension between them at upfronts was just a fluke, the last of the residual poison working its way out of their systems. Maybe they'd both changed. Grown up. Now that she was in her thirties, having a nemesis felt slightly undignified, anyway.

Once she got closer to the coffee station, though, all thoughts of a cease-fire evaporated. On the table, lying open next to the mugs, was a pink cardboard box with pale green flowers around the border. An identical box to the one she had braced against her hip.

That motherfucker.

She dumped the box on the table, not even bothering to open it before turning on her heel and making a beeline for Shane, who still seemed oblivious that she was even in the room.

Don't say anything. Don't say anything. You can still take the high road. Just brush it off.

"You're such a dick," she muttered as she slid into her seat, the high road so deserted there were probably tumbleweeds blowing across it.

"Nice to see you, too, Lilah," he replied coolly, his eyes never leaving his script.

"*I* told you about Mitzi's donuts. You knew I'd bring them today. This is petty, even for you."

"And this is self-involved, even for *you*. I wanted to do something nice for the first day back. Who says it has anything to do with you?"

"It's not even in your neighborhood. You had to go totally out of your way to get them."

"Oh yeah. I guess I did." He finally looked up at her, that familiar lopsided smirk creeping lazily across his face.

She kept her tone nonchalant, though inside she was seething. "Well. I hope it was worth it."

He shrugged, returning to his script. "I don't know what you're so upset about. All I see are two identical boxes of donuts. Unless you had each of yours inscribed with 'Courtesy of Lilah Hunter' in icing so everyone knows who to thank." He punctuated his sentence with an enormous bite of the half-eaten vanilla-lavender donut in front of him, releasing a moan so loud it bordered on orgasmic. A few heads turned in their direction.

It was uncanny how quickly he had her careening from angry to gaslit to belittled to ashamed—all over something as insignificant as donuts. He was right. It didn't matter that he'd brought his own box. But there was no doubt in her mind that he'd done it to rile her up and then make her feel ridiculous for even caring; and, of course, it had worked. It always did.

No one else knew how to push her buttons quite like Shane. She just wished he didn't feel the need to pounce on every opportunity to do so.

Lilah pushed her chair back with a dull scrape against the

carpet and took off in the direction of the bathroom without another word.

She wasn't going there to hide. That would be beneath her. She was thirty-one years old, and, as much as it might feel like it right now, she wasn't in high school anymore. She just needed to be alone for a second. And if that second happened to last all thirteen minutes before the table read started, well, that was just a coincidence.

She locked herself in the farthest stall from the door, plunked herself on the toilet, lid down, and scrolled idly through her phone. She was halfway through responding to a text from her sister asking how things were going (which mainly involved searching for the GIF of Real Housewife Dorinda Medley shouting "Not well, bitch!") when she heard the door of the bathroom open, along with the tail end of a conversation.

". . . that they showed at upfronts. Apparently it was the Kate and Harrison show."

Lilah froze as a stall door swung shut near the bathroom's entrance.

"I mean, what did you expect? We might as well be extras now that she's back." This voice sounded closer to Lilah, next to the sink.

"I know. It's such bullshit. And here I thought I might actually get a decent storyline this year."

"Wanna trade? *I* get to be the bitch that's keeping them apart."

The first woman laughed, flushing the toilet and emerging from the stall. "Noooo thank you. You better lock down your Instagram now, before the Karrisons come for you."

The second woman groaned. "God. Maybe I should go into witness protection. Just, like, fuck it, new identity."

Lilah's stomach twisted, her mind racing. Her first instinct was to get defensive. *Fuck 'em*. If they wanted to resent her for something that was out of her control—tilting the balance of the show back toward her and Shane—there was nothing she could do about it. But maybe that was unfair. It wouldn't hurt her to be the bigger person in this situation, especially since they were upset about the *idea* of her, not anything she'd done.

Should she go out there and confront them, break the ice, get it all out in the open now? Or just pretend she'd never heard it, and try to kill them with kindness once she met them? She sat, stone-still, paralyzed with indecision, as the two of them laughed and chattered their way back out of the bathroom.

After a long, slow count of ten, she followed them.

· · ·

Shane had always had a thing for redheads.

Not that he was weird about it or anything. For the most part, he didn't have much of a physical type, his mind wandering whenever bro-talk inevitably turned to debating the hierarchy of tits versus asses. It felt like a Frankenstein-esque approach to attraction, one that had never resonated with him. He'd dated and slept with women of a variety of shapes, sizes, and backgrounds (and hair colors, for the record), and found it was usually the complete package that did it for him, rather than any individual piece.

But all that aside, there was only one feature guaranteed to turn his head every time. Real or fake, it didn't matter. He wasn't sure if he'd always been wired that way, or if he'd just seen *Who Framed Roger Rabbit* one too many times at an impressionable age. Whatever it was, it had started early, it was embedded deep, and it was completely out of his control.

Which was why, the first time he'd met Lilah, it had felt like some kind of cosmic plan—which would later feel more like a cosmic prank. Like the *Intangible* creative team had reached into the depths of his subconscious and pulled her right out of his horny teenage fantasies.

The worst part was, her hair was just the cherry on top, so to speak. She didn't have a bad angle—not to be taken for granted in their line of work. He should know. He'd logged more than enough hours spitefully studying her, trying his damndest to catch a glimpse of something weak or drooping or asymmetrical.

But unfortunately, no matter the perspective, she was all angular jawline, cut glass cheekbones, eyes and lips that were about 30 percent bigger than they rightfully should've been. His Botticelli wet dream come to life, sent from hell to drive him crazy.

And, since she was a natural redhead, her skin was covered head to toe in a constellation of golden-brown freckles that were only visible up close. More than once, he'd attempted to count them all as she giggled and squirmed beneath him, always getting too distracted somewhere in the low double digits to finish. But that might as well have been a lifetime ago at this point.

That was the problem with fantasies. They were shallow, passive, one-sided. Easily controlled. They always crumbled under the revelation that the object of your desire was not, in fact, an object but a flawed, willful, three-dimensional human being. No fantasy could withstand what the two of them had been through: the years of grudges and ego clashes and betrayals, amplified by a demanding schedule that had them spending every waking minute together.

Lilah wasn't his dream. She was just a person. A person who, most of the time, he couldn't fucking stand—and it was no secret the feeling was mutual. For the most part, they'd become experts at ignoring each other whenever they were off camera.

It was the only way to survive working in such close contact with a hostile ex.

Still, he'd never been able to shake his constant, involuntary awareness of her, like there was some Lilah-specific radar burrowed deep beneath his skin that couldn't help but ping out a warning whenever she was in close proximity. Worse, it seemed like their time apart had only made it stronger: without even looking up, he immediately knew when she'd returned to the bullpen. But maybe he could just tell from the way the chatter around him suddenly dipped in volume, full-throated conversations turning to murmurs several long moments before she slid back into her seat beside him.

Walt stood up from his seat on Shane's other side and cleared his throat, prompting the last stragglers to find their spots.

"Morning, everyone. I'm so thrilled to see all your gorgeous faces here to kick off season nine. The big finish." The furrow in his brow and the hard set of his mouth made him look anything but thrilled. "First of all, I'd like to welcome back Lilah Hunter. For those of you who don't know Lilah yet, she's incredibly talented, hardworking, and professional, and we're very lucky to have her back in the *Intangible* family."

Shane looked down at his script as a modest smattering of applause traveled around the room. He didn't join in.

Walt had them all go around the table and briefly introduce themselves before kicking off the reading without much fanfare. Shane struggled to keep his focus, feeling uncharacteristically self-conscious.

He'd sat beside her at dozens of table reads, of course, but this one felt different. Before, even if they hadn't gotten along, she'd still belonged there. Now, she felt like an interloper, sitting there in stiff, judgmental silence. He could practically feel her scrutinizing his every line reading, whether he'd gotten worse in the three years she'd been gone.

But when they reached her one and only line—the final line of the episode—it was obvious she hadn't been paying as close attention as he'd assumed. She still appeared to be studying her script, but as the silence stretched, every eye in the room turning toward her, she was clearly zoned out, lost in her own world. When she looked up again, it was to meet his gaze with a scowl—though it only took a second for her to realize her mistake.

"Oh! Um. Sorry." She fumbled with her script before looking over at Shane again, her eyes wide and limpid. "Wh-where am I? Who are you?"

Her transformation was so seamless that he'd almost believe she wasn't flustered, if her cheeks and neck weren't stained scarlet. She'd always blushed easily—her only tell. He used to relish his ability to trigger it: undeniable physical proof that she wasn't as unflappable as she appeared on the surface.

As Walt took over again to wrap things up, Shane slid his glance back over to Lilah just in time to see a split-second flash of misery cross her expression before she composed herself again, the color draining from her face. He felt a stab of something undefined in the pit of his stomach at the sight of it. He wanted to blame it on scarfing that donut down too fast, but he knew that wasn't all it was.

For the first time in years, he found himself questioning why he felt the urge to antagonize her. What he wanted from it, what he got out of it. She'd given him more than enough reasons to dislike her, but even the most recent one—her parting shot before she'd left, arguably the worst of all—was years behind them at this point. Besides, there was no doubt that he had the upper hand in this situation. Maybe it wouldn't be the worst idea to extend an olive branch. Try to leave the past in the past, and move on like they should have long ago.

The room dissolved into murmurs and chatter as everyone stood, stretched, and gathered their things. He looked over at Lilah, who'd shoved her script in her bag and gotten up in one abrupt motion. He hurried to his feet, too.

Say something nice. Something supportive.

"Good job today," he blurted out, unable to think of anything else.

He realized immediately that was the worst thing he could've said under the circumstances. She shot him a look that could've stripped the paint off a car.

"Yeah, you, too," she said. "It's comforting, really, always being able to predict exactly how you're going to deliver a line. I'm sure half the audience would die of shock if you switched it up and did something different for once. Versatility is such an overrated quality in an actor, don't you think?"

She swept out of the room before he could respond.

Well, he'd given it a shot. Now he could go on hating her with a clean conscience.

. . .

When he arrived back home, his younger brother, Dean, was watching TV in the living room. Dean had been his stand-in on *Intangible* since season two but was somehow still "crashing" in Shane's "guest room" as if he'd just moved to L.A. the week before.

"How'd it go?" Dean asked, his eyes never leaving the TV.

As Shane's stand-in, Dean wasn't needed at the table read—he notoriously never read the scripts at all. But then, he didn't have to. His job was to be roughly the same size and coloring as Shane and stand on Shane's marks as they adjusted the lighting and cameras. No context required. Sometimes he'd even played the back of Shane's head when he and Lilah were having a particularly bad day. It hadn't happened that often, but it had happened more than Shane was proud of.

"Fine," Shane said curtly, sitting on the couch and dropping his bag of Mexican takeout on the coffee table. "You just get in?"

"Yeah, about an hour ago. I was over at Colin's."

Colin was Shane's stunt double—yet another person whose job it was to look vaguely like Shane. On the days that all three of them were on set, it was a little uncanny. When he'd found out that Colin and Dean had an occasional friends-with-benefits arrangement, Shane had been slightly unnerved, unsure if it crossed the line into pseudo-incest or was just regular narcissism.

Shane unwrapped the first of his tacos. "Oh yeah? Is that back on?"

Dean shrugged, leaning over to grab a few tortilla chips from the bag. "He was seeing someone for a while, but I guess it's over."

Shane's phone buzzed in his back pocket. He shifted to the side to pull it out.

"Mind if I take this? It's Renata."

Dean shook his head, muting the television. Shane answered the call and put it on speaker, setting the phone down on the table as he wiped his hands on a napkin.

"Hey, Renata."

"Hi, angel. Where are you? Can you talk?"

"Yeah, I'm just here with Dean."

"Hi, Renata," Dean drawled in a singsong voice. "My offer's still on the table, by the way."

"What, to marry you and take you away from all this? Forgive me for not jumping at the chance," Renata said dryly.

"Your loss. I'd make a great househusband. Just say the word."

Renata chuckled. Shane had asked her years ago if she wanted him to tell Dean to cut out the flirting, but she'd waved him aside. She didn't wear a wedding ring, but other than that, her personal life was something of a mystery to him, as was her age—she could've been anywhere from forty to seventy. But if it didn't bother her, it didn't bother Shane, and it always stayed playful enough that they both seemed to be having fun.

Shane tried to steer the conversation back on track. "So what's up?"

"They want you and Lilah for the cover of *Reel*'s big fall TV preview issue. It shoots two weekends from now."

"That's great," Shane said weakly.

Dean snorted. "They probably can't Photoshop him into that one, huh?"

"Well, that's the other thing. My impression is that they want the shoot to be a little . . . risqué. How do you feel about showing some skin?"

Dread brewed in the pit of his stomach. "How much skin?"

"As much as they can get away with without having to sell it in a brown paper bag, from the sound of it. Are you okay with that? Do you need me to make a stink? Because I'll make a stink."

Shane stared down at his taco, feeling Dean's eyes on him.

"No. No, it's no problem."

"Great. Better start doing your planks now."

Dean groaned, swiping the bag of tortilla chips out of Shane's reach entirely. "He always gets so grumpy when he's dieting."

"Maybe you can tag along, Dean, and they can superimpose your abs onto his body."

"Don't tell me you've been thinking about my abs again," Dean replied with a grin.

Shane cracked a smile, too, despite himself. "I don't think we need to go that far. They can do amazing things with makeup these days. I'll just get them painted on."

Renata laughed again. "Sounds like a plan. I'll let them know you're up for it."

When Shane hung up, Dean turned the volume back up on the television, and the two of them sat in silence that bordered on uncomfortable. Lilah had been a touchy subject ever since the season-five wrap party—the last time Shane had seen her until upfronts. The night that had shown him once and for all what kind of person she was.

It was obvious they were both thinking about it. Shane considered saying something, but the idea of hashing it all out again this long after the fact felt both exhausting and unnecessary. He wasn't really the confrontational type, anyway, especially when it came to Dean. Even though he was pushing thirty, Dean was still the baby of the family, and no matter how annoyed Shane got with him, his protective instinct always won out.

Almost always.

4

Whenever people asked Lilah why she'd started acting, she had a few standard responses.

Because her childhood asthma had prevented her from playing sports.

Because she'd seen a community theater production of *Annie* when she was seven that had left an indelible impression on her.

Because her grandmother had been an actress, too—just a bit player, retired by twenty-five, but one of the last signed to Paramount before the dissolution of the studio system.

None of them were lies, exactly, but the real answer was both simpler and far more complicated: because of her anxiety.

She couldn't remember a time before it. She'd been born into chaos, the product of a union of two profoundly incompatible parents who'd divorced when she was eleven—twelve years too late, she'd thought even back then. She'd never been able to figure out what they'd seen in each other in the first place, other than the fact that they were both Jewish and ready to settle down (or ready to settle, more likely).

Her mother was extroverted and impulsive, a supernova of charisma who could talk her way into or out of anything, with a mean streak a mile wide and a constantly expanding list of grudges with no expiration date. The polar opposite of her father, whose stoic, detached façade concealed a mountain of neuroses they were all constantly at the mercy of. It wasn't until Lilah was older that she understood how being born male and conventionally handsome in a different era had enabled him to avoid getting the help he'd needed, that his rituals of checking every plug and lock and light switch before they left the house and circling the block in the car three times before they came home couldn't be written off as standard fatherly quirks.

Though Lilah loved them fiercely, she sometimes felt like she'd inherited the worst of each of them. Both nature and nurture had conspired against her: she didn't know whether she should blame her temperament on the two mismatched halves at war inside her, or whether she'd just soaked up the household's dysfunction like a carton of baking soda in the fridge. Her younger sister had her own share of issues, but as the oldest—the first undercooked, misshapen pancake on the griddle—Lilah had borne the brunt of it.

She'd been bullied a fair amount in school, too, though she obviously downplayed it in interviews. She knew everyone rolled their eyes at now-gorgeous and glamorous actresses who complained that they were ostracized while growing up for being too skinny with disproportionately huge tits or whatever.

And while that had never been her particular cross to bear, the physical features she'd resented for preventing her from blending in at the time (sprouting to her full adult height of five-eleven by the end of sixth grade, on top of her Technicolor hair) were things she'd come to appreciate as an adult. Even so, traces of that miserable, gawky, awkward kid still lurked in the rafters of her self-perception, like a brace-faced Phantom of the Opera.

Things had come to a head when her parents had announced the divorce, the turmoil at home reaching its peak at the same time the bullying did, the group of friends she'd had since kindergarten dropping her without explanation practically overnight. She dreaded getting up for school in the morning, and she dreaded coming home in the afternoon.

After she'd cried herself sick the night before she had to give a presentation in front of one of her classes, her mother, at the suggestion of Lilah's school counselor, had forced her into after-school acting classes. Lilah had expected it to be a nightmare, her mind racing and stomach in knots in the car on the way there. Instead, it had changed the course of her life.

It was sort of ironic, the way that slipping into someone else's skin had allowed her to discover herself. Having the road map of a script in front of her, secure in the knowledge of exactly what she was supposed to do and how everything would unfold, gave her the freedom to let go, to exist purely in the moment. It got her out of the house, away from the offstage drama of her family. And she finally had some control over when and why people were looking at her.

As she'd made new friends in the drama department and snagged the lead in play after play, her offstage confidence had grown, too. By the time she'd graduated from high school, she was pretty much done giving a fuck what anyone else thought of her.

Her therapist at the time had introduced her to a concept called "the spotlight effect": the idea that you think people are paying much more attention to you than they actually are. Assuming that a friend didn't respond to a text because they hated you, that a group that burst out laughing as you walked away was making fun of you. But the truth was, most people were focused on themselves, wondering what everyone else thought of *them*. The idea had liberated her.

Until she'd gone and fucked it all up by becoming famous.

Once *Intangible* had taken off, the odds were pretty good that the whispers *were* about her. That she wasn't imagining the furtive stares. That complete strangers were concocting conspiracy theories about her personal life, sneaking pictures while she was out and about, spreading stories about what a stuck-up bitch she was whenever she didn't feel like making conversation. But after a few years—and plenty more therapy—she'd learned to adapt, to the point where it almost felt normal. Staying off social media helped; her management team ran her official accounts. She didn't even have the passwords.

There were still some things that triggered her—talk show appearances were always accompanied by sweating hands, a racing heart, and zero memory of anything she'd said. And occasionally someone would catch her off guard when asking for a picture or autograph, and her small-talk skills would completely desert her, leaving her an awkward, stammering wreck.

But it could've been worse. Though *Intangible* had been everywhere for the first few seasons, at the end of the day, she was just TV famous. Which meant that, more often than not, when a stranger approached her, they were calling her Kate. She clung to the thin layer of protection that provided her. It was "Kate" they wanted a piece of, and "Lilah" was still allowed to belong mostly to her.

. . .

The only thing that sustained Lilah during that first torturous week back on set was the promise of her plans on her day off: trekking out to Calabasas for brunch at her friend Pilar's house.

Before *Intangible,* Lilah's only major credit had been *H.A.G.S.,* a teen dramedy she'd shot between her first and second years at Juilliard about four estranged childhood best friends—now in different high school cliques—who rekindle their bond while working as counselors at the same sleepaway camp the summer before their senior year. Lilah had played The Alternative One, complete with magnetic nose ring and taped-in purple streaks in her hair.

The movie had been made on a shoestring but became a quiet hit, building enough momentum as a perennial sleepover favorite to spawn two sequels (the overzealously punctuated *H.A.G.S. 2: L.Y.L.A.S.* and *H.A.G.S. 3: B.F.F.L.*). But, more important, the casting director had gone above and beyond when selecting the four of them: they'd begun the monthlong summer shoot as strangers, and left as lifelong friends.

More than ten years later, their group chat (obviously called "The Hags") was as active as ever; but while they still regularly saw each other in combinations of two or sometimes three, getting all four of their schedules to align was a rarity.

Their lives had, inevitably, spun off in different directions over the past decade. Yvonne (The Smart One), a multi-hyphenate graduate of the Disney child star machine, had shifted her focus to her music career with wild success, her marriage to a superstar hip-hop artist cementing her A-list status as half of the reigning First Couple of Music. Pilar (The Hot One) still took the occasional acting or spokesmodel gig but had mostly pivoted to full-time mommy influencer, showering her millions of followers with aspirational lifestyle content about her, her gorgeous wife, and their two equally gorgeous children. And Annie (The Athletic One) had quit the industry for good shortly after they shot the third movie and was currently preparing to enter her final year of law school, on track to become a public defender.

When Lilah let herself into Pilar's airy, farmhouse-minimalist kitchen, Yvonne was already there, leaning against the marble kitchen island, watching as Pilar finished assembling an exorbitant, multitiered fruit plate. Pilar's six-year-old-twins, Luz and Paz, were nowhere to be seen, which meant they were probably off with their nanny somewhere. Both women exclaimed in delight as soon as they noticed Lilah, who dropped her bag and immediately wrapped Yvonne in her arms.

Every time Lilah was reunited with her friends, she was struck by the competing sensations of them looking exactly as she'd always known them and completely different at the same time, her mind automatically filling in the gaps between the unruly teenagers they'd been and the poised thirtysomethings they'd become.

Today, Yvonne wore a flowing dress in a color that would've been impossible for anyone else to pull off, a bright mustard yellow that made her skin glow. Her hair was wrapped in a colorful silk scarf, and as Lilah pulled away, she paused to coo over the delicate new tattoos twining between the slender gold rings on her fingers.

She moved around the island to hug Pilar next, who was swathed in clouds of floaty white linen, the dark roots of her hair fading immaculately into a loose, honey-blond bun.

"Can I get you something to drink? Seltzer? Mimosa? Kombucha?" Pilar asked, heading over to the fridge.

Lilah shook her head. "I have that nude shoot tomorrow, I should probably skip the bubbles. God forbid I bloat." She delivered the last part with a self-deprecating eye roll.

"Oh, right. Bummer. Want a green juice, then?"

"No. But I'll take one anyway."

Pilar laughed, sticking her head in the fridge.

Annie arrived just then, looking a thousand times calmer and better rested than the last time Lilah had seen her. The dark circles had disappeared from under her eyes, the locked-in-the-library pallor gone from her complexion. She was even dressed in color, surprisingly—a pale blue sundress—with her light-brown hair, usually pulled out of her face, falling loose and curly down her back.

Annie refused Pilar's offer to make her coffee, instead buzzing around the kitchen to make it herself, complaining good-naturedly that Pilar had rearranged everything since the last time they were all there.

Yvonne reached over the counter to pluck a cube of mango from the fruit plate before turning to Lilah. "You're doing a nude shoot tomorrow? For what? The show?"

"Yeah, for *Reel*. The cover of the fall TV preview."

"Just you?" Annie asked.

Lilah sighed. "Me and Shane."

Yvonne's nose crinkled. "Did you try to get out of it?"

Lilah shook her head. "Everyone already thinks I'm difficult. And it'll be good exposure."

"How much exposure?" Pilar laughed.

"Based on the deck they sent over, I think it's going to be one of those things where we start out clothed and end up naked."

Lilah didn't have many reservations about nudity. Her body

was her tool, and she wasn't shy about stripping down for work when it was required. It wasn't the getting naked part that bothered her—it was the getting naked with Shane part.

Annie blew on her coffee. "That sounds like porn. Are you sure you're not just doing porn?" she deadpanned.

"Dario Rossi is shooting it, so unless he's switched industries . . ."

Yvonne's eyes widened. "Oh, I *love* Dario. He's shooting my next album cover. He's gonna take such good care of you. I bet those pictures will be *hot*."

Lilah felt a flash of anticipation shimmer over her, which she quickly pushed away.

"Yeah, maybe. So, wait, what's this new album?"

Yvonne filled her in as Pilar put the finishing touches on the fruit plate, standing on top of a stool to get the perfect overhead shot. Lilah felt her social battery recharging as they fell into the rhythm of their familiar chatter, the four of them weaving in and out of various side conversations without missing a beat.

It was sometimes surprising to Lilah that they were still in touch at all, let alone as close as they were. Most of her other friendships in the industry felt shallow and transactional, people whose cheeks she kissed at parties but whom she never saw in daylight, whose small talk felt like a calculated investment they were making in her that they would eventually try to cash out in the form of a favor.

But the four of them had been thrown together at exactly the right time, in exactly the right situation. They'd rubbed calamine lotion on one another's bug bites, held one another's hair back after drinking too much cheap beer, and passed out on one another's shoulders after long, sun-sick days of shooting. Every time they reunited, Lilah would be filled with nervous anticipation that they'd finally grown too far apart to have anything to talk about, but within minutes, she'd be wheezing with laughter at some wordless inside joke that she'd forgotten until that exact moment. They spoke the secret language of old friends, that unconditional love and acceptance that could only come from years of shared history.

It made her even more bitter about the situation with Shane. The fact that she had to fight so hard to find time for the people she loved, while someone she hated was allowed to monopolize such a large chunk of it. Even after she'd done everything she could to diverge her path from his, fate—and the whims of the UBS executives and the viewing public—had shoved them right back together again.

"So, how is it? Being back on the show?" Pilar asked once they were seated at her dining room table, French doors thrown open to let in the breeze off the pool. She'd outdone herself on the meal, laying the table with fresh-cut flowers, homemade pastries, and a mouthwatering quiche. They'd all filled their plates except for Lilah, who had her green juice, which she begrudgingly had to admit was pretty good.

Lilah groaned, flopping her head dramatically onto the table. The others laughed.

"Is it just Shane being Shane? Or is it everything?" asked Yvonne.

Lilah lifted her head and settled back against her chair. "It's everything. All the new cast members hate my guts, too." She turned to Yvonne. "How do you manage working with Adam all the time? Do things ever get weird?" Yvonne's ex-boyfriend still produced all her albums.

Yvonne shrugged. "Not really. Well, not anymore. But we never had the kind of drama you two do."

"Have you tried to talk to him? Shane, I mean? Clear the air? It seems kind of counterproductive to let all this old bullshit still bother you," Annie said.

Lilah felt a stab of guilt as she shook her head. "We've been pretty much ignoring each other since we started shooting. And when we do talk, it's . . . not good."

Pilar raised her eyebrows. "Do you think . . . is it, like, sexual tension, or . . . ?"

"No," Lilah replied forcefully before Pilar could even get the words out. "Definitely not."

"Okay, calm down, it's not like that's so out of the realm of possibility." Yvonne grinned. "You all of a sudden don't find him attractive anymore?"

"Of course he's attractive. I'm just so repulsed by his personality that it neutralizes his looks."

Annie picked up her phone and started scrolling as if to find something. "So you're saying you didn't write this *BuzzFeed* list, 'Eighteen Times Shane McCarthy's Smile Literally Put You into Cardiac Arrest and Sent You to an Early Grave'?"

Lilah reached over to grab playfully at Annie's phone. "Shut up. It does *not* say that."

Annie giggled, holding it up out of reach. "It's on the front page and everything."

"Maybe you just need to bang it out. Hate sex is always a good option, have you tried hate sex?" Pilar asked. Lilah sipped her juice, her face heating, internally grateful when Yvonne jumped in before she had the chance to respond.

"See, I've never understood why people are obsessed with that. It seems so toxic. The best sex I've had has been with people I was in love with, people I felt super connected to. Not people I hated."

"Proud of you that the wires for 'hot' and 'wrong' aren't

fused together in your brain. We should all be so lucky," Pilar teased, raising her hand-squeezed blood orange mimosa in a mock toast. She turned her attention back to Lilah. "If you have to have all that tension, you should at least be getting laid for your inconvenience. Maybe it would chill you both out a little bit."

Lilah sighed. "Or it would just make everything worse." She rested her elbows on the table and leaned forward, cradling her head in her hands. "I know we should try to move on. I don't know why we can't. It's like . . . every time I look at him, it makes me feel like the same dumbass twenty-two-year-old I was when we met. Everything that happened . . . everything I did. It's humiliating. And the worst part is I know *he's* thinking about it, too. I can't let it go."

Yvonne reached over and rubbed her back. "It's not humiliating. Or, I mean, it's okay if it is. Try to have some compassion for twenty-two-year-old Lilah. Remember, you're in a group of people who love her. You're not allowed to talk shit about her."

Lilah smiled, her eyes growing misty. "Thanks. Sorry I'm such a downer today. I should know better than to come to brunch when I'm not allowed to eat anything."

The others laughed. "Better whiny, dramatic, low-blood-sugar Lilah than none at all," Annie said. Yvonne and Pilar raised their glasses in agreement. Lilah buried her face in her hands.

"Stop, you're gonna make me cry for real," she choked. She typically wasn't much of a crier, though of course she'd done it in front of them plenty of times over the years. She'd been in denial about the extent to which the tense environment on set was already getting to her. About how badly she'd needed to spend some time around people who actually liked her.

The other three rose out of their chairs as one, crowding in on every side to wrap her in their arms where she sat, in an

awkward—but somehow still gratifying—group hug. If she'd
been slightly less frazzled, she would've joked about the resem-
blance to one of the more saccharine scenes in *H.A.G.S.*, but
instead, she shut up and let herself appreciate it.

She took a long, deep breath, as if the affection that surrounded her right now could be stored inside her long-term,
doled out in regular doses to fortify her during the long, lonely,
hostile days ahead.

Yvonne released her and reached across the table for her
phone. "Let's get a picture of us all together before we forget. I
bet that'll bump Shane's stupid face right off the front page."

5

The *Reel* shoot was in Beverly Hills, at a historic hotel that was both a tourist attraction and an industry hot spot. Shane had eaten at the restaurant a few times, but this was his first time upstairs. They'd reserved three rooms on the top floor: an enormous luxury suite for the shoot itself, and two smaller rooms across the hall for Lilah and Shane to get ready.

Earlier in the week, Shane had gotten a call from a woman named Mercedes, who'd identified herself as the intimacy coordinator for the shoot. He'd been a little surprised; he was familiar with the concept, but he'd never worked with one before and was under the impression they were mostly for choreographing sex scenes, not still photography.

Mercedes had explained that Dario, the photographer, had recently started bringing her on any shoot that featured either nudity or intimate physical contact. She'd asked if he had any hard limits when it came to either.

"Did you talk to her already? What did *she* say she was uncomfortable with?" He wasn't going to be the one who blinked first.

"You don't need to worry about that. This is just about your own boundaries."

"I'm fine with anything she is," he'd replied promptly. But the reality of what was in store for him hadn't fully set in until he'd arrived at the hotel and the stylist had shown him his three looks—a designer suit, black boxer briefs, and a beige dance belt (a cross between a jockstrap, a Speedo, and a thong). Better than a cock sock, he thought ruefully, but not by much.

Mercedes came by to visit him after he'd gotten dressed in the suit (in his own underwear, they'd specified). She looked like she was in her midfifties, with a broad, warm face, curly dark hair streaked heavily with gray, and the most calming aura Shane had ever encountered.

"Normally, I'd get you both together and do some bonding warm-ups before the shoot and go over the ground rules again, but Lilah seemed to think it wasn't necessary since you've worked together for so many years. I'm okay with deferring to you two, if you agree. How do you feel about that?"

"Great," he said, with a little too much verve.

"Perfect. Since this is a photo shoot, we don't need to choreograph everything out beforehand. We can stop and take as many breaks as we need, figure it out as we go. Just don't hesitate to let me know if there's anything I can do to make this experience more comfortable for you."

He resisted asking, *Could you find me a different partner to do it with?*

Dario stopped by to introduce himself next; he was tall and bald with a deep, rich voice and an impressive black beard. He reiterated that he wanted them to feel comfortable and relaxed and, most important, to have fun. Shane was pretty sure he'd have more fun getting his entire body waxed—which, thankfully, they hadn't asked him to do—but he smiled and nodded and said everything he was supposed to say.

As Dario headed out the door, he turned back to Shane. "By the way—big fan of the show. Do you know yet if they're finally going to get you two together?"

Shane smiled weakly. "That's the whole point of today, right?"

Dario grinned. "Exactly. See you out there."

When Shane crossed the hall to the set, Lilah was already there, getting final touch-ups on her makeup. Someone must have cranked down the thermostat in an attempt to offset the heat from the lights, because it was fucking freezing.

They'd both been styled in an ambiguously retro aesthetic: his hair slicked back, beard freshly trimmed, her with long hair extensions teased high, eyes smoky with dramatic cat-eye makeup.

She was wearing a thin silk slip dress, and as he gave her a quick once-over, he could tell she was cold, too. He refused to let his eyes linger, since she was staring directly at him; he wouldn't give her the satisfaction of catching him checking her out.

She did look good, though. Better than good. He thought about walking the few steps over to her and telling her that, trying to break the ice between them that couldn't be blamed on the temperature, but those steps might as well have been miles. The words stuck in his throat, and he turned away as one of the makeup artists came over to give him a touch-up of his own. Someone turned on some mood music, sultry, ambient trip-hop pulsing low and steady through the room.

They started in the suite's outer room, on a pale pink crushed-velvet couch opposite the fireplace. Lilah sat in the center of the couch, Shane standing behind it, his hands braced on the back. At Dario's direction, she reached up and grabbed hold of his tie, pulling him closer. When he met her eyes, her expression was guarded and wary, tension vibrating through her neck and jaw.

These pictures probably weren't very good, but it wasn't like they'd use them, anyway. This was just about getting the two of them warmed up before they were asked to start shedding layers and crawling all over each other.

Click-click-click. "Good, good. You both look gorgeous. Try to relax a little. Take a deep breath, and exhale. I know we're still finding our way into it. We have plenty of time."

Next, Shane sat on the couch, in the corner, his legs spread wide and a lazy arm resting across the back. Dario lowered the camera and called out instructions, gesturing with his free hand.

"Now, Lilah, can you scoot closer—yeah, under his arm, head on his chest, you got it. Stagger your knees a little, point that bottom foot—perfect. Shane, now bring your arm down and look at her."

She was lying almost completely on her side, nestled flush against him, her legs stretched toward the other end of the couch. She placed one of her hands on his chest, and, against his will, he felt his heart rate speed up. *Fuck.* If she was already getting to him while they were still fully clothed, this was going to be a long goddamn day.

He stared down at the top of her head, keeping his breathing slow and controlled, trying to narrow his focus to the patterns of the individual strands of hair on her scalp. Nothing sexy about that. But even so, his mouth went dry as he caught a familiar whiff of her lavender shampoo.

"Shane, you're holding a lot of tension in your face. The bad kind. Try to unlock your jaw a bit."

Dario had them change positions again. Lilah settled onto her back, against the side of the couch, one arm slung over her head. Her legs were parted, her skirt drifting up her thighs, and he placed one knee between them—not touching her, but still, she shifted uncomfortably, putting even more space there.

With Mercedes checking in every step of the way, Shane loomed over her, his other leg planted on the ground, her free hand clutching his lapel. When he moved his hand to cover her other wrist, the one draped across the arm of the couch, he saw her eyes widen briefly, almost imperceptibly, as his fingers closed around it.

"Lilah, is it okay if he puts his other hand on your thigh?" Mercedes asked.

Her eyelids fluttered slightly, but she nodded. Shane hesitated for a moment before splaying his fingers across the cool, tender skin of her inner thigh, his fingertips brushing the hem of her dress. He looked back up at her face and saw color rising to her cheekbones, and just like that, he was half-hard. *Goddammit*. Why did she always have to be so fucking responsive?

When he met her eyes, whatever she saw there had her immediately looking away again, her blush deepening.

Dario snapped a few more pictures then glanced over at the display. "You okay, Lilah? You look like he's about to murder you."

She laughed, but it came out as more of a choked gasp. "All good over here."

"Just checking. I think it might be the hand on the jacket. Why don't you put it on his face instead?"

Lilah released his lapel and brought her hand to the curve of his jaw. Even though he was expecting it, the contact almost made him jump out of his skin—and not just because her hand was freezing. He was so fucking on edge, it was embarrassing.

The only consolation was that he could tell Lilah wasn't nailing it, either. Her gaze tracked her own hand as she moved her thumb lightly against the grain of his beard, her brow furrowed, like she was trying to solve a complicated equation in her head.

Dario moved around them, making minor adjustments to their poses as he photographed them from various angles, before leaning over to confer with his assistant. The two of them spoke for what seemed like an eternity, leaving Lilah and Shane frozen awkwardly on the couch, avoiding each other's eyes.

"Let's set up in the bathroom while you get into your second looks," he said finally. Shane jumped off Lilah as if he were spring-loaded, his cheek burning where she'd touched him.

He retreated to his dressing room, stripping out of his jacket as soon as he walked in. To his relief, the stylist handed him both the briefs and the dance belt. When he put them on, it seemed like the belt's padding and compression would do a decent job of keeping his dick as unobtrusive as possible, even if he did end up getting hard again. He clung to that "if" like it wasn't just a "when" in denial.

As Shane pulled on his robe, there was a knock at the door. Dario entered, followed by Mercedes. They both smiled warmly at him.

"How are you feeling so far?" Dario asked, perching on the arm of the easy chair in the corner.

"Fine. Good. Is everything okay?"

"Actually, we were coming here to ask you the same thing,"

Mercedes said. "Is there something going on between you and Lilah?"

"What do you mean?" Shane asked, in his best attempt at nonchalance.

"You haven't said a word to each other all day."

Not just today, he wanted to reply. "Oh. We, um. We just like to stay focused when we're working. Not get distracted with chitchat."

Mercedes and Dario exchanged looks.

"Right," Dario said. "The thing is . . . we're not feeling the chemistry. We know you two have it, obviously. But that connection is missing right now. That's what this whole shoot is about. Without that, it's just vulgar."

Shane scrubbed his hand over his face. "Shit. Sorry." He gestured to his robed body. "I guess I'm a little nervous."

Dario's expression cleared. "Of course. Totally understandable. We'll be closing the set for the rest of the day, if that makes a difference." He stood back up. "Also . . . no pressure at all, and I'm not suggesting you get wasted or anything, but if you want, there's always the option of having a shot of something to help you loosen up a little."

"Like what? Morphine?"

Dario chuckled. "I was thinking tequila, but I can check the first aid kit for something stronger."

Mercedes cleared her throat. "We could also get you two together and take a few minutes to do those bonding exercises I was talking—"

"I'll take the tequila," Shane interrupted.

The shot warmed him from the inside out, the tension in his body instantly dissipating. Not all of it, obviously. That would've taken the entire bottle. He tossed another one back for good measure.

He strode back onto the set, a little more swagger in his step. Lilah showed up a few minutes later, looking slightly more relaxed, too. They were herded into the bathroom, which was almost as big as the bedroom, with an ostentatious chandelier dangling over a detached claw-foot tub in the center. True to his word, Dario had closed the set, clearing the room of everyone except the three of them and Mercedes.

At least it was warm in there.

"Whenever you're ready, you can take off your robes," Mercedes instructed. Shane turned away from Lilah to take his off, not that it mattered.

To start, Dario shot Lilah in the mirror as she pretended to do her makeup, the reflection catching Shane sprawled in the (empty) bathtub, watching her.

The vintage theme of the shoot extended to her lingerie, which she definitely hadn't been wearing under her dress earlier— a strappy bra that stretched down her ribs, high-waisted briefs, thigh-high stockings, garter belt, and heels, all black. Shane had never really understood the appeal of fancy lingerie—it always seemed like more of an obstacle than anything—but she was making a hell of a case for it.

Even though the bra gave her an almost cartoonish level of cleavage, his eyes kept drifting down to the sliver of midriff between her waistband and the bottom of her bra, the stretch of exposed thigh revealed by the tops of her stockings. It was less skin than she'd show in a bathing suit, but something about the negative space of it all made it feel obscene.

All he could do was stare as she arched her back and leaned over the counter, reapplying her lipstick. His brain was immediately hijacked by fantasies of smeared lipstick, fingers digging into those taunting flashes of skin, her serene expression in the mirror turned glazed and undone.

His first instinct was to suppress them. But there was no point in trying to hide it, trying to hold back. As disturbing as it was that she could still get under his skin like this, this was, ultimately, what they wanted from him. To see how much he wanted her. Fuck it. He could give that to them, no acting required.

"Amazing, Shane. Keep looking at her just like that. Lilah, toss your hair over your shoulder and look back at him."

She did, and when her eyes locked on his, a jolt went through him. He knew that look. She wasn't nervous anymore, either.

"Stunning. You two are killing me. Lilah, go over and sit on the edge of the tub. Take your time, though."

She capped the lipstick and turned around, pausing for a beat to lean against the countertop. Dario circled them as she sauntered over to Shane, her heels clacking out a leisurely rhythm against the tile. He let himself drink her in, bringing his thumb to his mouth and lightly brushing it across his lower lip as he watched her. Her gaze tracked it, her breasts rising and falling with a heavy exhale.

Under Mercedes's instruction, she perched on the side of the bathtub, ankles crossed demurely, like her ass wasn't inches from his shoulder. She placed her hand on the nape of his neck, pleasurable goosebumps rippling across his skin as she slowly spread her fingers across his scalp. Once she had a solid grip on his hair, she used it to guide his head back as she looked down at him hungrily.

He'd thought he was hard before, but it was nothing compared to now, his cock throbbing and heavy underneath the layers of restraints. He felt his back muscles bunch and tighten against the tub as he stopped himself from reaching for her, from sinking his teeth into the flesh of her hip where the hard edge of the bathtub pressed it out toward him.

"Perfect. That's perfect." Dario beamed, lowering his camera. "I think we're ready to move into the bedroom, don't you?"

Lilah released his hair so suddenly that he had to catch himself before he smacked his head on the ceramic. She had her robe on before he had even gotten out of the tub.

Shane knew what that meant: the final stage of their wardrobe. They took another break for the crew to break down the lights and set them back up again in the bedroom. Once the hair and makeup people left his room, he considered going into the bathroom and jerking off to relieve his misery somewhat, but that felt like admitting defeat. Admitting that she still had that kind of hold on him. He couldn't exactly ignore the evidence, though.

Mercedes stopped by to visit him again.

"Just want to confirm one more time, before we get back out there. Is there anywhere you don't want Lilah to touch you?"

It was all too easy to answer truthfully: "No."

In the center of the bedroom was an enormous four-poster bed, covered in pristine white sheets and a billowing duvet. They stood in opposite corners of the room and dropped their robes in silence, like boxers waiting for the first-round bell to ring.

As they climbed under the covers from either side, it occurred to him that they hadn't been naked together since they were, well, together. The last time they'd had sex, it had been rushed and ferocious, without time to remove anything more than was absolutely necessary. He had to stop his eyes from roaming, cataloging the spots where her body had changed in the subsequent years—filled out, become softer and more lush—not extreme enough that he'd noticed when she was clothed, but enough that he fisted the sheet in his hands so he wouldn't be tempted to map the differences himself.

She wasn't totally naked, though. She had on nipple pasties and a spandex thong that were so close to her skin tone that his dick was confused for a minute by the uncanny Barbie aesthetic of it all. Then again, with his Ken Doll groin, he supposed they were a matching set.

They started with Dario climbing to the top of a ladder parked next to the bed to shoot them from above. Shane lay sprawled on his back, Lilah on his chest, his arm curled tightly around her, pulling her flush against him. He shouldn't have been surprised by how natural it felt. They'd found themselves in that position countless times—but not for years, and never in front of a camera.

It was kind of funny, in a ghoulish way: the two of them forced to reanimate the corpse of their former intimacy, without even the barrier of their characters to hide behind. To his body, it was like nothing had changed. But it wasn't any deeper than muscle memory and pheromones, the sense memory triggered by the scent of her vanilla body lotion.

He rested his hand behind his head and stared down the camera, as she pressed her cheek to his chest, presumably doing the same thing.

"Lovely. Now, look at each other for me. Let's see that connection."

Lilah shifted herself further up his body, his arm automatically sliding down around her waist. When their eyes met, her expression was tender and unguarded. Their faces were inches from each other now, his other hand reaching over to push a lock of hair behind her ear. And that was how he knew he had truly lost his mind: with practically every inch of her body bare and pressed up against him, the thing he was aching to do the most was kiss her.

After that, things got a little hazy.

His back was up against the headboard, his legs slightly spread, Lilah sitting sideways between them, sheet clutched to her chest, both her legs draped over one of his. She leaned forward to nuzzle her face into his neck, his hand flying up to stroke her back almost of its own free will.

"Shane, is that okay with you?" he dimly heard Mercedes ask.

"Mmph," he grunted, in a way he hoped was affirmative without making Lilah too pleased with herself. When he felt the hot drag of her tongue as she pressed an open-mouth kiss to the side of his throat, he was barely able to swallow his groan.

As soon as she did that, he realized her game: she could tell exactly how turned on he was, and she was messing with him. The annoyance that swept over him was nothing compared to the heat that had been pounding through his veins for hours, but it was enough to clear his head somewhat.

"Okay, Lilah, let's take it down a notch," Dario said. "I appreciate your commitment, but we don't want to get sleazy with it."

Lilah glanced back at him, lowering her lashes modestly. "Sorry."

"No need to apologize. Glad to see you're both feeling it. Better to go too far and pull it back than try to drag it out of you."

Shane could think of at least one major reason it would be a bad idea for her to go too far, but he kept his mouth shut.

Finally, Dario and Mercedes rearranged them into the position he was dreading: Shane sitting upright as Lilah straddled him.

She stayed hoisted on her knees, hovering above him as Mercedes arranged the sheets. Once she was appropriately covered, he assumed she would leave a gap between them as she lowered herself down. Instead, she inched her knees forward, sinking down flush against his lap.

Shane couldn't help but hiss like he'd been burned. She shifted and smirked, flicking her eyes down and then back again.

"Don't flatter yourself," he murmured into her ear, low enough that Dario and Mercedes wouldn't hear.

She draped her arms around his neck, dipping her head down until her cheek brushed his. "Don't flatter *yourself* by thinking I would find it anything other than totally unprofessional." Her voice was low and husky.

"Just keep talking. It's going down already," he lied through gritted teeth.

Dario guided them through a few variations: Her looking coyly back over her shoulder. Their foreheads pressed together. Dario crouching beside them, with both of their faces turned toward the camera. Every now and then, she would rock her hips slightly—not enough for anyone else to notice, but enough to make his vision go white at the edges.

"Now who's being unprofessional?" he grumbled, tightening his grip on her hips in an attempt to hold her in place.

"Still you, it feels like." She adjusted her thigh, dislodging the sheet, and her gloating smile disappeared.

Shane followed her gaze down, but he already knew what she was looking at, peeking out from under the strap of the dance belt: the small black linework tattoo of a cartoon ghost on his hip, no bigger than a quarter, slightly blurred with age.

When she looked back up at him, her self-satisfied expression had been replaced by genuine shock.

"You never got it removed." It was a question, but it wasn't.

He pushed the rest of the sheet aside to see her opposite hip. She did have a tattoo there, but when he looked closer, it was a symbol he didn't recognize.

She'd gotten hers covered.

Of course she had.

. . .

"This doesn't need to be anything more than it is."

That's what she'd said to him the first time they'd had sex—the first time they'd done anything besides flirt and eye-fuck, really—in her hotel room after upfronts. He'd nodded in agreement, but since she'd said it straddling him while his hands diligently worked at her bra clasp, he probably would've agreed if she'd said "chicken salad sandwich."

Later, once enough blood had returned to his brain to belatedly process it, he was relieved. It wasn't that he was opposed to commitment. But he'd been living in L.A. for less than a year at that point, and his life had already been upended by unexpectedly landing on the show. Adding a new relationship on top of that would've been a disaster. Plus, he barely knew her, and they were co-workers, for fuck's sake. Keeping it casual was the only option that made sense.

In retrospect, the option that would've *actually* made the most sense would have been to not sleep together in the first place, but for some reason, that hadn't crossed his mind.

He was grateful she'd been so direct about her expectations, saving him the trouble of trying to decode what she wanted from him. True to their word, he hadn't slept over afterward, and they didn't talk at all between upfronts and the start of production on season one. He'd been ready to write it off as a one-time thing. But then, their first week on set, he'd gone to her trailer to run lines and ended up going down on her instead.

Their only attempt to define the relationship had been about a month after that, when they were already spending two or three nights a week together—but only after work, never weekends. He'd been drifting off to sleep, lulled by the soft drone of the TV in her darkened bedroom.

"Are you seeing anyone else right now?" she'd asked casually, her warm breath ghosting against his chest.

He wasn't.

"Have you been tested recently?"

He had.

"Do you want to stop using condoms, then? I have an IUD. Just let me know if . . . if anything changes."

It wasn't very romantic, but then, that was their deal. And to be fair, he never took her on a real date the entire time they were together. The two of them dating in public would be a whole Thing with a whole other set of pressures, more trouble than it was worth. Their arrangement was about superficial attraction, convenience, and stress relief. Romance was never a factor.

So there was really no explanation for why, after a few more months, when he looked at her—when they sat side by side, half-asleep, in the makeup trailer; when she slipped inside herself with terrifying focus while studying her script or waiting for them to call "Action"; when she slid into bed next to him at the end of the night, draped in one of his T-shirts—his heart stuttered out a pattern that almost felt like *forever*.

Not every time. Not enough to do something about it. But enough to mess with his head.

To add to his confusion, his friends at the time had been pulling him in the opposite direction. Not only did they disapprove of Lilah in particular, they felt like he was wasting his time being tied down by *anyone*. He should be keeping his options open, taking advantage of his freshly minted status as the star of the hottest TV show in the country. With Lilah, they reasoned, he had the worst of both worlds: all the burdens of monogamy, with none of the benefits.

The tattoos had been his wake-up call. That half-suppressed *forever*, etched on his skin.

He had no fucking idea why he hadn't gotten it removed, though. He'd meant to. But he had to wait six to eight weeks for it to fully heal before he could make an appointment, and after that he kept putting it off, and putting it off, until he barely even noticed it anymore. Now, though, his stomach turned at the sight of it. Even though they'd broken up, their chance at forever destroyed before they'd even made a real go of it, she was still branded on him.

Shane knotted the sheet in his fist.

"Don't read anything into it," he growled. He was surprised by the ferocity of his reaction, but he'd been edging all day, courtesy of one of his least favorite people on the planet, who was currently still clinging to him like a barnacle. Sweat beaded at the edges of his hairline. This might be the thing that finally broke him.

Lilah said nothing, just ran her fingers over the tattoo one more time, lashes downcast, her expression cryptic.

Suddenly, he couldn't take another second of it. Of any of it. He stood up abruptly, tumbling Lilah off his lap and onto the bed.

"We got what we needed here, right?" he asked gruffly, pulling his robe back on and storming out of the room before anyone had a chance to respond.

6

Lilah woke up the morning after the season-one wrap party with a burning sensation on her hip and the worst hangover of her life. She blinked a few times, heavily, painfully, her whole body aching, her fuzzy teeth and rancid mouth making her stomach lurch. Shane's warmth and weight around her, usually a comfort, felt smothering. As she shrugged out from under him and rolled herself upright, she heard a crinkling noise.

She stood, swaying a little as the pounding in her head intensified, and glanced down at the bed for the culprit. Judging by how terrible she felt, it wouldn't surprise her if they'd been binge-on-junk-food-then-fall-asleep-on-the-wrappers wasted.

The show had provided drivers to escort them to and from the party, and she knew Drunk Lilah wasn't above asking them to stop at a gas station or take her to a drive-through. But there was nothing in the bed other than a prone and still-unconscious Shane.

Lilah pulled up the bottom of the oversized T-shirt she was wearing and did a brief inspection of her body, anticipating an Oreo wrapper stuck to her ass or something.

What she found was much, much worse.

"*Fuck,*" she croaked, dropping the hem and staggering to the bathroom to vomit. In between heaves, she heard Shane stir.

"Y'allrightinthere?" His voice was thick with sleep.

She responded by blindly kicking her leg out to shut the door the rest of the way. Once she felt capable of standing again, she rinsed her mouth out with water before brushing and mouthwashing thoroughly.

Her reflection was sobering: hair matted and greasy, skin blotchy, eyes raccooned with smeared makeup. She leaned in closer. Was that a *hickey*? Not just one, she realized, pulling her hair back to get a better look. A whole constellation of them. Thanks to her complexion, it was all too easy to mark her up with minimal effort, but by now Shane usually knew better than to leave them where they'd be visible. She couldn't even bring herself to get mad about it, though. At least she didn't have to worry about going into work today, facing the knowing smirks in hair and makeup. And, unlike the throbbing reminder at her hip, they were temporary.

She stumbled back toward the bedroom. Shane looked practically dead himself, sprawled across the bed diagonally, facedown, clutching her pillow to his chest the same way he'd been clutching her moments earlier.

He craned his head to look up at her, a lazy smile spreading across his face once he saw the state of her neck. "Damn, I really got you. Sorry." His self-satisfied tone made it clear he was the opposite of sorry. Ordinarily, she might have thought it was kind of cute. In her current state, it infuriated her.

"Look at this." She sat next to his head, and he automatically reached out to squeeze her butt. She swatted him away, lifting the edge of her shirt to reveal the small square of black plastic wrap taped over her hip.

"What's that?"

"I think it's a fucking *tattoo*," she said, peeling the tape off slowly, wincing as it snagged on her skin.

Shane pushed himself upright, suddenly alert. Since he was naked, it didn't take long for them to home in on the corresponding spot on his hip that was also taped and plastic wrapped. In contrast to her tentative approach, he ripped his off all at once, so they both revealed their mystery tattoos at the same time: tiny, matching cartoon ghosts, so sickeningly cute that Lilah thought she might need to run to the bathroom again.

They looked up at each other for a long, loaded beat. Shane's expression was hard to read, like he was waiting for her to tell him how he was supposed to feel about it.

Lilah struggled to piece together the events of the night before, which were trickling through the fog of her hangover more slowly than she'd like.

The venue had specialized in "elevated" frozen cocktails, waiters circulating with trays of fluorescent rainbow shot glasses. She'd sampled three flavors in a row with Max, the head of the hair department, as soon as she'd arrived: cold and sticky and dangerously sweet.

She wasn't normally a big drinker, especially during filming—

it was unprofessional (not to mention unpleasant) to work hung-over, plus it made her look puffy and tired on camera. With the summer hiatus looming and her alcohol tolerance in the gutter, it was no wonder she'd overdone it.

Anxiety sizzled through her. So far, she and Shane had some-how managed to keep their whatever-this-was under wraps, but there was a nonzero chance that the two of them had gotten a little too friendly in front of their co-workers last night. Both of them tended to get handsy when they'd been drinking. Months of sneaking around, taking separate cars, avoiding being seen in public together, politely deflecting gossip—all undone by a few too many frozen margarita shots.

She dropped her face into her hands, groaning. "*Fuck.* Do you remember anything that happened last night? We didn't— when did we even *do* this?"

He scrunched up his forehead. "I don't know," he said. Lilah groaned again, even more dramatically this time.

"This is a fucking *nightmare.*" She knew even as she said it she was being way over the top, but she was so hungover she'd prob-ably cry over a stubbed toe. She stood up, her fatigue suddenly overtaken by nervous energy, and began pacing. "Do you think we're the only ones who got them? Can we even ask anyone? Or will it just seem suspicious?"

"I don't know," Shane repeated, closing his eyes.

"That's all you can say?"

"What do you want me to say?"

"I don't *know,*" she said, and the corner of his mouth twitched.

"What are you worried about, exactly?" He sounded ex-hausted.

Lilah stopped pacing abruptly. "That people will know. About us."

He rubbed his hand over his face. "I'm sure they already do. The ones we work with, anyway."

"What? Really? You think?" Her voice got higher and higher pitched with each question.

"Probably. We're in each other's trailers all the time. I don't think it's that hard to put it together. Plus, you're always undressing me with your eyes."

She cast a sharp glance at him. He was grinning up at her mischievously, obviously trying to defuse the situation. How was he so fucking calm about this? She'd always had a hard time understanding people like him, the perpetually unruffled, who inspired envy and frustration in her in equal measure.

To be fair, that type never seemed to know what to do with her, either, other than inform her she was being neurotic or overreacting or thinking too much—as if she didn't already know. Even his hangovers seemed to hit him differently, making him chill and cuddly, whereas she currently felt like her skin had been removed, the volume and brightness of the world turned all the way up.

She flopped back onto the bed next to him, unable to tell whether she was annoyed or grateful that he didn't move to touch her again. She closed her eyes and dug the heels of her hands into them, trying to fight off the swirling visions of the two of them, wasted and sugar-high, cackling like idiots at the bar, Shane sucking on her neck in the bathroom, the ominous buzz of a tattoo machine.

Another dire thought settled over her. The possibility that they hadn't just been sloppy in front of their co-workers—they'd been sloppy in public. All it would take was one picture. Then the constant, insistent drone of attention she'd just barely learned to live with would amplify into a roar, swallowing her whole.

Lilah propped herself on her elbow, leaning over to inspect

Shane's hip again. "How soon do you think we can get them removed? Probably not until they're healed, right? Do you know how long that takes?"

His amusement faded. "You want to get them removed?"

"You *don't*?" she asked, eyes widening.

He looked away. "I didn't say that."

"Why wouldn't we get them removed?" She knew her voice was going all shrill again, in the way her worst high school boyfriend had told her made his dick feel like it was shriveling back up inside his body.

He shrugged, still unable to meet her eyes, his gaze drifting to her own exposed hip. "I dunno. I mean . . . a couples tattoo isn't exactly the end of the world, right?" He reached out to stroke her thigh, and she jerked away.

"We're not a couple," she snapped, and it was like he turned to stone before her eyes.

It was only supposed to be one time.

But one time had turned into a dozen had turned into a hundred, and against her better judgment, she'd let things carry on way past their expiration date. It was just so easy. *He* was so easy.

Not in the sense that it was easy to get him naked, which, yes, there was that. But they had the same unpredictable schedule, he was laid-back and sweet, and, most important, she could trust him. He was the only person in her life who understood what she was going through, because he was going through it, too: the surreal, thrilling, terrifying, one-in-a-million experience of going from nobody to capital-S Somebody practically overnight.

After the year they'd both had, easy was all she could handle. And there were more than enough reasons why being in an actual relationship with him would be really fucking hard.

Maybe they'd blurred the lines by spending the night as often as they did, but that was just about logistics: they left work late, started early, and didn't live particularly close to each other. They never *slept* together without sleeping together, though, a boundary Lilah had been careful to keep intact.

Until last night.

Looking down at his stricken expression, she was hit by a wave of something worse than nausea. Something closer to disgust, crested with despair. She hurt all over, inside and out, exhausted and weak and embarrassed enough that her most self-destructive impulses had wrestled free of their chains and clawed their way to the surface. She wanted to hurt him, too. To punish him for the unforgivable crimes of caring about her, of wanting more from her, of assuming he knew her.

"What do you think this is, exactly?" Her voice already didn't sound like her own, caustic and sharp, a warning to herself that she was about five seconds away from saying something she'd deeply regret.

"I don't—" He caught himself just in time, but she pressed on, unable to stop herself.

"Have I ever said anything to make you believe I would want a fucking *couples tattoo* with you?"

"No, but—"

"But what?" She wasn't sure when she'd gotten to her feet, but she was standing again, arms crossed defensively, shifting her weight like she was seconds away from bolting out the door of her own damn bedroom. "You want to be my *boyfriend* now? Is that it?"

He met her gaze, his voice frustratingly calm. "Not when you're acting like this, I don't."

She lifted her chin. "And how am I acting?"

He didn't respond, just kept looking at her with those wounded golden retriever eyes.

Lilah sometimes felt like she was walking around with a snake coiled in her belly just waiting for her to open her mouth, ready to strike at the slightest provocation. She knew she was out of control—skin flushed, heart beating wildly, regret already brewing in the distant part of her mind that held her better judgment.

She was practically daring him to take the bait. To dump her, to call her a bitch, to give back whatever she deserved and then some. Plenty of men would—and had—with less.

But he didn't. He just shook his head, casting his gaze to the ground. When he spoke, his voice was weary. "Maybe I should get out of here. We probably both need to cool off a little."

"Or you could go, and we could just call it." It was out of her mouth almost before she realized what she was saying. She still didn't feel like she was fully inside her body as she continued. "I think this . . . whatever this is . . . has run its course."

He raised his eyes back to hers. His brows were knit together, lips pursed, face hard and closed off. He'd never looked at her that way before. It felt wrong on him, somehow.

"So I guess that's that, then."

"That's that." She looked down at her feet as she said it.

There was no movement in her peripheral vision for several long seconds.

"Right," he said at last. The mattress creaked as he eased himself off the bed and began hunting around for his clothes.

She didn't know why she'd expected him to argue more. To try to fight for her, for them. That wasn't really Shane's style. He was easy, after all.

Still, his quiet acceptance was a punch in the gut.

She sat on the edge of the bed, watching him pull on his jeans, self-loathing curdling in the pit of her stomach.

Once he buckled his belt, he made his way back over to her. She just stared up at him.

"That's my shirt," he said.

Lilah looked down at the faded, unfamiliar logo across her chest.

"Oh. Right."

She stood, pulling the shirt over her head and handing it over. She wasn't wearing anything underneath it besides a thong, and she crossed her arms over her breasts self-consciously as he took it from her, leaving her exposed. She noticed his eyes flick down, his nostrils flaring slightly. For a brief, desperate moment, she considered trying to seduce him into goodbye sex. But she'd never felt less sexy in her life, and besides, if he rejected her, she'd probably shrivel up and die of humiliation on the spot.

She threw on a shirt of her own and a pair of leggings as Shane finished gathering his things; they both averted their eyes, giving each other a wide berth as they moved around the room. When he reached her bedroom door, he hesitated, looking back at her.

She met his gaze, her skin prickling with unease. The aggression had drained out of her almost as quickly as it arrived. All she wanted to do now was climb back under the covers and stay there, trying in vain to hide from the remorse that already threatened to overwhelm her.

She heard herself say, quietly: "I don't want to lose you as a friend."

He let out a short exhale through his nose, the ghost of a laugh, then shook his head resignedly before meeting her eyes again.

"We've never been friends, Lilah."

She'd been wrong earlier. *This* was the punch in the gut.

Then he was gone.

After he left, she did her best to distract herself by pulling out her laptop and frantically searching their names over and over, trawling every social media platform and gossip site she could think of, her heart in her throat. Fortunately, to her shock and relief, it seemed like they'd managed to stay under the radar as far as the general public was concerned. *Un*fortunately, from what she could gather from her texts with Polly—her favorite writer on the show—and Max, it seemed like no one else had joined them on their little tattoo adventure. They had, in fact, gotten couples tattoos. She shut her laptop and curled up on her couch under a blanket, letting herself drift off into a sullen nap.

Later, after she was rested and showered and caffeinated and rehydrated enough to think straight, she allowed herself to replay the events of that morning, marinating in her guilt and embarrassment. But there was something else there that unsettled her most of all: the sharp sting of loss.

She'd tried to ignore the tiny intimacies that had piled up over time. The inside jokes. His toothbrush in her bathroom cabinet. The way he had her coffee waiting for her in the morning. The unfortunate fact that the best sleep she'd ever gotten was with him curled around her, his lips pressed to the nape of her neck.

He'd told her he loved her only once, four or five months ago. Almost inaudibly, into her shoulder, in the middle of the night, after they'd both inexplicably woken up at the same time and reached for each other, during sex that was half-dreamy and unusually tender. She was so overwhelmed she'd pretended she hadn't heard him. If he'd said it again in daylight, looking directly at her like he actually meant it, that would've been one thing. But he hadn't.

Mostly, though, she'd ignored it because she hadn't believed him. Not that she thought he was lying or anything. They spent a lot of time together, obviously, but they were usually working or fucking, their conversations rarely delving deeper than banter or small talk. She believed that he loved the idea of her, he loved sleeping with her, he loved that she fit into his life in a way that was both seamless and undemanding. But he didn't love *her*. He couldn't. She hadn't shown him enough of herself for that to be possible.

Sometimes she'd catch him looking at her in a way that made her chest seize, because she could tell he wasn't actually seeing her but whatever flawless, impossible fantasy woman he'd invented long ago and superimposed her face onto. He deserved to be with the woman he thought she was—someone soft, like him, whom he could hold as tightly as he wanted without finding himself sliced to ribbons when he pulled away.

There was a sick sense of relief in that, too. At least now he finally knew who he was dealing with. She wouldn't have to spend the next few months pretending not to notice him slowly growing disenchanted with her the more she opened up to him.

No matter what, though, they needed to find a way to put all this behind them, for the sake of the show. The worst thing they could do was allow their breakup to affect their working relationship.

Tomorrow. She'd call him tomorrow and apologize, and they'd figure it out.

The next morning, she woke up to a notification in the Hags group chat.

ANNIE: Did something happen with you and Shane?

Lilah felt her stomach drop.

LILAH: Why?

PILAR: Just trying to figure out if we need to kill him or not

Pilar's next message was a link to a gossip site. When Lilah clicked on it, she was greeted with a series of pictures of Shane out at a club with his friends: a group of other up-and-coming twentysomething actors he'd fallen in with after *Intangible* had blown up, whom the press had semi-derogatorily nicknamed "The Poon Squad."

The first time she'd met them, at a New Year's party she and Shane had attended as "friends," one of them had looked her up and down and then leaned over to ask Shane, without bothering to lower his voice, if the carpet matched the drapes. She hadn't reacted, just turned on her heel and walked out. She'd heard it enough times that the unoriginality pissed her off more than the vulgarity.

Shane had run after her and coaxed her into staying, demanding an apology from his friend once they returned, which had been enough to placate her. By the time he pulled her into an empty bedroom just before midnight, she'd almost forgotten about it. Almost.

But now, it was all she could think about as she scrolled through the pictures of Shane wrapped around a Victoria's Secret Angel so tightly it looked like they'd been welded together with a blowtorch. He was clearly trashed, sloppily making out with her as she stuck her hands up his shirt, the rest of the guys laughing, jeering, and raising their glasses in the background, their arms around modelesque women of their own.

Lilah felt her vision black out around the edges. She should've trusted her gut about them. Hating someone's friends was never a good sign for the longevity of a relationship—birds of a feather, and all that. And it was no secret they fucking hated her, too.

They'd likely been hounding him to dump her for months. Given what they felt comfortable saying to her face, she didn't even want to think about how they talked about her behind her back.

But, of course, Shane was a grown man. No one was forcing him to stick his tongue down that woman's throat. He was doing it because he wanted to.

He was doing it because now he could.

She stared at the picture for what felt like hours.

Finally, she willed her fingers into action, trying to compose a text that was much more chill than she felt.

LILAH: lol

Good start. She forced herself to continue.

You don't have to kill him
We're not a thing anymore
I might die of embarrassment from letting myself be associated with someone who would act that tacky, though

PILAR: omg wait what

ANNIE: Since when???

YVONNE: Are you okay?

LILAH: yesterday
I was the one who ended it
and no, I'm not really okay
But I will be

She assured her friends that they didn't need to come over, assured herself that the devastation she felt was unjustified. It was her pride that was bruised, that was all. She'd forget about it by next week.

Except he didn't stop.

For the next several days, Shane was photographed out and about with a different woman every night—some famous, some not. Even though the PDA got slightly more tasteful after that first night, it was obvious that they were purposely showing up where they knew there'd be paparazzi or hungry fans. There was no other way to interpret it: he was doing it to hurt her.

She visualized her heart hardening like a stone and tried to distract herself from how well it was working.

The worst part was, she couldn't even do the same thing to him. If she was out with a different guy slobbering all over her every night, she'd be seen as trashy, branded a slut, her image and potentially her career irrevocably tarnished. And though a few feminist-skewing gossip outlets called out Shane's behavior for what it was (pathetic, messy, try-hard), the biggest sources lauded him as a stud and an icon, a one-man Poon Squad all on his own.

On the fifth day, alone in the middle of the night, she finally allowed herself to cry about it.

7

Now

When Walt called Lilah and Shane into his office during their lunch break the week after the photo shoot, Lilah was sure she knew why. They'd shot their first major scene together a few days before, and it had taken them all day to get through three pages—a disaster on a strict TV schedule, causing them to run behind for the whole week.

She'd been mortified, painfully aware of how many people's days she was ruining as she fucked up one take after another. Shane's barely concealed amusement at her struggles had only made things worse. Her embarrassment had compounded on itself, making it impossible to recover, getting in her head so badly that eventually she was messing up lines that she'd delivered perfectly before.

After a while, the director had come up to her and kindly asked her if she needed to take a few minutes to regroup, bringing in her stand-in while they shot coverage of the other actors. Her cheeks had burned as she'd slunk off the set.

But when they sat down in Walt's office, both of them bearing guilty sent-to-the-principal's-office expressions, Walt flopped a tabloid onto the desk without a word. Lilah glanced at Shane, who seemed equally confused.

"Sorry to hear about Peyton's . . . baby drama?" he said tentatively, looking up from the cover. Walt grabbed the magazine and thumbed to a dog-eared page, folding it back onto itself and sliding it over to them again.

MATCH MADE IN HELL: *Intangible*'s Dream Team is
Back—and a Behind-the-Scenes Nightmare!

Lilah's stomach lurched when she saw the photos. One of each of them, taken at completely different times and locations, but superimposed together in a way that implied their unhappy expressions were directed at each other. Based on the fact that Lilah was in her Hangoveralls (the oversized Carhartt overalls she wore whenever she had an especially bad hangover, as dubbed by Pilar), her picture was from three months earlier, when she'd gotten a flat tire on her way to pick up breakfast tacos. Of course she looked annoyed.

Flicking her eyes to Shane's photo, she idly wondered what had made him look so tormented. Probably racked with guilt that he'd had to tell a waiter they'd messed up his order or something.

They both inched forward in their seats so they could read

the article without picking it up from the desk. It was mostly padding—basic facts about her return to the show—ending in a breathless claim from an anonymous source that their photo shoot had *allegedly* been cut short after the two of them got into a furious screaming match on set.

"It's not true," Lilah said meekly. "We didn't scream at each other." Even though Dario and Mercedes had been the only people in the room with them at the time, there were at least a dozen witnesses to Shane's hasty exit through the main area of the suite. The story could have been fabricated by any one of them.

Walt sighed. "It doesn't matter if it's true. The network is pissed. We need to nip this in the bud."

"You don't want us to pretend we're dating, do you?" Shane grumbled.

"Of course not," Walt said. "Nobody's trying to meddle in your personal lives. They just have a big old press tour lined up for you two, but it's going to be a big old waste of everyone's time if it's obvious you hate each other."

"We don't hate each other," they replied, robotically, in unison.

Walt sighed again. "Right. Well, I've been talking to the network, and they think it might be a good idea for you to do a few sessions of couples counseling to work out whatever . . . whatever's going on here."

"We're not a couple," they said, once again in unison.

"That's very cute. You should take it on the road," Walt said with a humorless chuckle. "Yes. I know you're not a couple. You're a couple of pains in my ass, is what you are." He took off his glasses and rubbed his eyes. "It's not just the story. It's how you've been on set, too. At this rate, we're going to be shooting this season for the next three years. I know you've had some personal issues in the past, and that's none of my business. But once it affects your work, *then* it becomes my business, and my problem."

Lilah stared down at her hands, abashed. She'd never been reprimanded like this before. That was something she'd always taken pride in: no matter the circumstances in her personal life, she showed up and nailed it. She burned with resentment toward Shane for fucking that up for her, too—though, of course, she had to accept responsibility for her part in it. A match wouldn't light without something to strike it against.

"Okay," she said abruptly. "We'll go to therapy."

She glanced over at Shane, who was already looking at her.

"Sure," he said, his voice gravelly. "Right. Sorry. Whatever you want." He actually sounded remorseful. He should—it was his tantrum that had landed them in the tabloids, exaggerated or not.

A few minutes later, Lilah followed him out of Walt's office, pulling the door shut behind them. They both paused there, his eyes searching her face with an indecipherable expression. She thought he might say something, but instead, he turned and strode down the hall. She scampered to catch up with him.

"Well?"

He didn't even turn his head. "Well, what?"

"Don't you have anything to say for yourself?"

"You were the one who needed all those takes the other day."

His nonchalance infuriated her. "Yeah, because *you* kept messing me up. But this wouldn't be happening without you freaking out about the tattoos."

Honestly, it was still a sore subject for her, too.

A few weeks after their breakup, she'd left town to shoot the second *H.A.G.S.* movie during their hiatus before season two. Instead of a lonely summer moping around L.A., she'd escaped to upstate New York for six weeks with her best friends and little to no cell service, which was exactly what she needed. She was grateful to have the work to distract her; an actual vacation would've given her too much time alone with her thoughts.

Once they'd wrapped, the four of them piled into Yvonne's rented Jeep and drove forty minutes to the nearest tattoo studio, where they'd all gotten matching tattoos of the logo of the fictional summer camp where their characters worked. If Lilah looked closely enough at hers, she could still see the faint outline of the ghost underneath—but then, she rarely looked closely at it these days.

By the time she had to return to production on *Intangible*, she was at peace with the whole situation—as much as she was ever going to be. If Shane wanted to live out his douchey little *Entourage* fantasy and fuck his way through Los Angeles, that was none of her business.

But as soon as she was back in the real world, she'd been blindsided by breathless nonstop coverage of the hottest new celebrity couple: Shane and Serena Montague, fresh off her divorce from her equally A-list husband—and seventeen years Shane's senior. She'd been one of the highest-paid actresses in Hollywood when Lilah and Shane were kids, but now that she was on the other side of forty, her career had hit an inevitable stalling point.

The tabloids had been obsessed with them, painting Serena as a desperate cougar and Shane as her fame-hungry boy toy. As much as Lilah's wounded pride wanted to believe their relationship was rooted in a mutual need for attention, they'd stayed together for several years—and the handful of times she'd interacted with Serena, she'd been nothing but kind and gracious to Lilah.

As for Shane, at least he seemed appropriately guilty about

his exploits once they were back on set, tiptoeing around with a sheepish puppy-dog look that infuriated her. She could've coasted on her moral high ground as the wounded party, and maybe things would have eventually cooled off between them.

But that wasn't who she was. Of course she had to retaliate.

Shane had helped Devon Dillon, the infamous carpet/drapes offender, land a ten-episode guest arc on the show, with the potential for more if his character was well received. She was already dreading the prospect of working with Shane for the next four years of their contracts; the thought of adding Devon to the mix was unbearable.

Somehow, after a few casual-but-pointed suggestions during a night out with Polly and a few of the other writers, she managed to get Devon written off permanently after only three episodes. It was the next best thing to getting Shane himself fired. The first time she saw Shane after he found out, that puppy-dog look was gone, replaced by contempt. Neither one was ideal, but she'd take being hated over being pitied any day.

After that, there was no turning back. Once the rose-colored glasses of their relationship had been smashed, she saw with perfect clarity that the easygoing charm that had initially drawn her to him was actually a mask for spinelessness, for insecurity, for the pathological need to be liked. And through his eyes, she became the ugliest version of herself: the tightly wound, vindictive, humorless shrew.

Whatever therapist they'd end up seeing certainly had their work cut out for them.

Shane stopped abruptly and turned on his heel. "It wasn't about the tattoos."

She stepped closer to him until they were almost nose to nose. "Then what?"

His jaw tightened. "You know what you were doing."

"What? What was I doing?" She made her eyes wide and innocent.

"You were trying . . ." He looked away before starting again. "Everything's a competition with you. You always need to win."

"Your dick is not the prize you think it is, Shane," she snapped.

He smirked a little, his voice dropping low. "That's not what you used to say."

"Well, I also used to have Lean Pockets and Red Bull for breakfast, but thankfully my standards for what I allow in my body have gotten a little higher since then." She pushed past him, trying to fight back her blush.

Okay, yes, she had been teasing him a little at the shoot, but just to deflect from her own discomfort about how weirdly hot and bothered she was getting, too. It was the only way to feel like she had some control over the situation. But she'd paid for it later. It wasn't until she'd woken up in the middle of the night, on the verge of orgasm after hours of anxious, sexually charged dreams, that she allowed herself to reach between her legs and finish the job they'd started.

Her one consolation as she brought herself over the edge was that, judging by Shane's tortured reactions, there was no way he'd been able to hold out as long as she had. She told herself the only reason she was seeing stars as she came was because it had been building all day, and not because her friends were right about it being hotter because she hated him.

They exited the building practically side by side. She at least had the maturity not to fight with him when he held the door for her, muttering a begrudging "thank you" under her breath. She cringed at the prospect of walking with him all the way back to their trailers, so instead of turning right, in the direction of the set, she went left toward the parking lot, to take a lap around the building and give herself a chance to cool off.

"Where are you going?"

She whirled around. "What do you care?"

He blinked, a look of genuine confusion passing over his face. "I don't. You're right. Sorry." He turned and walked off without another word, leaving Lilah perplexed in his wake.

8

"So, how long have you two been together?"

Shane and Lilah exchanged uncomfortable glances.

The two of them were sitting on either end of a couch that wasn't nearly as big as Shane would've liked. Perched in a plush armchair opposite them was their network-assigned couples therapist, Dr. Deena, a slender sixtysomething South Asian woman with cropped white hair and oversized purple-framed glasses. The glasses seemed to be an anomaly, though, since everything else in her office, from the furniture to the décor to her outfit, was aggressively neutral, running the gamut of shades from cream to beige.

"We're, um . . . we're not together," Lilah said. "We're not a couple, I mean." She said it with some hesitation, like she was unsure if it was a trick question.

Dr. Deena blinked a few times then glanced down at her notepad. "Oh, I'm sorry. There must have been some kind of miscommunication with my intake coordinator. So, what *is* your relationship, exactly?"

"Co-workers," Shane said tersely. Dr. Deena looked even more confused.

"We're actors. On a TV show," Lilah supplied. "The network wanted us to see you. We've been having some . . . issues."

Dr. Deena's eyes crinkled warmly at the edges. "I see. I don't watch much television, so you'll have to forgive me for not recognizing you." She sighed, leaning back in her seat. "Okay. Got it. Just bring me up to speed, then—what's your relationship status outside of each other? Are either of you married?"

They both shook their heads. Dr. Deena made a note on her pad.

"Dating?"

They eyed each other briefly before returning their gazes straight ahead.

Shane hadn't been in a relationship longer than three months since he and Serena had broken up, but not for lack of trying. Despite his sporadic attempts at playing the field over the years, he'd always been a girlfriend guy. It was just hard to maintain a serious relationship with his schedule, especially if he was dating someone equally as busy as he was.

His last attempt, with a woman who worked in the art department on another UBS show, had petered out sometime around the end of last season. The two of them had stolen as many moments as they could during production, counting down the days until their summer hiatus and the promise of plenty of uninterrupted time to spend together—but when it had finally rolled around, they'd realized that neither of them really wanted to.

"No," he said at last, glancing over at Lilah again, who he was surprised to see was studying him intently. He didn't want to admit how curious he was to hear her answer.

After she and Shane had stopped seeing each other, he knew she'd gotten back together with her ex-boyfriend from New York, a playwright who regularly spent months in L.A. on the writing staff of one short-lived prestige show or another. From what Shane could gather from passive thirdhand gossip, their relationship was fairly chaotic, with the two of them breaking up every time he left, then taking another crack at it whenever he returned.

But, he realized with a twinge, other than the tabloids briefly linking her to her *Without a Net* costar in a transparent attempt to drum up some positive buzz for the movie (which had backfired, since he was playing her adult son and everyone just thought it was creepy), Shane had no idea what her personal life had looked like since she'd left the show.

Lilah looked straight ahead again. "No. I'm not seeing anyone."

"And have either of you been in therapy before? Couples or otherwise."

Lilah answered first, without hesitation. "I have. By myself. On and off, since I was around . . . eleven, I guess? I have GAD."

Shane kept his gaze resolutely forward, trying to camouflage his surprise. He wasn't sure what that meant, but he knew the "A" in the middle probably stood for "anxiety." She'd mentioned it in passing—and he'd borne the brunt of it firsthand before, of course—but he didn't know it was bad enough that she'd been in therapy for it since she was a kid. He felt a pang of sympathy toward her, which he quickly suppressed.

Dr. Deena nodded. "And you're able to manage it effectively now? I'm sure it's not easy in your line of work."

Shane thought he caught her glancing over at him before she responded.

"Mm-hmm. All good," she said crisply.

Dr. Deena turned to him. "What about you, Shane?"

He shook his head. "No. Never."

Lilah made a derisive noise under her breath. Either Dr. Deena didn't notice or she chose to ignore it. "So, how long have you two been working together?"

"The show started eight years ago, I left after five seasons, and I just came back a few weeks ago," Lilah rattled off.

"And that's when the conflict started? When you came back?"

"Ah . . ." Lilah clicked her tongue. "No, it was . . . before that."

Dr. Deena shifted in her seat, tapping her pen on her chin. "What would you say your biggest issue is? If you could narrow it down."

"We spend too much time together," Shane said, his voice flat. If he added it up, he'd probably logged more hours at Lilah's side than anyone else's, including any of his girlfriends.

"Can you pinpoint when things started to decline, though? It couldn't have been like this from day one," Dr. Deena persisted.

They looked at each other, Lilah's face reflecting the unease he was feeling.

"It was after . . . we used to . . . we were involved. For a little while. And it . . . ended badly," Lilah said at last, like it was being extracted from her under interrogation.

Dr. Deena nodded slowly. "I see. Let's walk it back to the

beginning, then. Tell me about your relationship. When did it start?"

They sat in silence for a long moment, neither of them looking at the other. Shane sensed Lilah was about as eager to rehash all this as he was. But that was why they were here, he supposed. He sighed.

"It started at the beginning. I mean, it started when we met, pretty much. After the show got picked up."

"And how long did it last?" Dr. Deena asked.

"Um . . . eight, nine months? Something like that?" He allowed himself to glance at Lilah for confirmation, and she gave a brusque nod.

"So what happened?"

Shane rested his elbows on his knees and leaned forward, running both hands over his face and through his hair. "Well. We were spending a lot of time together, like I said. And from the beginning there was . . . um. A spark, I guess. So we started seeing each other."

"It was just physical, though," Lilah interrupted. "Nothing serious."

Shane felt something flare inside his chest. Of course she would say that. He was the one who'd been stupid enough to tell her he loved her, his heart sliding into his stomach when she'd ignored it. But he'd thrown the word around too easily. He'd just been high on sex brain chemicals or something. Sitting next to her now, it was hard to believe he'd ever had any strong feelings for her besides loathing.

"You want to take it from here?" he asked, his voice sharp.

She held up her hands in surrender. "No, please, keep going. I want to hear this part."

Shane shifted in his seat, trying to recapture his train of

thought. "So, things were fine. Good. I thought so, anyway. But then after we wrapped the first season . . ." He paused, feeling Lilah's eyes on him. It felt so fucking stupid saying it out loud. "We, um. We drank a little too much at the party and woke up with . . . matching tattoos."

"You two have matching tattoos?" Dr. Deena asked, eyebrows raised.

"Not anymore. She covered hers up." He glanced at Lilah. "What is that, by the way? Is it a Hags thing?" He tried in vain to keep his voice friendly, prickling with irritation all over again about the whole situation.

Lilah flattened her lips into a tight line. "I think that's beside the point."

"Right. The point. The point is, Lilah made it pretty fucking clear that whatever was going on wasn't working for her anymore."

Lilah sighed heavily. "Okay, yes, fine. I overreacted. But twelve hours later you were sticking your hands up every tube top in L.A., so obviously you weren't *that* torn up about it."

Shame coursed through him, hot and thick. He pushed it down, trying to tap back into that self-righteous anger simmering in the background whenever he was in Lilah's presence.

"*You* broke up with *me,* Lilah," he said, turning to face her directly, trying and failing to keep his frustration from boiling over. "Stop trying to make me the bad guy."

Something resembling pain flashed across her face, just for a second, turning to anger so swiftly he wasn't sure if he'd imagined it.

"You're right, all you did was go out of your way to hurt and humiliate me as much as possible immediately afterward. Truly a prince among men." She shook her head wearily before turning away, her next words escaping under her breath. "There *are* no good guys here. You haven't figured that out yet?"

Guilt pooled in the pit of his stomach. He forced himself to keep his mouth shut before it slipped out: that back then, he hadn't been sure he *could* hurt her. But she was right that he'd damn well tried his hardest.

Getting involved with her had been the biggest mistake of his life—tied with every other subsequent mistake he'd made regarding her. He knew he was far from the only person who'd made bad, impulsive decisions when they were young and stupid, but he'd never been allowed to make a clean break and move on. He had to face her every day, rip off the scab over and over again before the wound had a chance to heal. Even her leaving the show turned out to be only a temporary fix, since here they were again, worse than ever.

She couldn't exactly be the one that got away if he could never fucking escape her.

"Okay. Well. I can see there's clearly still a lot of emotion here, on both sides," Dr. Deena interjected, startling Shane. He'd almost forgotten she was still in the room. "So, things have been like this between you for the past seven years? I'm surprised you've been able to shoot a single episode."

Shane shook his head, suddenly self-conscious that they'd gotten so carried away in front of her.

"No, we were able to put it behind us enough to work together. I mean, we basically just avoided each other as much as possible." He cast a sidelong glance at Lilah. "But then, right before she left the show . . ."

Lilah was staring out the window now, palpably tense. He lost his nerve at the last second, choosing to keep things vague. "Things kind of . . . escalated again. Worse than before."

Dr. Deena leaned forward, studying them both intently for a moment before obviously deciding not to push it. "I see. Let's put a pin in this for now. You're both carrying a lot of resentment over things that happened in the past, but neither of you knows how to make the first move to push past it. Our goal for these sessions is going to be to try to break the holding pattern that you're in. I want to refocus our energy on that. You've known each other for a very long time and obviously used to get along. I don't see why we can't get there again."

Both of them sat in skeptical silence. Dr. Deena turned to Shane.

"Now, Shane. I want you to tell Lilah one thing you like about her."

Shane allowed himself to study Lilah. She watched him impassively, eyes hooded, before turning the other way to look out the window.

Better make it something superficial, something obvious.

He turned back to Dr. Deena. "She's very attractive."

"Let's try to stick to nonphysical attributes, if we can," Dr. Deena replied gently. "And tell her, don't tell me."

"Oh. Sorry." He glanced at Lilah. "Forget I said that."

Her lips were pursed in barely concealed amusement. "Forgotten."

Shane considered taking a passive-aggressive swipe at her perfectionism, her coldness, her stubbornness, but he knew Dr. Deena would just make him come up with something else. If they were going to get through this session, he'd have to pay her a genuine compliment.

"She's—I mean, you're—" he corrected, twisting his head toward Lilah again. "You're a good actor. Really good."

"Because I've pretended to be in love with you for so long?"

she asked drily. She, too, had been expecting a backhanded dig from him.

He shook his head. "No. Not that. You just . . . when we first started. I was really intimidated by you, because you were so . . . you knew what you were doing, and I didn't. Working with you made me step my game up a lot. I learned so much. Just from being around you."

Lilah stared at him, her lips parted slightly.

"Thank you, Shane, for your honesty," Dr. Deena said.

"Yeah. Thanks," Lilah muttered.

"Lilah, I'd like you to do the same for Shane. One thing you like about him."

She shifted on the couch and looked at him for a long time, legs crossed, fingers clasped around her top knee.

It felt like hours ticked by.

Finally, Dr. Deena intervened. "It doesn't have to be anything big. Just the first thing that comes to mind."

Lilah glanced at her. "Sorry." When she spoke again, he could tell she was working hard to keep her voice steady. "It's just . . . you're *very* likable, Shane. You're friends with pretty much everyone. You can be really kind, and funny, and charming, and generous. You have a lot of amazing qualities." Her expression tightened. "It's just been years since I've experienced any of them personally."

It shouldn't have been a revelation to him. Of course he knew how he'd been treating her—and most of the time, she'd been giving it right back. But something about hearing it laid out like that had him speechless, guilt twisting his stomach. Or maybe it was the look on her face that did it: hard and impassive at first glance, but her pink cheeks and shining eyes betraying her.

It could have been an act, an attempt to get Dr. Deena on her side. But that wouldn't be like her. As good an actress as she was, she wasn't one to waste energy faking her emotions off camera if she didn't have to. Not like this, anyway; not to try to manipulate someone else's opinion of her.

That was the thing about Lilah that had always scared the shit out of him: that she was fully, terrifyingly, immutably herself, whether anyone else liked it or not. Whether they liked *her* or not. She was fearless in a way that he, a people pleaser to his core, never could be, which from the very beginning had intimidated him ten times more than her already formidable talent.

So really, her reaction could only mean one thing: if she'd never cared about him—if she still didn't—she wouldn't be this upset.

He had no idea what to do with that information.

When the hour was over, the two of them filed silently through the empty waiting room. As soon as Shane pushed the button for the elevator, Lilah made a beeline for the emergency stairwell. Without thinking, he tagged along after her. When she looked back at him with an accusatory glare, he shrugged.

"Never hurts to get a little exercise."

She didn't say anything, just held the door open behind her so he could squeeze by. The stairs were narrow enough that he had to lag a few steps behind her. They didn't say a word to each other all four flights down, their footfalls echoing off the cement walls.

When they reached the parking lot, he placed his hand on her arm—nonaggressively, he thought, but she still jumped. He dropped it as soon as he had her attention.

"What are you up to right now?"

She eyed him with suspicion. "I was going to go to set early, work on the scene. We have a ton of pages to get through. I don't want to be out there all night."

He looked down at his shoes, feeling ridiculous for even asking. "Do you want to grab something first? Coffee? Or lunch?"

A handful of emotions crossed her face—astonishment, annoyance, then a flicker of that same hurt he'd seen earlier. She glanced down at her feet, and when she looked back up again, it was pure distrust.

"You want to get *lunch*? What, I give you one compliment and suddenly you like me again?"

He shifted his weight. "No. I mean—I don't know. That's what this is for, right? I thought maybe we could . . . keep talking."

She looked at him for a long time before slowly shaking her head. "I think I'm all talked out for the day," she finally said, her voice coming out quieter and more tired than he'd expected. "And I think . . . not without Dr. Deena. For now. It's just . . . there's too much, still."

He nodded mutely. She was right. They'd barely scratched the surface of their issues.

She turned and walked to her car. His own car was a few spaces over, but he just stood there, watching her.

"Stop staring at me, you fucking weirdo," she called as she slid into the driver's seat, but he could hear the trace of laughter in her voice, see the flash of a rueful smile before she shut the door.

9

By the time they began production on the fourth episode, Lilah's attempts to ingratiate herself with the rest of the cast had, thus far, been met with mixed results.

It wasn't like she *needed* to be friends with everyone she worked with. Obviously, she'd been spoiled by her experience on *H.A.G.S.,* but she knew better than to expect that every time. And they weren't outright hostile—to her face, anyway. They were just vaguely distrustful, moderately unfriendly.

She understood it: nothing united a group like a common enemy. With her return upsetting the dynamic of the ensemble—plus whatever Shane had been saying about her—she made sense as a target.

If she hadn't been in the exact position she was in, she would've kept her head down and kept to herself. But she knew she had to be the bigger person—or at least try. It was a fine line to walk: attempting to make genuine overtures toward people who, on the surface, seemed to want nothing to do with her, while avoiding the type of cloying industry-standard fake niceness that made her skin crawl.

If they still disliked her once they got to know her better, that was fine. She'd accepted long ago that she wasn't for everyone. But she wanted to be disliked on her own merits, at least.

Apart from her and Shane, there were four other actors rounding out the principal cast: Margaux Lang, Natalie Barton, Brian Kim, and Rafael Espinosa. Once Lilah had returned to her seat at the first table read, it had been obvious that the voices she'd overheard talking about her in the bathroom belonged to Margaux and Natalie.

But shockingly, Margaux—who played Harrison's long-lost daughter, Rosie—had been the first to crack. At lunch during their second week of shooting, Margaux had sidled up to Lilah in line for catering.

"Are you really still friends with all the *H.A.G.S.* girls?" she'd asked shyly.

At twenty-two, Margaux was in the exact demographic to have grown up watching the trilogy religiously, and that deeply implanted nostalgia was clearly enough to override any misgivings she had about Lilah stealing her screen time. They'd wound up sitting together and chattering a mile a minute all through lunch.

Back at the table read, Lilah had marveled at what a good job they'd done casting her. She was strikingly beautiful, with the heart-shaped face and full lips of Bree (who played Harrison's late wife in flashbacks) combined with Shane's mischievous eyes, her light brown complexion the midpoint between their skin tones. She was good, too, especially for her age; it was like she lit up from within whenever the camera was on her.

As soon as they had the chance to talk one-on-one, Lilah was immediately charmed by her—how candid, funny, and wickedly observant she was. She had Lilah in stitches with her impression of Walt, mimicking his hangdog cadence with uncanny accuracy.

Brian Kim also hadn't seemed to have much of a personal problem with Lilah, probably because he was the most recent addition to the cast—newly bumped up to series regular after appearing as a guest star toward the end of season eight. He played Ryder, a brooding, mysterious vampire, who was obviously being set up for a juicy romance subplot with Margaux (which was likely the other reason she'd warmed up to Lilah so quickly).

Even though he was way too young to normally be on her radar, Lilah's stomach had still fluttered involuntarily the first time she'd seen him: long and lanky with a pouty mouth, cheekbones to die for, and a perfectly tousled head of glossy black hair. He seemed to have that effect on everyone on set, though, sending PAs and producers alike swooning in his wake. If she hadn't been trying to stay on her best behavior around Shane, she would've teased him about aging out of the Hot Young Eye Candy role—but then again, so had she.

Intangible was Brian's first major role out of school, so Lilah soon realized what she'd initially clocked as standoffishness was just nerves and shyness. After the two of them had a long heart-to-heart between takes about the whiplash of going from the bubble of a drama school environment to working on a set, he'd loosened up around her considerably, letting his sweet and goofy side come out.

She knew Rafael Espinosa a little better. He was the oldest of all of them, midforties or so, a veteran character actor with a craggy, interesting face and a salt-and-pepper beard. He'd started recurring on the show in the fourth season as Will, an operative at the government agency that had been antagonizing them for years—now turned double agent, assisting their team.

It was obvious that he and Shane had become close in the interim, though. He'd been barely holding back a smirk on that miserable day when she could barely get her lines out. Given his loyalty to Shane, he was probably a lost cause.

Natalie Barton, unsurprisingly, had proven to be the wild card. Her character, Carla, the quirky, deadpan computer hacker of the group, had been brought in primarily as a new romantic interest for Harrison, which meant as Lilah's ostensible replacement, Natalie was now redundant. She was in jeopardy of being sidelined at best, prematurely written off at worst. Out of all of them, she had the most legitimate reasons to resent Lilah's presence.

Which was why Lilah groaned to herself when she received the script for the fourth episode: the writers were finally diving headfirst into setting up the love triangle between Kate, Harrison, and Carla. The episode was dominated by the three of them—Lilah and the two people she dreaded sharing scenes with the most.

On the morning they were set to shoot their first scene together, just her and Natalie, Lilah sat through makeup with a nervous quiver in her stomach, Natalie one seat away from her, ignoring her. She was around Lilah's age, shorter and curvier, with platinum hair and skin almost as pale, striking blue eyes completing the ice queen aesthetic.

They were on location that day, shooting exteriors at the motel that had served as the group's base of operations for the past few seasons. When they arrived, they quickly blocked out the scene with Paul, the director.

"Are you good to go, or do you need more rehearsal than that?" Paul asked.

Lilah and Natalie eyed each other. Rehearsal was a luxury most of the time—especially for exteriors, where natural light was a factor—but it often ended up saving time on the back end, since they could catch problems early without wasting takes. However, this scene was short and straightforward enough that they probably didn't need it.

"I'm . . ." Lilah began, nodding slowly, still looking at Natalie. "If you . . . do you?"

"No, I'm good. Let's do it," Natalie said, her tone curt.

They got final touches on their makeup and made their way to their starting marks inside the room.

"Roll sound . . . roll camera . . . mark it," the assistant director called from the other side of the door, the slate clapping.

"Action," Paul yelled.

Natalie burst out of the door faster than Lilah was anticipating, forcing her to speed walk to catch up so she could deliver her first line. They barely got through a page and a half of dialogue before Paul called "Cut," both their heads snapping toward him.

"Nat, you're playing it kind of aggressive," he said. "I think you're wary of her, but you don't need to ice her out that much. Try to find a little more warmth, a little curiosity in it."

Natalie took the note without reacting, but Lilah could feel the tension radiating off her. "Sure. Okay. Sorry, Paul."

"I know you'll get it. Let's reset, back to one. Lilah, you're doing great, don't change a thing."

Lilah winced internally as she saw Natalie stiffen further at Paul's praise. Sure enough, the next take wasn't any better, and with each subsequent take, she could tell Natalie was getting more and more psyched out.

"Hey, do we have time for a five?" Lilah finally called out, after yet another unsatisfactory attempt. Natalie shot her a glance that was halfway between embarrassed and grateful as Paul agreed, the crew dispersing. Lilah turned to her.

"Can we talk?"

They walked alongside the motel until they reached the wall farthest from the set. Lilah stopped, leaning her shoulder against the stucco. Once Natalie's wary gaze settled on her, Lilah felt a flutter of nerves, but she forced them aside. It was now or never.

"I think we need to clear the air a little," Lilah said. "Maybe I'm imagining it, but I've been feeling some weird tension between us since the first table read."

"No," Natalie said, her eyes trained on her feet. "You're not imagining it." Lilah waited, but she didn't elaborate any further.

"Okay. Well. It's fine if you don't like me, or you don't like that I'm back on the show, or whatever it is. But if there's anything you want to say to me, or anything I can do to fix it . . . let's talk it out. Or, as much as we can in—" Lilah checked her phone. "Three and a half more minutes."

Natalie was silent for a moment. Then she brought her hand to her eyes and groaned in frustration. "God. I'm sorry. It's not you." She dropped her hand and crossed her arms. "You know your fans are fucking scary, right?"

Lilah blinked, surprised. "My fans?"

"Yeah. You and Shane. I can't open my phone now without someone harassing me for getting between you two. Saying the most fucked-up shit you can imagine. Telling me to kill myself, telling me they know where I live. And this season hasn't even started *airing* yet."

Lilah's stomach lurched. "Are you serious? They know it's not real, right?"

"You'd think."

"Fuck." Lilah exhaled heavily. "I'm so sorry. I had no idea it was that bad. I don't run any of my social media, I haven't looked at any of that stuff in years. Is there anything I can do to make them calm down? Like, post a picture of us together or something? Tell them to chill the fuck out?"

Natalie smiled wryly. "Maybe I should just leak a behind-the-scenes video of you and Shane. Then they'd see that *I'm* not the one keeping you guys apart." Her expression turned earnest. "I'm sorry I've been taking it out on you. It's hard not to think about it whenever I'm around you. But it's not your fault. Although I guess it doesn't help that it kind of feels like the writing's on the wall. Like the show isn't big enough for everyone." There was no arrogance in Natalie's delivery, just an aura of defeat. Lilah's chest tightened in sympathy.

"That's not true," Lilah said, shaking her head emphatically. "They're really lucky to have you. *We're* lucky, I mean."

Natalie looked like she was about to protest, but she met Lilah's eyes, and something in her whole countenance softened. Like she could tell Lilah was being sincere.

"Not today, you aren't," Natalie deadpanned, her eyes flicking back toward the set.

Lilah waved her hand dismissively. "We all have those days. You saw me fighting for my life last week." Her phone alarm buzzed, notifying them their break was over. She silenced it with a swipe. "Should we get back to it?"

When they returned to set, they nailed the two-shot in one take.

10

Shane's birthday fell in early August, which, for most of his childhood, had meant an opportunity to make new friends. It wasn't that his birthday parties were anything special—if they even happened at all. But year after year, when he inevitably found himself yet again starting at a new school where he knew nobody, it helped to break the ice.

As an adult, he usually didn't do much to celebrate. The big exception had been his thirtieth, when Serena had thrown an extravagant masquerade ball for him at her house. But as he'd floated through room after room filled with smoke and colored lights and more famous people than he'd ever seen in one place (except maybe at the Golden Globes), clutching an elaborate cocktail served to him by a dancer wearing nothing but body paint, he'd had a strange, queasy feeling, like the party wasn't really about him at all.

He was turning thirty-five this year, though, so he felt compelled to do *some*thing. He'd rented out the generously sized back room and paid for an open bar at Gold Rush—the closest thing he had to a neighborhood haunt, considering how little he went out these days. It was cozy and unpretentious, while still a few steps above a dive.

Even though he'd been in L.A. for almost ten years at this point, most of his social life still revolved around *Intangible*, which was reflected in the guest list. He'd drifted apart from his party friends once he'd started dating Serena, who, like Lilah, had despised them—but unlike Lilah, she hadn't even bothered trying to hide it, and since she was actually his girlfriend, her opinion held more weight.

He'd started to pull away from them even earlier than that, though—ever since his week of debauchery after he and Lilah had broken up. He hadn't gone home with most of the women he'd taken out, but he'd still woken up each subsequent morning feeling grimier and grimier, more hungover, more strung out, more embarrassed, until he'd finally had enough. Anyway, it had been a distraction, not a cure. Lilah's role in getting Devon fired from the show had only sped up the inevitable. Within a year, he wasn't in touch with any of them anymore.

As he sipped his beer and glanced around the room, he was heartened by the turnout, cast and crew alike. At the same time, though, he couldn't ignore the bittersweet pang at the thought that they'd all be going their separate ways after this year.

He'd invited Lilah, of course, but only because it would've been too much of a statement not to. They were supposed to be getting along now, after all. But it was the definition of an empty gesture. He knew she wouldn't come.

Which was why, when he saw her stroll into the bar right as he was lining up a shot on the pool table, he was so startled that he sent the cue ball straight into the corner pocket. Shane glanced over at Dean on the other side of the table, who gave Shane an appraising look before retrieving the cue ball.

"What?" Shane asked.

Dean shook his head. "Surprised you invited her."

"I invited everyone."

"Guess things must be better, then. Since she came."

"Or she's here to start shit," Shane grumbled. Even as he said it, though, he knew it wasn't true. It wasn't her style. She could be vicious, for sure, but she usually didn't lash out unprovoked. The two of them had an uneasy truce. For now.

Shane caught Lilah's eye. She raised her hand in a small wave but didn't approach him.

In fact, she steered clear of him all night. Her motivations behind showing up became increasingly apparent, though, as he watched her work the room like a pro: gossiping in a corner with Margaux, refereeing an arm wrestling match between Brian and the key grip, conferring over the jukebox with Natalie before sending the Bee Gees blasting through the bar. As hard as he tried to push down his annoyance at the whole scene, it popped back up with equal force, like a beach ball held underwater.

Later in the evening, Shane handed the bartender a few hundred bucks in cash and told him to take a break before slipping behind the bar himself.

Even though he'd been working as a waiter when he'd been cast in *Intangible,* most of his service industry experience had been as a bartender. It was still his favorite job he'd ever had. All the sitting around he did as an actor was luxurious, but it was also incredibly boring. And now, as he sank into the rhythm of it again, his muscle memory taking over, he felt useful in a way he hadn't in years.

Not that he romanticized getting people drunk as some kind of humanitarian outreach or anything. And he didn't take for granted the enjoyment and escape that *Intangible* brought to the people who watched it. But there'd been a level of human connection with his customers that he could never replicate with some distant, faceless audience. And on slow nights, when he'd get drawn into a long conversation with a stranger or a regular, his relative anonymity allowing them to confide in him in a way they couldn't with anyone else, he'd felt the most useful of all.

Tonight, though, tending bar provided the perfect setting for Shane to hold court, flitting from one conversation to another. As he chatted with several of the writers, popping the tops off their beers in a series of fluid, practiced motions, he felt more at ease than he had all night.

But there was something off about it, too. It had been ten years since he'd been behind a bar for real, and he likely never would be again—unless he was playing a bartender. A photocopy of a real person, who ceased to exist when no one was looking at him or telling him what to do.

Anxiety gripped him suddenly at the thought that maybe the others would see it as some kind of smug joke. *Look how out of place I am back here, ha ha. How ridiculous for me to serve rather than be served.* Like he was gloating about a life he'd never have to return to, instead of grasping desperately at one he missed.

As if he'd manifested it out of the depths of his subconscious, he heard the opening notes of "Common People" cut through the room. He jerked his head up to see Lilah by the jukebox again, eyebrows raised mockingly in his direction before she turned away.

Of course she could tell exactly how he was feeling. She'd always had a preternatural ability to hone in on his insecurities— almost before he could name them himself. She'd think it was funny, naturally, to let him know she knew, needling him with a song about rich people playacting at being poor.

She was one to talk, anyway. He knew she'd grown up in a wealthy suburb and attended a private arts high school before her stint at Juilliard. *Her* childhood birthday parties probably had four-figure budgets.

He watched as Lilah returned to her game of darts with Dean and Rafael, forcing himself to tamp down the surge of betrayal he felt at seeing the three of them being so buddy-buddy. He knew Raf wasn't that fond of her, but get a couple of drinks in him and he'd cuddle up to a rattlesnake. And as for Dean . . . well.

It looked like a close game, but Rafael triumphed in the end, Lilah throwing her hands up good-naturedly as he slapped her on the back. She collected their empty glasses—obviously her penalty for losing—and headed toward Shane.

"Bulleit neat, water, and whatever IPA Dean's drinking. *Please,*" she said, dropping the glasses to the counter with a clink. She eyed the pitcher on the bar next to her, overflowing with tips. "This isn't going to you, is it?"

He cleared the glasses and leaned a fresh pint glass under the tap. "Of course not."

"Just checking." She dug a twenty out of her pocket and dropped it in.

As he poured the whiskey, she turned away until she was in profile, pointedly ignoring him, scraping her hair into a make-shift ponytail with one hand. Over the past few hours, the temperature in the bar had crept up to somewhere between "muggy" and "stuffy," leaving everyone looking like glazed donuts. He tried to ignore the flush staining her cheeks; the stray lock of hair, damp with sweat, that clung to her neck; the way the position of her arms made her breasts swell above the neckline of her tank top.

"What's with the Miss Congeniality act?" Shane asked casually, placing Rafael's whiskey next to Dean's beer.

She raised an eyebrow, dropping her hair and turning back to him. "You mean being friendly to my co-workers? Who says it's an act?"

Shane filled a pint glass with ice and aimed the soda gun into it. "I dunno. Seems a little out of character, working this hard to get people to like you."

He expected her to bristle, but instead, a slow smile spread across her face, sending an unexpected (and unwelcome) surge of heat through his veins.

"Of course. Because if I don't make an effort, I'm a bitch who thinks I'm better than everyone. But if I *do* make an effort, I'm being fake. What do you want from me, exactly?" She wasn't drunk; he hadn't seen her have a drink all night. There was nothing to explain the playful challenge in her demeanor— other than the possibility that she actually *was* having a good time and refused to let him ruin it.

"I'm just waiting for my turn in the sun." He moved to put her water on the bar, but she held out her hand, so he passed it right to her. When their fingers brushed, he thought he saw something spark in her eyes. She looked away before he could parse it.

"You already had your turn." She tilted her head back and took a long drink before placing the glass back on the bar, half-empty. He dutifully refilled it.

"It does make things easier, though. If we all get along," he said. "That's why you're doing this, right?"

She glanced over at him and gave a long, exasperated exhale.

"Maybe I genuinely like them. Maybe they like *me*—as hard as that might be for you to believe." She gracefully scooped up the drinks, meeting his eyes again, her gaze as chilled as the ice in the bin in front of him. "And maybe you don't know me as well as you think you do."

With that, she sauntered back over to the dartboard. Obviously, he watched her walk away, but he didn't realize how intently he'd been staring until an unexpected voice next to him made him jump.

"So, who dumped who?"

He turned to see Natalie nursing the end of her whiskey sour.

When Natalie had first joined the cast, he'd reflexively kept a polite distance from her, not wanting to make the same mistake twice; however, once they'd established they weren't really attracted to each other, the two of them had become good friends. Shane had even introduced her to her now-husband, a private chef he'd met through Serena.

They'd never discussed the specifics of his history with Lilah, though.

He cleared his throat, taking a sip of his own beer behind the bar. "Sorry?"

"Come on." She slid onto the barstool in front of him. "The last time I was on a set this tense, the director was in the middle of divorcing the star. He tried to fire her, the producers intervened, it was a whole thing. They wouldn't even speak directly to each other, they just had their assistants pass messages back and forth."

Shane winced. "Are we that bad?"

Natalie's expression turned triumphant. "So it *is* true."

He paused. He'd never told anyone who worked on the show about him and Lilah—besides Dean, of course. That didn't mean other people hadn't figured it out on their own, but it was still probably best to play dumb.

"What's true?"

"You two. You had a thing way back when, and that's why you hate each other now."

Shane looked down at the bar. Suddenly, he was struck with a need to confess, to confide. Who was he protecting? Lilah? Himself? Whatever they'd had back then was long dead and buried, even if its ghost refused to leave them alone. It didn't seem like it would make much of a difference at this point, finally confirming what everyone had already assumed.

"Yeah. Yeah, it's true. But it wasn't anything . . ." He trailed off before starting again. "It was over by the second season."

He held out his hand for Natalie's glass, and she passed it to him. She rested her chin on her hand. "Wow. So that was, what, seven years ago? And you're both still this weird around each other? Not that your little *Scenes from a Marriage* role-play isn't fun for all of us, but it kinda seems like it's time to get over it."

Shane hunted around for the sour mix, considering. He shouldn't say anything else. He shouldn't.

"It's not just about that."

"What, then?"

He mixed Natalie's drink thoughtfully, buying some time. He didn't want to seem like he was trying to turn her against Lilah. But it was the truth. It wasn't his fault if it made Lilah look bad.

"She slept with Dean."

Shane placed the drink in front of Natalie, but she ignored it, her eyes wide with shock. "What? When?"

"At her last wrap party."

Her jaw dropped. "*At* the party?"

"After, sorry. After. They left together. That was the last time I saw her. Until upfronts."

He still saw it, sometimes. The two of them headed toward the exit, Dean's arm slung around her shoulders. He must have had a few too many at that party, though, because he remembered it two distinct ways. In one version, she glanced back at him, making sure he was watching. In the other, she didn't bother.

Three and a half years later, he still wasn't sure which one was worse.

Dean had stumbled home the next morning, shirt inside out, shamefaced, mumbling about how nothing had happened, unable to meet Shane's eyes. That was the thing about Dean, though: he'd never grown out of that little kid impulse to lie his way out of trouble.

Shane had forgiven him, obviously. Eventually. But he hadn't believed him for a second.

"Damn." Natalie craned her neck to look across the bar, and Shane followed her gaze. At that exact moment, Lilah and Dean were dancing to the eighties hair metal playing on the jukebox—in a manner that was decidedly goofy, not sexy. Not even touching. Still, Shane felt something hot flare behind his rib cage, and he quickly looked away.

"Can't blame her for having a type, I guess," Natalie mused.

Shane shook his head a little too emphatically. "It was only that once. She just did it to get back at me. They both did."

"Get back at you for what?"

His mouth tightened. "Doesn't matter."

Natalie's eyebrows were in her hairline as she sipped her drink. "It matters what they did, but not what you did?"

Just then, Margaux came to his rescue, appearing out of nowhere with a plate bearing an array of cupcakes, "three" and "five" candles stuck haphazardly into the two in the center. Shane ducked out from behind the bar as the rest of the group crowded around him, singing "Happy Birthday" boisterously in a variety of keys and tempos.

"Make a wish!" someone shouted.

He didn't put much stock in birthday wishes. Even so, as he bent over the candles, he racked his brain, only to come up empty. At the very last second, he glanced up, catching Lilah's eyes in the back of the crowd right before he blew them out.

11

Backstage at *After Hours with Joey Masters,* Lilah was trying her best to keep her cool—or look like she was, at least. If she'd still been in her own dressing room, she probably would've been pacing, trying to work off some of her nervous energy. But once she'd gotten her hair and makeup touched up, she'd been brought to a shared greenroom with Shane to await their interview together.

The network had put them on a red-eye to New York less than a week before *Intangible*'s season premiere, their *After Hours* appearance serving as the centerpiece of a press tour that had seemed endless. Thankfully, they'd been making the rounds separately as much as together. But out of everything they'd done so far—the magazine spreads, the newspaper profiles, the soul-searching podcast interviews, eating hot wings on YouTube—this appearance was the one she'd been dreading the most.

After Hours was an entertainment industry dinosaur, a legendary late-night talk show that had been on the air since the fifties. Its current host, comedian Joey Masters, had gotten famous for his filthy, misogynistic stand-up, his hard-core coke habit, and his extramarital hookups with barely legal fans. But once he'd done the bare minimum to clean up his act, he was rewarded, in classic smarmy-white-guy fashion, with a show that brought him into fifteen million homes a night.

Talk shows had always made her skittish, though she wasn't sure why. It wasn't being in front of an audience—she'd done plenty of theater. The show was pretaped, not live. All their talking points had been approved in advance. She'd been a professional actress for over a decade now; there was no reason that her hands should be this sweaty, her heart racing like she'd been running stairs at the Empire State Building.

Maybe it was because she was playing her least favorite character: herself, but not herself. Blander, glossier, smilier, all her sharp edges sanded off, eyelids heavy under fake lashes and skin thick with foundation, channeling a level of perky falseness that left a bitter aftertaste in her mouth. Or maybe it was the persistent reminder that a hell of a lot of people's jobs—her own included—were riding on whether a critical mass of strangers wanted to either be her friend or fuck her.

This was the kind of thing that made her feel the most under the microscope, even more so than when she was secretly photographed out and about with no makeup and greasy hair. It was the ultimate paradox: She was there to show the audience how relatable she was, that she was just like them. But the fact that she was up there to begin with meant she wasn't very much like them at all.

When she'd arrived in the greenroom, Shane was already there, standing with his hands in his pockets, looking idly at the pictures on the wall of previous guests spanning the past half century. When he glanced over at her, she'd felt a jolt that was certainly just nerves, and nothing to do with the way he looked in his suit: dark blue, no tie, crisp white shirt unbuttoned enough to see a hint of chest hair. He gave her an appreciative once-over in return, then planted himself in the middle of the couch and pulled out his phone, leaving her to spiral in relative peace.

Joey had stopped by soon after to shake hands and make small talk, briefly going over the topics for the interview one more time: the photo shoot, the season premiere, how great it was to be back together. Lilah nodded and smiled and didn't say much, distracted by the soft buzz filling her head, thankful that Joey mostly ignored her in favor of bro-ing down with Shane. Her emergency Ativan called to her from her clutch, but she knew it would be a mistake to break into it. She needed to stay sharp.

After Joey left, she leaned against the long counter that lined the wall opposite the couch, drumming her fingers on it rhythmically.

"Man. I forgot how much you hate this."

She glanced up to see Shane staring at her.

"I'm fine." She cringed at the tremor in her voice, audible even in two terse syllables.

He slid his phone into his jacket pocket and settled against the couch, stretching his arms wide across the back. "I don't think I'd last five minutes in there."

"Where?"

"Your brain."

To her surprise, there was nothing derisive in his tone—just quiet bemusement.

She closed her eyes, taking deep, deliberate breaths, forcing her lungs to do their job, despite what felt like a hundred pounds of wet sand sitting on top of them.

The show's muffled theme music filtered through the walls, alerting her that the taping had started. When she opened her eyes again, she directed her gaze at the monitor next to Shane's head, watching without really watching as Joey silently mugged his way through his monologue.

"Do you still have stress nightmares all the time?"

She glanced sharply back at Shane. She'd forgotten she'd ever told him.

She'd been plagued by them since she was a kid, vivid and disorienting, causing her to wake up with her heart racing or her pillow wet with tears. In the first recurring one she could remember, she was sitting in the back seat of a car in the dead of night, hurtling along a narrow forest road at breakneck speed, crawling up to the front seat in a panic only to find no one driving. As an adult, she was often on the run, a variety of relentless pursuers hot on her tail, the consequences once they caught her ominous but unclear.

The fact that he'd even remembered, let alone brought it up at all, had her on high alert.

"Are you trying to tell me I look tired?"

"Just curious."

She considered ignoring him—but the alternative was going back to the interminable silence, drowning in her own thoughts.

"Not always full-on nightmares. But anxiety dreams, yeah. Most nights."

"And you don't have any way to manage it? After this long?"

"No, I do. Sort of."

The caginess of her answer didn't deter him. In fact, it seemed to do the opposite, his posture straightening. "What? What is it?"

She shook her head.

"Come on," he said, breaking out his most charming grin. Lilah's stomach did an involuntary flip, and she sighed.

"Sometimes it's, like, lucid dreaming. Where I can control it. Especially if it's one I have a lot. So if that's the case, I just . . . do my best to turn it into a sex dream."

Shane burst out laughing. She felt something flutter in her chest, distinct from her jitters. Something almost pleasant.

"And how does that work, exactly?"

She shrugged, doing her best to keep a straight face. "I try to have sex with whatever's coming after me. Or, like, a random bystander, if I'm not being chased by anything. It kind of depends on the situation."

He leaned forward, resting his elbows on his knees, his gaze direct. "Anyone I'd know?"

"You know, it did look a little like you under the Pennywise makeup the other night."

He laughed again, a quick, surprised bark. "You fucked Pennywise?"

"Well, I tried. He wasn't really that into it."

"You got *rejected* by Pennywise? That is a nightmare." Shane reclined back against the couch again, crossing an ankle over his knee, appraising her. "For what it's worth, you're way out of his league."

"Thanks. I'll tell him that next time he shows up." She shifted her weight, crossing her arms. "Other kids used to call me that sometimes, when I was growing up. You know. The hair."

Shane frowned, tapping his finger to his lips. "Hmm. And

now he haunts your nightmares and turns down your sexual advances. I wonder what that means."

She suppressed a smile. "Stop trying to analyze me."

"I could never. I'll leave that to Dr. Deena."

Shane leaned over to the monitor and turned up the volume, Joey's voice gradually becoming audible.

"After the break, we have two very special guests—you're in for a treat tonight, folks." He grinned, displaying more teeth than should reasonably fit in a human mouth. "The stars of *Intangible* are here: Lilah Hunter and Shane McCarthy." The applause that followed was so thunderous it felt like it shook the greenroom. "Yes, yes, we're all very excited. We'll be right back!"

It wasn't until her heartbeat kicked into double time again that she realized how much their conversation had calmed her—if only temporarily.

A production assistant came to herd them to their spot in the wings, behind the band, hidden by a curtain, to wait out the short break while they reset everything for the interview.

Lilah could hear a flurry of commotion around her—the audience chattering, crew members murmuring into headsets, the band riffing—but their pocket of the wings was relatively peaceful. It was just the two of them, plus a lone PA stationed a few feet in front of them, facing the stage, attention elsewhere.

The anticipation was always the worst part. Once she got out there, she'd be fine. That's what she told herself, anyway, as her heartbeat grew bigger somehow, until she was one giant pulse, her head so light she thought it might float off her shoulders.

"Are you okay?" Shane's voice cut through her reverie. She glanced at him, and whatever he saw on her face had his brow creasing in unfamiliar concern.

She nodded, her hand flitting up to brush her hair out of her face, which was a mistake. One, because it had already been perfectly arranged by the stylist and wasn't in her face whatso-ever. And two, because it drew both of their attention to how badly her hands were shaking.

He took a step closer, and she instinctively backed away, her shoulders brushing the curtain.

"Hey," he said quietly, in an obvious attempt to soothe her. But it just freaked her out even more, because the last time he'd used that tone with her was—actually, she didn't think he ever had. "C'mere."

He reached out to touch her bare shoulder, soft and un-sure, and if she'd felt even marginally less frazzled, she would've brushed him right off. Instead, she stepped forward and allowed herself to be folded into his arms, her body overriding the pro-tests of her brain in a desperate search for comfort before she shut down completely.

She slid her arms around his lower back, inside his unbut-toned jacket, a sigh escaping her as his scent and warmth envel-oped her on all sides. His own arms flexed in response, pulling her closer. She half expected to tense up, but instead, the aching familiarity of it all had her melting into the embrace like a stick of butter on a hot skillet. She nestled her forehead into his neck, careful to avoid smearing makeup on his collar. Her shallow breaths began to match the pace of his, deep and even, gradually syncing up.

And then, to her astonishment, she felt his face turn slightly, until his mouth was pressed against her hair. But it must have been an anxiety-induced hallucination, because there was no fucking way Shane McCarthy was kissing her on the fucking head.

Something shifted between them then, something she didn't want to think about. Something that made a fully clothed hug suddenly feel exponentially more intimate than when she'd been naked on top of him a couple of months ago. His breathing became heavier, almost ragged, at the same time as her heart began to pound again.

Vaguely, she heard the band break into the theme song, signaling their return from the break. The PA next to them cleared his throat.

She and Shane released each other, slowly enough that it could be considered reluctant. When she got a look at his face, his brow was creased even more deeply than before, which made her feel a little better. Less alone in her confusion.

As they pulled apart, his fingertips skated down her bare arm, leaving goosebumps in their wake. At the last second, she caught hold of his hand.

He looked down at it, then back up at her, his expression difficult to parse. He didn't let go, though, just gave her hand a quick squeeze, which she was grateful for, because it felt like the only thing keeping her from passing out.

The curtain in front of them opened, the audience howling with excitement as they walked onstage to an instrumental cover of "Superstition." She realized too late that they were still holding hands, that people could actually see them now. Shane seemed to have the same thought at the same time, and they separated halfway to the couch, settling on the cushions—close, but not too close—as the band played their final sting.

After exchanging a few generic pleasantries, Joey leaned back in his chair.

"Now, listen. Let's address the elephant in the room here. There's been some rumors going around that the two of you don't get along, but honestly, I'm having a hard time believing that. Was I hallucinating, or were you holding hands when you came out just now? Ronald, did you catch that?" He lobbed the last question at Ronald, his bandleader.

"I did see that, yeah," confirmed Ronald.

Lilah and Shane exchanged conspiratorial glances, though inside she was still as bewildered as ever.

"I thought she looked cold," Shane said innocently.

"I see. So you were warming her up, one hand at a time?" The audience tittered.

"Every little bit helps."

"He's very considerate," Lilah said.

"Are you cold, Lilah?" Joey asked, returning his attention to her. "I'm sorry, that's probably my fault. I'm always asking them to crank the AC. The suit, the lights, it can get a little moist in sensitive areas."

"Well, not all of us are lucky enough to be wearing suits," Lilah said, feeling her smile turn sickly sweet.

"You're right, you're right. Shane, why don't you give her your jacket?"

The audience whooped and cheered. Lilah demurred, but it didn't stop Shane from immediately shucking off his jacket and leaning over to drape it around her shoulders. Her fingertips brushed his as she reached up to pull it tighter around her, the warm satin lining like an embrace against her chilled skin, a tangible reminder of the one they'd shared backstage a minute ago. She shivered.

"Thank you," she murmured, gazing up through her oversized eyelashes at him, feeling obligated to ham it up a little for the camera lurking in her peripheral vision.

"How are we doing now?" Joey asked. "Comfortable?"

"All better."

"Great, great. See? This is what I'm talking about. We're all friends here, right? Now, speaking of. Everyone's been talking about these pictures of you two." Joey turned to the audience. "Have you guys seen these? Can we get them up on the screen?"

The audience oohed and aahed, scandalized, as pictures from their *Reel* photo shoot faded onto the monitors.

Lilah had been sent proofs through her agent a few weeks ago, but the prospect of looking through them had been so unappealing she'd approved them without opening the email. Seeing them now, though, took her breath away. Dario had done an incredible job: like he'd promised, they were sexy without being sleazy. Her eye was drawn immediately to their faces, rapt with desire, their naked bodies almost beside the point.

"So, level with me," Joey said. "What's it like, shooting that kind of thing? Gotta be a *little* awkward, right?"

Lilah and Shane both opened their mouths to reply, then made eye contact and hesitated, intentionally drawing out their knowing looks a beat too long, making the audience laugh.

"It's just part of the job," Lilah finally replied, with a coy smile.

"It was kind of boring, honestly," Shane added. "I almost fell asleep a few times. I mean, we were already in bed, you know?"

"Right. Right. Just another day at the office," Joey said. "Ronald and I have a shoot like that every morning before we get our coffee, right, Ronald?"

"You didn't tell me there were cameras," Ronald replied, and the audience hooted.

Lilah felt like she was watching herself from outside her body after that, as she, Joey, and Shane discussed her return to the show and what fans could expect from the final season. She saw herself gush about how welcoming everyone had been, how much she'd missed playing Kate. They played a clip from the premiere, her resurrection scene.

"That was from the ninth season of *Intangible,* premiering next Tuesday, September twenty-third," Joey said as the audience cheered. "Don't go away, we'll be right back with Lilah Hunter and Shane McCarthy, and we're gonna play a little game. Stay tuned!"

A few days before the taping, Lilah had been sent a brief questionnaire to fill out about Shane, and he'd presumably had to answer the same questions about her. During the break, a producer handed each of them a small stack of cards containing their answers, so they could try to match them, *Newlywed Game–*style.

"Now, you two have known each other a long time," Joey said after the break. "Today, we're going to test out just *how* well you know each other."

They started out simply, just the facts—how many siblings Shane had (two) and where Lilah had grown up (Philadelphia)—which they both answered correctly.

Joey consulted his cards. "Lilah, this next one's for you. What's your go-to snack when you're on set?"

Lilah blinked. It hadn't occurred to her that the sets of questions they got would be slightly different, that her own answers would have to be off the cuff. She grabbed onto the first thing that crossed her mind.

"Um . . . almonds?" She regretted it the moment she said it. It was true, but she knew it made her sound like an out-of-touch diet article in a women's magazine, like she was just another neurotic actress obsessed with maintaining her weight. Which maybe she was, but only to the extent that she had to be. Either way, it wasn't an answer that would endear her to anyone, which was supposed to be the point.

"All right, solid choice," Joey said. "A little boring, but solid. Shane, let's see your answer. What does Lilah like to eat on set?"

Shane turned over one of his oversized cards to face Lilah and the cameras. When she saw what he'd written, she shocked herself by throwing her head back and laughing—her first genuine reaction of the night.

The card read **LEAN POCKETS AND RED BULL**.

Joey laughed, too, clapping like a trained seal. "Your cover's blown, Lilah. I knew that 'almonds' thing sounded fishy."

Lilah exchanged looks with Shane. "No comment."

"All right, all right, I see what's happening here. Let's keep it moving, then. Shane, who was your first celebrity crush? Getting into the really hard-hitting questions now," Joey added under his breath, shooting the camera an exaggeratedly world-weary glance.

"My first celebrity crush?" He took a moment to think about it. "I gotta say . . . Ginger Spice."

Joey nodded emphatically. "Good choice, man, good choice. Right there with you. Lilah, did you get it?"

Lilah felt a smug thrill in her stomach as she revealed her card: **GINGER SPICE**.

"Nice work," Joey said. "You know, Lilah, you've got kind of a Ginger Spice thing going on yourself." He addressed the next question to Shane. "Does she ever wear that little Union Jack dress for you?"

Lilah laughed, but in every way except physically, she was already in the scalding hot shower she knew she'd need later to scrub this interview off her.

Shane's face was somber. "Actually, I'm usually the one wearing it."

The crowd hollered and whistled as Joey grimaced. "Now, *that's* an image I didn't need."

Lilah rolled her eyes. "Can we move on, please?" She meant

it to sound playful, but as soon as it came out, she felt the caustic edge to it.

Joey straightened his cards. "Okay. I'm sensing this game is wearing out its welcome, but luckily we're on the last one. This is for you, Lilah." He assumed a serious expression, delivering every word with melodramatic gravitas. "Most. Embarrassing. Moment."

Lilah froze. She looked at Shane, trying to figure out what he might have said. The answer was obvious: her movie. Her agent had told Joey's producers that the topic was off-limits for interview banter, but Shane could easily go rogue. But he wouldn't actually write that, would he? It would just make *him* look bad.

"Uh . . ." She stalled for a moment, praying something else would come to her. Suddenly, it did. "Oh! One time when we were shooting, I was wearing these really tight pants that were made out of this, like, thin satiny material, and we were doing a scene where I kept having to crouch down over and over, and then finally . . ." She trailed off, scrunching up her face.

"You ripped 'em?" Joey supplied.

"I ripped 'em," she confirmed with a self-deprecating laugh, the audience following suit.

They both looked over at Shane. It seemed like he was turning the card over in slow motion, her heart pounding in her ears, her brain struggling to unscramble the letters written on it: **RIPPED HER PANTS ON SET.**

She felt a rush of relief so intense that she was dizzy for a moment. Declining to humiliate her on national television was a pretty low bar for him to clear, but she appreciated it all the same.

The crowd cheered at their success, Joey pausing for a minute to wait for it to die down. "I'd like to see *those* outtakes, if you know what I mean," he said, waggling his eyebrows at the camera.

She smiled, frozen. She knew the good-natured lech thing was part of his shtick, but it also felt like every hair on her body was standing on end. In any other circumstance, she'd have no problem dressing him down or removing herself from the situation altogether, but right now, she had two options, neither of them good: call it out and look like a humorless bitch, or say nothing and look like a doormat.

But to her astonishment, Shane swooped in with a third option she hadn't considered.

"No, I don't know what you mean," he replied, without a trace of humor in his voice.

Joey's smile faltered. "Hey, come on. It was just a joke."

"I don't get it," Shane said evenly, fixing an unwavering stare on Joey. "Explain it to me."

The audience tittered uncomfortably.

Finally, Joey pulled at his collar exaggeratedly. "Jeez, tough crowd." He switched back to address the camera, smoothly transitioning them out from the segment, thanking them for appearing, and bumping the show back to commercial. She had no doubt that that last exchange would be cut from the final episode before it aired that evening.

The music swelled and the cameras panned back, Joey leaning in to make fake small talk with them until the moment his producer called "Cut." Then, they were swept off the couch with little fanfare.

As they headed backstage again, Lilah glanced over at Shane. "Thank you," she murmured.

He met her gaze but didn't say anything. He didn't have to. To her surprise, she felt the pressure of his hand between her shoulder blades, just for a second, through his jacket, which she was still wearing. There was something in the gesture reminis- cent of their earliest days, back when it felt like the two of them against the world.

She didn't know what to make of any of it. All she knew was that she was grateful.

The next morning, Walt emailed them both a link to a *Vulture* article, accompanied by two words: *Nice job*. She didn't even have to click the link to know what it was, based on the fact that the URL ended with *karrison-shippers-assemble.html*. But she clicked on it anyway.

When the page loaded, she was greeted by a header image of her and Shane on the couch, him frozen in the process of drap- ing his jacket around her shoulders as she gazed up at him with an expression that, if she didn't know any better, she'd say looked a lot like adoration.

12

Shane had meant to find a real date for the season-nine premiere party, but since he barely had time to breathe with the whirlwind of promo stuffed into the gaps in their shooting schedule, it snuck up on him before he knew it. For once, Dean didn't have a date, either, so the two of them shared a car to the first venue of the evening—a theater that the network had rented out to screen the episode—which would be followed by an after-party at a historic nightclub nearby.

On the ride over, Dean was uncharacteristically quiet, staring out the window.

"You good?" Shane asked.

Dean turned to him, shaking his head a little. "Just thinking about how this is the last one of these."

"Yeah," Shane said. "But you know I'm taking you with me, right? Whatever happens next. If I have a job, you have a job."

Dean's face clouded over unexpectedly.

"Right," he said, looking back out the window again.

Shane frowned, but he didn't push it.

Honestly, he'd been a little surprised that Dean had lasted so long as his stand-in in the first place. It wasn't hard, but it was still early mornings and long hours. He'd half expected Dean to blow it off after the first week to go to Burning Man without even a heads-up text. But his instinct to protect his brother, to take care of him, had overridden the (very reasonable) fear that he'd fuck it up—and Shane was beyond proud that he hadn't.

There was a two-year gap between Shane and his older sister, Cassie, and five between him and Dean—none of them had exactly been planned, Dean least of all. As the oldest, Cassie had been forced to step up whenever their parents couldn't, during the first nine years of Shane's life. Because of that, she'd always felt more like another parent than a sibling. Even after things in their family had stabilized, Shane had still gotten the sense that she saw the two of them as a burden, the pain and resentment she felt toward their parents redirected at him and Dean. Though his relationship with her had gotten better in adulthood, they'd never been that close.

But while Shane's friends complained about their annoying younger siblings, he had never minded Dean tagging along. He'd been the one who taught Dean how to ride a bike—by pushing him down a hill and yelling, "pedal," but still. And when Dean was in middle school, Shane had been the first person he'd trusted to confide in that he didn't think he was totally straight.

Once Shane had booked the job on *Intangible* and it looked like it was actually going somewhere, it had been a no-brainer to bring Dean out to share in his success.

But he was unsure what Dean actually wanted to do with his life, even less sure than he was about himself. Dean had never shown much passion or aptitude for anything in particular—nothing he'd stuck with for longer than a week, anyway. He'd always been spontaneous, the risk-taker, reaping the benefits of having two older siblings who doted on him and little memory of the period before their parents got their act together.

As the car deposited them in front of the theater, Shane tried to push his concerns out of his mind.

Focusing on the episode wasn't much of an escape, though. He didn't love watching himself onscreen—he'd tuned in during the first season, just for novelty's sake, but soon realized it made him overly self-conscious on set.

It was a strange experience, though, watching it with an audience, especially one that was so receptive, filled with the people who made the show and their loved ones. When Lilah appeared onscreen at the very end, the whole auditorium erupted in whoops and applause. Shane resisted the urge to sneak a look at her, sitting a few seats down, so he could see her reaction.

It seemed like their therapy sessions were actually working. When he'd seen her face backstage at *After Hours,* he hadn't felt any kind of gloating satisfaction at how much she was clearly struggling. He'd just wanted to fix it, and fast. And not because he was worried about her embarrassing him, or having to carry her through the interview, or anything like that. Because they were a team.

It shocked him, that feeling. Both the fact that he'd had it at all and how powerful it still was—like it had never gone away.

Like the place in his heart where she used to fit had been drywalled over rather than bricked up.

And then there was the way he'd felt when she'd curled up inside his jacket, her body flush against his, his hands on her bare skin, her heart thrumming so hard against his chest that it felt like it was pumping his blood, too.

He was still attracted to her, that was all. It was fucking annoying, but it wasn't new. He had been since the first time he saw her. He couldn't help it. But acting on it had, historically, brought them nothing but trouble. The only thing to do about it was to continue avoiding her as much as possible.

"As much as possible" was relative, though, since as soon as he arrived at the after-party, the show's publicist sent him to track down Lilah for cast photos.

It didn't take him long to spot her once he went inside. She'd brought a friend as her date, one of the women from those summer camp movies she'd done—Annie, he wanted to say? He'd never heard of the series before he met her, but he'd stumbled across the first one on a streaming service a few years back and accidentally ended up watching the whole thing. It wasn't great, but it was clear that the four of them had had a blast shooting it, the kind of chemistry that was impossible to fake. He should know.

The two of them were facing away from him as he approached, caught up in animated conversation. He felt a pang as he saw how relaxed Lilah was, her body language carefree and easy. He'd been allowed a glimpse of that, once: what she was like when she was truly comfortable around someone. He knew it was something she didn't give up easily.

As he got closer, he could overhear their conversation.

"So, who here should I nail?" Annie asked, scanning the room.

Lilah laughed. "What are you in the mood for? Above or below the line?"

"Ugh, below. I never want to fuck an actor again. Fetch me your best boy!" Annie proclaimed, slipping into a fake British accent.

"I'll drink to that." Lilah clinked her glass against Annie's. Shane was glad neither of them could see him flinch.

When he came up beside them, he was startled to see a flash in Lilah's eyes that looked almost like guilt before she composed herself, her guard raised sky-high in an instant. He addressed Annie instead.

"Annie. Nice to see you. It's been a while."

Annie nodded, in a curt I-dislike-you-by-proxy way. "Sure." She sized them up next to each other. "Did you two coordinate?"

They'd both worn classic black tuxes, with one major difference: Lilah wasn't wearing anything under her jacket—except possibly double-sided tape.

He shrugged. "Just on the same wavelength, I guess." He turned to Lilah. "Hey, could I borrow your jacket? It's a little chilly in here."

"Ha." She rolled her eyes, but he could see she was suppressing a smile. "You can tone it down, it's just Annie."

He cocked his head toward the door. "They want us outside for pictures."

Lilah drained her glass and set it down, excusing herself as Annie waved them away. She was drinking tonight: white wine, so it wouldn't stain her teeth. Shane offered her his elbow automatically. Thankfully, she took it without comment—but not without hesitation.

"Nice to see the Hags are still going strong," he said as they made their way over to the step and repeat.

"Mmm. Sorry your toxic-masculinity support group disbanded."

"I'm not." Out of the corner of his eye, he saw her glance at him, so he changed the subject. "So, how do you decide which one to take to something like this? Do you have a little wheel that you spin?"

"Well, first of all, law students really know how to party. But Pilar's in Bali, and Yvonne's rehearsing for her tour, so she's not allowed to do anything fun for the next three months."

"Yvonne's probably too famous to be a plus-one now anyway, right? Wouldn't want to get upstaged at your own party."

"I dunno," Lilah said. "Might be nice. I'm getting a little sick of being the center of attention these days, aren't you?"

"It's what we signed up for," Shane said, but it was halfhearted.

"Yeah," she said quietly, and he knew she was thinking the same thing he was: there was no way they could've known back then what they were actually signing up for.

They reached the step and repeat, where most of the cast had already assembled. They started with group shots, Shane and Lilah at the center, the rest of them slowly peeling away until it was just the two of them, his arm around her waist.

"Who wore it better?" one of the photographers called.

"I did," Lilah said, at the same time as Shane said, "She did."

They turned to each other and laughed, perfectly in sync. She probably assumed he was playing it up for the cameras, which was fine by him, but it was true: she looked fucking incredible. Her face was sunny and open, eyes sparkling, not a trace of strain in her smile. It shouldn't have surprised him; she was an actress, of course she was good at that. Maybe what really surprised him was that his own smile didn't feel forced at all.

. . .

After a few hours, Lilah slipped outside to the enclosed patio to get some air. She should've known better than to hope she'd be alone, though—there was already a small group huddled in a circle, passing around a joint, by the smell of it.

One of them lifted his head out of the shadows. Dean.

"Hey, Lilah," he said on an inhale. "You want a hit?"

She opened her mouth to decline, then paused. "Sure. I'd do a shotgun."

"Oh yeah?" Dean asked, opening the circle so there was an empty space next to him. Lilah stepped into it, suddenly self-conscious about the intimacy of what she'd asked for—and who from. She realized too late that maybe she'd had one drink too many, her inhibitions lowered, her tongue looser than she'd like.

"Sorry, is that weird? I haven't smoked in a long time."

Dean shrugged. "Nah. Not weird." But instead of taking another hit, he reached across her, passing the joint to the hand on her other side, already outstretched.

She knew it was Shane before she even looked up.

The first time she'd gotten high wasn't with him—that would've been when she was fifteen, at the cast party for *The Miracle Worker,* after which she'd spent the rest of the night hiding in the host's laundry room, fending off a panic attack by reading the back of the fabric softener bottle over and over—but she was with him the first time she'd enjoyed it.

One night early on, when they'd gotten home at an ungodly hour, their next call time pushed to the afternoon to accommodate the mandatory twelve-hour turnaround, they'd lounged on his living room floor as he'd rolled them a joint. Lilah, already punch-drunk with exhaustion, hadn't been able to take her eyes off his hands, nimble and assured, handling the fragile paper as delicately as if it were a butterfly's wing.

When he was done, he'd shifted so they were sitting facing each other, legs bent and overlapping as he sparked it. He'd taken a long drag, then leaned forward, gently cradling her jaw in his other hand. She'd opened her mouth for an endless, bottomless moment, the two of them suspended in the split second before a kiss, breathing in as he blew out, bringing the smoke deep into her chest and holding it. It was like they'd transformed into a single organism, four long legs and one set of lungs: *Inhale. Exhale.*

The high that followed was soft and safe, enveloping her like a hug, her mind quieting rather than shifting into overdrive. When they'd had enough, he'd stubbed out the joint and closed the gap, kissing her slow and deep, the taste of smoke lingering on their tongues. He fucked her that same way, right there on the floor, every sensation so heightened it was almost too much.

Okay, she'd thought as she'd lain beside him afterward, rug burn on her back and sweat cooling on their skin, *I get why people like this.*

She snapped back to the present as she watched the cherry flare at the tip of the joint, twin embers smoldering in Shane's eyes to match. And that look in them, the one she knew well, like he was trying to burn her, too. Did he think she was trying to provoke him by asking Dean? It wouldn't have meant anything with him.

Shane pinched the joint between his fingers, his hand dropping back to his side. She wasn't sure if she moved into place or if he did, but suddenly his lips were inches from hers, his face cloaked in shadow again. She took a shaky breath, bracing herself.

What she didn't expect was for his hand to come to her jaw, lightly tilting it toward him. The gesture was so comfortable, so familiar, so intimate, that Lilah jerked back involuntarily, stumbling a little. Shane's brow creased as he stepped back, too, dropping his hand and stuffing it in his pocket, like he didn't trust it.

"Sorry," he said, the word escaping in a cloud of smoke.

"Sorry," Lilah repeated automatically. "I just—I'll do it. I can do it." She held out her hand and Shane passed her the joint, and she took a sharp, too-deep inhale, already coughing before she was even finished.

"Thanks," she managed to choke out, handing the joint to Dean before turning on her heel and fleeing the circle. She knew it was rude to hit and run, but her cheeks were burning, her face likely as red as her hair.

She sagged against the railing on the outer edge of the patio, trying to collect herself, already feeling more light-headed than she'd like. Her gaze snagged on the Edison bulb string lights, bobbing gently in the wind, going blurry and shimmery as her eyes slipped in and out of focus.

Out of the corner of her eye, she saw the group disband and make their way inside. A lone figure doubled back, heading toward her.

"Hey." Shane's voice was thick and slightly raspy from the smoke. He reached his arm out, like he was about to touch her on the back, then dropped it awkwardly. She still felt the ghost of it there.

"Hey," she said, a sliver of wariness threading through her tone.

He came up beside her, resting his drink on the railing, not looking at her. "Weird night, right?"

"Yeah." It came out under her breath.

"Have you been thinking about it?" he asked. She shot him a sharp look, as if he could somehow sense she'd been thinking about the season-one premiere party, when they'd narrowly avoided getting caught dry humping in the coatroom.

"What?"

He shook his head. "Sorry. I mean . . . about what's going to happen after. What we're going to do next. On our own."

"Oh. Yeah. I mean, of course." She turned her back to the railing, resting her elbows on it. "I guess it depends how all this goes. If it works. If I get another chance."

"To do what?"

"To do anything else. Anything interesting, I mean. To stretch myself. Not just scraps, playing someone's wife or mom for the rest of my life."

"What would you want to do? If you had your pick."

She cut her gaze sideways, unnerved by the sincerity of his question. Even more unnerving was the fact that she actually wanted to answer.

"I don't know. If you'd asked me a few years ago, I would've said . . ." She trailed off, reluctant to dredge up her false starts and failures. "Someone different from Kate. Someone unlikable, maybe."

"I thought you said you wanted to stretch yourself." Even the insult lacked the bite it normally would, an audible smile in his voice.

She laughed, a small hum in the back of her throat. "I guess I set myself up for that one. What about you, then?"

She was surprised to see the amusement drain from his face. "I'm not sure there's much to stretch." He looked off into the distance, lost in thought for a moment. "I'll figure it out, though. I kinda have to. It's not like I can go back to The Vine, right?"

"Don't underestimate yourself," she said before she could

think too much about it. He turned his head slowly to meet her eyes, his face still mostly in shadow. Sensing the moment was on the verge of becoming too earnest, she added, "I'm sure you could still handle the lunch rush with the best of them."

He cracked a smile. "I used to dream I was back there all the time, during the first few seasons. Like they'd realized they'd made a huge mistake and dumped me back where I belonged. Or sometimes it was like I never even moved out here in the first place, and I'm back in Oklahoma, helping my dad run his body shop. Even after all these years . . . I don't know." He shook his head, looking out over the railing for a few long seconds. "Do you feel like you deserve it?"

"What?" she asked, startled.

He half turned and gestured back toward the party. From the catch in his voice and his troubled expression, she knew what he was really asking: if *he* deserved it.

Lilah almost deflected it with a quip, but something— probably the one-two punch of that third glass of wine on an empty stomach and her accidental monster hit—compelled her to answer seriously.

"No. Yes. I mean . . . as much as anyone deserves anything in this industry, I guess? So much of it is out of our hands. I know so many people from school, or classes, or auditioning, who were—*are*—so fucking talented, but never got a break. I don't think I'm here and they're not because I deserve it more. But since I *am* here, all I can do is my best, you know? Show up on time, know my lines, take it seriously, try not to be an asshole to the people I work with . . ." He raised his eyebrows. "Well, most of them," she amended, sheepish. "Sorry. I think I lost the thread of that question."

"No, no, that was a good answer. But this was your dream, right? What you always wanted."

She turned to face him fully. His expression was serious, searching.

His star-is-born origin story had been a huge part of the promotional push for the first season: landing in L.A. by chance as a roadie with a friend's band, couch surfing and waiting tables with no ambitions beyond the next night's party, then plucked to star in the top-rated show in the country without so much as a credit as a tree in a school play.

He'd brushed it off in his aw-shucks way at the time, and as the years went by, she'd assumed he'd bought into his own hype—that he really was *that* fucking special. But as she studied him now, she realized she'd been wrong. He'd never stopped feeling like a directionless fraud, he'd just gotten better at hiding it.

Out of nowhere, she was struck by the woozy sensation of time folding back in on itself, suddenly granting her the ability to see him—*really* see him—as he was now, free of the vestiges of the younger man she'd known a decade ago. Her gaze tracked across his face, taking him in anew: the faint lines in his forehead and beside his eyes, the furrow in his brow, the way he held himself with a gravitas she didn't know he was capable of.

Something in her chest constricted, and she pushed it aside, trying to refocus on his question. "Yeah," she said, drawing it out slowly, unsure. "Yeah, it was my dream. I never thought my career would look like this, though."

"Like what?"

"Playing the same character forever. Being known for this one thing. Being part of something so huge. I mean, I'm grateful for it, but I would've been satisfied just being a working actor. I didn't need to be a celebrity. Even a B-list one," she added self-deprecatingly. "Sometimes I wonder if I would've been happier staying under the radar, even if I made less money."

She saw his expression tighten, subtly, almost imperceptibly in the dim lighting. "What?" she asked.

"Nothing." He shook his head. "It's just nice that's not a factor for you. The money."

It was impossible to ignore the bitterness that had crept into his tone. Lilah bit the inside of her cheek, fighting the urge to get defensive. If she'd been even 10 percent more sober, she would've ended the conversation there and gone back inside.

"When I was in high school," she said, her voice calm and measured, "I found out my mom was in a ton of debt. Like, hundreds of thousands of dollars. I had no idea until I started applying for college."

Even more than a decade later, long after she'd worked through it with a string of therapists, the same emotions shuddered through her in a rush of heat. The betrayal. The fear. Dozens of happy memories turned retroactively grim with this new context, every clue she'd brushed off and ignored falling into nauseating place. The terrifying realization that the person she'd trusted to guide her through the world was, in fact, no better equipped than she was—and possibly worse. She supposed she was lucky she'd been able to maintain the illusion for that long.

She glanced over at Shane, whose jaw had gone slack. "What? Why? I mean, how?"

She shook her head. "She'd been a stay-at-home mom our whole lives. She went back to work part-time after she and my dad got divorced, but . . . I think it was really important to her that she could give us everything my dad could. Even if we didn't ask for it. Even if we didn't *need* any of it. But she cared a lot about what other people thought of her; the two of them were constantly trying to one-up each other. So, yeah, we had more than we wanted growing up, but it wasn't real. It wasn't even about us."

Shane was staring at her intently, his drink down to melted ice in his hand, forgotten. "So what happened?"

Her mouth twisted. "What do you think? I paid it all off after I booked the show. I still have to bail her out every now and then, but less, ten or twenty K maybe." She shrugged, a little helplessly. "What else am I gonna do?"

He didn't say anything else, just kept looking at her, that same intense gaze. She felt self-conscious all of a sudden, unsure why she'd told him, wishing she could take it back.

"I had no idea," he said at last.

"Why would you?" she asked, her tone light. "She doesn't owe you money, does she?"

The edge of his mouth curved up. He pushed himself off the railing, and she did the same, falling into step beside him as the two of them slowly walked along the perimeter of the terrace.

"It's not like *you* need to worry about money anymore, either," she said. "You never even have to act again if you don't want to. Just get an endorsement deal for one of those midlife-crisis cars, or some macho-man liquor brand. You've got nine seasons of residuals, plus the convention circuit. You're set."

They both received invitations to do panels and meet and greets at various conventions multiple times a year. Shane did them regularly—likely for the fat paycheck that came along with it—but Lilah had gone only once, during the first season, to the biggest one of all, held every spring in San Francisco. She'd found the whole thing so overwhelming that she'd drifted through the weekend in a Xanax haze, which she regretted after she'd been visibly zonked out of her mind in all the photos.

Shane snorted. "I don't know if I'm ready to be put out to pasture like that just yet."

"Well, I'm sure *Dancing with the Stars* would be happy to have you."

"If you want to see my moves, you could just say so."

"I've already seen them."

"Maybe I've learned some new ones."

She glanced over and met his eyes, the two of them slipping into a slightly awkward silence.

"So, why'd you come alone tonight?" he asked, averting his gaze again.

"I'm not alone. I'm with Annie."

At that moment, they passed by one of the floor-to-ceiling windows lining the back of the venue and were treated to a perfect view of Annie making out heavily in a corner with Kenny, the camera operator she'd been talking to when Lilah had gone outside.

"Not anymore," Shane said.

"You know, good for her." She glanced over at him. "Why'd *you* come alone?"

He shrugged. "Couldn't find anyone who wanted to sit in the splash zone."

"That was an accident," Lilah protested, her face heating at the memory even as she laughed.

The first time she'd met Serena, at the season-two premiere party, Lilah had turned around too quickly and bumped into her, spilling her drink directly down the front of Serena's dress. Lilah had been mortified, offering to pay Serena's dry-cleaning bill—which of course was an empty gesture, since Serena was worth more than Lilah and Shane combined.

"Sure," he said with a grin.

They passed one of the doors, and she expected him to break off from her and go back inside, but instead, they continued walking in silence, making their way to the other end of the patio. Even though it wasn't cold, Lilah wrapped her arms around herself in a protective gesture. Her head felt pleasantly fuzzy around the edges, the intrusive worries that were constantly running through it dulled to a low hum.

She followed Shane's gaze through the window, where Margaux and Dean were absorbed in an animated conversation, Dean's hand going to the small of Margaux's back.

"I know she's not really my daughter, but part of me wants to go over there and break that up for some reason." There was a hint of conspiratorial humor to his voice, low and husky, that made her feel warm all over. She forced herself to focus on the part of it that irritated her.

"God. Are you going to be one of those dads who gets all weird and controlling about his daughters dating?"

"If they're dating my brother, yeah."

"Well, good thing she's not really your daughter."

They watched as Dean pulled Margaux closer, whispering something in her ear, and the two of them headed toward the exit.

"Man. Is it just me, or is everyone extra horny tonight?" She felt Shane's eyes on her, felt her cheeks go pink. "I mean. It's like none of them ever heard that you shouldn't fuck your coworkers."

"It's the last season, I guess it's now or never." He looked at her for another beat, then looked away. "You want to catch up and tell her?"

"Nah. That's a mistake she has to make on her own."

A spark of tension crackled between them.

Shane pushed his jacket aside, resting a hand in his pocket. "Well. Now you two can compare notes."

Lilah was so startled that she turned to face him fully. "What? You mean about *Dean*? Nothing happened between me and Dean." Aside from a few stilted minutes of making out that had gone nowhere, during which she'd felt nothing.

No, not nothing. Nothing would've been preferable to the ache she'd felt somewhere deep in her chest—the realization that, even though Dean looked uncannily like Shane, had a similar voice and smile and overall demeanor, he wasn't Shane.

That glimmer of understanding about what she'd actually been looking for had been so disturbing that she'd shut the whole thing down before Dean's hand could even make its way up her shirt. He hadn't seemed to care much, but he'd been drunk enough to take her up on her offer to crash there for the night, stripping off his shirt and passing out facedown on her couch before she'd finished brushing her teeth, out the door by the time she woke up the next morning.

She didn't blame Shane for being pissed that they'd made a scene by leaving together, but she'd assumed Dean had told him that it ended there.

Shane's brow creased. "You went home together. He spent the night."

"Yeah, on my *couch*. He didn't tell you?"

He looked even more stricken. "He, um. He did. I just . . . I didn't believe him."

The words hung in the air for several long seconds as Lilah struggled to process them, the thick, syrupy muddle of her thoughts no longer a comfort.

"So, wait a minute. This whole time, you've been mad at me for something I didn't even *do*? That Dean *told* you I didn't do?"

Shane put his drink down on a nearby table and ran his fingers through his hair in agitation. "Yeah, but you were *going* to."

"What are you, the thought police? Fine, yes, I was going to, but I *didn't*. I couldn't." She saw something shift in his expression and hurried to continue. "The point is that *you* are so fucking obsessed with hating me that you didn't even believe your own *brother* that we didn't. Which, by the way, I assume you haven't been holding this same grudge against *him* the whole time."

"No, but—"

"And why is that? Bro code? Double bro code, because he's your actual brother? Guess I can't compete with *that*." Even as she said it, she knew she should back off, that she'd made her point, that her lacerating tone was unnecessary. But she was drunk, she was pissed, and she could never fucking quit while she was ahead.

"Because he didn't *know!*" Shane thundered, just as worked up as she was.

She suddenly noticed how red his eyes were, the hazy, unfocused look in them. Neither of them was in a state to be having this conversation. She couldn't stop herself, though.

"Didn't know what? That we were"—she lowered her voice just in time, conscious that they were still in public—"*together*? You didn't bother to tell him?"

Shane exhaled in frustration. "No, he didn't know that I— that we—" He gestured between them. "Just—everything. With us. He didn't get it. Doesn't."

Lilah stared at him, baffled. "Okay, well, he and I have that in common, because I don't know what the fuck you're talking about."

It seemed like maybe he was about to say something else— his face flushed, posture tense—but instead he just shook his head resignedly before turning and skulking back toward the party.

"Use your *words,* Shane!" she hollered at his back before she could stop herself. She winced as a few heads turned toward them from inside, her outburst clearly audible through the glass. *Fuck.* Hopefully this wouldn't wind up in some fucking tabloid.

She took a few deep breaths and headed back inside, too, making a beeline for the bar once she clocked that he wasn't anywhere near it.

"Sounds like therapy's going well," she heard Natalie say dryly over her shoulder.

Lilah choked out a laugh. "Glad I'm not the one paying for it." The bartender handed her her seltzer, and she dug around in her purse to find a few bucks to tip.

Natalie leaned against the bar next to her. "It's pretty wild. I've been working with him for two and a half years now, and he's one of the most laid-back people I've ever met. Except around you."

"Well, lucky me. He must like me the best, then," Lilah snarled, her frustration flaring again.

Natalie laughed, holding up her hands defensively. "Whoa, okay. I'm not the one you're mad at, remember?"

Lilah let out a full-body exhale, the bar at her back the only thing preventing her from totally collapsing. "Fuck. I'm sorry." She took a long drink of her seltzer. "I think that might be my cue to get out of here."

Natalie frowned sympathetically. As if she'd been summoned, Annie sidled up to Lilah's shoulder, high heels dangling from one hand.

"Ready to go?"

Lilah turned to look at her. "You're still here? What happened to Kenny?"

Annie grimaced. "He kept trying to stick his fingers in my armpits."

"*What?*" exclaimed Lilah and Natalie in unison.

"I know. I don't want to talk about it. Do you think the driver would take us through Del Taco?"

"Never hurts to ask." Lilah turned to Natalie. "Wanna come?"

Natalie grinned. "Sure."

Head held high, Lilah left the party flanked by Natalie and Annie, pretending she didn't notice Shane glowering at her from the corner where he stood alone.

13

Three and a half years ago

The *Deadline* announcement had dropped at dawn, the only thing anyone on set had been able to talk about all morning. Shane shouldn't have been surprised Lilah hadn't told him herself. They hadn't spoken an unscripted word in months.

Still, when he'd seen the article, it felt like something in his brain had fried, erasing his ability to process the written word. But no matter how many times he looked at it, it still said the same thing.

He'd tried his best to push it out of his mind as he'd gone through hair and makeup, but it consumed him, like a needle trapped in a record's groove, unable to move past the same section and repeating over and over.

Sitting in his trailer, failing to absorb the revised script pages in front of him for thirty minutes straight, he knew he had to talk to her. It was the only way to clear his head, get it out of his system. He wasn't sure what exactly he wanted to say, but he'd figure it out in the fifteen seconds it took to get from his trailer to hers.

He strode over to the door and flung it open—only to find Lilah already standing on the other side, her feet staggered sideways on the stairs, like she was talking herself into (or out of) knocking.

They froze, staring at each other.

What are you doing here? was what he meant to say. What he actually blurted out was, "You're leaving?"

She didn't say anything at first. She didn't have to. Her cheeks went pink and her eyes dropped to the ground, and Shane felt like his chest was about to burst open.

"Can I come in?"

He stepped to the side without a word. She shut the door behind her then hovered in front of it, arms crossed. "I got another job," she said, her mouth tight.

"And you didn't tell me?"

"Must've slipped my mind during our last heart-to-heart."

"It's professional courtesy."

She cocked her head, her brow creasing with a faux-confused expression. "Professional courtesy? You mean like when you sent Dean in to play the back of your head last week?"

Shane felt heat creep up his neck, but he said nothing. Neither of them moved for a long moment.

"I assume you weren't on your way to congratulate me," she said.

"So you're going."

"I'm going."

"And I'll just . . . be here. Still. Without you."

She met his eyes, her face placid and impenetrable. "That's really none of my business anymore."

Her stoicism only made him more agitated. He shook his head, running his fingers through his hair. "This is pretty fucked up, Lilah. Even for you."

"I thought you'd be happy about it," she shot back, which made him start. Why *wasn't* he happy about it? Why had his first instinct been to barge into her trailer like she owed him an explanation?

"I *am* happy. It's just hard to put together a parade on such short notice. Still trying to work out the permit situation, might need to call in a favor."

The corner of her mouth quirked up, and something wound tighter inside him, ready to snap.

"That seems excessive," she said. "I'm sure 'bye, bitch' spray-painted on my trailer door would get the same point across for a fraction of the hassle."

"You deserve a better send-off than that."

"What did you have in mind?" The look on her face was a challenge and an invitation all at once.

It was fucking dangerous, was what it was.

He took a step closer, then another.

"I don't know. Skywriting, maybe."

She didn't back away, didn't object. She just uncrossed her arms, her gaze flicking to his lips—only for a split second, but long enough to start his pulse pounding in his ears.

He paused, a breath away from brushing against her.

"Or fireworks," he murmured. She lifted her chin and met his eyes, the provocation in them bright and burning.

He'd have to initiate, of course. She never would. She'd see it as a sign of weakness, admitting defeat before they even began. Even that first night, in the corner of that dark hotel bar in New York—back when things between them were as close to simple as they'd ever been—she would've rubbed herself all over him and then gone upstairs alone if he hadn't made the first move. He'd been oblivious enough to believe that pulling her into his lap was his idea. But really, the choice had always been to either play by her rules or not play at all.

So he reached out, unsure at first where he was going, almost surprised when his hand came up to cup her jaw—the first time he'd touched her in nearly four years. He held it there for a moment, their gazes locked. It wasn't too late to turn back. Nothing had happened yet, not really.

But then she closed her eyes and turned her face into his touch with a soft exhale, and that was it. His blood turned molten as his fingers spread and shifted, tangling in the hair at the nape of her neck, his other arm banding around her lower back to pull her flush against him. He was already hard before he even kissed her.

Considering how slow the buildup was, the first kiss was ferocious, both of them diving in so quickly that Shane was shocked nobody got hurt. But no, they'd always been good at this, their faces fitting together like they'd been made that way, the taste of her mouth too familiar as he plunged his tongue inside it.

He slid his hand possessively to the base of her throat and walked her back against the door, their kisses becoming more desperate, him sucking on her tongue, her biting his lower lip and sighing into his mouth as she clawed at the back of his T-shirt.

Shane broke away, both of them breathing heavily. "Do

you . . . do you want to do this?" Five minutes ago, he'd had no idea this was even within the realm of possibility. Now he felt like he would die if she said no.

Her eyes narrowed. "Do *you*?"

Only Lilah could turn consent into a standoff. But instead of annoying him, it just drove his desire higher, and he gripped her jaw to dive back in for another hungry, ravaging kiss, nudging her legs apart with one thigh and rocking against her, making her gasp.

This wasn't the way he really wanted this to happen, he realized with a pang. If he had a choice—if he'd known he'd get one more chance at a last time with her—he'd do it differently. On a bed, for starters. He'd lay her down and take his time. Show her he wasn't some overexcited twentysomething kid anymore. But if this was his only option, going at it fevered and fumbling, he'd take it in a heartbeat.

He ducked his head down to suck at the sensitive spot just behind her jaw—too hard, probably, but he couldn't bring himself to care with the way it made her breath go ragged, her head lolling helplessly on her neck.

"Careful," she gasped. He barely heard her, too preoccupied by the feel of her hands groping at his belt.

His own hands traveled down, sweeping over the indent of her waist, the flare of her hips, and he kissed her again, groaning as he grabbed two generous handfuls of her ass through the thin, stretchy material of her skirt.

Fuck. He needed to be inside her, right fucking now.

He was so disoriented that he hadn't realized he'd said it out loud until she laughed against his lips.

"Wow. All these years, and you still think foreplay is optional. I thought Serena would've trained you better than that."

He knew she was just talking shit, trying to rile him up by

taking jabs at his sexual prowess and his recent breakup all at once—and it was working.

He released her, dropping to his knees and pushing her skirt up her thighs. She braced her shoulders against the wall and watched him, her pupils blown-out and her expression hazy, as he ran his index finger along the elastic seam of her underwear, slipping it underneath and finding her soaking.

"Foreplay, huh?" Even as he teased her, he knew the rasp in his voice gave away how affected he was, how his cock was hard as iron, chafing uncomfortably against his fly.

She gave an exasperated huff that almost sounded convincing. "It's about the *principle*."

But he wasn't listening. He nuzzled his face between her thighs, giving one long, slow lick over the fabric. She bit back a moan, but her legs were already shaking before he pushed the material aside.

It was gratifying that he barely needed to think about it, that he could just let his instincts take over. He still knew exactly how she liked it, even after all this time, all the ways to make her gasp and tremble and cry out, and she slung one of her legs over his shoulder and gripped his hair with both hands for support.

When he felt her orgasm building on his tongue, those telltale whimpers and shudders that had him on the verge of coming himself, he pulled back, ignoring her protests. He stood up and kissed her again, wrapping her tightly in his arms and guiding her away from the door.

As the backs of her calves hit the couch, she pulled away.

"Wait," she said breathlessly. "My hair. Max will kill me."

"What?"

"I need to be on top."

"Okay. Right. Okay."

He sat down, palming himself through his jeans, groaning

loudly at the sight of her bending over to pull her underwear off in one fluid motion before climbing up and straddling him.

"You better be quiet, or these are going in your mouth," she said, dangling the lacy fabric from one finger.

"Promise?"

She threw her head back and laughed, and something about it sent a strange twinge through him. Fuck, he'd missed her. Missed making her laugh just as much as he missed the rest of it.

She reached down to stroke him through his pants, and he felt like he'd never been this hard in his life, like he was about to go out of his mind from wanting her. He got dizzy as he watched her undo his fly and slide her fingers under the waistband of his boxer briefs, his cock springing free so enthusiastically it was almost embarrassing.

When she reached out and wrapped her hand around it, thumb sweeping lightly over the tip, his hips bucked involuntarily and he shuddered. "*Fuck*. Lilah . . ." he moaned, his vocabulary reduced solely to those two words.

Her tongue darted out to moisten her lips, swollen and pink from where he'd sucked and bitten them, and he swallowed a moan like he could practically already feel them enveloping him, sucking him down, even though they had no time, even though they were running out of time already.

"Condom?" she breathed, and he gestured absently toward a side table. She glanced sideways at him like she was about to say something, give him shit for having them so easily accessible, probably. But she just leaned over to rummage through the drawer, rolling one on and positioning herself above his lap without missing a beat.

He pushed her skirt up to her hips so he could have an un-obstructed view as she braced one hand on his shoulder and used the other to position him against her. She slid down agonizingly slowly; it felt like it took ages for just the tip to notch inside her. Then she stopped. He tried to thrust up, desperately, but she only lifted her hips with him, preventing him from sinking any deeper.

When he collapsed back down again, growling in frustration, she finally started to move, fucking herself on him shallowly, slowly, teasing him. Down an inch, up an inch, but no more. He felt like he was going to go out of his fucking mind.

"God*dammit,* Lilah," he choked, digging his fingers into her hips, dragging his eyes back to her face.

She was unbelievable, looming over him, face flushed, eyes sparkling, teeth sunk into that full bottom lip, like she should be in a fucking museum or something. Gloating down at him with an expression that could only mean *I own you.*

He couldn't argue with that.

"Ask me nicely." The sternness in her voice made his cock pulse.

"*Please,*" he groaned, but he didn't wait for her response before his grip tightened around her hips and he slammed her down flush against him, making her take him all the way.

The moan that ripped out of her was powerful enough to make her fall forward against his chest, but when she rolled upright again, she was smirking. Like he'd played right into her hands, like baiting him into losing control had been her plan the whole time.

He knotted his hand in her hair, tightening his grip, making her wince. "Be *quiet,*" he growled. Her breath hitched in response, and she ducked down to catch his lower lip in her teeth so hard he thought she might draw blood.

She started to ride him, lazily at first, then finding her pace, and all he could do was try to keep up, electric currents sizzling up his spine, his jaw going slack. She was in charge, she'd been in charge from the moment he'd met her, and he fucking loved it. He loved *her*.

No. Fuck. What? It was enough to make him lose his rhythm for a second. He didn't love her. He didn't love her. He hated her, but he was also fucking her, and it was so goddamn good he could barely remember his own name. Of course everything was all mixed up. It didn't mean anything.

But why did he hate her, again? Because she'd gotten his friend fired, someone he didn't even talk to anymore? Because he'd been in love with her all those years ago, and she hadn't felt the same way?

He forced himself to abandon that train of thought before it completely derailed him, surrendering instead to his animal instincts, his heart hammering so hard he swore he could hear it rattling his rib cage, blanking out everything but the sensation of her squeezing around him, slick and hot, taking what she needed from him. He kept his hands firmly on her hips, not trusting himself to touch her anywhere else, both grateful and disappointed that they were still fully clothed.

"Stop looking at me like that." Her voice was shaky as her eyes fluttered shut, then open again.

"Like what?"

"You're being all . . . intense."

"Sorry."

"No, don't *stop* stop," she said, and exhaled in frustration. He realized he'd unthinkingly slowed the movement of his hips, so he picked up the pace again.

She leaned over him, her hair brushing against his shoulder, one hand clinging to his neck as she ground against him at an angle that made them both groan. He wasn't sure who found whom, but suddenly her other hand was brushing his, their fingers interlacing, palms pressing together. He looked down at their hands, then up at her face to see her watching him, her eyes heavy-lidded and glassy, then back at their hands again. For some reason, that felt like the most intimate place they were joined, by far. He pushed that out of his mind, too.

He heard the rhythm of her breathing change, felt her grip on the back of his neck tighten, and he willed himself to hold on long enough for her to finish, even as that familiar tingling pressure built at the base of his spine.

He shouldn't even care if she came or not, he realized dimly. He could be selfish if he wanted. Maybe that was what she deserved, to get all wound up and then left unsatisfied. But what he craved even more than his own release was to feel her tumble over the edge, to force her to give up some of that tightly held control for just a moment. To grasp at some kind of tangible proof that he could make her half as crazy as she made him.

He felt her shudder and clench around him, gasping and whimpering as she came. He gave her a second to come apart against him, his hand reaching beneath her shirt to stroke her back. When she opened her eyes again, though, the heat was still there, which was all he needed to thrust up into her, fast and hard, drawing more cries out of her as she let go of his hand to wrap both arms around his neck.

It wasn't long before he came with a groan, harder than he had in years, possibly ever, hard enough that his vision went black for a second, feeling like he'd been wrung out of everything he had. He collapsed against the back of the couch, still holding her tightly to him, her head buried in his neck, their breathing slowly returning to normal.

Once the haze cleared, though, he couldn't push the truth away any longer.

She was leaving.

She was fucking leaving.

She didn't even tell him. She didn't give a shit about him. And she was fucking leaving. Even *this* was probably just some weird power move, trying to prove something to herself, or to him.

He must have tensed up, because she shifted against his chest, pressing her damp palm to his shirt as he sat them both upright. Her expression was still relaxed and peaceful. She leaned forward to kiss him.

Instinctively, he jerked his head away, feeling his gaze go hard.

She looked confused for only a split second before her face immediately clouded over with hurt, followed closely by embarrassment, her hand on his shirt tightening to a fist.

He stood so suddenly he practically pushed her off his lap, fumbling with the condom and his zipper before turning back to look at her, annoyed and disheveled on the couch.

"Why did you come here, Lilah? What the hell was this? One last chance to fuck with my head? Is that it?"

She was breathing heavily again, looking up through her lashes at him. "No."

He waited to see if she would elaborate further, but she didn't, just kept staring at him with that same haunted look in her eyes.

"Then what? What do you want from me?"

"I don't know," she said quietly, defeated.

"Well, fucking figure it out," he snapped, his voice rising. He never yelled, couldn't remember the last time he'd lost his cool, but it was like a stranger had taken over his body and trapped him outside, unable to do anything but watch. "You know what? I *am* happy you're leaving. You're the worst goddamn thing that ever happened to me. And if I never see you again, it'll be too fucking soon."

She stood slowly, without looking at him, bending down to clutch her crumpled underwear in one hand. She walked toward him until they were toe to toe, eye to eye.

"Fuck you, Shane," she spat, her voice ragged. All the amusement was gone, all the playfulness. He'd ruined their game, but he couldn't bring himself to care.

He swallowed the obvious response.

"Congratulations," he murmured instead.

She shot one last, fiery look at him—lips swollen, cheeks red, mascara smudged below her eyes, and her hair a mess despite their best efforts—before stalking out, slamming the door behind her.

As soon as she was gone, he got straight into the shower, taking care to keep his hair and face out of the spray. No matter how high he cranked the temperature, no matter how hard he scrubbed, he could still smell her on him. And instead of calming him down, that churning, restless feeling only got worse, pressure building inside his chest like a shaken soda can.

When he got dressed and returned to the main area, Dean was sprawled on his couch, one shoe off, an open bag of chips on his chest, playing *Call of Duty*. It wasn't an unusual sight, but in Shane's state of agitation, it was the last straw.

"Get out." The bitterness in his own voice startled him.

Dean craned his neck to look at him. "What's with you?"

"Nothing. Nothing," Shane said, scrubbing his hand over the back of his neck as he paced back and forth. "Maybe I'm just tired of seeing you every time I turn around."

Dean blinked, stunned, the controller hanging forgotten from one hand. "What?"

Shane felt his stomach twist at Dean's expression, one he didn't think he'd ever seen before, let alone caused. In a dimly lit back corner of his mind, he was already mortified, barely able to recognize himself. But when he opened his mouth, instead of an apology, what came out was "You need to move out. It's way past time, it's fucking embarrassing. Get your own life. Stop mooching off mine."

Dean tossed the controller aside and stalked toward Shane, and for a split second, Shane thought he might be about to hit him. A perverse part of him hoped he would: give him some actual, physical pain to focus on, something sharp and immediate to distract him from the confusing jumble of feelings that had been sitting in the pit of his stomach since that morning, that had only gotten worse since he'd opened his door and seen Lilah standing there.

Dean didn't even give him the satisfaction of getting angry, though. It was like he knew exactly what Shane was trying to do—attempting to alleviate his own misery by spreading it. But Dean had always been too even-tempered to bait like that.

"Fine" was all he said, quietly, shooting Shane a stony glare before shoving his foot into his other shoe and storming out the door.

Three weeks later, watching the two of them leave that wrap party together, there was no doubt in Shane's mind that he'd gotten exactly what he deserved.

14

Now

"So, Shane," Dr. Deena said, leaning forward in her chair. "Is it possible that your unwillingness to believe your brother stemmed from a subconscious attempt to relieve your own guilt about the way you behaved toward both of them after your last sexual encounter with Lilah?"

Out of the corner of her eye, Lilah saw Shane shift in his seat. *Good.*

"Sure," he said noncommittally. "I mean, anything's possible."

Lilah swallowed a frustrated groan. After their display at the premiere party, they'd been sent to an emergency therapy session, but their attempt to unravel what had caused the blowup in the first place was going about as well as expected.

Dr. Deena sighed. "Okay, let's try a different approach. *Why* do you think you reacted that way?"

Shane crossed an ankle over his other knee, jiggling it restlessly. "I guess I felt like she was using sex as, like . . . a power play. Like she was only doing it because she had something to prove."

"So you felt that, for her, the sex was divorced from any emotion."

"Yes."

"But not for you."

"Yes. I mean, no. I mean . . . I don't know. I just felt kind of . . . used."

Lilah rolled her eyes. "Oh, give me a fucking *break*."

Dr. Deena turned to Lilah, her gaze sharp. "Let's hear it from you, then, Lilah. What were *you* feeling that day?"

Now it was Lilah's turn to be evasive. "It's hard to say," she said tersely, crossing her arms. "It was a long time ago."

"Why don't you take a moment and try your best to remember."

Lilah tried to ignore both Shane's and Dr. Deena's stares as she cast her eyes to the ceiling, considering the question.

"I guess I just got caught up in the moment," she said after a long pause. "I didn't have any ulterior motive." And it was, to date, still the hottest sex of her life—even though she'd burst into angry, helpless tears the moment she'd slammed his trailer door behind her.

"And would you say there were emotions involved on your end?"

Lilah pursed her lips. "I thought this was about fixing our professional relationship, not our romantic one."

"Well, it does seem like those are more intertwined than we'd like them to be, doesn't it?" Dr. Deena said coolly, looking down at her notes. "What about when you were together initially? You've both said it was just casual. But I have to say, it's hard to imagine that you two would still have this level of hostility after all these years if there was no deeper emotional connection whatsoever."

Lilah and Shane exchanged uneasy glances. Neither said anything for a long beat.

"Yeah," Shane responded gruffly, in a tone she'd never heard before, like it was being pulled out of him. "Yeah, I was in love with her."

It wasn't a surprise, not really. Still, hearing him say it outright like that made Lilah feel like her lungs had been vacuum-sealed. She stared straight ahead, keeping her face as neutral as possible.

"And did you ever talk about it?" Dr. Deena prodded gently.

Out of the corner of her eye, she saw Shane nod. "I told her." He swallowed. "And she ignored it."

Lilah inhaled deeply and refrained from rolling her eyes again. He was obviously playing up the melodrama, trying to get Dr. Deena back on his side. "He told my *shoulder blade* he loved it. During sex. That doesn't count."

"Why not?" asked Dr. Deena.

"Because it's just . . . it just doesn't," Lilah finished lamely, before changing course. "He didn't love me, he barely knew me."

"Bullshit," Shane said. "I spent more time with you than anybody."

"So what? That's not how it works. You're not automatically an expert on me once you log your ten thousand hours, or whatever."

"You think you make it easy, Lilah?" he blurted out, turning to face her for the first time the whole session. She just looked back at him, stunned at the intensity behind his words. "You don't think I *wanted* to know you? Maybe I got tired of waiting around for the drawbridge to lower, to finally get permission to cross the moat to Lilah Island."

"Why would an island need a moat?" she muttered under her breath, unable to help herself.

Shane exhaled loudly, bordering on a groan, dragging his hand over his eyes in frustration. "See? This is exactly what I mean."

Dr. Deena held her hand up to silence them.

"I'm curious why you're so eager to invalidate Shane's feelings for you, Lilah."

"I don't doubt he had feelings for me. But it wasn't love."

"Why not?"

Lilah crossed her legs, adjusting herself to sit upright on the couch. She spoke slowly, selecting her words carefully. "To me . . . love needs a degree of reciprocation. Of mutual openness. Choosing to let someone in, letting them see all of you."

Dr. Deena nodded, making a note in her pad. "So you don't believe unrequited love is possible, then?"

She shook her head. "A crush, maybe. Infatuation, lust, whatever. But that's not love. It's not even about the other person, really; it's just about projecting some weird fantasy of who you *think* they are."

Shane scoffed, and both their heads turned toward him.

"You can't control other people's feelings, Lilah," he said. "If I said I fell in love with you at—I don't know—our first audition, you can't tell me I didn't."

"At our *audition*?" she exclaimed, louder than she meant to, unable to hide her irritation that he was obviously fucking with her while she was trying to take things seriously. Sure enough, his eyes were sparkling with mischief, even as the rest of his expression remained innocent.

"It was just an example."

"You're both entitled to have your own perspectives," Dr. Deena said before turning back to Lilah. "But as you were saying. You and Shane weren't in love—by your own definition—because you weren't open to it." It wasn't a question.

Lilah felt herself flush. "I think that's a little reductive."

"Did you ever develop any kind of romantic feelings for him at all, though? Ever consider pursuing something more?"

"Sure. I mean, yeah, of course." She shrugged, trying to keep her voice casual, like it wasn't her first time admitting anything of the sort in his presence. "I'm not, like, a *robot*. We were sleeping together for months. Of course I . . ." She trailed off, looking down at her lap. Next to her, Shane's gaze was fixed straight ahead, his posture tense.

She realized, then, what Shane had meant by his outburst at the party: *Because he didn't know.* It hadn't been an unforgivable crime for Dean to go home with her, because as far as he knew, things hadn't been serious between her and Shane. But as much as they'd tried to deny it—then, now, and every moment in between—they both understood, deep down, it was more complicated than that. *That* was why her betrayal had been worse.

"We're just . . . really different," she said after a long beat. "The only thing we had in common was the show. It happens all the time, people bonding in a high-pressure situation like that. That doesn't mean it's real. It can't sustain itself long-term."

"And that was the only thing holding you back from taking things to the next level?" Dr. Deena prodded gently.

Lilah glanced at Shane, who was already looking at her, his gaze impenetrable.

"That, and . . . taking it to the next level would have meant taking it public. Eventually. It wouldn't be ours anymore. It would be everybody's. And then, if it didn't work out . . ." She shook her head. "Things were so overwhelming during that first year. It just seemed like all this extra pressure to put on it, on ourselves. It would've been too much to handle."

"But that's part of the bargain you make as an actor, isn't it?" Dr. Deena asked. "That if you're successful—if you become a public figure—you give up a certain level of privacy in your personal life. That's no reason to shut yourself off from love and relationships entirely."

"No, I know. I only felt that way about *us,* me and Shane specifically. I think it was just, like . . . if we were *together* together, it would've been like our feelings were . . . a commodity, or something. Something they could sell alongside the show. That's not the kind of relationship I wanted."

Dr. Deena nodded. "Is that how you felt, too, Shane? Were you concerned about public scrutiny impacting your relationship?"

Lilah snorted. "Please. He jumped from me right into the most public relationship he could find."

"Oh really?" Dr. Deena asked, with mild curiosity.

"Um . . ." Shane shot Lilah an annoyed look. "I was with Serena Montague, yeah. For three years."

Dr. Deena stared at him intently for a moment, brow furrowed, before a look of comprehension dawned on her and she snapped her fingers. "You know, I didn't recognize you with the beard. You looked younger without it."

"I *was* younger," Shane muttered.

"I thought you don't watch TV," Lilah said, a hint of petulance creeping into her voice.

"Well, I've been to the supermarket and the doctor's office and had quite a few haircuts," Dr. Deena said with a smile.

Lilah slouched back against the couch. "I guess that proves my point, then."

"I suppose it does." Dr. Deena shifted in her seat, tucking her legs beneath her. "Have you ever been in love, Lilah? If not with Shane, then with anyone?"

Lilah's mouth went dry; she was intimately aware of Shane next to her. "I feel like we're getting off topic."

"Humor me."

Lilah's gaze flicked to the clock behind Dr. Deena's head, contemplating whether she could try to stall until they were out of time. But they still had a good twenty minutes left, so she was stuck.

"No," she said quietly. "I haven't."

"And do you think of yourself as lovable?"

Lilah recoiled like she'd been slapped. "What?"

"Do you think you're worthy of love?" Dr. Deena repeated.

Lilah opened and closed her mouth a few times, stunned into silence.

When Lilah was sixteen, her first serious boyfriend had dumped her the first time she'd had a panic attack in front of him. He'd at least had the decency to wait until the next day to do it, pulling her aside between classes and informing her that she was "too much drama."

Naturally, she'd retaliated by covering his car with mayonnaise: sneaking over to his house with a Costco-sized jar while his family was out of town, so that the acid would eat away at the paint as it baked under the hot sun, the stench seeping through the cracks and into the upholstery. If she'd already earned the label, she reasoned, she might as well live up to it.

She hadn't had much luck in the subsequent years, either. She was a magnet for men who would pursue her relentlessly, only to realize once they had her that they wished she was someone else. Men who'd coveted her for her appearance but resented everything she had to do to maintain it. Men who'd been attracted to her status and success, then complained that she was always busy, seethed with jealousy over her onscreen love interests, and grumbled about the attention she got when they went out.

But even before all that, she'd always been—as her bubbe had half-affectionately, half-derogatorily declared her many times as a child—a handful. Opinionated, self-righteous, stubborn, with a brain hell-bent on twisting every good thing in her life until it found the angle that made her miserable.

When she'd met Richard at Juilliard, performing in a reading of one of his plays, she'd recognized a kindred spirit—someone even pricklier and more difficult than she was (though of course, as a writer and a man, it was seen as proof of his brilliance and not an innate character defect). She'd been flattered to make the cut as one of the few things he didn't hate, addicted to the thrill of chasing his conditional, unpredictable approval. It had been enough to sustain their relationship for years, on and off and on again, his interest revitalized every time she ended things.

But she'd never felt truly *safe* with him. Her sense of security had come from knowing he was always just out of reach, that he'd never see her as anything more than a supporting character. That she'd never have the power to break his heart, or him to break hers. It wasn't love, but it was as close as she'd thought she could get.

After Richard, Shane had been such a shock to her system that she'd had her guard up practically from day one. It felt strange, now, to remember how worried she'd been about accidentally hurting him, when she'd spent the next several years trying as hard as she could to do it on purpose.

But then, she'd misjudged him, too. He had more edges than she'd given him credit for. Not only could he take it, he could dish it right back. Or maybe she'd just been the first person to bring out that side of him—maybe the impulse for cruelty could be sexually transmitted.

It wasn't the first time she'd behaved badly in a relationship— that honor went to her condiment-based vandalism—and it wouldn't be the last. She couldn't change any of that now. Over the years, she'd done the work to love and accept herself as she was, flaws and all. That didn't mean that anyone *else* would ever be able to, though.

"Sorry," she finally managed, laughing nervously. "I just . . . I feel like I've really been in the hot seat here today. I don't think I'm comfortable with"—she shot a sideways glance at Shane— "this situation. Going any further down this road."

Dr. Deena nodded. "I understand. We can move on."

When the session was over, they walked out of Dr. Deena's office in heavy silence, Shane holding the door to the emergency stairwell for her. By the time they reached the bottom of the first set of stairs, Lilah was still so shaken that she couldn't help herself.

"You were laying it on a little thick in there," she said.

Next to her, Shane kept his eyes forward. "What do you mean?"

She pouted dramatically and assumed an Eeyore-esque cadence. "'I felt so *used.*'"

He looked down, like he was suppressing a smile. "Well, what about you?" He turned to her, his voice becoming breathy and high-pitched, stopping just short of outright mocking her. "'I didn't want them to *sell* us.'" When they reached the third-floor landing, he stopped. "Was that all bullshit? You feeling some type of way about me back then? 'Cause this is the first I'm hearing about it."

Lilah stopped, too, a few steps below him. She looked up at him for what felt like a long time.

"No," she said softly. "It wasn't bullshit."

"Well. How about that." He looked a little too pleased with himself.

She braced her arm against the banister, peering up at him skeptically. "Come on. You're really telling me if I'd wanted to . . . if we'd decided to . . . you would've just . . ." She snapped her fingers. "What about your little friends?"

"I don't know. Fuck those guys, I haven't talked to any of them in years. I would've picked you."

"Why?" The question slipped out in a vulnerable exhale. She forced herself to stop there, the rest of it only implied: *Why did you love me?*

A hard line formed between his eyebrows. His gaze dropped to the ground, then back to her.

"How could I not?" he asked quietly.

The look on his face made the remaining air in her lungs escape in an involuntary *whoosh*.

She suddenly understood, with a nauseating surge of regret, what a precious thing she'd been so careless with all those years ago, too blinded by distrust and self-loathing to see it standing right in front of her, if she'd only been brave enough to reach for it.

"But that was before," she said, her throat tight, once again unable to finish the thought. Before she'd spent years systematically dismantling the pedestal he'd put her on, dead set on showing him what bad taste he'd had to fall for her.

He nodded slowly, then descended with purpose, closing the

gap one stair at a time. She pressed her back to the wall to create as much space between them as possible. Once he reached the stair she was on, he leaned against the banister on the other side.

Her heart thudded in her ears in anticipation of what he would do next. But he just stared intently at her for a long moment, his forehead creased.

"We really made a mess of it, huh?"

She raised one shoulder. "We were young. It was a weird situation. It happens. We just have to move on."

"Do we?"

"Yeah. We do. That's why we're here."

He shook his head slightly. "That's not what I mean."

It felt like the stairs had dropped out from beneath her. She leaned her full weight against the wall, resting her head on the rough cement. "What, then?"

"I mean . . ." He pushed himself off the banister, slowly moving closer to her. "You weren't being totally honest with her back there."

"I wasn't?"

"The show isn't the only thing we have in common." His gaze swept over her from head to toe, the sudden heat behind it making her light-headed.

He was messing with her again. He had to be. Or maybe he was deluded enough by the dangerous combination of post-therapy vulnerability and misplaced nostalgia that he thought they could get away with sleeping together a few more times.

It was a terrible idea, obviously. She shouldn't even consider it. She definitely shouldn't think about his hands, how she could practically feel how warm they'd be through the thin cotton of her shirt—or better yet, underneath it. She shivered, praying he didn't notice.

It was bad enough that she was entertaining the thought to

begin with, made even worse by the fact that she knew exactly how it would all go—how good it would be—if she wanted to.

No, not if she wanted to. If she let herself.

She realized with a jolt that she was still staring at his hands, so she forced her gaze north, snagging on his mouth for a beat too long.

The mouth she'd kissed hundreds of times. That had murmured filthy secrets in her ear. Traced every inch of her body.

The same mouth that had hurled insults, taunts, accusations. Twisted in scorn. Smirked at her misfortune.

Lilah choked out a disbelieving laugh, hoping the dim lighting camouflaged her burning cheeks. "You're not serious."

"Why not? I've tried just about everything else to get you out of my system." He said it playfully, but there was an edge of genuine frustration to it that made her heart stumble in her chest.

She fought to keep her tone neutral, conflicted about whether to play along. "We've already tried that, too, remember?"

His gaze never left hers, his voice low and gravelly. "I can't fucking forget it."

Lilah swallowed hard, her mouth suddenly dry. With effort, she broke the spell of their eye contact, glancing down at her shoes before her willpower eroded completely. She took a deep, ragged breath, then shook her head, meeting his eyes again. "We can't undo the last eight years. It's too late, the damage is done. Antagonizing each other, being constantly at each other's throats . . . it's toxic. Dysfunctional."

At the mention of throats, Shane glanced down at hers, and he took another step forward. Her pulse fluttered as he brought one hand to her neck, fingers sliding smoothly across the nape, thumb coming to rest along the bottom of her jawline. She felt like she'd forgotten how to breathe.

He slowly leaned down to the other side of her face, his beard rasping against her cheek, his voice low.

"I think you like having me at your throat. Sometimes."

She was grateful she was against the wall; otherwise she wasn't totally sure she'd stay upright. She knew for sure she wouldn't have a second later, when she felt his lips brush the pulse point behind her ear. She inhaled sharply, and his grip tightened on the back of her neck, just for a second.

Too soon, he pulled away again. She expected him to look smug about getting such an easy and obvious reaction out of her, but he seemed flustered, too, like he was fighting for control of himself. He slid his hand out of her hair and dropped it back to his side, and she followed its path with her eyes without thinking.

If she hadn't, she wouldn't have caught the brief, involuntary shake of his fingers before he turned and descended the rest of the stairs without another word.

15

Once the season began airing and the flurry of press surrounding the premiere died down, Shane quickly fell back into his normal routine, the next several weeks passing in a blur.

He'd been worried his encounter with Lilah on the stairs would make things even more awkward between them. When he'd slid into the chair next to hers in the makeup trailer a few hours later, he'd expected her to greet him as usual—that is, not at all. Instead, she'd glanced at him, raised her eyebrows for a split second, then turned back to the mirror, a hint of a smile on her lips.

It was like someone had opened a release valve, heading off the inevitable explosion just in time. Their therapy sessions helped, but that wasn't all of it. Maybe it was because he'd given a name to it at last, acknowledging out loud the connection that still sizzled between them like a live wire. They seemed able to relate only in extremes, either all over each other or each pretending the other one didn't exist. It made sense that, now that they'd finally started to work though their issues, they'd inevitably swing back toward the other end.

He hadn't really meant it, though. Like all their games, it was about trying to get her to blink first, admit something she'd rather hide. He told himself that even if he hadn't forcibly removed himself from the situation, it still wouldn't have gone any further—even though she'd been looking at him like she wanted to devour him whole.

But she was right. There was no way to undo the years of backbiting, sniping, and petty revenge they'd inflicted upon each other.

Probably.

In late October, they began prep to shoot the biggest episodes of the season, a moment nine years in the making: the climactic two-parter where Kate finally regains her corporeal form, culminating in a passionate kiss between her and Harrison. They'd be traveling to Vancouver for three weeks to shoot it, and, in something of a coup, it would be guest directed by Jonah Dempsey, the twenty-four-year-old wunderkind whose premium cable show, *Head Case,* had swept the Emmys the year before.

Shane wasn't sure it was necessary. *Intangible* had never been known for its directorial flair. Like most network shows, it was helmed by a small rotating group of regulars who were valued more for their ability to stay on schedule than their visual panache. But, like the location change, it was meant to send a message: these episodes were a Big Fucking Deal.

As the Vancouver shoot drew closer, the prospect of the kiss loomed large, casting a shadow over everything else. Their personal baggage aside, kissing someone onscreen was an unpleasant experience more often than not. It was tough to get lost in the moment with half his mind focused on how it would look from the outside, and the other half trying to ignore the dozens of people crowded around watching.

He wanted to believe it would be the same with Lilah. But if he was being honest with himself, he couldn't say there had ever been a time he'd kissed her without feeling anything.

The night before his flight, Shane dawdled around his room, throwing T-shirts and jeans into his open suitcase.

"Can I take the BMW tonight?"

He looked up to see Dean in the doorway.

Serena had given it to him, a sterling-silver roadster—the kind of flashy, ostentatious gift she was fond of. He'd always felt like a douchebag driving it, a feeling that had been confirmed when he'd pulled up to set in it for the first time. Lilah had passed as he was getting out, looked him up and down, and smirked without saying anything. After that, it mostly sat in his garage.

"Sure. You know you don't have to ask." Shane dug around in his hamper, looking for his favorite pair of jeans. "What are you doing?"

Dean shrugged. "I'm just going out." His shifty, faux-casual demeanor made Shane do a double take.

"Oh yeah? Where?"

"Dinner. Carlo's."

"With who?"

Dean shrugged again.

"Okay, then." Shane returned his attention to his suitcase, pulling out everything he'd haphazardly thrown in and sorting and rolling it. "Just don't trash the place while I'm gone."

Only the six principals and essential production staff would be traveling to Vancouver, with most of the crew—including stand-ins—hired locally.

Dean grinned. "You'll never even know I was here."

"What are you talking about? You're always here."

It was meant to be a joke, but when Shane looked up from his suitcase, the amusement had faded from Dean's face.

"I mean—not in a bad way," Shane quickly amended. "I like having you here. Obviously."

"Of course you do," Dean said, his expression lightening, to Shane's relief. "Someone's got to keep you company. Since you're so sad and alone these days."

"I'm not sad," Shane protested. He went into his en suite bathroom to pack up his toiletries, and Dean came into the bedroom, taking a seat on the bed next to Shane's suitcase.

"But you are alone."

"So?"

"So, I've never seen you single for this long. I think it might be a record."

Shane opened his mouth to protest but realized Dean was right. His last relationship had ended in May—almost six months ago, making it the longest stretch of time since high school he'd been not only single but celibate.

"What's wrong with that?"

"Just trying to look out for you, man. You're not getting any younger, and I'm not gonna be around forever."

"What? Why? Are you okay?" Shane asked, poking his head out of the bathroom in alarm. Dean laughed.

"Living here, I mean. Sorry. I don't know why I said it like that."

Shane laughed, too, ducking back inside the bathroom.

"I've been busy," he said, zipping up his dopp kit and returning to the bedroom to drop it into his suitcase. "I don't know if I want to try to date again until after the show's over. It's kind of pulling all my focus right now."

"Right," Dean said. "The show is what's pulling your focus."

Shane looked up at Dean, who held his gaze, as if daring him to ask what he was talking about—to try to deny it, force Dean to say her name first.

Shane exhaled, shaking his head.

"Listen," he said, closing his suitcase. "I'm sorry I didn't believe you. When you said nothing happened with her back then. That was really fucked up of me."

Dean's expression turned serious. "No, *I'm* sorry. I never should've gone home with her in the first place."

"I get it. I was an asshole. I deserved it. From both of you."

"Yeah, but . . . I don't think I really understood, not until after. The way things were between you two. Even now."

"What do you mean, now?" Shane asked, his mind immediately flashing to the premiere party: Lilah's request for a shotgun, how he'd reached his hand out for the joint without even thinking about it, Dean passing it to him without a word.

"Come on," Dean said. "What about the first table read? Didn't you drive, like, forty minutes out of your way to get those donuts she likes?"

Shane blinked. "Well, yeah. But I didn't do it because she likes them, I did it to mess with her."

Dean furrowed his brow in a fake-pensive expression. "I wonder what it would be like to have someone so obsessed with me that they arrange their whole day around finding incredibly specific ways to rile me up."

Shane scowled. "I'm not obsessed with her."

"Whatever you say," Dean said with an evil grin, standing up and stretching. "You're just lucky she hasn't taken out a restraining order against you. But it kinda seems like she's into it, so maybe you freaks really are made for each other."

Shane shook his head. "I think that ship has sailed. And sunk. That ship is at the bottom of the ocean, full of seaweed and skeletons in pirate hats."

"Guess it's time to get over it, then." Dean headed out of the room, pausing in the doorway. "When you get back, we're signing you up for one of those dating sites where they make you answer, like, a hundred different questions about your favorite pasta shape and what you want to do with your body after you die."

"I'm not doing that."

"Why not? Worried it'll just spit out a picture of Lilah at the end?"

Dean was already halfway down the hall before Shane had a chance to respond.

16

When Lilah turned her phone back on after landing in Vancouver, she was greeted by a missed call from Jasmine, her agent. She ducked into a corner of the terminal after deplaning, gesturing to Shane and the others to make their way to baggage claim without her.

Jasmine answered, as always, on the first ring. She'd started as the assistant to Lilah's previous agent but quickly worked her way up the ranks. When Lilah's agent had dropped her unceremoniously after *Without a Net* had flopped, Jasmine, now at her own agency, snapped her up so quickly that Lilah's ego barely had time to bruise.

"Great news. I have a lead on the *perfect* post-show project for you."

Lilah adjusted the strap of her bag. "Really?"

"Do you know *Night Call*?"

"Sure, I've read it." *Night Call* had been a true crime sensation a decade or so ago, a nonfiction bestseller chronicling the case of a serial killer who had terrorized Seattle in the early nineties. The book had been optioned before it was even published, but had been stuck in development hell ever since, with one big-name actress after another attached to the juicy leading role of the intrepid local journalist (and sister of one of the victims) who had finally tracked him down.

Lilah's stomach leapt once she realized what Jasmine was saying. "Wait. Is it finally happening?"

"They're trying to keep it hush-hush, but it's happening. And Marcus Townsend is adapting it."

Lilah's jaw dropped.

Growing up, she'd dreamed of working with her *Without a Net* director, but in retrospect, she could admit that his creative peak had come a couple of decades earlier. Marcus Townsend, on the other hand, was undoubtedly still at the height of his powers. He'd made five films over the past dozen years, each more critically acclaimed than the last—the first Black director to be a three-time Academy Award nominee in that category. She'd been burned by her previous grasp at so-called prestige, but starring in a Marcus Townsend movie was the closest she was ever going to get to a sure thing.

"You think you can get me an audition?" Lilah asked, once she could speak again.

"The sides are already waiting for you at the hotel."

Lilah leaned against the wall. "Holy shit. Okay. How long do I have to prepare?"

"They wanted you to come in next week, but I told them you were out of town. Do you think you can put yourself on tape while you're out there?"

"Absolutely, of course. Whatever they want."

After she hung up with Jasmine, her nerves buzzing, she power walked her way out of the airport on shaking legs, doubling back when she passed a bookstore to pick up her own copy of *Night Call*.

. . .

The hotel they were staying at for the duration of the shoot was clearly chosen for budget over comfort: scratchy carpet, confusing abstract art, thin comforter that she definitely shouldn't run a black light over. As Lilah dropped her bags and stripped down to take a quick shower, she brattily wondered if their accommodations had any connection to the undoubtedly outrageous cost of hiring Jonah Dempsey to direct these episodes.

The schedule had them hitting the ground running—the first table read was scheduled less than an hour after they arrived at the hotel, in one of the conference rooms downstairs. Lilah threw on a pair of leggings and a sweatshirt before rough-drying her hair, and her phone buzzed with a text on the bathroom counter next to her. When she leaned over to see who it was, she felt an unexpected thrill of nerves.

FUCKFACE: What room are you in?

She thought about ignoring it, but her curiosity won out, and she compromised by responding with the minimum amount of effort.

LILAH: Why

FUCKFACE: I have something to give you

LILAH: If it's what I think it is I'm not interested

FUCKFACE: Don't worry, they confiscated that at customs

LILAH: ?
They confiscated your dick at customs?

FUCKFACE: I don't know where I was going with that one

LILAH: Is that what you said right before they took it away

FUCKFACE: Not that I'm not having the time of my life with this
but are you going to tell me your room number or what

Lilah took a long moment to respond, turning off the blow dryer and flipping her head upside down to twist her hair into a loose bun.

LILAH: 816

A few minutes later, there was a knock at the door. Lilah opened it to find Shane, carrying a cardboard box she'd recognize anywhere: glossy pink with green flowers around the border.

"What is this?" she asked, even though she already knew. He glanced down at the box as if to double-check.

"It's donuts," he confirmed, looking back up at her.

"Why?" was all she could manage. He must have gotten them before they'd left, she realized dizzily, and hid them from her even as they'd sat next to each other on the plane.

He looked a little abashed. "For, um. For your birthday. It's on Tuesday, right? I thought about waiting to give them to you, but they'd probably be hard as rocks by then. They did get a little squished in my suitcase, though."

Lilah gaped at him. "Oh. Uh. Thank you." She took the box from him, and an awkward moment passed between them. In the silence, his stomach growled audibly, and she fought not to crack up as he winced.

"Sorry, I haven't eaten since before we got on the plane."

"Do you want one?" Now that he mentioned it, she was starving, too.

His glance flicked over her shoulder. "For here or for the road?"

"We have a few minutes, right?"

She stepped aside and he walked past her, his lingering glance telling her the gesture wasn't lost on him. She shut the door, placing the box of donuts on the counter next to the TV. She broke off half of a maple walnut and nibbled on it, leaning against the dresser, feeling jittery in a way she couldn't totally blame on low blood sugar. He gravitated toward the vanilla-lavender again before settling in the armchair next to the window.

They ate in silence for a moment.

"Thanks for this," she said. "Did I already say that?"

"You did, yeah." Shane popped the last bit of donut in his mouth. "I don't know. I figured you probably wouldn't be doing much celebrating, stuck up here working. And I wasn't sure if anyone else knew."

It was like he was trying to answer the question still hovering in the air: why he'd gotten them at all. It was the kind of gesture she knew he'd make for anyone. But her heart squeezed when she remembered the last time he'd shown up with them, what that meant.

It was something more than an early birthday present: it was a peace offering.

"I guess not. I'm not sure if I'd be doing much even if I was home, though. Other than changing my birth date on Wikipedia. Thirty-two feels kind of whatever, as far as birthdays go."

Shane cracked a smile. "Right. Sure." He brushed the crumbs off his hands. "Are you going home for Thanksgiving?"

She shook her head. "Doesn't really make sense. You?"

He shook his head, too.

"Should we do something?" He looked so startled that she hurriedly added, "All of us, I mean. And fuck Thanksgiving, obviously. But we have the long weekend, and I'm sure we're not the only ones sticking around."

"What would we do? Get takeout, eat it in one of our rooms? That sounds crowded."

"Yeah, and depressing." She took another bite and chewed thoughtfully. "Maybe we should rent an Airbnb or something. We could all cook."

He cocked his eyebrow. "You cook?"

"Don't sound so shocked."

"I just . . . I've never seen it."

She wanted to protest, but it was true. She'd never so much as toasted a bagel in his presence. In fact, she could probably count on two hands the number of times she'd cooked herself a real meal over the past nine years.

They lapsed into silence again, their strained small-talk quota apparently maxed out. Lilah finished her donut, too, marveling at the fact that the two of them still had the capacity to be this weird around each other after all this time. But then, every new wrinkle their relationship took on managed to surprise her, in its own way.

She was forced to accept that what they were to each other defied categorization: more than co-workers, no longer enemies, but not exactly friends, either. Even a few weeks ago, they would've filled the space by fighting; now, a different kind of tension flickered between them, more complex and unsettling than mutual animosity.

Maybe he was also painfully aware they were alone in a hotel room—their first time alone together since the stairwell. She cast her gaze down to the hideous carpet and swallowed, her throat suddenly dry, the last crumbs of the donut sticking uncomfortably. She crouched down and pulled a bottle of water out of the minibar.

Shane shifted his weight. "So, have you heard anything about this Jonah guy?"

"Honestly?" she said, straightening up and unscrewing the cap. "Nothing good. I mean, he gets results, which is probably why he still gets hired, but I heard he can be kind of an asshole. And he's not afraid to do a million and one takes if he's not happy."

Shane's forehead creased.

"What? Am I a terrible person for listening to gossip and judging him before meeting him?" she asked, rolling her eyes.

He shook his head. "No. Just . . . hopefully he's happy with the kiss within the first hundred thousand." The corner of his mouth lifted in a sardonic half smile.

Lilah's stomach plummeted. She'd known she'd have to kiss him over and over in front of the whole crew, but it hadn't occurred to her that she might have to do it dozens, maybe hundreds of times, at the whim of a hostile director.

She raised her eyebrows, refusing to show how much it rattled her. "Are you worried you've forgotten how?"

"I haven't had any recent complaints."

He met her eyes, and the temperature in the room spiked ten degrees.

She didn't want to think about any of it. The last time she'd kissed him. Who he may or may not have kissed since then. Whether anyone had ever kissed her better.

He looked like he was about to say something else, but instead he stood and stretched, brushing nonexistent crumbs off his shirt. Against her will, she felt her eyes grow saucer-wide as he approached her—then bypassed her completely, stopping in front of the box of donuts. He paused and glanced up at her, as if to ask permission, then did a double take.

"Are you wearing makeup?"

Lilah blinked. "What? No. Why?"

"What happened to your freckles?"

Her hand flew to her cheek, then dropped back to her side. "Oh. They got lasered off."

"You got them removed?" His brows knit together in concern.

"Not on purpose. It's a side effect. Trying to shave a few years off more than just my Wikipedia page."

He returned his attention to the donuts, flipping the lid open and studying the contents of the box. "Too bad."

"I still have plenty more," she said reflexively, but she regretted it when his gaze flicked back to her, taking her in from head to toe.

"I know," he said, in a tone that was matter-of-fact and not pervy in the slightest, but that didn't stop her from feeling like her entire body was blushing.

Without waiting for her to respond, he grabbed another donut. "See you down there," he said with a grin, sticking it between his teeth and heading out the door.

17

It took only fifteen minutes in Jonah Dempsey's presence for Shane to conclude that Lilah's secondhand reports about him hadn't been an exaggeration. If anything, they'd been too kind.

He seemed unassuming at first—thin and wiry, with a ruddy complexion and dirty-blond hair gelled firmly away from his face. But when Shane shook his hand, thanking him for coming in to help them, Jonah just tipped his head back and smirked. Even though he was a few inches shorter than Shane, he somehow managed to look down his nose at him anyway.

"Sure, man. You know, this is my mom's favorite show. It's cute."

He barely looked up from his phone during the table read, even leaving the room to take a call at one point.

However, that inattentiveness didn't carry over once they started shooting. The schedule on the call sheet quickly proved to be just a suggestion, as his overambitious camera setups and exacting direction led every scene to run over, sometimes by hours.

After the third day, when Jonah made a PA, an extra, and the head of catering cry in quick succession, Shane pulled Walt aside.

"This is ridiculous. He's making everyone miserable. There's no way he's talented enough for this to be worth it. What kind of set are you running here?"

Walt shrugged helplessly. "I don't have any say in it. The network hired him, and they're not budging. You know who his father is, right?"

Shane didn't, but the fact that the question was even being floated in the first place got the point across.

"There are a lot of assholes in this business," Walt continued. "And we got pretty damn lucky that none of them are with us on a regular basis. It's only three weeks. We're just gonna have to tough it out."

The van back to the hotel every night was dead silent, half the passengers sleeping, the other half staring moodily into the distance. Shane would lose consciousness the moment he tumbled into bed, his alarm jolting him awake what felt like minutes later.

Their second week of shooting kicked off with a scene that was shaping up to be an even bigger pain in the ass than his eventual kiss with Lilah: the restoration of Kate's physical body, followed immediately by her kidnapping. It was a long and technical scene, the second half of which would take place in the rain—something none of them were looking forward to in November in Canada.

To make matters worse, Jonah had announced that he was planning on shooting everything after the rain started—five complicated pages—in one continuous take. The sense of dread that settled over them, cast and crew alike, was palpable.

The morning of the shoot, they boarded the van when it was still pitch-black outside. Their location for the day was the lush rain forest of the Clayoquot Sound, four hours away. Locations had already been out to prep everything the day before, so a mini village of tents and trailers awaited them when they arrived, powered by an army of generators, cords snaking out of the backs and snarled like neon-orange rat kings.

After he stepped out of the makeup trailer, Shane grabbed a cup of coffee and took a moment to absorb the scene: the sun filtering through the rolling greenery, the blue of the sky. He closed his eyes, inhaling the fresh, crisp scent of cedar. Maybe today wouldn't be so bad after all.

He felt the hard clap of a hand on his shoulder.

"Didn't realize we were paying you to stand around." Jonah's oversized grin didn't match the flintiness in his eyes.

"I'm usually sitting around, actually," Shane said evenly, sipping his coffee.

. . .

Lilah knew it was optimistic to think that they'd get through it in under ten takes, but she allowed herself to hope for it, anyway.

The first take, the cameraman fumbled the transition from Steadicam to handheld.

The second take, the rain machines malfunctioned, leaving a long, awkward pause after the thunderclap and lightning strike.

The third take, Lilah was hit with a heavy slash of rain in her face right as she was about to say her line, leaving her choking and spluttering helplessly.

The fourth take, Brian tripped over the camera tracks while backing up.

Takes five through ten were concerned with the heavy action section at the end of the scene, in which hordes of faceless henchmen appeared through the trees to take out the members of the team one by one, before grabbing Lilah and carrying her away. After several rounds of trial and error, it was determined that it was impossible to switch them all out for their stunt doubles without it being noticeable.

The news sent an unhappy ripple through the six of them. Lilah opened her mouth to object but caught Shane's eye. *It's not worth it,* he seemed to say. She closed her mouth, took a deep breath, and participated in re-blocking the scene sans doubles without complaint.

It was clear, though, that Shane would be bearing the brunt of the change. Even though the henchmen were all played by trained stunt performers—experts in doing this kind of thing safely and painlessly—it was impossible to fake the way they had to drag him across the rocky terrain as he struggled to free himself. From the way his face stayed contorted in the same expression even after they moved on, it was evident that his discomfort was real. Lilah forced herself to avert her eyes so she wouldn't lose her own focus, the knot in the pit of her stomach growing larger the longer she watched.

She lost track of the number of takes they did after that. She'd never shot a scene with this many moving parts that had the potential to go wrong, and time after time, one part or another proceeded to do just that. As hard as she tried to stay present as Kate, she eventually went numb, her brain switching into pure survival mode as her body was drenched in icy fake rain and manhandled by the stuntmen over and over and over.

Around her, she could see Margaux's teeth chattering, Rafael limping slightly, Brian's shoulders sagging with exhaustion, finger marks blooming on Natalie's arms that had to be covered by the makeup department every time they cut. Even though PAs hurried to wrap them in down coats between takes, it didn't do much to mitigate the fact that they'd been shivering in the same soaking clothes for hours. Lilah had never felt this kind of cold before: clammy and damp and endless, seeping deep into her bones like she'd never be warm again.

As for Shane, it was obvious that each take was exponentially more painful than the last. He was doing a good job keeping it together when the camera was on him, but she could tell how much he was suffering: the subtle winces when he moved, the effort that seemed to be behind every ragged breath he took. During one take, a stuntman's boot slipped on the wet grass, kicking Shane hard in the ribs, making him cry out. Lilah's lips parted, her breath escaping in a rush, almost as if she'd felt the impact herself.

Impotent rage surged through her at the whole thing: at Jonah's arrogance, at how unnecessary it was to make them go through this, at how Shane was too much of a self-sacrificing people pleaser to ever complain.

"Action," Jonah called again, and Lilah took a deep breath.

She felt it immediately: there was something different about this take. Everything that had been hazy and sloppy snapped into perfect, crystalline focus. Her lines came effortlessly, she hit her marks without trying, every emotion coming to her as if it were the first time. Even the rain didn't feel quite as cold. She could tell the rest of them felt it, too, tapping into a kind of flow state, the six of them practically psychically linked.

Finally, finally, finally, they made it all the way to the end of the scene. It felt like everyone on the entire set was holding their breath until the second Jonah called "Cut!"

The rain machines shut off and the crew cheered. Rafael let out a whoop, picking Natalie up and spinning her around as Margaux collapsed against Brian, bursting into relieved tears. Shane and Lilah exchanged exhausted, affectionate glances. All the adrenaline drained out of her immediately, leaving her too tired to do anything but stand there and grin at him like an idiot.

The celebratory mood immediately fizzled as Jonah's voice cut through the chatter. "Let's reset to go again."

Lilah whirled on him before she could stop herself. "*What?*"

Jonah met her gaze, his face expressionless. "I said we're going again."

"Why?" Lilah spat, stalking toward him. "We got it."

He rose to his feet once she reached his chair, but it didn't do much to intimidate her, since she was still taller than him.

"It wasn't good enough, that's why," he said. "Just because you all *finally* got through it once doesn't mean we're done."

Lilah pushed a soggy lock of hair out of her face. "This clearly isn't working. Can't you find a way to sneak a cut in there? Change *something* about what we're doing to make it run a little smoother?"

"I think you're forgetting your role on this set," Jonah said, eyes narrowing, voice lowering in an impression of a threat. "I'm the director. You're the actors. You do what I tell you to do, and you do it until I say you did it right."

Lilah's cheeks grew hot. She fought not to raise her voice. "We've been doing *exactly* what you told us to do. Part of *your* job is to make adjustments so we can get it done and get out of here."

"Of course. I should've known," Jonah said, rolling his eyes.

"This kind of show is just, like, some soulless paycheck machine, right? You don't care about the work, all you care about is getting home in time for dinner. You all might as well be CGI or, I dunno, fuckin' *robots* or something. Maybe then you'd be able to get it right more than one fucking time."

The entire set had come to a standstill around them. There was a rustle of footsteps behind her, Shane slowly appearing in her peripheral vision. She thought maybe he was going to tell her to cool down, that she shouldn't escalate things any further. But instead, he paused next to her.

Not to talk her down. To back her up.

His wordless support was like a battery, her anger flaring with renewed force. "Well, unfortunately for you, we're not robots. None of us are." She gestured at the crew around her, all of whom were looking the worse for wear. "We can't take unlimited abuse and just keep going. But we *are* professionals. If we've been doing this all fucking day and just got through it for the first time now, maybe we're not the problem. Maybe it's your concept that's the problem."

Jonah's nostrils flared. He held Lilah's gaze for a long moment. "Let's take five," he shouted, turning his head to address the crew. "Then reset to go again. Same as before."

Lilah set her jaw and turned away, her stomach clenching. She felt Shane's eyes on her, but she looked straight ahead, afraid she might burst into tears if she looked directly at him.

"Fucking bitch," she heard Jonah mutter behind her.

Then Shane lunged at him.

Lilah pivoted on her heel so quickly her vision swam, practically tackling him, diverting his fist seconds before it made contact with Jonah's face. Their momentum knocked them both off-balance, sending her sprawling on top of him in the mud. He let out a hiss as her elbow collided with the side he'd been babying—his bad rib. At the same time, she landed on her wrist at an awkward angle, making her yelp in pain.

They lay there in stunned silence for a moment as Lilah waited for the air to return to her lungs. Shane moved first, pushing himself up to a sitting position with a groan, Lilah clinging to him as they struggled to their feet. Jonah watched them with an amused expression so punchable that, for a fleeting moment, she regretted pulling Shane back.

"You don't get to fucking talk to her like that," Shane said, still breathing hard. "You need to apologize. Now."

Jonah looked both of them up and down. "Sorry," he said, not even attempting to sound sincere. He turned away, addressing the crew. "Let's wrap this up. I don't need this shit. We're done here."

After a few uncertain seconds, the set churned into motion again.

Lilah and Shane trudged down the path that led to the trailers, Lilah slowing her pace to match his without thinking twice about it.

"You okay?" she asked, sneaking a sidelong glance at him.

"Yeah. I will be." His words slurred together with fatigue. "You?"

"Yeah."

They walked in silence for another few paces. To Lilah's surprise, she started to laugh, helpless, hysterical giggles bubbling up from deep in her chest.

"I can't believe you tried to punch him. I didn't know you were a punching guy."

He smiled ruefully. "Neither did I."

"I'm kind of surprised that's what set you off. What, no one's allowed to call me a bitch except you?"

"I've never called you a bitch."

Lilah scoffed. "Oh, fuck off."

"I'm serious," Shane said, and the forcefulness in his tone had her glancing over at him in surprise. "You're always calling yourself that, not me."

She raised her eyebrows, even as something in his expression had goosebumps prickling down her back—or maybe it was her soaked shirt that was causing them. "You expect me to believe you've *never* called me a bitch. Not once, even behind my back, in all these years."

He paused for a long moment. "Okay, maybe not *never*." His sheepishness had her cracking up despite herself. "But not in a long time," he continued. "Not any time I can remember. Really. And if I did, I'm sure you didn't deserve it, and I'm sorry. I was probably being as much of an asshole as he was."

She let the thought settle over her for a few more paces, the edge of the closest trailer coming into view. Remorse trickled through her. "*Did* I deserve it, though? Back there. Maybe I should've just kept my mouth shut."

He shook his head emphatically. "No. No. You were . . . thank you. For saying something." He glanced behind them, where Natalie, Rafael, Margaux, and Brian were slowly making their way down the same path. "I know they appreciate it, too."

Lilah looked down at the ground, uncomfortable. "Sure. It was nothing."

He ascended the stairs to the wardrobe trailer then turned back to her. "It wasn't nothing," he said simply, before pulling the door open and stepping aside. "After you."

Hours later, as the van approached the hotel, Lilah woke with a start, chagrined to find she'd nodded off on Shane's shoulder. With her tendency for motion sickness, it was unusual for her to fall asleep in the car at all. It was a testament to how run-down she was that she was passing out every time she sat still for more than fifteen minutes.

She probably should've known better than to sit next to him on the way back, but she'd slid into the seat automatically, too tired to think about it. At least he was out cold, too, his breathing slow and even.

But that wasn't the most disturbing part. It was the realization that, at some point during the ride, they'd started holding hands—her fingers fully intertwined with his, their hands resting between them atop their pressed-together thighs.

Slowly, her pulse pounding like she was defusing a bomb, she straightened one finger at a time and eased her palm out of his grip, dreading the prospect of him waking up before she was free. If he did, they'd both be burdened with the mounting evidence that something was happening between them that they might actually have to address. But if she was the only one who knew about it, maybe they could keep ignoring it a little longer. Run out the clock until the show ended and they could be done with each other for good.

He didn't wake up, though. He just shifted closer, letting out a soft, sleepy groan that made her heart ache with recognition.

18

None of them were surprised (or upset) when the day in the woods turned out to be Jonah's last. Through the grapevine, Lilah heard that the network had offered Jonah even more money not to quit, to no avail. The story of their confrontation had already started to spread, obviously planted preemptively by his team, since the coverage painted her as a lazy, entitled diva throwing tantrums over the slightest inconvenience.

She'd had an emergency triage call with Jasmine and her publicist the morning of Thanksgiving. The two of them had begged her to be on her best behavior going forward, the "or else" only implied. She didn't regret standing her ground with Jonah, but once she understood her chance at *Night Call* was now in jeopardy, she *did* regret holding Shane back from clocking him.

Luckily, their long holiday weekend—still union-mandated even though they were in Canada—arrived just in time. Everyone had embraced the idea of their pseudo-Thanksgiving dinner party wholeheartedly, the stress of the situation bonding them more than ever.

Lilah had taken care of booking the one-bedroom house, though Shane had insisted on splitting the cost of everything, the two of them waving away everyone else's offers to help pay for booze or groceries. The head count came out to around a dozen: other than the six of them, the only others who had traveled with them from L.A. were Walt and Polly (who'd cowritten the episodes), plus their significant others.

Margaux, Natalie, and Natalie's husband, Omar, declared themselves in charge of the menu. The three of them took care of the shopping while Lilah checked into the Airbnb.

At the suggestion of the set medic, Shane was off getting a chest X-ray. When she'd heard, Lilah was startled to realize her first impulse was to offer to go with him—which she'd obviously suppressed. She flipped through *Night Call* while waiting for the others to show up with the groceries, ignoring the equally irrational urge to text him to check in about it.

The three of them arrived laden with bags shortly before noon, Lilah dropping the book on the counter to go help them unload the car.

Omar, the professional chef among the group, began delegating tasks to all of them, and they set to work washing, chopping, and measuring, the kitchen quickly filling with delicious smells. Margaux took control of the playlist, rolling her eyes good-naturedly whenever a song came on that none of them were young or cool enough to have heard of.

The others slowly trickled in over the course of the day—Brian, Rafael and his wife, Walt and his husband, and Polly—and were subsequently put to work.

Shane showed up last, to exaggerated but affectionate applause from the rest of them. He waved it off, grinning sheepishly.

"How's the patient?" asked Rafael.

"All good. Just bruised," Shane said, making his way into the kitchen and leaning against the counter across from where Lilah was caramelizing onions. "This whole socialized healthcare thing is pretty cool, though. Have y'all heard about this? Instead of a bill, they just gave me a Tim Hortons coupon and a little kiss on the forehead."

The rest of them laughed, and Lilah bit her lip to keep from joining in. But when she looked up, she caught Shane looking away from her—like he'd been checking for her reaction first.

. . .

When the meal was ready, they all gathered around the table. Since none of them cared about Thanksgiving (not to mention the fact that they were in Canada), the menu wasn't exactly traditional, but Shane's mouth had been watering for hours, and he filled his plate to bursting with every dish on the table: baked kabocha squash stuffed with spicy hazelnuts and topped with burrata, slow-cooked lamb shawarma, mushroom-onion galette, couscous salad with roasted cherry tomatoes and fresh herbs. Though the plastic checkered tablecloth and paper plates gave the meal a ragtag aura, the food was exceptional, and they all ate in contented silence for several minutes.

Once they'd eaten their fill, Shane cleared his throat, catching Lilah's eye at the opposite end of the table.

"Should we go around and each say something we're thankful for? I feel like that's the one good thing to take away from Thanksgiving as an institution."

Everyone else murmured in assent, setting their forks down and glancing around to see if anyone would volunteer to go first.

Brian leaned back in his chair, half raising his hand. "I can start, if you want. I'm thankful we never have to shoot that damn scene again." He shot a worried glance at Walt. "Right?"

Walt shook his head, and the rest of the table broke into relieved laughter, a few of them raising their glasses in agreement.

"Honestly, though, I'm thankful to be here at all," Brian continued. "As far as first jobs go, this has kind of been the dream. And I know my parents are thankful that I'm actually going to be able to pay off my student loans."

The others laughed again, and they continued around the table: Rafael sharing his gratitude that his parents were able to retire and relocate to Los Angeles with his help, Margaux tearing up while describing how her cat, Tuba, was now thriving after emergency surgery the previous month.

When it was Lilah's turn, she looked down into her wineglass, taking a long moment before speaking.

"I know . . . I know it hasn't always been easy. And I don't think it's a secret that it wasn't exactly my choice." A self-deprecating smile crept over her face. "But . . . I'm thankful I came back. Really." She looked up at last, meeting Shane's eyes first before glancing around the table. "Getting to work with all of you . . . getting to *know* you . . . it's been really special. I'm thankful to have a second chance, I guess."

"I'm thankful you're back, too," Shane said, to his own surprise. He must have still been woozy from the painkillers.

Lilah raised her eyebrow, obviously waiting for the punch

line, but there was none. A few others exchanged glances, as if they were unsure whether he was being sarcastic, and a slightly uncomfortable silence settled over them.

"I'm just thankful you two are finally getting along," Walt said with a world-weary sigh, defusing the tension, the rest of the table cracking up. Lilah raised her glass to Shane with a rueful smile, and he matched the gesture, waiting for her to look away first before he took a drink.

. . .

After dinner, they settled in the living room, taking a break to digest before dessert. Natalie found a battered Taboo box in the cabinet under the TV, and they set about dividing into two teams.

"We need to split up all the couples," Margaux protested, pointing at Shane and Lilah.

"We're not a couple," they said in unison.

"But you've known each other long enough for it to be an advantage," Margaux said.

They looked at each other and shrugged, Shane moving to the couch to sit next to Brian.

After a few heated rounds, Lilah excused herself to the kitchen to start preparing dessert. To her surprise, Walt offered his help, and the two of them set about cutting and serving the spiced apple cake Natalie had made.

"What do you think about them?" Walt asked quietly, nodding his head over toward the living room. Lilah followed his gaze across the island to see Brian, sitting cross-legged on the floor, back against the couch, as Margaux rested her knees on either side of his shoulders, trying to French-braid his hair, both of them giggling at her sloppy, haphazard progress.

"What do you mean?" Lilah asked, carefully transferring a

slice of cake onto the paper plates they'd bought. "I . . . like them?"

"There's been some talk about spinning them off. Rosie and Ryder. Their storyline has been testing well. We might do a backdoor pilot later in the season, see how it goes over. If nothing else, it'll give you and Shane a break for a week."

"Oh. Huh," Lilah said, her eyes drifting back to the two of them. It was hard to deny they played well off each other. "I think it's a great idea. Would you run it?"

Walt shook his head. "I'd executive produce, but we've been talking about setting Polly up as showrunner. She's grown so much over the past few years. Plus, she really knows how to write for the two of them."

"Wow," Lilah said. "That's so exciting. And then whoever from the crew doesn't have a new job yet . . ."

"They'd probably come over, too, yeah." Walt stuck a corkscrew in a new bottle of wine. "Not to be indelicate, but . . . you don't know about anything going on between them, do you?"

Lilah glanced back to them automatically. "No? Not that I've heard, anyway. I think they're just friends."

"Good. That's good. I mean, this show wouldn't be what it is without you and Shane, obviously, but it *would* be nice not to go through a repeat performance of your greatest hits, if we can avoid it. Don't want to deal with one of them trying to break their contract and shut the whole thing down after the first season, right?"

Lilah did a double take that probably bordered on cartoonish, unsure if she'd heard him right. "What? *I* didn't . . . Shane tried to quit?"

Walt's brow creased deeply. "You didn't know?"

She wiped her hands on a dish towel, thinking back to that nightmarish summer after they'd broken up, whether anyone had said anything to her then. "Is that why we got those raises before season two? But why wouldn't they just give it to him, if he was the one who wanted to leave? Why did I get one, too?"

She'd questioned it at the time, but even her former agent hadn't seemed to know. As unknowns, their initial contracts had been for union minimum, and they weren't up for renegotiation until the end of season five. Her agent had brushed it off, telling her it was probably a reflection of the show's increased budget after its surprise success. Even back then it had sounded fishy that they would give her more money without her having to fight for it, but she chose not to push further, feeling ungrateful for looking a gift horse in the mouth.

Walt shrugged, pulling the cork out with a grimace. "Couldn't say. That was all before my time. You'd have to ask him."

He went into the living room to get a head count on coffee, and Lilah leaned against the counter, other hand on her hip, staring at Shane with what must have been a perturbed expression. As if he felt it, he glanced over at her. When he turned back a second later, he had a look on his face like they'd shared a private joke.

If only she knew what it was.

19

When the sun went down, Shane built a fire in the fireplace and sprawled on the couch in front of it, intending to just shut his eyes for a moment, lulled by the murmurs of laughter and chatter around him.

When he opened them again, the fire was still crackling, but the room was quiet apart from the soft turning of pages. He craned his neck to see Lilah curled up in one of the armchairs, reading. She looked up at the noise of his shuffling, her lips quirking in a half smile.

"How was your nap, Grandpa?"

"I'm on a lot of painkillers, okay?" he grumbled, the throb in his ribs alerting him they'd worn off. "Is everyone else gone?"

"Mm-hmm," she said, turning another page without break-ing eye contact.

They were alone, then. Again.

It seemed like they were pushing their luck, this many times without incident. It felt inevitable that things would eventually explode, one way or another.

With great effort, he swung his legs over the side of the couch. "Did I sleep through all the cleanup?"

"I *knew* you were faking to get out of doing the dishes." Her eyes glinted with good-natured mischief.

"I feel bad. I wanted to help, since I didn't do any of the cooking."

"You're in luck. There's still a few in the sink."

"Well, I didn't feel *that* bad," he mumbled, and she snick-ered.

With a sigh, he scrubbed his hand over the back of his neck and stood up, heading toward the kitchen.

"Want some company?"

He turned to see her looking at him over her book, her ex-pression hard to read.

"Sure," he said. "Yeah. I'd like that."

She closed her book and trailed after him, refilling her wine-glass before hoisting herself onto an empty stretch of counter.

Neither of them said anything for a long moment as he set down a dish towel on the counter next to him and turned on the sink, running his hand under the tap as it warmed up. But to his surprise, it wasn't an uncomfortable silence. It felt easy. Lived-in. Domestic.

It shouldn't have felt this natural. Playing house with her like this, in a place neither of them lived, when they weren't to-gether anymore, when they hadn't ever done this kind of thing even when they *were* together.

And yet somehow it felt like the thousandth time and not the first: lingering in the kitchen late at night after everyone they'd hosted had gone home, him doing the dishes, her drinking wine, both of them basking in the afterglow of good food and good company, quietly appreciative that they were alone again all the same.

He pushed the thought out of his head. "Do you need a ride back to the hotel after this?"

Out of the corner of his eye, he saw her shake her head. "I was planning on staying here tonight."

"Here?"

Lilah idly swung her legs against the side of the counter. "Yeah, I mean, why not? I paid for it."

He glanced over at her. "Actually, *we* paid for it. I have just as much of a right to that bed as you do."

He was teasing, mostly, but tried to keep his expression serious. In return, she arched an eyebrow.

"I'll pay you back for your half."

He grinned, turning back to the sink. "I don't know . . . spending the night somewhere other than that hotel is sounding pretty good to me right now. I don't think my back will ever recover from that mattress."

"How do you know this one is any better?"

"Only one way to find out."

She didn't respond, just sipped her wine. Maybe he was taking it too far, crossing into pushy. He looked over at her again. "I'll go back if you want me to."

She met his eyes, her tone neutral.

"I didn't say that."

He felt a ghost of a smirk cross his face but said nothing, turning back to the sink. He tried not to let his mind race about the implications of what that meant.

As if she could hear his thoughts, she added, "If you stay, you know nothing's going to happen tonight, right?"

"Isn't that jinxing ourselves? Now it's all tempting and forbidden."

"You're right," she deadpanned. "Maybe we should just have sex now to remove the temptation to have sex later."

"Now you're talking."

He could tell she was working to keep her voice stern, to fight the laugh bubbling up underneath it. "I mean it."

"I believe you."

"And I mean *every* definition of sex. No hand stuff. No mouth stuff. No loopholes."

"Well, stop talking about holes, then. You're getting me all worked up."

The laugh she was suppressing finally escaped, the sound sending a thrill through him. "I hate you."

"No, you don't." He glanced over at her after he said it, almost without meaning to. Her cheeks were tinged pink, though it was just as likely from the wine as from anything else. She took another sip, holding his gaze.

He turned back to the pan that had held the apple cake and scrubbed vigorously. "Who said *I* want to have sex with *you,* anyway? Kind of full of yourself."

She still didn't say anything, but out of the corner of his eye, he saw her drain her glass and slide off the counter. He tensed as she approached him from behind, feeling the nudge of her feet on either side of his, followed by the soft press of her breasts against his back. To his dismay, he fumbled with the dish in his hands, and the small, hot exhale of her laugh on his neck made every hair on his body stand on end.

Resentment rushed through him at how easily she could get a reaction out of him, calling his bluff—joke or not—without doing much of anything. But mostly he was just grateful that he was facing away from her, the lower half of his body blocked by the sink, hiding the full, humiliating extent of his innate response to her.

When she rested her chin lightly in the spot between his neck and shoulder, just for a second, it occurred to him that maybe her boundary was less of a boundary and more of a dare in disguise.

He wouldn't cross it without her permission, obviously, but there was plenty of leeway in the terms she'd laid down. Earlier, he'd peeked into the house's one and only bedroom and was suddenly overtaken by the vivid image of the two of them tangled in those sheets, dry humping like overheated teenagers, slowly stripping off one piece of clothing at a time in an attempt to hold out as long as they could, each waiting for the other one to break first.

It must have been a sign of how hard up he was after half a year of celibacy that his hands were shaking at the thought.

If she noticed, she didn't point it out. She just slowly reached around him, placing her wineglass in the almost empty sink.

"I'm gonna go take a shower," she murmured into his neck.

As he watched her disappear down the hall toward the bathroom, another, more uncomfortable idea settled over him: maybe he was wrong. Maybe she didn't deserve the manipulative seductress label he'd slapped her with—then, or now. Maybe, like Dr. Deena had suggested, it was another way to absolve himself of his own responsibility in their endless push and pull.

Maybe she was just as confused as he was about what they were to each other: unsure what she wanted, what was attainable, what was worth hoping for.

Maybe they both cloaked all that uncertainty in sex as a distraction, afraid of what they'd find if they bothered to look beneath the surface of their physical connection.

And as he heard the shower start to run, he wondered if maybe it wouldn't have been the smart move for him to go back to the hotel after all.

. . .

Lilah took her time getting ready after her shower. As she dressed in the sweats and tank top she'd packed for herself, she tried to figure out how her solo getaway had turned into a pseudo–couples retreat. He'd given her an opening to tell him to fuck off and leave her alone, and she probably still could, if she wanted to. But she realized that at some point over the past few months, disturbingly and without permission, he'd snuck his way back onto the very short list of people whose company she preferred to being alone.

On her way out of the bedroom, she caught a glimpse of herself in the mirror. Her shirt was thin enough that she considered putting her bra back on, but the idea of torturing herself with underwire for a second longer was less appealing than Shane's inevitable teasing about it. Besides, it wasn't like he was unfamiliar with the concept of her nipples. He'd just have to deal with it.

When she padded into the living room, Shane was on the couch, flipping through the channels. His brow furrowed as soon as his gaze fell on her, and she braced herself for what was coming next.

"Are those my pants?"

Fuck. She'd hoped he wouldn't remember.

"I don't think so," she lied.

He pushed himself off the couch and strode over to her, reaching down and tugging playfully at the drawstring. "Yes, they are. They're missing the little metal thing here. I thought they were gone for good."

"Well . . . do I have to give them back? They're my favorite pair." The hint of a whine crept into her voice—mostly out of embarrassment that she'd been caught.

"Maybe just for tonight. I don't have anything to sleep in."

"What about your underwear?"

"If that's what you'd prefer," he said, the corner of his mouth twitching.

She rolled her eyes. "Fine." She knew he didn't mean right that second, but she was annoyed enough that she hooked her thumbs into the waistband and stripped them off where she stood. He took them from her, his gaze locked on hers without straying downward.

While he was gone, she threw another log on the fire, then pulled a blanket off the back of the couch and swaddled herself in it from the neck down.

He returned shortly, dressed in the sweatpants and nothing else. She tried not to wince at the sight of the mottled bruising and taped-up spots on his torso. But once the shock wore off, she was struck again, like she'd been from afar at upfronts and from up close at their photo shoot, by how his body had changed in the time she'd known him.

The first season, he'd told her he'd never stepped foot in a gym, like that was supposed to impress her. That his lean frame and corded arms came from his time on the road with his friend's punk band—the one that had brought him to L.A. in the first place—loading and unloading their equipment, living off free beer and bar snacks, coasting on his youthful metabolism.

He wasn't a twenty-five-year-old dirtbag anymore, and it was clear he'd been taking advantage of the network-sponsored personal trainer and private gym membership. He'd bulked up and filled out, no longer lean—a body that told the story of hard work, but also of indulgence. Of someone who wouldn't—or couldn't—completely deprive himself of the things that brought him pleasure.

She realized too late her eyes were lingering, her face starting to warm.

"You're not getting my shirt, too, if that's what you're after," she said.

He grinned. "Just getting in your pants is enough for me."

"Technically, you got in your own pants."

"You wish."

"I don't even know what that's supposed to mean."

He settled next to her. "It means move over and stop hogging the blanket."

She unwrapped herself and they negotiated their positions carefully, taking spots at either end of the couch, the blanket large enough to cover both of them. As Shane stretched his legs out toward her, Lilah tucked hers underneath herself to prevent them from touching.

She grabbed the remote and began scrolling through the cable menu, pausing on one of the movie channels, which was just starting *Gravy Train*—Serena Montague's breakout role, thirty years earlier. She raised her eyebrows at Shane. As expected, he shook his head, and she kept going.

"Whatever happened with you two, anyway?" she asked casually, her gaze still glued to the screen. Out of the corner of her eye, she saw him shrug.

"Nothing interesting."

"So she didn't catch you in the hot tub with her daughter and her roommate when they were home for spring break?" she teased, racking her brain for the most outrageous of the tabloid rumors. He scoffed.

"Is that really what you think of me?"

"Well, I don't know *what* to think," she said, in a faux-scandalized voice.

He watched her scroll through the cable menu for a few more seconds. Just when she thought he was going to ignore her or change the subject, he said, "We just wanted different things."

"Like . . . you wanted kids?"

"Not necessarily." She snuck a look at him and was surprised to see the serious expression creasing his features. "She was just so *settled,* you know? Like, established. In her career, her life, everything. And at first, it was nice, because everything in *my* life was so fucking chaotic at that point." He glanced at her sardonically. "I mean, I guess I don't have to tell *you* that. Being with her kind of . . . stabilized me. But then, after a few years—around the time I turned thirty—it started to feel suffocating. Like, she could never compromise on anything. I think that's what she liked about me, that I was so flexible. She could just mold me into whatever she wanted. Eventually I started to feel like . . . like maybe I wanted to be with someone that I could actually build a life with, together, rather than someone who already had their life all figured out before I even got there, and I just got slotted into it."

Lilah grinned. "You say that now, but I bet you're going to end up with some flexible, unmolded twenty-two-year-old that you'll just slot into *your* life. The cycle continues."

"I wasn't twenty-two."

"No, but she will be. Trust me."

"Yeah. Maybe." He sounded slightly annoyed as he held out his hand. "You're doing a terrible job picking."

She tossed the remote at him. He picked it up and began scrolling so fast she got dizzy. "What about you and Dick?"

"You mean Richard?" She cast a sidelong glance at him, surprised that he was instantly able to summon the name of her on-again, off-again ex—who, unlike Serena, wasn't exactly a household icon.

Her legs were starting to cramp, so she stretched them out, one at a time, her bare skin sliding against the worn-in fabric of his sweats. He kept his eyes on the television, but she thought she saw a tendon in his neck twitch.

"Richard and I . . . we weren't good at compromising, either. Mostly about where we wanted to live. He hated being in L.A. if he didn't have to be, for work."

"Did you ever think about moving back to New York to be with him?"

"Sometimes. I almost did, after I left the show."

"But you didn't."

"No."

"Because you weren't in love with him."

She paused. "No."

He glanced over at her, holding her gaze for a moment before turning back to the television.

"But you kept getting back together." His tone was measured.

"Yeah. I mean, we were so similar. Too similar, probably. But it was . . . familiar. And it was nice that he wasn't famous, that we'd known each other since before . . . it made it feel normal, almost." She pulled one of the decorative throw pillows onto her lap and wrapped her arms around it. Shane didn't say anything, just kept flipping channels in silence.

"He really looked down on the show," she said quietly after a moment. "He'd always tell me I was wasting my talent, which I was deluded enough to think was a compliment. But he just thought he was better than all of it. Me included."

"What did he think you should be doing instead?"

"I don't know. Making a hundred dollars a week in some experimental off-off-off-Broadway play, probably."

"So he was an insecure snob who couldn't handle the fact that you were more successful than he was." He said it so matter-of-factly that she couldn't stop herself from grinning.

"Well, if you want to put it that way."

Shane finally put the remote down, settling on a rerun of an old reality show that centered around a group of bros hitting one another in the balls with various items. Lilah opened her mouth to protest. Instead, she asked, "Did you love her? Serena?"

He was still looking at the television, but she could tell he wasn't really watching it. His chest rose and fell, heavily, slowly. "I loved being with her, yeah," he said. "She's an amazing person. But she was kind of . . . impenetrable, I guess. I think being that famous for that long messes with you. And I know it got to her, what people said about us. About her. She didn't let her guard down much, even when we were alone. It was like she was always performing." Finally, he turned to face her, fixing her with a stare that made goosebumps scatter across her skin. "Maybe you're right. Maybe you can't really love someone unless they let you."

Lilah swallowed hard but kept her gaze steady. "Sounds like you have a thing for emotionally unavailable women. You should probably talk to someone about that."

He snorted a little, shaking his head wearily. "You're tellin' me."

The defeated edge in his voice made her heart squeeze. He wasn't looking at her anymore.

She turned back to the television, looking at it without absorbing anything.

"Shane?"

"Hmm?"

She hesitated. "Did you try to quit? After we . . . after the first season?"

He didn't say anything for a long moment, his face in profile, eyes in shadow. Finally, he exhaled heavily and shook his head, but she could tell it was a gesture of resignation, not denial.

"I don't know what the fuck I was thinking. I was just . . . I was out of my mind. After everything. The thought of showing up to that set again every day . . . I'm just lucky it was big enough that they offered me more money, instead of suing my ass for breach of contract. Really put into perspective how ungrateful I was being, trying to throw it all away over . . ." He trailed off, glancing at her uneasily, then back at the TV.

Lilah sat with that for a moment, unsure what to do with it. "Why did they give *me* a raise, too, though?"

He shrugged, but she could see the tension in his gesture, the feigned nonchalance. "It just didn't seem right. Me getting paid more, when we're doing the same job."

Even though she'd been expecting it, sort of, it felt like the air pressure in the room dropped. Lilah blinked, fighting to get her next words out.

"But you hated me."

He stretched one of his arms across the back of the couch, finally looking straight at her. "I don't know what you want me to say, Lilah," he said quietly.

She held his gaze, her stomach churning with unease. There was something about the look on his face—helpless, almost—that only made it worse. After a long beat, she turned back to the TV, and so did he.

They watched the rest of the episode in silence. She shivered, pulling the blanket up to her neck. He shot her a sidelong glance before tugging it back toward himself. As their half-playful power struggle continued, they slid lower and lower on the couch, until they were both snuggled fully under the blanket, legs entangled like a pretzel. Lilah wanted to be annoyed, but she was too cozy to care.

When the next episode started, she repositioned her leg more abruptly than she'd meant to, her heel making hard contact with something warm and firm. Shane hissed through his teeth, jerking upright.

"Jesus *Christ,* watch your feet," he said with a wince, reaching under the blanket and adjusting himself.

She stifled a laugh. "Sorry. They made that seem more fun on TV."

"They also say not to try it at home," he grumbled under his breath. "Just get over here, already, before you do any permanent damage."

She paused, unsure she'd heard him correctly. But he didn't take it back, just stared at her, eyes dark and bottomless, flickering in the light from the fire.

The blanket fell away from her shoulders as she sat up, folding her legs underneath her until she was kneeling. She crawled across the couch toward him, never more aware that they'd split one outfit's worth of clothing between the two of them, that her tank top was barely more than a technicality.

She assumed his hands would be on her as soon as she was within reach, but instead he flipped the blanket back, scooting over to create space for her between his body and the back of the couch. She slid in beside him, half relieved, half regretful that this was all he meant.

Once she was seated next to him, bare shoulder to bare shoulder, the long line of his lower body pressed against hers, she hesitated, looking over at him. He was studying her with a serious, almost troubled expression, his gaze flicking from her eyes to her lips to her chest and then back to her lips again.

She wondered if he was going to try to kiss her after all. He obviously wanted to, and it would be so easy, their faces already inches apart. They'd done it plenty of times before, they were days away from being forced to do it again, and once the idea entered her head, it was hard to make it leave.

But she knew if they did, it wouldn't matter what she'd said earlier—she wouldn't be able to stop there. And going down that road with him again would only lead to the same drama and mess and emotional carnage it always had, their work environment once again collateral damage. The tentative peace they'd fought so hard for over the last few months undone in a single night. They'd come too far to risk it.

So she slid down farther, Shane following her lead, until they were both lying flat: her cheek on his bare chest, her arm stretching across the span of his ribs, her breasts pressed into his side. He brought his arm around her, tucking her shoulder tightly into his armpit, before pulling the blanket back over them. Once they were fully settled, they both exhaled heavily, and Lilah felt the last bit of tension drain from her body as she relaxed against him.

There was nothing wrong with a little cuddling. It didn't have to mean anything. Considering how well their bodies fit together like this, it would be a waste if they didn't. Lilah couldn't remember the last time she'd felt this comfortable, warm and swaddled and safe, mellowed by wine and practically high off the scent of his skin. Her eyelids began to droop.

" 'S better." Even though she couldn't see his face, she could tell by the sluggishness in his voice that his eyes were probably closed, too. He stroked his hand back and forth over her upper arm absentmindedly, sending pleasurable tingles down through her toes.

"Now that you're safe from me?" she asked his chest.

"I don't think I'll ever be safe from you," he murmured, or maybe she hallucinated it, since she was already drifting off.

The next thing she knew, the room was dark apart from the flickering of the TV—and cold, too, now that the fire had gone out. But she was warm somehow, even though the blanket was half-off her. It didn't take her long to figure out the source: she was lying on her side, facing Shane, his arms wrapped around her, his weight pinning her to the back of the couch.

She took inventory of one body part at a time, her heart speeding up exponentially as she accounted for every limb: both her arms around his neck. Her bottom leg sandwiched between his heavy thighs. Her top one slung over his hip. There wasn't very much of her that wasn't pressed up against him.

He was still asleep, his brow creased deeply, like he was worried about something. She resisted the temptation to reach up and smooth it out with her thumb.

She must have tensed because she felt him stir, clutching her closer as he woke up. When he opened his eyes, he didn't seem surprised. He didn't say anything. He still seemed half-asleep, honestly. But his hands began to move.

The hand that wasn't pinned under her body trailed down her back, settling on the strip of skin below her tank top, then back up again. His fingertips grazed under the hem, the barest brush somehow sending electric currents straight to her core, her nipples tightening against his chest. He kept his gaze locked on her face, and she knew he was waiting for a signal to stop. One of her hands clenched—practically spasmed—giving her away, her nails digging into the muscles of his shoulder.

He moved with purpose then, freeing the parts of his body that were trapped underneath her, shifting her more fully onto her back, looming above her. His gaze swept over her, eyes glazed, before he slid his hand possessively over her stomach, skating it up over her shirt until he stopped short, just below the swell of her breast.

She struggled for air, her lungs feeling like they were operating at half capacity. In her borderline dream state, his weight and heat and scent crowding her on all sides, restless and greedy, all her earlier inhibitions melted away. There was something hazy and unreal about the whole thing, like nothing that happened would exist outside that moment.

That must have been what emboldened her to place her own hand over his and move it the rest of the way, her breath escaping in a helpless gasp when she felt the warmth of his palm cupping her, his thumb grazing her nipple, her whole body clenching with need.

She thought his eyes would turn her to ash on the spot. He bent his head, and she felt his breath ghost against her skin. "*God*. Please," he rasped, his voice desperate. "I know we can't. I just . . . need to . . ." He didn't finish his sentence before he closed his mouth over her other nipple, sucking through the ribbed fabric of her tank top, as hot and damp and electrifying as if he'd put his mouth directly between her legs. She arched her back and whimpered, lacing her fingers through his hair and holding on tightly.

At her encouragement, he gripped her breast roughly at the same time that she felt the sharp wince of his teeth, making her cry out harder. She wrapped her leg around his waist again and ground against him, her brain so clouded with lust she couldn't summon any rational excuse why she shouldn't. Like there was no way that anything that felt this good, that she wanted this badly, could possibly be a mistake.

Too soon, he groaned and released her, sliding his hand down to meet the other one at the small of her back. He rested his cheek against her lower belly, exhaling heavily, as if stopping took ten times more effort than action. She reached down to stroke his hair.

She knew, then, that they really weren't going to have sex that night.

They weren't going to have sex ever again, unless it was for keeps.

The idea didn't unsettle her as much as she thought it would. It must have snuck in and nested in the basement of her subconscious at some point over the last few weeks—or maybe it had been there for years, lying dormant, waiting for her to wise up and notice it.

That didn't mean it was going to lead anywhere. But it was there, all the same.

She thought maybe he'd fallen asleep again, his breathing slow, his head moving gently with the rise and fall of her stomach. But then he propped his elbows on either side of her waist and looked up at her, his hair sticking up where she'd messed with it.

"Should we go to bed?"

Lilah had already brushed her teeth, so she got straight into bed while Shane was in the bathroom. She sighed with pleasure as she slid into the cool, crisp sheets, feeling herself start to drift off again as soon as her head hit the pillow.

She heard the door creak, followed by Shane's footsteps. Felt the depression of the mattress as he climbed in next to her.

All of a sudden she was awake again, alert, waiting to see what he would do.

He shifted closer, until she could feel the heat of him at her back.

His lips brushed her ear. "Is this okay?"

She nodded, and he slid his arm over her stomach, closing the gap between them. She covered his hand with hers, loosely interlacing their fingers, shivering at the press of his lips to the back of her neck.

They were still in that position when she woke up the next morning.

20

Shane woke to the blaring of Lilah's phone alarm. They
didn't have anywhere they needed to be, so she'd probably forgotten to turn it off the night before—and knowing her, the
alarm was set at least a full hour before she intended to get up,
so she could keep snoozing it over and over. It had driven him
crazy when they were together, but now, there was something
oddly comforting about the familiarity of it.

Lilah groaned and leaned over the nightstand to silence it,
settling back against him and stretching languorously. He barely
restrained himself from grinding into her in return.

"It's not last night anymore," he murmured into her neck.
"Do the rules still apply?"

She didn't say anything, just sighed and nuzzled her face into her pillow, baring the long stretch of her throat to him. He couldn't resist gently raking his teeth over the spot where her neck met her shoulder, which made her sigh again, closer to a moan this time. He pressed a kiss to the same spot, and he felt her pulse race beneath his lips, felt himself get even harder in response. It was still second nature, touching her like this, knowing exactly how she'd respond, even after all this time.

He let his hand slide down her ribs, past the dip of her waist, onto the mostly bare skin of her hip, then rested it there, waiting. She exhaled shakily.

"I think we're past the 'sex without feelings' stage of our relationship," she said quietly, placing her hand over his and guiding it back to her stomach.

"So what stage are we in, then? Feelings without sex?"

It was meant to be a joke, sort of, but the words hung ominously in the air as soon as they were out of his mouth.

She was silent. They lay there, still, for another few breaths, before she rolled out of bed and padded to the bathroom.

He sat up, leaning against the headboard. "Do we need to talk about this?" he called after her.

A few moments later, the bathroom door swung open again. "Probably," she said through a mouthful of toothpaste. She disappeared to spit, and he heard the sound of water running.

"But are we going to?" he asked, not even bothering to hide the ripple of annoyance at how closed off she was being, as if the previous night—whatever the fuck it was—had never happened.

In the light of day, he almost thought maybe he *had* imagined it, with how unlikely it seemed that they'd spent the better part of the last eight hours wrapped around each other. But he couldn't remember the last time he'd slept that soundly and woken up so rested, so it must have happened after all.

She reappeared, leaning against the doorway. "I don't know what there is to talk about. We both agree that it would be a bad idea to start sleeping together again while we're still working together, right?"

"Right."

She shrugged.

"So . . . that's it? We're just going to forget it?" he asked, unsure what he even meant by "it."

"I think we need to focus on the show for now. Whatever this is . . ." She waved her hand between them. "It's a distraction. It always has been."

He felt his irritation swell. Of course she was able to compartmentalize like that. Put him and her feelings in a box, label it "distraction," and ignore it until it was convenient for her.

Fuck it. If she could, so could he.

She must have sensed the change in his demeanor, because she softened, her shoulders sagging. "It's just . . . I've done this before, you know? Trying the same thing over and over again and expecting a different result."

"With Richard, you mean."

"Yeah."

He bristled at the comparison, but he could tell by the way her posture had already gone rigid again that it wasn't worth pushing back.

"Right. Sure. You're right." He watched her go over to her overnight bag and dig around. "What time do we need to be out of here?"

"Not until eleven. I was going to head out now, but you can stay if you want."

If he didn't know better, he'd think she was talking to a mediocre one-night stand she was desperate to give the slip.

"No, that's okay. I'll get going, too."

His gaze fell on the unfamiliar pattern of black ink on her hip. The symbol of the failure of their first go-round, which she'd rushed to cover up and forget about as soon as she could.

Now that he knew what to look for, it was easy to understand how she'd never allowed herself to fall in love. With him, or with anyone. She still had that same tendency to snap shut like a bear trap at the first hint of vulnerability, leaving him grateful he'd escaped with all his extremities intact.

It was so different from his own approach to relationships, especially when he was younger—offering up his heart indiscriminately, perpetually optimistic that it would be taken care of. Like being consumed by the act of loving, the validation of being loved, would give him some clarity of purpose. Tell him who he was, who he was supposed to be.

But then, neither perspective seemed to have served them very well, since they'd both ended up in the same spot: still single, still messing around with their ex from a decade ago.

As he dressed in silence, folding his sweatpants and handing them back to her, trying to ignore the ache in his chest that had nothing to do with his bruised ribs, he brushed off the question that had popped into his head—one that now seemed too ridiculous to say out loud: *What if we're different now?*

· · ·

Lilah didn't see Shane again until production resumed the following Monday. She'd kept herself distracted over the weekend, tagging along with Margaux and Brian for some sightseeing when she wasn't trying unsuccessfully to sweat out her restlessness in the hotel gym.

She'd already gotten back in her team's good graces without even trying. Margaux had posted a handful of photos from Thanksgiving on her Instagram, captioned "ty mom&dad," the last slide of which was a candid of Lilah and Shane. Lilah had no memory of it being taken, but it must have been during the Taboo game; they'd somehow ended up next to each other on the couch, too close, their knees brushing. Shane's face was inclined toward her in midsentence, trying and failing to suppress a grin; Lilah's head was thrown back in genuine, unselfconscious laughter in response to whatever he was saying.

Seeing the picture for the first time had given her the same squeamish jolt as the screengrab from the *After Hours* episode—but worse. That had clearly been a performance—cameras shoved in their faces, studio audience staring them down, everything as inauthentic and manufactured as the skyline backdrop behind them.

This wasn't that. She didn't fault Margaux for taking or posting it, but there was something mortifyingly private about the moment she'd captured. Even though it was irrational, the more she stared at the picture, the more irritated she got. He had no good reason to be looking at her like that, like she was the only person in the room, or possibly the universe. It would just add fuel to the contingent of rabid, intrusive fans obsessed with figuring out what was going on between them offscreen.

Then again, maybe she could use their help, since she'd never been more confused about it herself.

Her publicist informed her in a tone of barely restrained glee that the photo had quadruple the engagement of any of Margaux's other posts, and several news outlets had already picked it up. Lilah had tried her best to sound excited. She *was* thankful that the Jonah stuff seemed to have blown over so quickly. But mostly, it was an unpleasant reminder that the most likable thing about her was Shane.

When they returned to work, they were introduced to the local director the network had hired to replace Jonah, a woman named Fatima Alami—fortysomething, petite, with a long braid of dark curly hair and a warm, dimpled smile. As soon as Lilah met her, she felt a wave of relief that Fatima would be the one working with them for their kissing scene, and not Jonah.

Once they began shooting again, Fatima quickly proved to be one of the best directors Lilah had worked with, equally adept at handling actors and keeping the set running efficiently. Within a few days, they'd made up a good portion of the time they'd lost from Jonah's dicking around.

When she'd expressed her sympathy that Fatima was being brought in to clean up the mess Jonah had made, Fatima had just grinned mischievously.

"Don't worry about it. My manager got me the same day rate he was getting, plus a bonus if I get us back on schedule. I'm cleaning up in more ways than one. Besides"—she'd winked— "I'm a fan."

The night before they were scheduled to shoot the kiss, Fatima called Lilah and Shane in to meet with her in one of the hotel conference rooms. Shane was already there when Lilah arrived, flipping through his script. He looked up and nodded but didn't say anything.

They hadn't been outright avoiding each other since their night together, but they weren't exactly sitting next to each other in the van anymore, either. She suddenly felt a wave of regret that they hadn't kissed that night after all—it would have been a terrible idea, but at least then the last time they'd done it wouldn't have been the day they fucked in his trailer.

Thankfully, Fatima arrived before she had a chance to spend too long weighing which option was worse.

"Thanks for meeting with me. I promise I won't keep you too long," she said, half sitting on one of the conference tables. "I thought we might want to do some extra preparation for this one, since this is such a crucial moment, and you know there's never enough time to work through it day-of. We weren't able to book an intimacy coordinator on such short notice, but I want to stress that your comfort is the most important thing here. How are you feeling about everything?"

"Fine," said Lilah, at the same time as Shane replied "Good." They exchanged uneasy glances before looking back at Fatima.

"Great." Fatima pulled out a chair and gestured to them to take a seat. "Let's talk through it a little bit, and then we'll run it up until the kiss. Now, Lilah, how do you think Kate's feeling here?"

Lilah eased into one of the rolling leather chairs as Shane did the same. "I think . . . I think she's frustrated that they obviously have these feelings for each other, but he can't admit it. Especially after everything they've been through. It's hard for her to understand why he's shutting down and pushing her away. I think it really hurts her."

She avoided looking at him as she said it, but her face heated under his gaze, the irony of the situation not escaping her.

Fatima nodded. "Absolutely, I think that's spot-on. And Shane, why do you think Harrison is so reluctant to pursue things with her?"

Lilah glanced over at Shane, meeting his eyes. He looked away first.

"He's afraid. Opening himself up to her means making himself vulnerable to getting hurt. I don't think he ever really got over her death. He doesn't want to take the risk of caring about her again. It's easier to just close himself off, even if that means sacrificing his own happiness."

"Well, we don't *know* they'd be happy," Lilah blurted out before she could stop herself. Shane and Fatima both looked at her with curious expressions. "I mean . . . they've never actually been together for real. We don't know what their relationship would look like. I don't think it's wrong for him to take that into account before jumping into things. Especially after all this buildup. There's no way it could live up to whatever expectations they have for it."

Fatima pursed her lips and cast her eyes to the ceiling, considering it. "Hmm. That's an interesting angle. If you want to play up the uncertainty, it could definitely add to the drama of the moment, but I wonder if it's denying the audience the catharsis they need."

"Right. You're right. Of course," Lilah said hurriedly. "Sorry. Just . . . thinking out loud."

"No need to apologize. No bad ideas here."

"For the record," Shane added, "I don't think Kate is that hurt by it. By Harrison being withholding, I mean. I think she finds it more annoying than anything. Like, when is this guy going to get over himself already?"

She whipped her head in his direction, embarrassed he'd caught her slip. He had that look he always got when he was messing with her, a gloss of wide-eyed innocence he never wore otherwise. Lilah rolled her eyes, but she couldn't help but feel a little destabilized by the whole conversation, unsure how much of it was real—from either of them. Fatima watched them with a pensive expression, her eyes flicking back and forth between them.

"Okay. Well. Good to know you have just as much insight into each other's characters as your own." She stood up. "Should we get it on its feet?"

They cleared the center of the room, rearranging the chairs and tables to give themselves some space. The scene was the last of the two-parter—Kate confronting Harrison about why he'd been so distant with her after rescuing her from her kidnappers.

Shane sat in one of the chairs, facing away from her, using his script as a stand-in for a prop book. Lilah approached the non-existent doorway, and they exchanged the first few lines of small talk. She paused, gathering her courage as Kate.

"Did I do something wrong?"

Shane's face was a blank mask. "What do you mean?"

"It kind of feels like you've been avoiding me."

"I haven't been avoiding you," he said in a monotone. He held her gaze for a long moment before closing his script and putting it aside. "Will said your memory's been coming back."

"Yeah."

"So? What do you remember?" His expression was cold, but she could see a flicker of emotion roiling under the surface. She was surprised he was bringing this level of intensity to what she'd assumed would be a glorified blocking session, but her competitive streak flared, pushing her to step her game up to match him.

She approached him slowly, without breaking eye contact. "I remember my name. I remember my tenth birthday. I remember the sound of my mom's laugh." She paused when she reached the desk, leaning against it and crossing her arms. "It's all pretty jumbled together, though. Like, it kind of feels like it all happened at once, and my brain is still straightening it out, trying to make sense of everything."

"Sounds confusing." He seemed almost bored.

"Yeah. It is." She paused. "You know the most confusing part, though?"

"What?" He wasn't looking at her anymore, but she waited to respond until he met her eyes again.

"Even when I couldn't remember any of that," she said softly, "I knew I was in love with you."

The script called for a long, loaded pause before Lilah's next line, so she gave it the space it needed.

Shane's gaze dropped to the floor. She watched his chest rise and fall. It felt like there was a string pulled taut between them—tighter every second, refusing to snap. He finally looked up at her, his expression so conflicted and stormy that her lips parted automatically, her heart rate speeding up, her stomach twisting. Those physical responses told her she was connected to Kate, fully present in the scene.

"Please say something." She was startled by the desperation in her voice, barely above a whisper.

He shook his head and looked away. When he spoke again, his voice was low and gravelly, sending a thrill through her. "What do you want me to say? That when you were gone, it felt like I was half a person? Like all the best parts of me were missing? Like I died all over again?" His Adam's apple bobbed as he swallowed hard, his jaw tense. He got to his feet abruptly, making her flinch, but she stood her ground as he slowly moved toward her, even though she felt like her legs might give out.

She uncrossed her arms and braced them against the table, his gaze bearing down on her, a force stronger than gravity. He continued, his thin veneer of control slipping. "Do you want me to tell you that I've been avoiding you because every time I'm around you, all I can think about is how badly I want to touch you? That it drove me half-crazy that you came back and I still couldn't?"

He stopped short in front of her, both of them breathing heavily. His hands hovered, then dropped to his sides.

"You can now," she murmured, her gaze flicking from his lips to his eyes. "Why won't you?"

Fatima's voice broke in, sounding like it was coming from another planet. "Okay, let's hold here."

Lilah blinked a few times, jolting back into herself. Shane

exhaled heavily as he stepped away, running his hands through his hair, not looking at her.

"Really good stuff, you guys. I appreciate you bringing it like this, even in a rehearsal." She flipped through her script thoughtfully. "Now, I know there's some description about how it goes from here, but I think we can do a little exploring to find what feels the most organic. You two know these characters as well as anybody. And it's not only about the kiss. That first contact has to feel just as explosive."

Under Fatima's guidance, they worked through the next few beats. Shane brought both his hands to Lilah's shoulders, then slid them slowly down her arms, drawing her closer. He caught hold of her hand and brought it up to cup his own cheek. She held it there for a moment before sliding it to the nape of his neck and nudging him forward until their foreheads were touching. He gripped her waist with both hands, the warmth of his palms radiating through her whole body.

"Okay, good, let's break again."

They dutifully separated, Lilah wrapping her arms around her midriff, suddenly cold despite her sweater.

"So, you have your last couple of lines here, and then . . . bam. The moment everyone's spent the past nine years waiting for. Is it tentative at first, or do they go all in?"

"I think they're all in," Shane answered immediately, without bothering to look at Lilah. "They've been waiting for this forever. Thinking about it forever. I don't think they're going to hold back once they decide it's going to happen."

Fatima turned to Lilah, who just nodded, not trusting herself to speak. Fatima clasped her hands together. "Let's give it a shot, then. Take it from your last line, Lilah."

They squared off again. Lilah wasn't sure if she saw nerves in his expression or if she was just projecting her own. She fought to stay focused, her hands trembling against the desk.

"You can now. Why won't you?"

They moved through their choreography carefully, fluidly: his hands trailing down her arms. Her palm on his cheek. Their foreheads pressing together.

Shane's mouth hovered millimeters from hers, drawing out the moment as long as possible.

"What if—what if this ruins everything?" he asked quietly. After the hard edge he'd brought to the rest of the scene, she was shocked by his softness now: the tremor in his voice, the genuine uncertainty in his eyes.

"What if it fixes it?" she murmured, and his mouth was on hers before she knew it, every muscle in her body immediately going rigid in response, as if she could somehow form a protective shell that would prevent her from feeling anything.

His tongue nudged the seam of her lips, but she kept them firmly closed, and he didn't try to force it. They continued that way, alternating smaller closed-mouth kisses with longer ones, hands planted in their starting positions like they'd been superglued in place, their bodies otherwise resolutely separate.

After a moment, they broke apart, looking at Fatima expectantly. Fatima had her hands on her hips, her brow creased, looking at them with dissatisfaction.

"Okay. That was . . . that's a start." She walked toward them slowly. "How do we feel about getting a little more . . . *passionate* with it? Tastefully, I mean. Not sloppy. And only if you're comfortable. I'm just not sure if the closed-mouth peck approach is really giving us everything the moment needs, you know?"

Both Shane and Fatima were looking at Lilah, who dropped her gaze to the ground, chagrined. She thought back to their photo shoot several months earlier, where they'd also been chastised for holding back.

But that had been different. Back then, her discomfort had stemmed from her physical attraction to him, but at least it had been safely swaddled in animosity. And though there was attraction now, too, there was nothing safe about the genuine fondness trying to hitch a ride on its back.

She forced herself to look at it objectively. At this point, there were very few places on her body his tongue hadn't been—and vice versa. There was no reason to get prudish about it now, especially since she wouldn't have given it a second thought if it were anyone else.

Lilah shook her head, trying to get herself back in the game. "Okay. Sorry. Yeah. That's fine. I just needed a practice run."

"Great. Not a problem, that's why we're here. Let's go again from that same spot."

This time, she pounced first, diving in with an almost animal ferocity. After a stunned, frozen beat, he followed her lead, digging his fingers into her waist and plunging his tongue down her throat.

Like the last time in his trailer, it felt more like an extension of one of their fights than anything else. Even though it was heated, it was clearly more about aggression than affection, as if they were waiting for Fatima to ring a bell, raise one of their hands above their heads, and declare a winner.

When it felt like they'd grappled long enough, Lilah broke away, wiping her arm against her mouth. Shane seemed slightly more affected by it than she was, rumpled and red around the ears and throat, verging on wild-eyed.

But when she looked at Fatima, she knew they hadn't fooled her.

"Well, I definitely felt the passion that time," she deadpanned. "But it's coming off a little . . . angry. There should be some softness to balance it out. Remember, they're madly in love. And they've been to hell and back, literally, to get to each other. They've waited nine *very* long years for this moment. We should feel all that, too."

Once again, they reset to the moment just before the kiss.

Lilah opened her mouth to say her line but made the mistake of catching Shane's eye first. Something about the way he was looking at her wiped her brain clean of not only her lines, but the reason she was even there in the first place, her stomach turning to jelly.

Fuck him for still being able to do that.

She glanced at Fatima, stalling. "Could we take it from the top for this one?"

Fatima nodded, and Lilah returned to her original mark, taking advantage of the few extra seconds to try to get her heart rate under control. At the last moment, she stripped off her sweater and tossed it on one of the desks, the heat of it suddenly unbearable.

Running the scene felt different this time. The nervous frisson of the unknown was gone, replaced by a heavy, pulsing inevitability.

The moment before he touched her for the first time, he hesitated, his hands close enough that she could feel the warmth radiating from them. When he finally wrapped his fingers around her bare shoulders, she exhaled involuntarily, eyelids drooping with sensation, the point of contact almost too intense.

Only then did she realize how long it had been since she'd let herself get this absorbed playing opposite him, tapping into that live-wire connection she'd never felt with another scene partner in quite the same way. In the early days of the show, their onscreen chemistry had almost annoyed her, since he was so green and untrained—like he'd skipped the line and lucked his way into something most people (herself included) had to work their asses off to learn. Now, though, she had enough experience to know it couldn't be taught.

The air thickened as they moved through all the places they'd been instructed to touch each other. Her arms. His neck. Her waist. Their foreheads. Lilah looked into his eyes, fighting to keep her breath steady.

How would Kate do it? Kate was brave. Much braver than Lilah. She'd jump in without a second thought.

This time, when Shane's tongue brushed against her lips, she opened her mouth to him, meeting him with gentleness, not force. And, just like she'd been afraid of, she felt the telltale heat brewing in her stomach, tingles chasing down her spine.

It would be different when they shot it, she told herself, when the set would be full of people watching them, and she'd be preoccupied with the lighting and the camera angle and whether she looked weird doing it.

But she didn't have any of that to distract her now. As the kiss deepened, she lost herself in the taste of his mouth, the hot slide of his tongue against hers unlocking something inside her, the last traces of her reservations melting away.

She slid her arm all the way around his neck, pulling him closer, and at the same time he wrapped his arms tightly around her, sealing their bodies flush against each other. He let out a sharp, needy breath and she inhaled it, nipping at his bottom lip, drawing a rumble from the back of his throat.

She was so in the zone that kissing him felt like a fucking revelation, like they were both brand new. She could never kiss him like this as herself: a kiss that was sweet with possibilities, not bitter with regret. It didn't feel like Shane was Shane, either, which helped. He was holding her with such care and affection, like she was something precious, but it didn't matter: she still felt like she was a breath away from shattering.

She let herself sink into it, deeper than she thought possible, Lilah and Kate and Shane and Harrison getting all jumbled up until her whole world was narrowed to the weight of his hands on her, the pressure of his lips, his tongue, his teeth, alternatingly soft and firm and hungry and tender. Blood rushed in her ears, her pulse drumming hot and insistent between her thighs as she fought to keep up, to match him, to show him how much she loved him, how long she'd been waiting for this—

How much Kate loves Harrison. How long Kate has been waiting for this.

Finally, Shane pulled away gently and planted a soft kiss on her forehead, bringing his thumb to wipe away a tear that had collected at the corner of her eye. She closed her eyes, too flustered to look at him, her face so hot she felt like that tear would've sizzled into vapor if it had made it down to her cheek.

When they turned back to Fatima, her eyebrows were in her hairline, a bemused grin creeping across her face.

"Wow. Okay, then. If that looks half as good on camera, we don't need to worry about disappointing *anyone*."

21

They broke for the holidays a few weeks after they returned to Los Angeles, Shane and Dean boarding a flight back to Oklahoma City the morning before Christmas. For Shane, it couldn't have come soon enough.

After working through it in rehearsal, shooting the kiss had been easy. The crew had burst into spontaneous applause after the first take, making Lilah blush. They'd only needed to do it a handful of times, to his relief—for coverage, rather than performance. But even though he could tell they'd delivered, nothing had matched their kiss in that conference room. The one where they'd finally gotten it right. The one he was still thinking about weeks later.

Even though he told himself the kiss was staged, the emotions behind it scripted, there was nothing fake about the feel of that bee-stung bottom lip between his teeth, the impossible softness of her skin under his hands, his body's uncontrollable response to her. He'd already known all that, of course, but the last thing he needed right now was a refresher. Now he had to fight to drag his gaze away from her mouth every time he was around her.

He knew Lilah was correct: nothing else should happen between them while they were still working together. They couldn't risk it. Which was why he was so relieved that he had an excuse to escape across state lines.

Their dad picked them up at the airport, driving the beat-up pickup truck he'd had since Shane was in high school. He brushed off questions about what happened to the car Shane had bought for him.

"Damn thing's in the shop," he grumbled. "Those computers these new cars have, they're always malfunctioning."

"Meanwhile this one is a sneeze away from breaking down for good," Dean said with a laugh.

Their Christmas celebration was small this year, his sister, Cassie, coming over with her family for a late breakfast and to open presents. Shane had brought an extra suitcase of gifts, mostly for the kids. They shrieked when they ripped the wrapping off the four-person laser tag set, the three of them immediately tearing the box open and heading into the backyard to play, Dean taking the last spot. The biggest reaction, though, had come when Cassie had opened Shane's card containing a blank check to stock all the classrooms at her underfunded middle school, his face heating in embarrassment as she burst into tears.

He sipped coffee and eggnog and ate himself sick on Christmas cookies as the day stretched into the evening. After helping his mother do the dishes after dinner, he ducked upstairs to his room for a quick breather, pulling out his phone for the first time all day.

He scrolled through his notifications, opening an email from Renata he'd ignored earlier. It took him a couple tries to process it: it was about a movie he'd turned down a few years earlier, an indie dark comedy set behind the scenes at a children's TV show. He'd passed on countless projects over the years, most of them long forgotten, but that was one of the few he still regretted. He'd loved the script, and had come close to taking it, but his self-doubt had won out in the end. They hadn't needed him, anyway; it had become a surprise hit, launching the career of the unknown actor who'd been cast instead. Now, it was being turned into a premium cable series, and that part was up for grabs again.

The executive producer behind the show was a legend in the comedy world, his empire anchored by his long-running sketch show, *Late Night Live*. That was the thing Shane had skipped over the first time, his stomach lurching nervously when he read the email over again and realized they wanted him to guest host *LNL* in January. If he did well, Renata seemed to imply, the part in the other show was his.

Shane lowered the phone and stared at the screen.

His first instinct was to say no, like he always did. Play it safe, stick to what he knew. But he didn't exactly have that option anymore. He tried to envision himself walking down this new road that had unfurled itself in front of him. It was the best offer he'd had so far, but there was no excitement there, only pure, undiluted fear.

What he really needed was a second opinion. From someone other than Renata, or his family. Someone he could trust to tell him the truth, who he knew would see the situation clearly, unclouded by their personal feelings for him, their unfounded faith in his abilities.

He scrolled through his contacts and hit "dial" before he lost his nerve.

The phone rang and rang, his heart sinking by the second. This was stupid. He should just hang up. As he lowered the phone, the call connected.

"Hey, fuckface," a voice said with a giggle on the other end. It sounded like Lilah, but there was something off about it. He opened his mouth to respond, then hesitated.

"Is this Rory?"

More giggling, then a short scuffle. He heard Lilah's voice, muffled, sounding like she was stifling a laugh. "I'm going to fucking kill you." Then, into the phone, unmistakably her: "Shane?"

"Lilah?"

"Are you drunk?" It was teasing, not accusatory. Borderline flirtatious, even—or maybe he was reading too much into it.

"Why? Because I called you?"

"Your accent. You called me *Lah*-luh. It always gets stronger when you've been drinking."

"It's probably just from being home. You should hear me around the guys in my dad's shop."

"Hmm, no thank you."

He laughed. On the other end of the line, he heard the sounds of a door sliding open, then footsteps climbing the stairs. "You calling to wish me a merry Christmas, then?" she asked. "Because you know I don't celebrate."

"Not exactly. I, um . . . I wanted to ask your opinion on something. I'm not interrupting anything, am I?"

He heard the soft *thump* of a door shutting. "No, Rory and

I were just out on the porch having our annual cigarette and talking shit. But we were about to head in anyway."

"Talking shit about who?"

"Everyone. That's what sisters are for." She let out a sigh, like she'd sat down. "So, what's up?"

He wondered which parent's house she was staying at. If she was in her childhood bedroom. Whether they'd left it a time capsule or wiped it clean of every trace of the teenager she was.

Shane had never lived in this house; he'd bought it for his parents a few years ago, after his season-six raise. All the furniture in the guest room he was staying in was new and unfamiliar. Other than the prize bass his dad had caught fifteen years ago, stuffed and mounted in a place of honor on the wall, it could've been a hotel room for how connected he felt to anything in it.

He wondered if she, too, felt untethered from her past, uncertain of her future, unsure what it meant to feel at home.

But that wasn't why he'd called.

After he'd explained the whole thing, she was silent for a long moment.

"Whoa," she said.

He sat down on his bed. "Yeah."

"That's big."

"I know."

"Are you gonna do it? Host, I mean?"

He exhaled. "I don't know. Would you?"

"Absolutely not," she said without hesitation.

He laughed, a quick, surprised burst. "Really?"

"No way. I'm not funny."

"What are you talking about? You're funny."

"I'm not good at comedy, though. Especially not sketch comedy. Plus the whole 'live' thing, doing it all in a week, everything changing up until the last minute . . . It sounds like my personal nightmare, honestly. I wouldn't do well under those circumstances." She paused. "I bet *you* would, though."

His breath caught. "Yeah?"

Her voice was quiet, almost dreamy. "Yeah. You're a natural, Shane. It's really annoying, but it's true. I mean, you literally had zero experience before you got on the show, and you carried it for three seasons after I left. Not everyone could do that. I don't know if I could've. I think you could probably do anything you set your mind to."

He closed his eyes, her compliment moving him more than he expected.

Not just the compliment. Her genuine belief in him. He knew she wasn't the type to dish out empty praise to fluff someone's ego—especially his.

To his surprise, she spoke again, still soft. "What are you afraid of?"

His throat tightened to the point that he needed to take a few deep breaths before he could respond. "Making an idiot of myself, I guess. Closing doors because of it. I've never been a big risk-taker. This feels like a pretty high-stakes way to figure out if I'm cut out for comedy or not."

He heard her chuckle under her breath. "I get that. But you know what makes you so good?"

"What?"

"You're an amazing listener. Whoever you're in a scene with, you just . . . connect with them, effortlessly. You know how to meet them where they are without even trying. I really don't think you have anything to worry about. You're capable of more than you think."

He couldn't help but laugh. "Are *you* drunk?"

"Why? Because I'm being so nice?"

"Well . . . yeah."

She laughed, too, low in her throat. "No. I'm not drunk. I guess I must mean it."

"So you think I should do it, then?"

"I thought we already covered this. Yes, I think you should do it. Guess you're not such a good listener after all." There was an exasperated edge to her voice, her softness from just a moment ago gone.

Ordinarily, her snapping at him like that would've irritated him, but he could tell there was no real malice behind it—just self-consciousness at giving him a glimpse of her sentimental side. When she got like this, she reminded him of a cat that had rolled over to expose its fluffy underbelly but was all claws as soon as someone tried to touch it.

God help him, he found it kind of cute. And he wasn't even a cat person.

"Okay. I'll do it."

"Good."

They lapsed into silence.

He should say thanks and hang up. There was no reason for the conversation to continue, but for some reason, he couldn't bring himself to end the call first.

Then, to his surprise, she spoke again.

"Will Dean go with you? Whatever you do next. Or does he have his own plans?"

"I'm not sure," he said. "It doesn't really seem like he's interested in staying with me."

She was quiet for a moment. "Did I make things weird between you two?"

"Kind of, yeah," he admitted. "But it wasn't just you. We all played our part in making it weird. I think it brought some things to the surface that he and I have never really dealt with."

"Like what?"

"I don't know. Just typical sibling stuff, I guess. He was the one who got all the attention growing up—quarterback, prom king, all that. I'm sure he never saw himself . . . I mean . . ." He hesitated, unsure how to finish the sentence without sounding like a dick.

"Living in your shadow?" Lilah filled in promptly.

He let out a gruff laugh. "I guess. But it's probably for the best that he's been kept so busy all these years, otherwise he'd probably be out in the desert leading his own cult or something by now."

"I was always jealous of you two, honestly. Getting paid to hang out all day. I tried to get Rory to come be my assistant after she graduated, but she thought it would mess up our relationship if she worked for me. Plus, she hates L.A."

"She was probably right."

"Oh, she was *absolutely* right. I still miss her like crazy, though." He heard rustling on the other end of the phone, like she was shifting positions. "Were you guys always this close? Even when you were kids?"

"Yeah. I was really protective of him. When we were younger . . ." He paused, seized by nerves all of a sudden. Why was he about to tell her this? Why did he *want* to? There was something about the detachment of being on the phone with her, no distractions besides her throaty, familiar voice murmuring in his ear, playing tricks on him, making him feel safe with her.

"When we were younger," he repeated, "our parents had . . . some problems. With, um. With drugs."

There was a long pause. "Oh," she said quietly. "I'm so sorry. I had no idea."

"It's okay. It was a long time ago. And it was on and off. They got clean for good when I was nine. Sorry, I mean they stopped using. Not supposed to say 'clean.' It's judgmental." He tried to clear the sudden hoarseness out of his throat. "I don't really like to talk about it. It feels weird, bringing it up. Or, like, unfair to them, almost. Because it was so long ago, and they're so different now. They're amazing parents—and grandparents—and they worked fucking hard to get there."

"It's not unfair," Lilah said, her voice gentler than he'd ever heard it. "It sounds like it was really tough."

"Yeah." His own voice sounded distant to him, the words tumbling out unselfconsciously. "It kind of feels like a dream, almost. Or like it happened to someone else. I mostly remember things feeling unstable all the time. We moved around a lot. Sometimes we lived with my grandparents. I don't know. My therapist told me trauma can impact your memory, but I don't really feel that traumatized by it. She calls it 'little "t" trauma,' which I guess can still mess you up as much as the bigger stuff. But she's been helping me see all the places it still pops up sometimes."

"Wait, you're seeing a therapist? By yourself? Since when?"

"Oh," he said. "I got some names from Dr. Deena, a couple of months ago. I just thought . . . since she's helped us so much. And it helped my parents, too. Might be worth a shot to help me figure my own shit out."

She was silent again, so he continued, filling the space, trying not to get self-conscious. "Anyway. I think that's why my relationship with Dean is the way it is. I don't know if I ever grew out of feeling like I was one of his parents."

"That makes a lot of sense. I'm sure he's grateful for it. Then, and now."

"Mmm. Maybe not so much now."

Lilah laughed a little in the back of her throat. "Maybe not." She paused. "Thank you for telling me."

"Yeah. Sure," he said.

He thought the conversation might end there, but for some reason, he still couldn't make himself get off the phone. He found himself telling her about how his dad's annual tradition of dressing up as Santa for Cassie's kids had been complicated by his decision to grow a long, white beard of his own over the past year, which had confused rather than delighted them. In return, she filled him in on how she, Rory, Rory's husband, and their newborn daughter would be shuttling back and forth between their parents' places practically daily for the duration of their visit.

"Divorced for twenty years, still live within five miles of each other, still fight every time they see each other. How's that for dysfunctional?"

"Sounds familiar, actually," he said, gratified when she laughed.

It turned out she was, in fact, currently in her childhood bedroom, which had been transformed into her dad's office—with the exception of a single shelf crammed with every ribbon, trophy, and certificate she or Rory had ever won.

"I think you could probably fit all my high school achievements on a coaster," Shane said ruefully. "Cassie went through first with straight A's, so all our teachers were set up for disappointment once Dean and I came around."

"Didn't you tell me you were a punk in high school? Did I make that up?"

"Yeah, I was. Kind of. I was pretty much over it by the time I graduated. I liked the music okay, but mostly I just wore a lot of black and rode around on an old Triumph motorcycle that my dad helped me fix up. The worst I ever did was give myself a mohawk, but my mom got upset, so I buzzed it off after, like, two days."

"But she was fine the motorcycle?"

"Go figure."

"That's pretty fucking sweet," she said. "But not very punk of you. I thought making your mom upset was the whole point."

"Actually, the whole point was to make girls think I was cool and tortured and mysterious."

"I'm not even gonna ask if that worked." He heard her shift, the phone rustling, like maybe she'd gone from sitting to lying down. "You know what I've always wondered?" she asked.

"What?" Shane lay down, too, staring up at the ceiling fan as it circled lazily above him. Maybe it was because they were already on the subject, but he was reminded of being back in high school, when he would fall asleep with his flip phone next to him on the pillow because he and his girlfriend could never agree on who should hang up first.

"How did you only end up with one tattoo? I feel like you should have a few basement stick-and-pokes, at least. Or an eighteenth-birthday mistake."

He paused, tracing his finger around the decorative groove at the edge of the headboard as he thought. "I don't know. I mean, I came close a few times. But I was always trying on different things when I was growing up, different personas, trying to figure out who I was supposed to be. I never really felt the urge to commit to anything permanently like that."

She went silent, and he wondered if he'd admitted something.

He changed the subject. "What were *you* like? Queen of the theater geeks? Star of every play?"

"Pretty much. I took myself *very* seriously."

"Shocker. You were right to, though. It's kind of amazing."

"What?"

"That you always knew exactly what you wanted. That you

made it happen. But I'm sure it's not surprising, to people who knew you back then. I bet it was obvious. What you had, what you were capable of."

He heard more rustling, like she was moving again. "What would you have thought of me, do you think? If we'd known each other at that age."

He considered it. "Honestly? I probably would've called you a nerd to my friends, then secretly thought about you when I was jerking off."

"So, the same as now, basically."

He snorted. "Fair enough." He paused, weighing whether it was worth pushing his luck, his hand sliding down to rest on his belt buckle. "Is this the part where I ask you what you're wearing?"

"Wanna see for yourself?"

His heart leapt at the seduction in her voice. Before he could respond, she'd already switched it to a video call. When he accepted and her face appeared on his screen, he burst into surprised laughter.

She was lying on her bed, propped against the pillows, no makeup, hair in a messy bun, wearing an oversized hoodie in a hideous shade of purple emblazoned with "Fort Washington High School Presents: *Cat on a Hot Tin Roof*" across the chest.

You look beautiful.

It popped into his head before he knew what to do with it. Thankfully, she spoke before he did something stupid like say it out loud.

"Wait, let me show you the best part." She turned the camera around so he could get a look at her legs, which were covered in baggy fleece pants printed with cartoon menorahs and dreidels. "Better not let these babies near a real menorah. Or any open flame, really." She flipped the camera back to her face. "How hard are you right now?"

"I already came," he deadpanned. "I thought you weren't religious, though?"

"*You're* not religious, and you still celebrate Christmas."

"Well, yeah, that's because it's—"

"—everywhere?" she finished. "Maybe us secular Jews deserve hideous holiday merch, too. This is how you know Hanukkah has really made it to the mainstream: you can buy as much polyester menorah garbage as you want." She heaved an exaggerated sigh. "Anyway. Are we having phone sex or what?"

"Are we?"

"I don't know, you asked what I was wearing."

"Well, in that case, can you put your hood up?"

"Why?"

"The sexy Grimace look is kind of doing it for me."

She snickered, pulling her hood over her head and tightening the drawstrings until there was just a tiny circle of skin visible through the purple fabric, her nose poking out over the edge. When she spoke, her voice was muffled.

"You like that, you sick fuck?"

"Ohhh yeah." He let out a moan, and she laughed harder, loosening the strings until the rest of her face came back into view.

He was still laughing when they hung up. When he looked down at the screen, he was startled to see they'd been talking for over an hour.

He wandered down to the kitchen, refilling his water glass in the sink. He turned and practically leapt out of his skin when he spotted his mother, sitting silently in her armchair in the living room.

"Jesus, Mom, I didn't see you."

His mother didn't say anything, just looked at him guiltily.

"What? What's wrong?"

Finally, she exhaled, a giant cloud of candy-scented nicotine vapor enveloping her face. Shane laughed. "I thought Dad doesn't like you vaping in the house?"

"I think what he really means by that is he doesn't like me doing it in front of him."

"Sure. Of course. I'll be sure to ask him about it tomorrow." Shane sprawled on the couch opposite her, resting his bare feet against the arm.

"Well, maybe it should be our secret," she said with a wry grin. "Speaking of, are you gonna tell me who you were up there talking to that's got you smiling like that?"

Shane felt the grin fade from his face. "Nothing. No one. Like what? I mean . . ." He fumbled with his words, his mother's grin widening. "I was just on the phone with Lilah. For a second. About a work thing."

"At midnight on Christmas? Must have been pretty important," his mother said, her eyes gleaming with amusement. "I called it, you know."

"Called what?"

"You two. After you took me to that awards show. Do you remember that?"

He did.

Intangible's first season had been an Emmy darling, garnering nine nominations covering every major category, including for Shane and Lilah—one of the few times they were nominated for the same award in the same year. Shane had known everyone was expecting him and Serena to make their red-carpet debut at the ceremony, but he'd brought his mother instead, thankfully only inspiring a fraction of the tasteless jokes he'd braced himself for about his affinity for older women.

He'd been seated behind Lilah, both of them on the aisle, so he was forced to stare at the nape of her neck for the entire show. Her upswept hair, the elegant line of her shoulders in her strapless gown—except when Richard's arm was in the way. Occasionally, one of them would lean over to whisper something in the other's ear, secrets that would make the recipient smile or raise their eyebrows or crane their head to look at something. He'd tried his best to ignore it, but it was right the fuck in front of him.

At one point, she'd reached over to place her hand on the back of Richard's neck, and he'd jumped, before shrugging her off. She'd dropped her hand back into her lap, chastened. Shane knew why: the theater was freezing, and her hands tended to be cold even under the best circumstances. He could practically feel her fingers sending chills down the back of his own neck as he watched the two of them. It made sense for Richard to react like that; Shane had done the same plenty of times. Still, for some reason, witnessing the whole interaction had irritated him so much that he'd had to get up and take a lap around the lobby before returning to his seat.

They'd both lost, which hadn't surprised him. But when they'd announced the winner in Shane's category, Richard had leaned over and murmured something to Lilah that made her laugh harder than she had at anything all night. That was the first time in Shane's life that he'd understood what it felt like to literally see red, acid churning in the pit of his stomach.

"I thought you were gonna burn a hole in the back of her head, the way you were staring at her," his mother continued, dragging him back into the present.

"Well, we didn't really get along back then."

His mother just smiled. "And what about now?"

"Now . . ." He exhaled, shaking his head. "Now we do, I guess. Sometimes. But it's complicated."

"It seemed complicated then, too," his mother said, laughing a little. "It's funny, huh? The life you've made for yourself out there. I don't think any of us could've seen it coming. I mean . . ." She gestured around at the house. "We wouldn't be here without it, for starters."

"Yeah," Shane said quietly. "It's amazing. I'm really lucky."

She turned to look at him, her gaze soft. "Forget lucky. Are you happy, baby?"

Something in his chest twisted painfully at the endearment, and he closed his eyes. "I don't know," he said finally. "I love doing the show. I do. I'd do it forever, if I could. But the rest of it . . ."

He trailed off. Even with the leg up of coming off a hit show today, he could easily become That Guy from That Thing tomorrow. If he wanted to stay in the industry, it would be a constant battle for the next job. The schmoozing, the hustling, the disappointments, the humiliations. He had no idea how anyone handled it without burning out and breaking down.

"Is it ungrateful of me? To think about getting out, throwing away this opportunity that so many other people would die for?"

"You gave them nine years of your life, that doesn't sound like throwing it away to me. And if you're so worried about other people, maybe the selfless thing to do would be to step aside and let them have your spot." Her voice was neutral, though she was obviously making fun of him. He laughed.

"Good point. But I have no fucking clue what else I would do. No degree, no other experience. Plus . . ." He waved around at the house, in the same manner she'd done earlier. "How else am I going to keep y'all living like this?"

"Now, listen," his mother said, her voice suddenly stern. "I don't want you to take us into account for a second when you're deciding what to do next. We don't need any of this stuff. If we had to sell this house tomorrow, we would. It's too damn big for just the two of us, anyway."

"But I *want*—"

"Shane." She cut him off, then chuckled to herself. "Well, we tried our hardest, but I guess we didn't fuck the three of y'all up too much after all. Lucky you grew up as well as you did, wanting to take care of us now."

"Mom—"

"Let me finish." He turned his head to look at her, her face as serious as he'd ever seen it. "As your mother, all I care about is that you're safe, and loved, and happy, and standing on your own two feet. Anything else is gravy. And I hope you know I'm so proud of you. Me and your dad both." She grinned self-deprecatingly. "Whatever that's worth, at your age. Your parents being proud of you."

Shane was speechless. All he could do was nod, his chest heavy.

"Thanks, Mom," he said, once he was able. "It's worth a lot. And . . . I'm proud of you, too."

She leaned over and stroked his hair.

"Although," he continued, "I kind of wish you'd said you wanted an even bigger house, and a Ferrari, and, like, a hat made of diamonds or something. That would make things a lot easier. You'd be looking at the new host of the American edition of *I'm Not Swallowing That*."

His mother threw back her head and laughed, full-throated and raspy.

A laugh that felt like home, even if the house they were sitting in didn't.

22

Yvonne's New Year's parties had been a tradition for as long as Lilah had known her. Naturally, over the past decade, they'd grown in scale and extravagance as Yvonne's star had risen. Lilah had only missed one, when she'd had the flu so badly she'd been hallucinating.

This year, Pilar and her wife, Wendy, had talked Lilah into agreeing to a blind date with one of Wendy's business associates, another venture capitalist.

"I don't know if I want to date a money guy," Lilah had demurred.

"Hey, watch it. My wife's a money guy," Pilar said with a

laugh. "It's just one night. And if he sucks, you can always ditch him and disappear into the crowd. I mean, as much as a six-foot redhead is able to disappear into any crowd."

Lilah had given in, but as she got ready, she found herself regretting it. In her experience, nine times out of ten, that type of man was looking for a trophy, and not just in terms of looks: they wanted a woman who was the most educated, the most successful, the most accomplished, so it reflected well on them when she gave it all up to raise their children and run their household.

But then, she had to admit that her dating pool was a little limited these days. He was in a totally different industry, so there was less risk of him being threatened by her success or trying to use her for her connections; plus, he had his own money, so he wouldn't feel emasculated by hers. As unenthused as she was about the prospect, he was the best (and only) option she'd been presented with in months.

She didn't want to think about Shane, so she didn't. She definitely wasn't wondering what he was up to tonight, whether he had a date of his own.

They hadn't spoken since their Christmas Day phone call, but he'd shown up in her dreams almost every night since, to her chagrin. Apparently, her brain didn't want to accept that their phone sex joke had been, well, a joke.

Thankfully, she had something more important to preoccupy her as she put the finishing touches on her makeup: she'd probably be hearing about her role in *Night Call* after the New Year, and she had a gut feeling it was as good as hers.

The week before she'd left to go home, she'd had her callback—one of the best auditions of her life. A few days later, she'd had a long lunch with Marcus Townsend and his wife,

Sareeta, with whom he was cowriting the screenplay. The three
of them had clicked instantly, chattering a mile a minute, Lilah
sharing her insights on the character as Sareeta and Marcus had
laid out their plans to bring the book to life. She'd left the meeting on a high, more invigorated than she'd felt in years.

She tried to channel that optimism as she walked into the
party, Yvonne's cavernous living room swarming with people
and thudding with music. It didn't take long before Pilar found
her, all in white with Wendy on her arm. Wendy, of course,
matched her perfectly, in an all-white suit and her signature
cropped platinum hair swooping over one of her eyes.

They introduced her to Kent, a dark-haired white man in his
midforties who was decently attractive and seemed perfectly
nice. Within five minutes, Lilah could tell she wasn't into him
whatsoever. As they sipped champagne and attempted to make
small talk, she had the sinking suspicion that, as often happened,
the two of them had only been set up because they were both tall.

"So, are you making any resolutions?" she asked in a light,
false tone.

Kent frowned. "I don't believe in New Year's resolutions.
Ninety percent of them fail. If you want to make a change in
your life, why wait until some arbitrary date to start? It just
shows you're not really serious about it."

Lilah laughed, but only because she didn't know how else to
respond. "Right." She gulped down the rest of her champagne,
then glanced around desperately for one of the waiters.

She was so distracted by her search that she was caught completely off guard when someone behind her tapped her on the
shoulder. When she turned around and saw it was Shane, she
was thankfully able to suppress her first instinct to gasp like she
was in a soap opera, but she could tell from the amusement in
his eyes that he knew just how flustered she was to see him.

"Sorry to interrupt," he said in a tone that indicated he wasn't very sorry at all.

He was accompanied by a stunning young blonde—the twenty-two-year-old she'd prophesied in Vancouver, by the looks of it. Though they exchanged introductions, the woman's name might as well have been white noise for how well Lilah was able to retain it.

"What are you doing here?" She directed the question at Shane, but his date answered.

"I work at the label."

"Bailey's a friend of Dean's. He introduced us," Shane filled in.

Bailey, Lilah filed away.

Shane's eyebrows lowered, his expression serious. "I didn't know this was Yvonne's party until we were on our way here. Really."

Lilah shrugged. "It's fine." She turned back to Kent, threading her arm through his. Shane's eyes tracked them, and he put his arm around Bailey's back a second later, but Lilah caught his hesitation, the slight flash of surprise in Bailey's eyes when he pulled her closer.

Suddenly, Lilah was hit with a brief, overwhelming sense memory of what it was like to be in Bailey's place. Shane always smelled amazing, unfortunately, whether he was fresh out of the shower or oozing pheromones after hours on set. It was the reason she was constantly stealing his clothes, back when they were together.

She blinked a few times to shake it away, cozying up to Kent, who glanced at her with confusion, since they hadn't touched at all up until that point.

"I just wanted to come over and say hello because Bailey's a big fan of the show. She was dying to meet you," Shane said.

Bailey smiled guiltily. "Sorry, I know I should probably play it cooler, but I was *so* obsessed with *Intangible* in high school. We used to have watch parties and everything."

Lilah smiled, too, forcing herself to relax. "Thank you. That's really sweet."

"We were all totally convinced you guys were banging in real life." Bailey clapped her hand over her mouth, her eyes going wide. "Oh, *fuck,* sorry," she said, raising her empty champagne flute and laughing nervously. "Guess this is my cue to slow down."

Lilah met Shane's eyes, all too aware that both Kent and Bailey were looking at them for a reaction.

"It's okay. That just means we were doing our jobs," Lilah said, her smile widening until she felt like she was showing every last one of her teeth.

Shane turned to Kent. "So, how long have you two been seeing each other?"

"This is actually our first date," Kent said, as Lilah stared at the ground, tension vibrating through her entire body.

"Us, too," said Bailey. "But you gotta have a date on New Year's, right?"

"Right. Lock down that midnight kiss," Shane said innocently, looking directly at Lilah. Lilah felt heat creep up her neck. Was it obvious even to him that there was no spark between her and Kent?

"Right," Lilah repeated, smiling brightly. "Well, I think I need another drink. It was nice meeting you, Bailey. Shane . . ." She just nodded at him, unsure what to say, and he returned it, his gaze unexpectedly intense.

She steered Kent through the crowd until they made it to the windowed back wall, swapping out their empty glasses for fresh ones en route. They stood there in awkward silence for a long moment, looking out at the view. Kent ran his fingers through his hair.

"I don't want to pry, but . . . is there something going on there? Because I don't want to get in the middle of anything. That seemed a little . . . complicated."

Lilah hesitated, a terse deflection on the tip of her tongue. She took a sip of champagne first, biding her time, weighing her impulse to be honest with him about it.

Or, at least, more honest than she was going to be.

"It's . . . 'complicated' is probably the right word for it, yeah. Working together so closely for so many years . . . it's an intense relationship, for sure. Almost like an arranged marriage, in some ways. We've definitely been through the wringer. But no, there's nothing going on."

Even as she said it, she flashed guiltily to that night in the Airbnb, their phone call on Christmas, the sweaty dreams she'd been having about him since. But for all intents and purposes, she was telling the truth: there was nothing going on between her and Shane. Otherwise, they wouldn't be here with other people.

Maybe saying it to Kent would help her believe it.

Kent nodded slowly. "It's a strange profession you're in. In my line of work, bringing emotion into things is seen as a sign of weakness. But for you, you have to keep yours easily accessible, all on the surface. I could never do that." He hesitated. "I actually almost backed out of this when I found out you were an actor. I've never been involved with one before. I always thought I'd get all jealous and insecure, watching them pretend to be in love with someone else."

Lilah cocked her head, surprised. She'd encountered that

brand of jealousy before, but usually not until it was too late and they were already fighting about it. Something about how candid and up front he was about it caught her off guard.

"So, what made you change your mind?"

Kent grinned. "Wendy spoke very highly of you. Said you were a real ballbuster."

Lilah bit back a smile, more charmed than she expected. "Not always. Depends on the balls. I'm surprised that was a selling point for you."

"Not always. Depends on who's doing the busting."

He met her eyes with a teasing glance, and for the first time all night, she felt a rush of attraction. Better late than never.

At that moment, his phone buzzed insistently in his jacket. He pulled it out and grimaced.

"Shit. I'm sorry to do this, but I actually need to head out."

Lilah was surprised to feel a stab of disappointment. "Really? You're not going to stay until midnight, at least?"

He shook his head. "I have to fly out to New York for some meetings tomorrow, wheels up at five A.M." He hesitated. "I would ask if you wanted to see each other again, but I'm not totally sure what vibe I've been getting from you."

Lilah brought her hand to her forehead. "God. Sorry. I'm really off my game. Can you tell it's been a while?"

He cracked a smile. "How about this," he said. "I'll give you my number. If you feel like giving me a call, I'd love to take you to dinner sometime. But if not, no hard feelings. Like I said, I understand if things are complicated."

"Sure. Okay. I'd like that. Really." Why was she writing Kent off before she'd even gotten to know him? Shane was obviously keeping his options open.

She handed him her phone and he tapped in his number.

He turned to go, then hesitated. "I don't want to push my

luck here, but if I'd stayed . . . what were my chances of getting that midnight kiss?"

Lilah pressed her index finger to her lips, pretending to think about it. "I'd say it was looking pretty good for you."

He smiled again. "Damn. You know, that's almost worse than getting shot down."

She stepped closer, emboldened by the champagne. "Maybe midnight came early."

He closed the gap between them, placing his hand on her waist, pausing for a respectful beat, then leaning in to give her a soft peck on the lips.

From a technical standpoint, there was nothing wrong with the kiss. His lips were neither too firm nor too soft, too dry nor too wet. His breath smelled nice, his hand was warm but not clammy on her waist, and he didn't try to push it any further. But Lilah felt nothing.

In fact, her only physical response came after he'd already pulled away, when her gaze snagged on Shane glowering at her from across the room and she jolted like she'd been struck by lightning.

After saying goodbye to Kent, she recirculated the party with renewed vigor. She tried not to pay too much attention to what Shane was doing, but it was hard not to. Maybe she was imagining it, but she swore she felt his eyes on her when she was toasting with Annie, laughing with Pilar, dancing with Yvonne.

But then, she saw something that knocked him out of her mind completely: Marcus and Sareeta, chatting in a corner.

When Lilah approached them, they greeted her warmly, and the three of them quickly fell into animated conversation about what they'd done over the holidays. Lilah was so on edge that she didn't retain a thing they were saying, adrenaline pumping through her, her nerves likely palpable.

Once the conversation hit a lull, Marcus's face turned solemn. "Listen, Lilah," he said, his clipped British accent softening. "I'm so glad there's no hard feelings. It really was quite close."

Lilah's stomach turned to stone. "Sorry?"

Marcus and Sareeta exchanged stricken glances. "Christ. I thought your agent would've notified you already. My apologies; of course it wasn't my intention to tell you this way."

Lilah blinked, a smile frozen on her face, the news washing over her like she'd been doused in ice water.

It would be typical of Jasmine to wait until after the New Year to deliver the bad news, so it wouldn't spoil Lilah's holiday. She probably hadn't thought Marcus would have the opportunity to break it to her personally.

Lilah managed to keep her composure long enough to excuse herself as gracefully as possible, her throat tightening. She barely made it out of the crowd before she started crying.

. . .

He'd felt it for a while, but tonight finally confirmed the suspicion that had been nagging at the back of his mind since Vancouver: Shane was in big fucking trouble where Lilah was concerned.

He'd tried to ignore it. Being unimpressed by the guy she was with—Clint? Brent?—wasn't jealousy. It was pity that she was stuck with a guy who seemed so goddamn boring. Shane could tell just by looking at him that he was the type who thought having money was a substitute for a personality.

But the feeling he got when he saw her kiss Len, like he'd been punched in the stomach and the dick simultaneously, was one he'd felt only once before, when he'd watched her walk out of that party with Dean. And back then, he'd had a very good reason to feel that way: they'd done it specifically to piss him off.

This had nothing to do with him, though, and he felt it just the same.

It wasn't even like the kiss was anything to write home about. Barely a peck. But she'd smiled at Clem as she'd pulled away, what he knew was a real smile—which had disappeared as soon as she'd met Shane's eyes. Maybe even from across the room she could tell what he was thinking—the way he wanted to stride over to her, take her by the hand, and haul her into an empty bedroom, like the last time they'd attended one of Yvonne's New Year's parties together.

"What are you looking at?" Bailey had asked, craning her neck, trying in vain to see over the heads of the people around them.

He'd almost forgotten she was there. "Nothing."

As hard as he tried, he couldn't stop watching her. Maybe "watching" was the wrong word; it was less premeditated than that. She stood out anyway, statuesque and attention-grabbing even when she wasn't trying; and tonight, strutting around in fuck-you heels, glittering practically from head to toe, she was trying.

She seemed to have ditched her date at some point and was mostly hanging out with her friends—having the time of her fucking life, from the looks of it. He fought the urge to approach her again. He didn't have any reason to.

But later in the evening, when he saw a flash of red hurrying out of the room, his feet carried him after her practically before he knew it. Bailey had long since disappeared, so he felt only the smallest twinge of uncertainty as he followed Lilah at a distance down one hallway after another, slipping past the boundaries of where guests were allowed, then disappearing through a doorway.

He hovered outside the door for a minute, debating whether he should turn around and go back to the party. Instead, he opened it.

It was a guest bedroom, by the looks of it—tasteful, immaculate, minimal, everything in it obviously ridiculously expensive.

He didn't see her, though.

"Lilah?"

A scrap of pale forehead poked up from the other side of the bed, nothing visible below her red-rimmed eyes. His stomach twisted at the sight, and he let out an involuntary exhale through his nose.

"What?" Her voice was thick with sobs.

"Are you okay?"

"Yep."

"Do you want me to get your friends?"

She shook her head.

"Do you want me to leave you alone?"

She hesitated, her gaze watery but unwavering, then slowly shook her head again.

He shut the door behind him and made his way to the other side of the bed. Lilah was seated on the floor, back propped against the bed, long legs askew like a beat-up rag doll. Next to her was an open bottle of champagne.

He'd never seen her like this. It stirred up the most bizarre cocktail of feelings in him: anger, empathy, protectiveness. He didn't know what to do with any of them.

He eased himself down onto the floor next to her. "Is it . . . did that guy do something? What was his name?"

"Kent." She shook her head. "No. He was fine. Good. He

had to leave early for a work thing." She rolled her head to look at him, the back of it never leaving the bed, like it was too heavy for her to lift. "Where's Bailey?"

"She went to try to find some coke around . . ." He checked his watch. "Ninety minutes ago? Haven't seen her since."

Lilah snorted through her tears. "Very cool."

"Yeah. I don't want to jinx it, but I think she might be the one." He glanced over at her. "*Are* you okay?"

She held the bottle on her lap, studying it. "I didn't get it. That part I really wanted," she said dully.

"Oh shit. I'm sorry."

She shrugged, taking a long swig from the bottle. "I feel so stupid. I've never cried like this over a role before. It's such a rookie move, getting invested before I knew for sure I had it. I shouldn't be this upset."

"It's okay to be upset." He glanced at her. "Actually, I don't think I've ever seen you cry before. Besides for a scene, I mean."

She cast her eyes over at him sardonically. "Any notes?"

"Not enough snot. You still look too pretty."

She laughed, which sounded more like a sob. "I'll try to work on it for next time." She passed him the bottle. He took a drink, then set it to his other side, out of her reach. She didn't object, just leaned her head back against the bed again and closed her eyes.

"I think I just let myself get carried away. You know when you have a really great first date, and you start planning out your whole future together in your head? And then maybe they never text you back, or you get to know them better and you realize they're not actually who you thought they were. You fell for their potential. That's what this feels like. It'll always be the perfect experience, because it never happened."

Shane nodded slowly. "You never know, though. Maybe it

would've been another . . ." He trailed off, not wanting to rub salt in the wound. Luckily, she smirked self-deprecatingly.

"Maybe. I'm sure if I'd lost out on that one, I would've felt the same way." Her smile disappeared and she groaned. "Fuck. Do you think *that's* why I didn't get it? Is that fucking movie going to haunt me for the rest of my career?"

"Nah. I'm sure everyone's already forgotten about it."

"I hope so." She sighed. "It just . . . it's scary, you know? The future. You get spoiled, having a consistent gig like this. Makes you forget what it's actually like out there."

"Yeah. I don't know how you do it, honestly."

"Do what?"

"Just . . . keep having faith like that. Putting yourself back out there, over and over, when it's all so out of our control."

She shrugged resignedly. "I don't know. I guess I love it enough that it feels worth it."

Shane took another swig from the champagne bottle, then rested it on his lap, his thumb toying with the foil. "Would you still have done it? *Without a Net,* I mean. If you'd known back then how it would turn out."

She was silent for a long time. "Yeah. I would've. I learned a lot from that experience. And . . . I don't know. It feels right, that I ended up back here."

It was the way she looked at him as she said it that emboldened him to say the next part:

"What about us?"

Her gaze turned sharp. "What?"

"You know." He looked down at his lap. "If you'd—if *we'd*—known. How things would go. Do you think we still would've . . . ?" He looked up at her as he trailed off, unsure.

He was relieved when she chuckled, then sighed wearily,

closing her eyes. "I don't think there's much that could've kept us away from each other back then."

She looked back at him, and something unspoken passed between them. Something he couldn't quite name.

"I'm so sorry, Lilah," he said softly.

"For what?"

"For everything."

She held his gaze for a long moment, then rolled her head to face forward. "Yeah," she said, even more quietly than he had. "I'm sorry, too."

Maybe he was reading too much into it, but it didn't just sound like an apology. It sounded like a lament. For the lost versions of themselves they could've been, for the different future they could've had, for every choice they'd made along the way that had carried them further away from each other.

"You should do the convention with me," he blurted out. "With all of us, I mean. In March."

The other five principals, plus Walt, were all scheduled to travel to San Francisco to make appearances at the biggest pop culture convention of the year. Lilah, as always, was the only holdout.

She scooted herself up from where she'd slumped down until she was sitting upright again, brushing the last stray tears from her eyes.

"What? Why? You know I hate that stuff."

He felt a pang as he remembered the only one she'd gone to, during the first season—her vacant stare, how uncharacteristically quiet she'd been, her hands laced together so tightly her knuckles went white.

"Yeah, but that was then. It was all still so new. You're more used to handling it now, right?"

She nodded, a little reluctantly. He continued. "Who knows? You might actually have a good time. It's fun, meeting people who love the show that much. Enough to take time out of their lives to come see us. Getting the chance to connect with them . . . it's really special. They always ask about you, you know."

"They do?"

"Of course they do." He shrugged. "Just think about it. It'll be the last one with us all together like this. Until we're washed up and doing the nostalgia circuit, I guess. But you deserve to feel some of that love now."

Her gaze slid sideways, but she didn't say anything. He cleared his throat. "Anyway. Since you talked me out of my comfort zone, I thought I might as well return the favor."

She perked up. "You're doing *LNL*? You decided?"

"Yeah. It's pretty much a done deal."

"Scared?"

He cracked a grin. "Extremely."

She laughed, and to his relief, the thickness was gone from her voice. "That's a good thing. That means you're challenging yourself."

"Or I'm about to make a complete fool of myself."

"I doubt it. Worst case, you'll just do *okay*, and no one will care by next week. But making a complete fool of yourself every once in a while is kind of a guarantee as an actor. Even if it happens, you'll survive. Speaking from personal experience here."

He sat with that for a moment.

"Lilah?"

"Hmm?"

"I thought your movie was good, actually."

She snorted. "Don't patronize me."

"I'm not," he insisted. "Okay, yes, the movie sucked. But *you* didn't. Honestly, you kind of blew me away. I forgot I was even watching you, most of the time."

"That was the prosthetics," she muttered under her breath, but it was clear she was biting back a smile.

He let out an exasperated laugh. "Will you just let me give you a fucking compliment? Jesus."

She turned to him, tears glinting off her eyelashes again, color high in her cheeks, but she didn't say anything else. He continued. "You were great in that, and you probably would've been great in this one, too. Fuck 'em, it's their loss. I'm not worried about you. Whatever happens, you're going to be fine."

He saw tears fill her eyes again before she quickly looked away, her voice trembling. "Yeah. Maybe."

"No, you are," he said, his voice becoming more impassioned. "Because you're fucking talented, and you work really goddamn hard, and you're tough as hell. And brave, too. Much braver than me. You're going to have an incredible career after this, I know you are. You're . . ." He paused, searching for the right word. "You're undeniable."

She was still looking away, her eyes downcast. Slowly, her hand shifted off her lap, sliding across the floor toward him. It slipped over his, colder than he'd anticipated, their fingers interlacing tightly and seamlessly. Without thinking, he brought his other hand over the top of hers, sandwiching it between both of his, rubbing gently for a few moments until it warmed up.

He lost track of how long they sat there, backs against the bed, legs sprawled in front of them, palms pressed together, fingers intertwined. For some reason, all he could think about was a picture Dean had shown him once of a pair of sea otters holding hands as they slept, to prevent them from being swept away by the current and separated forever.

He shut his eyes, listening to the sound of her breathing, the murmurs of the party far away from them. He didn't open them again until he heard the countdown, voices shouting loud enough to carry.

"EIGHT! SEVEN! SIX!"

He turned his head to Lilah, who was already looking at him.

Of course he wanted to kiss her. It was all he'd been thinking about since Vancouver—even before then, if he was being honest with himself.

But something about doing it now felt wrong. Like it would cheapen the moment, make it all about sex, crush the delicate, valuable thing fluttering and blooming between them. It wasn't worth it if there was even the slightest chance she'd think he'd been buttering her up to try to take advantage of her in a moment of vulnerability.

As he looked into her eyes, he knew without a doubt, down to the marrow of his bones, that he wasn't just in trouble. He was completely fucking in love with her. A love that felt old and new at the same time.

He loved the things that had drawn him to her nine years ago: her beauty, her talent, her drive, her self-possession. He loved the pieces she'd only recently allowed him to see: her loyalty, her courage, her resilience, her tender heart.

He even loved her bad sides, each and every quality that had once repelled him, because she wouldn't be Lilah without them.

That knowledge didn't bring him any comfort, though, just a vague feeling of unease. Because it didn't matter what he felt if she didn't feel it, too. And on the off chance she did, he suspected she was constitutionally incapable of admitting it. But even if they never saw each other again after the show ended, he knew she would never, ever work her way out of his system.

She'd been his other half since the day they'd been cast, their bond as unique as a fingerprint and just as much a part of him.

They ran out the clock without moving, distant cheers drifting over them.

She smiled at him, a little sadly, and squeezed his hand.

"Happy New Year, Shane."

"Happy New Year, Lilah."

She hesitated for a moment before angling her body toward him, still holding his hand, reaching for his face with the other. His breath caught in his throat as she cradled his jaw.

"I really do like the beard," she murmured, her voice sending a ripple of electricity through his veins. "But I miss . . ." She trailed off, running her thumb across his cheek, pressing it gently into the spot where his dimple would've been.

It felt like she was pressing it directly onto his heart.

He swallowed hard before reaching out, too, bringing his hand to her temple, running his fingers through her hair. He thought he saw her shiver at the contact.

"And you were still the most beautiful person in the room, even with that haircut," he teased.

She laughed, easing some of the tension, but didn't pull away.

"Don't remind me. I thought it would never grow out."

He laughed, too, deepening his grip on her hair without thinking. The amusement drained out of her expression, her eyes going dark and glassy.

Before he had time to react, he heard the door swing open abruptly, followed by a worried voice.

"Lilah? Are you in here?"

They both poked their heads above the bed at the same time. Yvonne, Pilar, and Annie were standing in the doorway, their expressions turning instantly from concern to shock as soon as they saw Shane.

"What the fuck," Annie blurted out.

Yvonne raised her eyebrows. "Are we interrupting something?"

"No," the two of them said in unison, Shane reluctantly releasing her hand and getting to his feet. The other three women regarded him skeptically as he approached, stopping halfway between Lilah and the doorway.

"Someone was saying you left crying, and then you were gone for so long . . . we just wanted to make sure everything was okay," Pilar said.

"Actually, we kind of thought *you* might be responsible for it," Annie said pointedly to Shane. Lilah got to her feet, too, wobbly as a baby deer, perching on the side of the bed like she didn't trust her legs to hold her.

"Not this time," she said breezily. It was only when he looked back at Lilah's flushed face that the implication settled over him, heavy and queasy: she'd cried over him before, and they all knew it.

"Looks like you're in good hands now," he said. "I should head back out there."

Lilah nodded mutely. Her friends eyed him up as he passed, and he met each of their gazes in turn, confident, but not confrontational. They clustered around Lilah, but she was looking only at him until the moment he closed the door.

23

After Shane left, Lilah's friends tried to grill her about what was going on, but she was too drunk and exhausted to give them any kind of coherent response. Soon enough, they'd bundled her into a car and sent her on her way. She leaned her cheek against the glass of the window, eyes half-shut, teetering on the edge of sleep.

She had thought she'd pass out as soon as she crawled into bed, but she'd tossed and turned for hours, her headache worsening, throbbing in time with a single word: *Shane. Shane. Shane.*

When she woke up the next morning, she lay there brooding for a long time. The loss of *Night Call* stung even worse in the light of day, a congealed lump of fear and self-pity and hope-lessness lodged beneath her ribs. She ruminated over every step of the audition process—the lines she could've delivered differ-ently, the missed opportunities to charm in conversation. But she was too exhausted to sustain her self-loathing spiral as long as she wanted to. Once it ran its course, she was able to let it go.

She sat up, her hangover hitting her like a frying pan to the face, and she knew immediately that the whole day would be a wash. As she trudged through the steps to make herself feel mar-ginally more alive—shower, coffee, toast, gallons of water—she tried to ignore the low, persistent throb of loneliness that ac-companied her, like an old injury that had never fully healed.

These were the times she most missed having someone. Spending the day cuddled on the couch or lounging in bed, no obligations besides napping, fucking, watching bad movies, and eating takeout. Something more attainable, in theory, than nearly every other facet of her life, something painfully mundane—but still somehow perpetually out of reach.

For as long as she could remember, her approach to relation-ships had been driven by the fear that she'd make the same mis-take her parents had, finding herself trapped with someone who barely tolerated her out of fear of being alone—which meant, by extension, she'd accepted she might always be alone.

Instead, she'd prioritized her career, seeking fulfillment via the escape of losing herself in a character, the security of finan-cial independence, the fleeting validation of success before the goalposts shifted once again. But that, too, was a relationship that often felt just as toxic, breaking her heart harder and more frequently than any man ever could.

The prospect of one day finding a romantic connection that nourished rather than drained her, that added value to her life, that made her feel safe and accepted and understood, sometimes seemed like even more of a fantasy than the most ridiculous storylines on *Intangible*. The brief glimpses she'd caught of it— last night; over the holidays; in Vancouver; nine years ago— made its absence all the more painful. The fact that those moments had all been with Shane—*Shane*—felt like a cruel joke.

As if he could sense she was thinking about him, her phone buzzed with his name—his real name now—as soon as she settled on her couch.

SHANE: how are you feeling?

Lilah rolled her bottom lip between her teeth, unsure how to respond.

LILAH: better
Still bad, but better

She hesitated, then added:

Thank you for last night

SHANE: glad to hear it. & anytime
I saw TBS is doing a best of Kate and Harrison new year's day marathon, in case you're in the mood for a walk down memory lane

LILAH: you know I don't like to leave repression avenue

Still, she found herself flipping to the channel anyway. Her own face immediately filled the screen—the third season, she could tell immediately, based on the length of her hair and the jacket she was wearing.

She was behind the wheel of a car, Shane in the passenger seat. That fucking car. They'd spent hundreds of hours crammed in there, shooting pages and pages and pages of dialogue. Whenever they weren't rolling, they'd sit in icy silence, without even their phones to distract them, staring out the window at the motionless landscape.

She vividly remembered all the times she'd seethed in annoyance as he joked around with the crew, jealous of how easy it was for him to keep everyone's spirits up when the day ran long, self-conscious about how standoffish she must seem in comparison, when she was just trying to preserve her energy and stay focused between takes so they could all go home as soon as possible.

But watching it now from the outside, years later, she didn't see any of that. All she saw was Shane, devastatingly charming, and funny, and charismatic—and all of it directed at her. How was it possible she'd found him so irritating back then? And the way he was looking at her . . . it wasn't real, obviously. He couldn't stand her in those days, either. But on camera, it read as undiluted yearning.

As the episode continued, she realized which one it was. Kate had been possessed by the ghost of a scientist who was unable to move on until she completed the study she'd been working on for years. Lilah had been stuck rattling off so much technical jargon she was sure the writers must have been messing with her. To make matters worse, she'd been fighting a miserable cold, her head feeling like it was stuffed with cotton, making it a struggle to retain even her easiest lines.

They were in the scientist's lab now. Lilah practically had war flashbacks from how long it had taken them to shoot this scene.

After finally getting the two-shot, they'd reset for her solo coverage, Shane out of range of the cameras. As soon as they'd called "Action," he'd held up his palm, where he'd Sharpie'd the buzzwords she'd been stumbling over, grinning wickedly as the crew cracked up. It had ended up on the blooper reel at the wrap party, of course, and she'd laughed along, even as humiliation brewed in the pit of her stomach all over again at the pleasure he took in openly mocking her.

But what if she'd had it wrong?

What if he'd been trying to help her?

She drew her knees to her chin, wrapping her arms around them, something unfamiliar aching deep inside her. Close to loneliness, but more pointed. Emptier. Like her rib cage had been replaced by a black hole.

She wished he was there with her now. The urge to invite him over was so powerful that she had her phone in her hand before she knew it. She stared at it for a long time.

Sure, she could text him, but then what? He'd come over with food, and he'd make her laugh, and he'd smell so fucking good, and she'd fall even more in love with him than she already was.

She sat upright with a jolt, nausea surging through her.

No. She didn't love him. She didn't. It was impossible to be in love with someone she wasn't even dating. Someone she'd hated for years.

And even if she did, she had no idea how she'd begin to tell him. To dig up the courage to lay herself bare in front of him like that, after everything they'd been through. After pushing him away again so recently. The prospect felt impossibly heavy, like she was a beached whale, crushed from the inside by the weight of her own tangled emotions.

Despite her best efforts, he refused to be consigned to a messy, complicated footnote in her past.

She let herself consider, just for the hell of it, what it would mean for him to be her future, too.

Obviously, their chemistry had always been explosive—to the point where it sent other people running for cover. She wasn't interested in that kind of chaos anymore. But, while she'd never stopped feeling that spark, it was hard to deny that the past few months had felt different, and not just from the way things had been with him before. From the way they'd been with any-one.

As she tossed around the word "boyfriend," though, it didn't quite fit. It felt too juvenile, too simple, barely skimming the surface of everything their relationship had come to encompass.

But the only other title she could come up with was "part-ner," and he was already her partner. Even after they'd stopped sleeping together, even when the sight of him made her blood boil, they'd still spent the better part of a decade side by side, sharing scenes and screens and red carpets and interviews and magazine covers, her name linked with his above all others. *Not for much longer,* she realized with a pang.

And then there was the last and biggest thing: the show. The fact that the two of them together, for real, would attract the kind of invasive attention that made her stomach turn. That would reset all the work she'd done to balance her mental health with the reality of being a public figure.

There was something about the inevitability of it, too, that grated on her now as much as it did then. It had poisoned her relationship with Shane from the very beginning; she'd resented him for how badly she wanted him, and resented herself for being so predictable.

Her phone buzzed again.

SHANE: you're watching, aren't you

LILAH: maybe

SHANE: you looked really cute in that lab coat

Her throat tightened.

She couldn't tell him. Not right now, anyway. Not until she figured out what the fuck she even wanted from him—from *them*. The last thing they needed was to complicate things again.

And maybe she wouldn't ever have to. Maybe, if she was very, very lucky, it would pass.

24

Shane's *Late Night Live* episode was scheduled for their second week back in production after the holidays. *Intangible* had arranged it so his time in New York would coincide with shooting the backdoor pilot for Rosie and Ryder's potential spin-off, so neither he nor Lilah would have much to do that week. He tried not to wonder how she planned to spend her time off, whether she'd be seeing that guy from the party again.

He couldn't stop himself from texting her after his first meeting with the *LNL* writers, though.

SHANE: hey
Were you planning on coming out to New York to watch the show?

She replied almost instantly.

LILAH: ummm maybe
I haven't bought a plane ticket yet or anything
Why?

SHANE: Would you want to make a cameo?
In the monologue, I mean. Maybe a sketch if you're feeling adventurous

She started to type something, then stopped. He added hurriedly:

It was their idea

LILAH: haha
No sketches
I'd do the monologue though
When would I have to come out?
And would they pay for it

SHANE: Just for the dress rehearsal on Friday, if you can. And probably

LILAH: deal

SHANE: you're the best

He hit "*send*" before he could stop himself, then put his phone back in his pocket, immediately self-conscious. To his surprise, it buzzed again immediately.

LILAH: So how's it going out there?

SHANE: good, I think. We haven't really done anything yet,
but everyone's cool so far
Doesn't seem like they're going to humiliate me on purpose,
at least

LILAH: idk
You know what they say
Never trust a comedian
They'll do anything for a laugh

Five nights later, as Shane was sweating his way through the
live show, he regretted not taking her warning seriously.

He couldn't even blame sabotage, though. He was bombing,
and it was nobody's fault but his own.

Things had started out okay. The monologue had gone over
well; he'd stumbled over the cue cards a few times but managed
to get laughs everywhere he was supposed to.

The highlight had, of course, been Lilah's cameo. One of the
cast members, Faith, had come onto the stage dressed up as an
uncanny Lilah-as-Kate, and the two of them flirted heavily,
moving closer and closer, complete with smoldering, meaning-
ful eye contact, and dramatic music not unlike the score of *Intangible*.

"Sorry, am I interrupting something?" Lilah's entrance had
been greeted with cheers and applause, Shane biting the inside
of his cheek to keep from grinning.

He rode into the first commercial break on a high, pulling
Lilah into a dazed hug as soon as he left the stage, his heart hammering wildly in his chest. Maybe it was his nerves, but it felt

like she was holding on extra tightly. But too soon, he was rushed off to wardrobe to get ready for his first character.

It was all downhill from there, though.

During the brainstorming phase early in the week, he hadn't wanted to seem like a diva, so he'd enthusiastically agreed to every idea that the writers had thrown out, whether or not he liked it. There hadn't been much time to second-guess during the breakneck rehearsal period, with sketches being added, dropped, and rewritten every hour. Throughout it all, they'd assured him that, as chaotic as the process seemed, it always came together in the end.

He started to doubt it halfway through the first sketch, in which he played the father of one of the show's signature recurring characters: an awkward tween girl who always got her period at the worst possible time. That one had gone fine, since the character was inexplicably popular, and all he had to do was play the straight man.

But next, he had to carry his first character sketch, playing a taxi driver who overshared about his sex life with his passengers. They'd given him a huge fake mustache that itched like crazy, pulling his focus, his New York accent fading in and out. He tripped over the punch lines, earning mostly polite, embarrassed laughter.

After that, he was so psyched out, it was hard to recover. The executive producer came over to him during a commercial break and clapped him on the shoulder, telling him he was doing great and he just needed to relax, which only freaked him out more.

He'd never experienced anything like this before. If nothing else, he was confident. Now, though, he had to admit that he was totally out of his depth. He could practically feel the other role—the one that, despite his better judgment, he'd let himself get attached to over the past few weeks—slipping through his fingers. He knew he was stiff, his energy low, but the train was too far off the tracks, each flubbed joke landing worse than the last.

He felt like a cartoon character, running off the edge of the cliff only to find there was nothing but air beneath him, legs pinwheeling hopelessly for several long seconds before he plummeted to the ground in a cloud of dust.

. . .

From her vantage point in the audience, watching Shane struggle through the show, Lilah felt physically ill.

As he stumbled through one misguided sketch after another, his timing off and his delivery wooden—playing Borat as a courtroom judge; dressed in full granny drag in a knitting circle; pulling off tearaway pants and dancing to Europop in a silver Speedo—it struck her how, six months ago, she would've relished this. That he was finally getting his first taste of failure in the charmed career he'd stumbled ass-backward into. Instead, it almost felt like *she* was up there instead of him: blanking at the cue cards, lights roasting her skin, the uncomfortable silence of the audience pounding heavily in her ears.

He'd be able to bounce back from this. The next week or two would probably be bad, but beyond that, it would quickly fade from public memory—at least until it was time to aggregate a new "Worst *LNL* Hosts of All Time" clickbait list.

But if this was supposed to be an audition for his next job, there was no question that his performance tonight had killed his chances. The two of them had that in common now, at least. Still, watching it happen in real time was viscerally painful, her whole body tense, a boulder of anxiety where her stomach used to be.

And, worst of all, she knew his confidence in himself was rattled in a way that would stick with him long after the public forgot. However badly he was doing, she could tell *he* thought he was flopping ten times worse. She was so attuned to his every microexpression that a single helpless twitch of his eyebrows was enough to make sweat bead at the base of her spine.

Something clicked into place then. Something she should've realized a long time ago.

She'd spent years resenting him for his easy charm, how effortless it was for him to make people love him—but for the first time, she understood it *wasn't* easy. It wasn't effortless. It was how he survived. He didn't know who he was without it.

When she looked at him now, trying as hard as he could to win over an increasingly disengaged audience, all she could see was that scared little boy he'd once been, convinced he could fix everything if he was just agreeable enough, accommodating enough, lovable enough—whatever he thought everyone around him wanted him to be.

Her hands trembled from how badly she wanted to reach for him, to jump on that stage, wrap him in her arms, and tell him that he was enough.

It fucking killed her that she couldn't help him. That she was powerless to do anything but sit there and watch.

But she wasn't powerless, she realized. There *was* something she could do. The idea took shape all at once, grabbing hold of her and refusing to let go.

She expected panic to follow, but instead, she felt strangely light. Peaceful. It was as if she'd been trudging around in head-to-toe armor for so long that she no longer noticed the burden, but now that it was suddenly lying in pieces at her feet, she was left both weightless and defenseless. She slipped out of her seat, her feet carrying her backstage without a second thought.

. . .

Shane dragged himself to his dressing room, back in his street clothes again after his last sketch. There were still a few minutes left in the show: a second performance by the musical guest, one more commercial break, and then the good nights. For better or worse, he'd made it through in one piece—physically, at least.

He opened the door, and Lilah was there, sitting on the counter, leaning against the mirror.

Until he saw her face, he'd been holding out one tiny bit of hope that his performance hadn't been as tragic as it felt from the inside.

"I know," he said weakly.

Her expression cleared as she quickly tried to regain her poker face.

"The writing was garbage. You were just doing your best."

He collapsed on the couch.

"Fuck. *Fuck.*" He covered his face with his hands and groaned. "This is exactly what I was afraid of. This is all everyone is going to be talking about tomorrow, isn't it? That I blew it?"

She didn't say anything, just braced her palms on the edge of the counter and leaned forward, her shoulders pushed up to her ears. "Maybe," she said carefully. "Or we could give them something else to talk about."

He was so agitated that it took him a moment to process what she was saying. Or what he thought she was saying. He sat upright. "*What?*"

Her head was still angled toward her lap, but her gaze slid up to meet his. Her chest rose and fell. She said nothing.

He stood up suddenly, pacing, impassioned, as he groped for

words. "Isn't that—we can't—wouldn't that be . . . I don't know. Manipulative? If it's not—if *we're* not . . ."

She looked down again, saying it almost to herself. "What if we *were*, though?" Her eyes flicked back to him.

He felt like he was frozen to the spot. He opened his mouth, then closed it.

"Huh" was all he could manage.

He sat back down on the couch with a thud. Neither of them said anything, their eyes locked for an interminable moment. He shook his head, as if that would knock everything back into the correct place and make this suddenly make sense. "And *this* is how . . . ? Shouldn't we . . . like . . . talk? Or something? First? Before we just . . ." He trailed off, gesturing vaguely with his hand.

"You don't want to?"

"Of course I want to," he blurted out immediately, ignoring the satisfied smile that played across her lips. He felt his voice rise against his will, his emotions already heightened after the stress of the past few hours. "But this would be a big fucking deal, Lilah. For me, anyway. And I don't want to be fucked around. Are you just doing this because you feel bad about talking me into it? You feel *sorry* for me? Because I don't need your pity."

She let out an exasperated sigh, eyes flashing with irritation, her voice rising even louder than his. "No, Shane, I'm doing it because I'm in love with you."

The words rang out like a slap, sharp and harsh. She looked almost surprised she'd said it, her face flushed, mouth slightly open. All he could do was blink at her, unable to move. Barely able to breathe.

"What?" His voice came out tight and strangled.

She took a deep breath, her hands twisting in her lap. When

she spoke again, her voice was quiet, careful. "I love you. I want . . . I want to be with you. And I don't care if the whole fucking world knows this time. I *want* them to know."

He felt dizzy, suddenly so light-headed that he wished there were a way to sit down while already sitting down. Of all the things he'd expected her to say to him—not just tonight, but *ever*—that was pretty much dead last on the list.

He wondered whether this was the first time she'd said it to anyone. Whether she'd said it to her ex while they were together. Whether she'd believed it then.

Whether he should let himself believe it now.

But then it hit him. The full gravity of what she was suggesting.

She'd torpedoed their relationship the first time around at the first hint that they might have to go public. And over the past few months, she'd made it clear she was too stubborn to ever admit she might want to try again—which was the only thing stopping him from getting down on his knees and begging. But now, she wasn't just asking, unprompted, for a second chance—astonishing on its own—she was offering it up as a lifeline. A distraction. Drawing attention away from his performance, so he wouldn't have to suffer even a fraction of the same public humiliation that she had.

Which meant it must be true.

She really was in love with him.

If he *were* a cartoon character, the revelation would've been an anvil to the head, birds and stars circling in the aftermath. Or maybe a piano, leaving him smiling dizzily with a mouth full of keys.

She groaned, scrubbing her hands over her face—a noise of frustration with herself, not with him. "God. I've never done this before. I'm not good at it, it's coming out all wrong. I shouldn't have just sprung it on you, this is totally the wrong time. You're right, we should probably talk about it first. And we don't have to do it like this, make a whole public thing out of it right away."

Her hands fell to her lap again, her gaze following them. She shook her head resignedly, voice cracking with emotion. "But I couldn't wait another fucking minute to tell you. I'm sorry. I just couldn't."

At that last part, she finally met his eyes, and his breath caught when he saw the mask was gone. The studied archness, the annoyance, the smugness at shocking and destabilizing him. It was just Lilah, cracked wide open, as unguarded as he'd ever seen her.

Dimly, in the recesses of his mind, he realized he should probably say it back. But he also understood, as brave as she was to confess, she never would've done it if she wasn't completely confident he was in just as deep as she was. He could see it in the way she was looking at him. She wasn't waiting for it. She already knew.

So he bit it back, letting her have her moment. He had the whole rest of his life to tell her. To show her.

Besides, now they were even.

"You know that was never my problem," he said quietly, holding her gaze. "Going public, I mean. If it'd been up to me, I would've shouted it from the rooftops from day one."

She dropped her gaze, presumably to hide the flushed smile creeping across her face. "I guess there wouldn't be any point trying to keep it a secret, anyway. It seems like we're the last to know."

"Speak for yourself."

Her smile widened, verging on giddy. "You weren't going to say anything?"

"Can you blame me?"

He felt something kick to life inside his chest as he reached her, her thighs parting so he could stand between them. He was going to kiss her, already cradling her jaw in his hands, but once he got up close, he could see she was shaking, her pulse fluttering wildly beneath his fingers.

So instead, he took her hands in both of his, running his thumbs softly over their smooth backs, over each knuckle. A shiver ran through her, her eyes flicking shut, then open again. She looked heartbreakingly vulnerable in that moment, like she was going to cry, and he tightened his grip on her hands.

"No. I can't blame you," she said quietly.

A loud rap sounded at the door, startling them—a PA sent to herd them into place for good nights. Shane let go of one of Lilah's hands but kept hold of the other as she eased herself off the counter, still holding on as they wound their way to the stage and took their place front and center among the cast members. He had a vague sense of people talking to him, congratulating him, slapping him on the back, but all he could focus on was the weight of Lilah's hand in his.

The prospect of what was about to happen—what they were about to do—filled him with an eerie sense of calm. It was like the rest of the evening had been a nightmare, a distant, unpleasant memory that held no power over him now that he was awake.

He released her hand and wrapped his arm around her shoulders instead. She flicked her gaze up at him before edging closer, placing her hand on his chest, then dropping it self-consciously to her side again as a producer counted them down. The band began to play, and Shane looked into the camera.

"Thank you to Lilah Hunter, Andromeda X, the cast . . . it's been an amazing week. Good night!"

He looked at Lilah as the music swelled behind them. If he'd seen even a trace of apprehension in her face, he wouldn't have done a thing. But all he saw was excitement, anticipation, a simmering ache—an expression that probably matched his own.

Just the smallest curl of his biceps around her shoulders and she was in front of him, her chest pressed to his, his mouth on hers without hesitation, his other hand floating up to cradle the back of her head.

He was dimly aware of the applause around them heightening to an earsplitting roar, but it faded to white noise as her arms slid around his waist and her lips parted, her tongue seeking his. It wasn't a raunchy kiss, though. It felt sweet and hopeful and perfect, the two of them wrapped tightly around each other, rocking gently back and forth, a self-contained loop, their own secluded island, unaffected by the chaos around them. Public, but intensely private at the same time.

He had a feeling that even if they'd been completely alone the first time he kissed her again—*really* kissed her—he would've heard a cheering section anyway.

He pulled back slightly. In his peripheral vision, he could see the shocked, gleeful expressions of the cast hovering around them. He ducked down to murmur in Lilah's ear.

"So you were thinking something like that?"

She laughed. "Yeah. That's pretty much what I had in mind."

"Guess you're stuck with me now."

Lilah pressed her cheek against his. He could hear the smile in her voice. "I've been stuck with you for the past nine years."

She tilted her head and caught his lips again, and everything besides the two of them ceased to exist.

25

Shane had wanted to skip the *LNL* after-party and go straight to the hotel, but Lilah insisted they make a cameo, at least. Mostly so the main topic of conversation at the party (and after) wouldn't be the two of them fleeing immediately to go have sex.

It seemed like their stunt had worked: instead of a funereal vibe, anchored by vague and insincere compliments of the "better luck next time" and "at least you tried" variety, the mood that greeted them was buoyant and congratulatory, almost like they were attending their own wedding reception.

They moved through the crowd as a single unit, never separating. His palm lingering on the back of her neck. Her fingers snaking around his wrist. Like if they stopped touching each other, the spell would be broken, and things would go back to the way they had been.

They didn't talk much just the two of them, but as they reached the bottom of their second round, they let themselves sneak a kiss here and there—each one a little deeper, a little longer—when they thought no one was looking. It reminded Lilah of the first night at that hotel bar, in a way—the air crackling with possibilities, all her nerves on end.

Finally, they disentangled themselves guiltily from what they thought was a secluded corner when the head writer for *LNL* snuck up behind them and yelled "Get a room" good-naturedly in their ears. Shane cocked his head toward the exit, linking his hand through hers as they left.

The January air blasted them in the face as they left the restaurant, knocking the breath from Lilah's lungs. Shane's hotel was closer than hers, just a few blocks away, and they clutched each other tightly against the wind. Still, it took them longer than it should have to get there, pausing to kiss and grope at stoplights until it wasn't just the wind leaving her breathless.

When they entered the hotel lobby, though, it had a sobering effect. The discreet lighting, the tasteful decoration, the muted music, the lack of people due to the late hour—all of it unsettled her. Her anxiety stirred and stretched, whispering poisonous questions in her ear: *What have you done? Did you really think this through? What happens now?*

They shrugged off their coats as they waited for the elevator, the aggressive heat of the lobby sending an instant trickle of sweat down Lilah's spine. When they stepped into the elevator, she expected Shane to reach for her again, but he must have sensed the shift in her mood, because he just placed a comforting hand on her lower back.

She felt him looking at her, but she stared straight ahead. His room was near the top floor of the hotel, the numbers ticking up agonizingly slowly. Finally, she allowed herself to glance his way, and the look on his face, concerned and searching, made her stomach twist. He looked exhausted, the dark bruises under his eyes and fine lines on his forehead thrown into sharp relief in the unflattering light of the elevator. She was sure she didn't look much better. He turned his attention forward again, so she did, too.

"I feel like Simon and Garfunkel should be playing right now," she muttered.

"Why?"

She glanced at him. "You've never seen *The Graduate*?"

He shrugged. "I know the basics. We used to get a lot of Mrs. Robinson jokes, me and Serena. So I never watched it out of spite."

The elevator finally dinged open, and the two of them stepped out into the hall.

"So you don't know how it ends?"

"I assume it's not happily ever after."

"Not exactly," Lilah said. "Dustin Hoffman crashes her daughter's wedding, and they run away together and get on a bus."

"Him and Mrs. Robinson?"

"No, the daughter. And the last shot is just one long take of them sitting in the back of the bus, like, 'Oh shit, what did we just do?'"

They reached the door to his room, and he fished around in his pocket for the key. "Is that how you feel? You regret it?" He studiously avoided her eyes as he asked it, and she felt her heart squeeze.

She shook her head emphatically. "No. I mean, I think it's supposed to be ambiguous. Not regret, necessarily. Just, like . . .

we did something big. Something that can't be undone. And I have no fucking idea what's going to happen tomorrow." She couldn't stop the quaver from creeping into her voice.

He had the key now, but instead of opening the door, he turned to her, cradling her face in both hands before leaning in to kiss her gently.

"Don't worry about tomorrow. Or about anyone else. Right now, it's just us. It's just tonight."

She suppressed a laugh, ruining the moment.

"What?" he asked.

"You just accidentally quoted *Rent* at me. Kind of."

He groaned, scrunching up his face to try to mask his grin. "God, you really *are* a theater nerd. You're right, this whole thing was a mistake. I gotta go."

He feinted like he was going to walk back toward the elevator, but she grabbed his sleeve and easily pulled him back into her arms, both of them laughing. "Okay, okay, just open the door already, cool guy."

Their laughter stopped abruptly as soon as they got into the room, Shane pinning her against the door before they even turned on the light. Their coats fell forgotten to the floor as they groped for each other, trading fierce, bruising kisses. He tangled his fist in her hair and scraped his teeth beneath her jawline, turning her whole body boneless.

She let herself sink into the rhythm of it, the push and pull of their mouths and breath and hands. Against her will, drowsiness began to overtake her the longer her eyes were closed, her movements becoming lazy and languorous. He pulled away once he sensed her slowing, and she opened her eyes to see him watching her with concern.

"Hi."

"Hi," she breathed.

He reached out to push her hair out of her eyes, his fingers tenderly skating across her temple. "Are you tired?"

"Kind of," she admitted.

"Do you want to wait?"

She considered it, then shook her head. "Do you? You must be about to drop."

He leaned in and pressed a soft kiss to her lips. "I think we've waited long enough, don't you?"

The rasp in his voice made her breath hitch, and she nodded, understanding him perfectly. He wasn't talking about sex, obviously. He meant how long it had taken them to get out of their own fucking way. How much time they'd wasted. How close they'd come to living out the rest of their lives hating each other for reasons she couldn't even remember.

Okay, maybe she could remember. But she didn't care anymore. She hadn't cared in a long time. All she cared about now was not wasting another second.

She leaned forward and caught his lower lip in her teeth. He groaned and pressed himself into her again, anchoring her to the door with his body, gripping beneath her thighs until he'd lifted her legs off the ground, which she obediently wrapped around his waist.

She gasped when she felt how hard he was against her, the ache between her legs already unbearable. He bit down on her collarbone and pressed a feverish line of kisses back up to her mouth, and she slipped her tongue between his lips without hesitation, making him moan in the back of his throat. She felt delirious with need, torn between wanting him inside her immediately and wanting to draw each moment out as long as possible.

Too soon, he pulled away, setting her back on her feet as she whined in protest.

"I think I need to shower first. Wash the flop sweat off me," he murmured into her mouth before turning and heading toward the bathroom. She leaned against the door, dizzy, blinking, unable to do anything but watch as he pulled his shirt over his head and dropped it on the ground. He craned his head back to look at her. "You coming?"

She pushed herself upright, kicking off her boots. "Soon, hopefully."

They both stripped down to their underwear, leaving a trail of clothes in their wake. He reached the bathroom first, already running his hand under the spray by the time she shut the door behind her.

"You probably want this a few degrees above boiling, right?"

"It's okay. I can *compromise*," she said with a dramatic sigh. He turned back to look at her, grinning, before doing a double take, his expression slackening as his gaze swept over her from head to toe. She crossed her arms over her stomach and leaned against the counter.

"What?" Based on the look on his face, she had a pretty good idea what, but she wanted to hear him say it anyway. It certainly wasn't a reaction to her bra and underwear, which were plain and functional and had both seen better days.

He shook his head and stood upright, moving toward her slowly. "I guess I always forget. Like, I convince myself my memory is playing tricks on me." He stopped short in front of her, curving his hands around her ribs before running them slowly down the edges of her silhouette, his eyes following their progress, making her shiver. "But you really are this fucking beautiful."

She rested her hands on his biceps for a moment, then slid them up to his shoulders, leaning down to press her mouth to the warm skin there. "Mmm. You'll do."

"Well, I'm no Pennywise."

"Good. His dick was really weird."

She caught his laugh against her lips, light and sweet, before he pulled back to look at her again.

"I thought you were going to give me a heart attack at that shoot," he murmured, splaying his hands wide around her hips, finding the spot where she was the softest and squeezing possessively.

"Sorry."

"No, you're not. They didn't let you keep any of that, did they? The stockings and stuff?"

"No, but I could probably track down something along those lines, if you want."

He pressed closer to her, skin against skin. "I do want."

She ran her hands up his smooth back and nuzzled into the side of his neck, taking a long inhale of his natural musk before the shower washed it away. "Just so you know, it took two other people to help me get into everything."

"I bet it would only take one to get you out of it, though. If they were motivated enough." His voice went low as his hands skated up to ease her bra clasp open, his erection pressing insistently against her hip. She reached her hand beneath his waistband and let her fingers wrap around him, hot and hard, stroking gently, reacquainting herself, feeling a thrill deep in her stomach at the confirmation that her memory hadn't been playing tricks on her, either. He groaned and rested his forehead in the gap between her neck and shoulder, sliding her bra straps down her arms.

She brushed her lips against his ear. "I think we're wasting water."

He grunted, half amusement, half regret, and they untangled

again, discarding their last scraps of clothing, Lilah tying her hair up before stepping in after him.

They both knew better than to even discuss attempting shower sex, which was high risk, low reward. Instead, they just held each other, their kisses soft and lingering, hands exploring leisurely under the guise of lathering up. Lilah swallowing a gasp as Shane's soapy fingers brushed over her nipples. Him groaning deep in the back of his throat as she lightly ran her palm over the hard length of him, base to tip.

Once they'd rinsed off, she dropped to her knees, ducking her head out of range of the spray. His eyes went dark and hazy as he braced one arm against the wall in anticipation, forearm flexing.

But the only place she touched him was his hip, placing a soft kiss on his tattoo. Her heart had leapt as soon as she saw it was still intact, the lines almost as dark as the day they got them.

"I would've thought you'd run straight from that set to the nearest laser," she teased, brushing her thumb across it.

"You know, I never did get around to that," he said with a throaty chuckle.

"Weird." She moved her head over a few inches, looking up at him mischievously before sinking her teeth into the firm curve of his ass—not as hard as she wanted to, but hard enough to make him yelp and jolt.

"*Ow!* Fuck." He was laughing, though, reaching down to rub the spot, which was already turning pink. She planted a kiss there, too.

"Sorry. Do you know how long I've been thinking about doing that?"

He turned off the water and helped her to her feet, pulling her into a kiss so deep and dirty she felt it in her toes.

"Let me show you what *I've* been thinking about."

They'd only turned on the bathroom light, so the bedroom was dark apart from the hazy late-night glow sifting through the open drapes. After the shower, Lilah felt wide awake, her skin sensitized and tingling pleasantly from head to toe, her pulse pounding heavily between her legs.

She didn't go straight to the bed, though. She wandered over to the window, pausing to look out at the street below—quiet, but never fully empty, the buzz of the city dampened to a soft, dreamy hum. In the muted reflection, she saw Shane come up behind her, his towel already discarded. He wrapped his arms around her, holding her close for a moment before moving to untuck her towel. She let it fall and kicked it aside, relishing the sensation of him at her back, warm and solid, the air in the room suddenly chilly in comparison, her nipples hardening even before his hands found them.

She whimpered as he cupped her breasts, massaging roughly, plucking at her nipples, his breath hot against her neck. "You might want to put your hands on the glass," he murmured, dragging his lips up the line of her throat to catch her earlobe in his teeth.

She leaned forward, flinching at the first touch of her palms against the cold window, a shiver rippling through her. He pressed his mouth to the top of her spine, keeping one hand on her breast, slowly trailing the other down her stomach until it settled between her legs. The first brush of his fingers against her clit made her jolt, and she dropped her head down, unable to hold it upright anymore.

He still knew exactly how to touch her. Like he'd been thinking about it for years, waiting patiently for the chance to do it again. That thought on its own was enough to get her pulse racing twice as hard, pleasure lighting her up from the inside, her skin turning flushed and feverish. Before long, she was delirious enough to wonder how it was possible there was really only one of him behind her when it felt like he was everywhere at once: his fingers slowly teasing between her legs, his other hand still toying with her nipples, his hot mouth nipping and sucking at the most sensitive parts of her throat, low noises of satisfaction rumbling in her ear at how easily he could make her fall apart.

She rocked against him, shameless, desperate. When his index finger finally slid inside her, she gasped, clenching around him involuntarily, and he groaned against her neck.

"Fuck, you're so wet." His voice was ragged. All she could do was moan as he added a second finger and fucked her harder with them, both of them breathing hard and fast, his other hand moving to rest on the base of her throat. "Does that feel good?"

You know it does, she wanted to say, aching pressure building in waves that already had her trembling, but it came out closer to "Unngh"; his laugh was dirty and rough and intimate. He shifted his arm and found an angle that had her crying out immediately, the heel of his hand pressing against her clit, crooking his fingers to stroke the spot inside of her that had fireworks popping behind her eyes, so good that it was almost too much.

She came quickly, sharp and surprising, her whole body seizing as the unbearable tension inside her crested and released, breaking her open. Shane held her tightly through it, his heart racing against her back. Once she recovered, though, she shrugged out of his embrace, pushing away from the window and turning to face him.

"Get on the bed." She forced herself to sound stern, though every part of her still felt wobbly.

He obeyed so quickly that it would've been comical if she didn't actually find it extremely fucking hot. He stretched out on the sheets, looking at her with hooded eyes as she stalked toward him, his hand coming down to idly stroke his erection, as hard and straining as she'd ever seen it.

"I didn't say you could touch yourself."

Heat flared behind his eyes as he held his hand up in surrender, before tucking them both behind his head, his biceps flexing, a husky edge to his voice. "I like it when you're bossy."

"I know." It delighted her, that the push and pull between them didn't have to end just because their animosity had.

They'd always been good together, and neither of them had exactly been virgins when they'd met, but there was something different about their dynamic now. The thrill of discovery and rediscovery. The comfort and trust that still lingered from the past. The confidence and experience they'd gained in the years apart. The gratitude that they'd had the chance to sample what else was out there but had still found their way back to each other in the end: taking what worked for them, discarding what hadn't, ready and eager to shape it into something that was theirs and theirs alone.

She knelt between his legs and was still for a moment, drinking in the scene in front of her, the gorgeous man sprawled at her mercy.

The gorgeous man she was completely, staggeringly, once-in-a-lifetime head over heels in love with.

Something expanded in her chest, and to her chagrin, she felt tears spring to her eyes. She blinked them back. She'd never cried during sex before—other than the time in high school she'd gotten a black eye from accidentally catching a stray elbow to the face—and she wasn't about to start now.

She refocused on the task at hand, gripping the base of his cock and giving it a long, slow lick with the flat of her tongue. His whole body jerked, and he made a noise like he'd stepped in a bear trap, the sound sending a bolt of pleasure straight between her thighs.

She still knew what he liked, too, teasing him with her lips and tongue and hands, savoring his soft, desperate moans, the way his hips twitched and bucked, his breath coming hard and fast. When she wrapped her mouth around him, relaxing her throat to take him deep, he swore loudly, his hands floating up from behind his head, one gripping the sheets, one winding tightly in her hair.

"*Fuck,* Lilah, you're gonna kill me. I don't know how much longer I can last," he gasped, tugging on her hair. She released him with a wet *pop.*

"Maybe that's good, though. Get this first one out of the way, take the edge off."

He shook his head, laughing a little, still panting. "I'm flattered you think I have more than one round in me right now. I'm probably going to pass out as soon as I come. But I need to fuck you tonight."

"No arguments here." She crawled back up over his body, leaning down to kiss him, slow and deep. "You have a condom, right?"

She assumed he wouldn't have let it get this far if he didn't, but all the same, she was relieved when he nodded.

"Yeah. In my bag." He rolled off the bed and went to his suitcase, rummaging around in an outer pocket before retrieving a strip and ripping one off. He squinted at it in the dim light. "Wait. Shit. How long before condoms expire?"

"I dunno. A couple years?"

"Oh, okay. We're good, then."

She smiled wryly, watching him rip open the foil and roll it on. "Been a while?"

He grinned, crawling back onto the bed beside her. "Maybe." He nudged her onto her back, kneeling next to her and sliding his hand up her thigh. "I might've been a little distracted the past few months."

She felt her face flush. "Me, too."

Something earnest crossed his expression, and he moved his hand up to stroke her face.

"Lilah," he breathed. "I—"

He cut himself off, shaking his head, then repositioned himself between her legs, braced on either side of her ribs.

"What?" she prompted.

He smiled bashfully, then shook his head again. "Nothing. Someone told me it doesn't count during sex."

She felt that same swelling in her chest, the tightening of her throat, tears pricking at the corners of her eyes again. She tried to clear her throat, but her voice was hoarse all the same. "Well. Let's hope you can still remember it later, then."

The intensity in his gaze sent a thrill through her. "I will."

She forced herself to laugh, though she felt like she was in pain. "Are you going to get all corny on me now that we don't hate each other anymore?"

When he smiled, there was something pained about it, too. Longing, maybe. "I'll be whatever you want me to be."

She felt her expression grow serious, the lump in her throat expanding as she reached up to cup his face, running her fingers through his beard. "I just want you," she said quietly.

He smiled, ducking down to nuzzle against her collarbone. "Now who's getting corny?"

She responded by shifting beneath him, raising her knees to

cradle his hips, and reaching down to guide him into place. He pushed into her slowly, both of them exhaling heavily, Lilah wrapping her arms tight around his neck and burying her face into it.

She felt raw and exposed, turned entirely inside out. For what might have been the first time, she felt relieved of the burden of performance during sex, of embodying the fantasy of whatever her partner expected. It was all too easy for her to protect herself that way, to intuit what they wanted from her and slip into it seamlessly—taking her work home with her, intentionally or not. There was pleasure in that, too, in its own way.

But as he moved inside her, carefully at first, his breath catching, her goddamn tears once again threatening to spill over, she finally understood the power of letting her guard down, of letting herself be known. It was the kind of connection she'd never felt before. With him, or with anyone. No games, no personas, no manipulation, no detachment. Just the two of them, stripped bare and clinging to each other, as nervous and vulnerable as if it were their very first time.

Lilah let her head drop down to the mattress and met his eyes, her arms loosening around his neck and sliding up to his face. There was hunger in his gaze, but tenderness, too—tenderness she would've found unbearable if not for the overpowering awareness that she was likely looking up at him in exactly the same way. Now it came close to unraveling her.

He shifted his weight back so he could press his palms to hers, interlacing their fingers as she stretched her arms high above her head. The gentleness was gone already, his gaze hot and dark; groaning how good she felt as his hips rolled harder and faster, sending pleasure sizzling up her spine. She felt another orgasm building, unhurried, a gathering storm as she wrapped her legs around him and rocked her hips up to meet his.

Once she felt herself start to plateau, she freed one of her hands and tapped his hip gently. They rolled over in one fluid motion until she was straddling him, barely losing their rhythm. It was always easy for her to come this way, especially with him. She closed her eyes and braced her hands on his shoulders, waves of sensation mounting as she ground against him, his hands all over her—her breasts, her waist, clutching her hips so hard she was sure she'd wake up with eight finger-shaped bruises on her ass.

As she got close, her eyes fluttered open again and she caught a glimpse of his face, looking up at her with an expression that could only be described as reverence. She leaned over until they were chest to chest again, and he wrapped his arms around her and thrust up from underneath as she dragged her tongue up the side of his neck.

"God, I fucking missed you," he growled, and it was the crack in his voice, thick with emotion, that ultimately toppled her over the edge—and, okay, yes, maybe a few tears finally slipped out, too, but only because it sounded like he was on the verge of crying himself. Where her first orgasm was acute and intense, this one felt deep and shimmering and bottomless, her body practically vibrating in slow motion, at a secret frequency only he could access.

He rocked them up so they were both sitting upright, still holding her, stroking her back, planting featherlight kisses on her neck and shoulders. But before the last aftershock had even passed, he'd flipped her onto her back again, slinging both her legs over one shoulder, his strokes turning deep and relentless, his head falling back in unselfconscious ecstasy. She could tell he wouldn't last much longer, but it didn't stop electricity from starting to coil inside her lower belly again anyway, from the feel of him, the sight of him, the sounds that were coming out of both of them.

He slowed, his thrusts becoming jerky and unsteady. "Fuck. *Fuck*." He dropped his head forward, panting.

She reluctantly let him get up to deal with the condom, but he tumbled back onto the bed soon enough, collapsing into her arms.

Eventually, he raised his head to kiss her, and she ran her hands through his hair, damp from both the shower and sweat.

"Lilah?"

"Hmm?"

He rolled them over so they were on their sides facing each other, clutching their hands between their chests like they'd been arm wrestling. He brought his other thumb up to trace her cheekbone. She could tell by the look in his eyes what he was going to say before he said it.

"Would you believe me if I said I loved you now?"

Warmth bloomed in her chest, and she closed her eyes. "Yes."

"What about if I said I loved you before, too?"

"When?" Her voice was barely above a whisper.

"On New Year's Eve." She felt his lips press to her forehead. "In Vancouver." Her cheekbone. "When you walked through the door at upfronts." The tip of her nose. "In my trailer before you left." Her jaw. "When we got the tattoos." Her shoulder. "The first time I kissed you." Her neck. "When you forgot your lines at our first audition." Her lips again, at last.

She thought about fighting it, even now. Insisting that he couldn't possibly have loved her from the day he'd met her.

But it didn't matter, she realized. There was no satisfaction in being right about this—if it was even possible. That wasn't the point. The point was that he loved her now, and she knew it as surely as she knew her own name. The kind of love that cast a warm glow back through time, all the way to their first meeting, reframing the past through the lens of the present. Powerful enough to illuminate the protective shell she'd thought surrounded her heart, revealing that it wasn't a shell at all, but a cocoon. Her heart hadn't been calcifying, it had been biding its time, breaking down and rearranging on a molecular level until it was finally safe to burst free and reveal itself, trembling and brilliant and brand new.

She opened her eyes.

"I'd say, 'Me, too.'"

He broke into a grin, so wide and unrestrained it was almost childlike. "Told you I wouldn't forget."

"Yours was a lot better than mine."

"Yours was perfect." He stroked her hair. "But I think I might have been working on mine for longer."

"Well, it was worth the wait."

His smile faded slowly, his expression turning serious. "Was it, though?"

She bit her lip. "I think we needed it. We weren't ready for each other back then. We both had some growing up to do."

"Maybe *you* did," he muttered, but she could tell he was struggling to keep a straight face, especially as she giggled. He leaned forward and kissed her deeply, thoroughly. "Please tell me this was the last morning I'll have to wake up without you," he said quietly when he pulled away.

"Codependent much?" she teased, even though his words sent goosebumps of pleasure skating up her arms.

"We have a lot of lost time to make up for; I'd say we've earned a little codependency. But I won't tell Dr. Deena if you won't." He nudged her onto her side, fitting her back against his chest, and she sighed.

"Shane?" she murmured, already drifting off.

"Yeah?"

"Can you still fuck me like you hate me sometimes?"

He laughed, bringing his hand down to give her a sharp smack on the ass, followed by a soothing squeeze. "I'll try my best."

26

Considering how little sleep he actually got, Shane woke up surprisingly rested. His humiliation the night before was barely on his mind—not with Lilah curled up naked in his arms. If he'd had his way, they wouldn't have left that bed for another few days at the earliest. But they were due back on set on the other side of the country early the next morning, so moments after waking up, they were propped against the headboard, limbs still entangled, sorting out the logistics of the day ahead: packing up his room, grabbing Lilah's things from her hotel, trying to change their tickets to get on the same flight back to L.A.

Lilah's alarm blared relentlessly from somewhere in the outer room of the suite, so he dragged himself out of bed to dig their phones out of their discarded clothes. When he slid back under the covers and handed Lilah hers, he caught a glimpse of her screen, flooded with notifications, the Hags group chat right at the top (forty-seven unread messages). She looked at it and groaned, dropping her head back against the headboard with a clunk, which was his cue to lean over and nip at her exposed throat, unable to contain himself, overwhelmed that he could.

They didn't really have time to have sex again, but all it took was Lilah innocently asking what he wanted for breakfast, and before he knew it he was flat on his back, her thighs straddling his ears, her breath escaping in helpless gasps as she gripped the headboard. Once she came, he flipped her onto her stomach and slid into her from behind, sinking his teeth into her shoulder as he pinned her to the mattress.

After that, they *really* had to hurry.

Somehow, they made it to the airport with time to spare. As they waited at the counter to check his bag, he developed a gradual awareness of something that had slipped his mind in the mania of the past twenty-four hours.

He was comfortable with the level of fame he had now. He'd had years to get used to it, and it was nowhere near its most frenzied peaks—the first season of *Intangible,* his relationship with Serena. For the most part, he was able to live his life relatively unbothered, minus the awareness in the back of his mind that he might be photographed at any time. But he could handle a sneaky picture here, an approach from a fan there. He liked talking to fans, actually, because he liked talking to pretty much everyone.

But the level of attention they were getting as they made their way through the terminal almost felt like that first season again. People were openly pointing, taking pictures without even trying to hide it, giving him that caged-zoo-animal feeling

for the first time in years. It made sense: the two of them together were of much greater interest than either of them were
separately, even to people who didn't watch the show. After last
night, they were kind of asking for it.

He glanced over at Lilah, who was still wearing her sun-
glasses, her posture rigid, mouth set in a thin, humorless line. He
wanted to reach for her hand to reassure her, but he wasn't sure
if that would make things worse. She returned his glance and
smiled tightly, taking his hand herself, giving it a squeeze.

"It's okay," she said quietly. "We knew this was going to happen, right?"

Once they made it through security, they were able to escape
into the airline's VIP lounge. Shane hunted down some snacks
and coffee as Lilah scouted a secluded corner by the window.
When he returned, she was scrolling through her phone, a perturbed look on her face.

"You better not be reading about us," Shane said, settling
into the armchair next to her. She scrunched up her face guiltily.

"It's wild. Like, I knew people would care, but I didn't think
they'd care *this* much. Jasmine just sent me a fucking *New York
Times* thing about it." She turned off the screen and placed it
facedown on the table next to her, gratefully accepting the paper
cup of mixed nuts he offered her.

"It's just because it's new. I'm sure people will get over it in
a week."

She shrugged, but her gaze was distant. "Yeah."

He stretched his legs straight out in front of him, unscrewing
the cap of his water bottle. "Is it time for us to talk now?"

"About what?"

"You know." He waved his hand between them. "Us. The
future. We kind of just dove headfirst into everything."

The corner of her mouth twitched. It was possible she wasn't thinking about everything they'd literally dove into headfirst over the past twelve hours, but now *he* sure was. "Right. That would probably be the responsible thing to do."

"What about marriage?"

She raised an eyebrow. "Is that a proposal?"

"Trust me, if it was, you'd know. But it *has* been nine years, some might argue it's overdue."

He could tell she was fighting back a smile. "So, what? You just want my thoughts on the institution in general?"

He shrugged. "I don't want to assume. I could see you as the live-together-for-decades-without-ever-putting-a-ring-on-it type."

She settled back into her chair, casting her eyes to the ceiling as she thought about it. "I'm not against it. But I'm not taking your name."

He snorted. "I don't care about that. I'll take *your* name, who gives a fuck."

"Maybe we should just take each other's names. Like, fully switch. First, middle, and last."

"We can save that for when things quiet down and we really need some attention." He took a sip from his water bottle. "So, do I need to start looking into converting to Judaism?"

"Not unless you want to get in good with my grandparents. And they're all dead, so. That's gonna be an uphill battle already. What are you now? Catholic?"

"In theory. But I'm like you, I really only ever went to Mass with my grandparents."

"Of course you are," she said with a wry smile. "Catholic guys are always obsessed with me for some reason. Maybe they can sense we have that shared culture of guilt in common. Or maybe they just think I'm Irish."

"Well, all those other Catholic guys are gonna have to get in line."

"At least they're used to it."

He leaned in, his voice dropping low. "They're used to being on their knees, too."

She grinned, but he could see her cheeks redden. "Don't sound so excited. We're in public, remember."

"Get your mind out of the gutter. Maybe I'm still talking about proposing."

She laughed again, her blush deepening, her eyes meeting his with a warmth that made his stomach do a strange flip.

She loves me.

The thought popped into his head involuntarily, for what felt like the thousandth time since the previous night. It was still so hard to wrap his mind around that all he could do was repeat it over and over like a mantra.

Gradually, though, her smile faded.

"What about kids?" She glanced down as she said it, and he sensed her apprehension behind the studied casualness.

He leaned back, scrubbing his hand over his beard. "I don't know. I've never felt like it was my life's purpose to be a parent or anything. Or like something would be missing if I didn't. But I'm not against it, either. I kind of assumed it would depend on whoever I ended up with. Whether they wanted them or not."

He saw her shoulders relax. "Okay. Good. That's good." It was only when he heard the relief in her voice that he understood how nervous she'd been to hear his answer. "I think . . ." she continued. "I think it can be easier to want them if you're not the one who would have to give anything up."

He lay his palm upright on the arm of the chair, and after a moment, she set her hand over his.

"I'll never pressure you into anything you don't want to do. You know that, right?" he asked quietly. She didn't say anything for a moment, still looking into her lap. Finally, she looked up, her face sincere.

"I know."

The trust and gratitude packed into those two words hit his chest like a battering ram, practically cracking him open. He turned her hand over and kissed it before setting it back on the chair, still intertwined with his. "Well," he said. "Looks like we agree on the big stuff, at least."

"That's a relief. It would be pretty embarrassing if we went through all that bullshit for nine years just to break up after twelve hours." She was smiling again. "Any other concerns we should get out of the way now?"

"Just one. Are you gonna let me take you out on a real date, or what?"

Her smile grew wider. "Like, in public?"

"That's the idea. I don't know if you heard, but the cat's kind of out of the bag about us."

"Hmmm. I'll consider it." Her expression turned mischievous. "There's a lot of things I want to do to you in private first."

He grinned, too, leaning in to kiss her. When they pulled apart, though, she looked annoyed. He turned his head and followed her gaze, catching a glimpse of one of the lounge employees hurrying away, slipping her phone into her pocket. He glanced back at Lilah, who smirked humorlessly.

"Should we ask her to send it to us? Maybe we can start a scrapbook."

27

Even with the best of intentions, Shane and Lilah's new relationship quickly began to look a lot like their old one, the two of them rarely going anywhere other than the *Intangible* set and their houses. Not that either of them minded—their schedule was as exhausting as ever, plus they were ten years older. He wondered how it was possible to be so happy from doing so little, just because it was with her. That he could spend practically every waking minute with her, both on set and at home, and still feel like it wasn't enough.

He'd expected the general reaction to their relationship amongst their co-workers to be positive, but wary—a collective holding of breath, since they all knew what would happen if he and Lilah stopped getting along again. But to his surprise, everyone seemed to be genuinely, unreservedly happy for them. He knew they'd all bonded over the past several months, but this was the first time it truly struck him what a unified front they'd become.

Basking in the glow of their reignited flame was the perfect distraction from the uncomfortable truth that neither of them had any idea what the end of *Intangible* held for them. It seemed like every day they arrived at work to the news that someone else had found a new job: Margaux and Brian's spin-off was moving forward with a real pilot, Rafael had booked a supporting role in a superhero franchise, Natalie was joining the ensemble of a big-budget streaming sci-fi show.

In the short term, they discussed spending the summer traveling—meeting each other's families, knocking international cities off their respective bucket lists, renting a house in the woods or on a secluded island so they could really be alone. For the first time since he'd found out the show was ending, the prospect of the future filled him with more excitement than terror.

It was uncanny how natural it felt to stop thinking of his plans as singular, only concerning him, and open his life up to encompass the two of them as a unit without missing a beat. He'd never felt so in sync with a partner before—ironic, considering how at odds they'd been even a few months ago. But maybe that had been necessary, the friction sanding down the last edges that had prevented them from fitting together as seamlessly as they did now.

One night in early February, cuddling on Lilah's couch after work, she brought up the upcoming convention in March so offhandedly that Shane did a double take.

"What? You're going? Since when?"

She craned her head to look at him, confused. "I didn't tell you? Jasmine just confirmed with them this week."

He shook his head in disbelief. "And you're doing everything? The panel and the meet and greet and everything?"

"Do you not want me to?"

He pulled her closer, planting a soft kiss on her forehead. "Of course I want you to." She settled against him with a sigh, and he ran his fingers absentmindedly up and down the bare skin of her upper arm. "Are you nervous?" he murmured against her hair.

She hesitated, then nodded. "Yeah. I mean, I think you're right, that it'll be easier for me now. I'm just worried that people will be extra . . . intense. About us."

He was silent for a moment, his hand moving up to stroke her hair. A knot of anxiety tightened in his stomach—both for her fears and for the fact that they were well founded.

"Whatever happens, we can handle it."

She craned her head to look at him, a smile playing at the corners of her lips. He leaned in to kiss her, slowly, tenderly. He was still getting used to being able to kiss her like this, a kiss that had nothing to do with sex. A kiss that felt like a confession, a confirmation, an appreciation, all at once.

. . .

The week before they were set to leave for the convention, Shane grabbed a quick coffee with Dean during a break on set. They'd barely seen each other lately—Shane spent most of his nights at Lilah's, and even when he was at his own place, Dean was scarce.

There was a slight frisson of awkwardness between them as they placed their orders, Dean visibly distracted, answering Shane's questions with terse one- or two-word responses.

When Dean went to the bathroom, he left his phone sitting on the table. It buzzed and lit up, Shane's eye drawn to it automatically.

It wasn't like he was *trying* to snoop. But even upside down, he could read his own name in the text message preview.

RENATA: Have you told Shane yet?

Shane's heart skidded in his chest. He turned the phone toward him, rereading it right side up, just to be sure. But it still said the same thing. Immediately, he flashed back to the night before he'd left for Vancouver—how evasive Dean had been about who he was going to dinner with, how elusive he'd been since. Was it possible he'd taken his flirting with Renata to the next level?

He looked up to see Dean approaching the table, his brow already creased when he saw Shane with his phone.

"Are you sleeping with Renata?" Shane blurted out before he could stop himself.

Dean frowned even deeper, incredulous, as he snatched his phone out of Shane's hand and sat down again. "*What?* No, I'm . . . I'm her client now." He delivered the last part without looking at Shane, his defensiveness giving way to embarrassment.

Shane blinked. "You're her *client*? Since when?"

Dean shrugged, still avoiding his eyes, and sipped his coffee. "A few months."

"And you just weren't going to tell me?"

"I was waiting until I booked something." Dean shifted uncomfortably in his seat.

Shane realized his mouth was hanging open, so he forcibly shut it. "Why?"

"You mean, why didn't I tell you?" Dean raised his eyebrows sardonically. "Maybe because you were more willing to jump to the conclusion that I was banging her than working with her?"

Shane felt his face heat but didn't say anything. Dean continued. "And if you mean, why am I working with her . . ." He looked down into his cup. "Don't get me wrong, man. I'm grateful to you for bringing me out here, for setting me up with this gig all these years. But . . . you were right that day, even if you were a fucking asshole about it. I can't just keep following you around, being your shadow forever." He glanced back up, meeting Shane's eyes. "And I don't want to be your excuse, either."

Shane frowned. "My excuse?"

Dean smirked, shaking his head. "I know you. You'd take a job you hated just so you could bring me along. Not that I don't appreciate it, but I don't *need* it. Whatever you do next, I don't want you worrying about me to be a factor."

Shane's throat tightened. "Right." He took a sip of his coffee to stall for time, settling into this new reality. To his surprise, his annoyance had already begun to fade, replaced by something that felt a lot like pride. And only the slightest twinge of jealousy that Dean felt so optimistic about pursuing a future that Shane had never felt more ambivalent about. "So, what has she been sending you out for?"

Dean's face cleared, the last traces of apprehension dissipating. "Mostly commercials, so far. Some modeling stuff. Renata says I'd be great for unscripted, but she's still looking for the right fit. And I've been taking acting classes on the weekends. Improv, too."

"That's great," Shane said, with unforced enthusiasm. "I'm really happy for you."

"Yeah?"

"Yeah. I've never seen you get this excited about anything work-related."

Dean grinned. "Believe it or not, this is slightly more appealing than scooping ice cream at Braum's or standing around waiting for them to set up the lights for you." He raised an eyebrow. "But can your ego handle it?"

Shane laughed. "I think I'll survive."

28

In the weeks leading up to the convention, it was easy for Lilah not to dwell on it too much. She was too wrapped up in Shane, filming, Shane, hunting for her next job, and Shane. But before she knew it, they were boarding a flight to San Francisco, checking into their hotel, clutching their itineraries as they rode the elevator up to their suite in silence.

Their schedule wasn't too demanding—meeting fans and signing autographs in the morning, the panel in the afternoon, a party in their honor at night—but it was all crammed into a single day, rather than spread out over the weekend. She was preemptively exhausted by the emotional energy it would take to be *on* all day, meeting hundreds of fans, second-guessing everything she said, ensuring no one walked away disappointed while still protecting her own boundaries.

But, of course, now that she and Shane were together, she hadn't thought twice about agreeing to do it. She didn't want to be apart from him a minute longer than she had to. Plus, the fact that he would be by her side the whole time was enough to ease some of her nerves. She'd had an emergency session with her old therapist the week before, working through every possible worst-case scenario in excruciating detail, coming up with strategies to calm herself without resorting to drugs—but with a freshly refilled prescription of benzos in her purse just in case.

She slept fitfully, waking up long before her alarm, lying there wrapped in Shane's arms as he snored softly next to her. At breakfast, she was able to choke down some coffee and most of a banana before her stomach tightened like a fist. She pretended not to see Shane's worried expression as he watched her.

In the van on the way to the convention center, Lilah sat silently in the back as the rest of them chatted and joked around her. Shane joined in, but kept her hand tightly in his the whole time.

The building spanned what seemed like an entire block, with a capacity of hundreds of thousands—hordes of people in brightly colored wigs and costumes were buzzing around the outside. Even though they were brought in through a back entrance, the distant roar of activity on the main floor was already oppressive. Lilah toyed absently with the laminated badge around her neck as Raf and Brian discussed which panels they were hoping to sneak away to catch in between their own commitments.

Before leading them onto the floor, the convention staffer who'd been assigned to them gave them a rundown on the rules: They weren't obligated to sign anything they didn't want to.

They could take pictures and chat, but the priority was keeping the line moving. If they felt unsafe at any point, they should alert the security guard posted next to the table. Lilah's heart thudded beneath her collarbone, her eyes slipping out of focus as the door opened and she was swallowed whole by the noise of the crowd.

She'd expected the autograph table to be in its own room, but it was right in the center of the action, the roped-off lines of waiting fans practically indistinguishable from the masses of other passersby trying to shove their way through. The table was at least a dozen yards away from the door, and Lilah fought to keep her nervous system from getting overwhelmed at every step.

She could vaguely make out people screaming their names—*LilahKateShaneHarrison*—as an endless sea of phones pointed at her from all directions, but the only time her extra-wide smile faltered was when she felt someone yank on her arm. She whirled around, but whoever it was had already been absorbed back into the crush.

Once they were seated at the long table—Shane on one side of her, Natalie on the other—Lilah was able to relax a little, her smile turning genuine as she waved at the long line of fans beaming back at them. She leaned over to Shane, her lips by his ear.

"Is it always like this?" Her memories of the one and only time she'd done this were beyond hazy at this point, but this still seemed exponentially more intense.

He glanced out at the crowd. "Never," he murmured back, giving her forearm a quick squeeze.

"*KISS HER!*" someone yelled, and Lilah jerked away from him like she'd been tased. A cheer rose up from the crowd, a handful of others taking up the chant: "*Kiss HER! Kiss HER! Kiss HER!*"

Lilah's face burned as she fought to keep her expression neutral. Shane turned back to the crowd and shook his head, waving the request away with a self-deprecating smile—as always, knowing how to strike the perfect balance of firmly shutting it down without looking like an uptight asshole. Her heart ached with gratitude for him.

Once the signing got under way, though, Lilah found herself enjoying it. The majority of people who made their way through the line were sweet and respectful. She got genuinely choked up as one person after another gushed that *Intangible* was their comfort show, that bingeing it had gotten them through chemo, or divorce, or the first lonely weeks in a new city. That Kate had inspired them to be bolder and more outspoken and unafraid to chase what they wanted. That the show's exploration of the long tail of grief had helped them work through their own.

Still, there was no ignoring the fact that there were more than a few fans there whose interest in the show—and the two of them—bordered on extreme. She knew to brace herself for them because they would either give Natalie a death glare or ignore her completely en route to Lilah.

One fan turned their nose up at everyone else at the table, only to shove a homemade shirt in Lilah's face to sign. Her stomach dropped when she realized what was on it: "#KARRISONFOREVER" in big block letters, over a picture of the two of them kissing on *LNL*—as themselves, not their characters.

For a split second, she considered refusing to sign it. *But we asked for this,* she thought ruefully, flashing the fan a brilliant smile as she scribbled her autograph above her own head.

Toward the end of the hour, a woman in her late thirties dumped a pile of memorabilia spanning the entire run of the show in front of Lilah. As Lilah began to work her way through it, the woman crossed her arms, her gaze flicking back and forth between Lilah and Shane.

"I knew it the whole time," she said with a smirk.

"Knew what?" Lilah asked, barely looking up from the copy of the original pilot script she was autographing.

"That you've been married since the first season, and all your other relationships since then were faked to try to throw people off."

That got Lilah's attention. She looked up abruptly. "Excuse me?"

The woman pressed on. "Is it true you left the show because you were secretly having his baby? And that's why you didn't work for the next few years?"

Lilah gaped at the woman, lost for words. "Uh . . ."

The fan seemed to take her shock for confirmation. "Don't worry, I don't think most people figured it out. But you left so many clues, it was easy to put it all together once we started looking for them. I have this blog . . ."

Lilah buried her face back in the stack, signing the last few items as quickly as possible as the woman rambled on. "Thanks for watching," she mumbled, avoiding the fan's gaze as she pushed the pile over to Shane, who remained oblivious.

Once their time at the autograph table was up, Lilah skipped lunch in favor of taking a nap in their hotel room, the adrenaline leaving her body so fast that she passed out practically as soon as her head hit the pillow. She woke a few hours later to Shane's hand on her shoulder, gently coaxing her into consciousness.

"How are you doing?" he asked, his voice tender, his gaze even more so. "Did you grab something to eat?"

"I'm okay," she said, in response to both.

He nodded, though the look on his face was skeptical. "The panel's in an hour. I wasn't sure if you set an alarm."

"I did, but I must have slept through it." She stretched, making no attempt to get up yet. He slid his hand down her collarbone, resting on her stomach, bare from where her tank top had ridden up. He looked like he was about to say something, then bit it back, smiling to himself.

"What?" she asked.

He shook his head. "Nothing. Just . . . you can hardly tell you had my secret baby."

Lilah half laughed, half groaned, burying her face in the pillow. "She brought that up to you, too, huh?"

"Yep. Although she was mostly grilling me about how my relationship with Serena was all an elaborate cover-up."

Lilah sat up with a sigh, shaking off the head rush. "God. I hate that this has to be part of it. Of us being together. I know I should just brush it off, but . . . it's fucking weird, right? Doesn't it bother you?"

He shrugged, taking her hand, rubbing his other palm lightly over her knuckles. "It bothers me because it bothers you. Of course I think it's weird, but it's not really *about* us, you know? They don't actually know us. We shouldn't let it affect us."

"Yeah. You're right." She knew it didn't sound convincing. He let go of her hand so he could wrap his arm around her waist, drawing her closer to where he sat on the edge of the bed, and she rested her head on his shoulder.

"I'm sure this is the worst of it," he said. "It's still so new, plus the show ending, plus Kate and Harrison getting together at the same time . . . but I don't think things will be like this for much longer." He dropped a kiss to the crown of her head. "Besides, can you blame them? I've been obsessed with the idea of us for just about as long as they have."

He felt her smile against him. "So when can I see your blog?"

"Trust me, you don't want to. It's filthy. Unhinged. You'd never speak to me again."

She laughed and tilted her head to kiss him. "Save it for our vows, then."

. . .

Lilah's strategy for getting through the panel was simple: smile. Wear her Engaged Listener face. Nod affirmatively and laugh where appropriate. Say as little as possible unless asked a direct question.

So far, it seemed to be working. With seven of them up there—the six principals, plus Walt—there was always someone ready to jump in and respond so she didn't have to. When the moderator asked her what it had been like to return to the show, she recited the same rote response she'd been giving for months, though now it triggered a round of knowing chuckles from the audience when she mentioned how much she enjoyed working with the rest of the cast.

Shane, of course, was nailing it. Charming, funny, confident without dominating. It was all Lilah could do not to sit back and watch in admiration. Even when someone asked a question lightly poking fun at Shane's *LNL* episode, Shane didn't flinch. He threw his head back with genuine laughter before playing it off with the perfect self-deprecating joke.

As the moderator prepared to wrap it up, inviting one last audience member to ask a question, Lilah let out a long sigh of relief that she'd made it through without incident.

The man who stepped up to the microphone looked like he was in his early forties, with a scruffy brown ponytail and a beard to match.

"Randall Meyer. I write for *The Geek Sheet*. I was wondering if any of you could comment on the rumors that *Intangible* is getting a last-minute renewal for another two seasons?"

Shocked murmurs rippled through the crowd. Lilah briefly glanced around at the other cast members, who seemed as confused as she was, before her gaze shot straight to Walt. His brow was creased, his expression troubled, though that didn't necessarily mean anything.

He cleared his throat. Lilah waited for him to shut it down, to drop a few hints about the spin-off. Instead, he asked, "Where did you hear that?"

Her blood ran cold.

"I don't feel comfortable revealing my sources," Randall said with a smug grin. The chatter in the audience increased.

Lilah's eyes were trained on Walt, but it didn't seem like he was going to say anything else. She leaned forward to speak into her microphone. "We've worked very hard to give the show the perfect send-off this season. It's not easy for any of us to say goodbye, but I think everyone will be very satisfied with the ending."

Randall's gaze flicked to her, an unmistakable challenge in them. "But viewers have waited so long to see you two get together, and now the show is ending as soon as it happens. Isn't that kind of a tease? Don't you think you owe it to the fans to continue Kate and Harrison's story?"

"Actually, I don't think we owe the fans anything," Lilah said crisply, before she could stop herself. Out of the corner of her eye, she saw Shane flinch. "Sorry, I didn't mean it like that," she hedged, trying to recover, the crowd already buzzing with disapproval at her answer. She dropped her hands to her lap so no one could see how much they were shaking. "Of course we're very grateful to everyone who loves the show. But our first priority is always doing what's best for the characters and the story."

"Great answer," said the moderator hurriedly, sensing an opening. "Thank you, Randall. Let's give it up one more time for the cast of *Intangible!*"

They headed offstage to significantly less enthusiastic applause than they'd entered to. As soon as they made it into the empty greenroom, the six of them huddled around Walt, fizzing with nervous energy.

"Is it true?" Margaux asked immediately, wide-eyed.

Walt sighed. "Yes, it's true." They all began speaking at once, so he held up his hands. "It's true we've been *discussing* it. Nothing's set in stone yet."

"Why now? Why did they change their minds?" Shane asked.

With eerie synchronicity, Margaux, Natalie, Brian, Raf, and Walt all turned their heads to stare at Shane and Lilah. The two of them exchanged an uncomfortable glance.

No one needed to say anything. The answer was obvious.

"So who makes the final decision?" Lilah asked with trepidation.

Walt took off his glasses and rubbed his eyes. "Well, this isn't exactly how we wanted to break the news. But the network is extremely interested. Apparently the ratings these last few months have been . . . very persuasive." He cast a weary glance around at the rest of them before returning his gaze to Lilah and Shane. "You two are the only ones who aren't locked into your contracts yet if we decide to continue."

The implication settled over the rest of them instantly—the color draining from Natalie's face, Margaux and Brian looking at each other, stricken.

"And it has to be both of us?" Shane asked, his voice rising in pitch.

Walt nodded. "Both of you, or no deal."

The room was silent for a long, loaded moment, before everyone abruptly started talking again, splitting off into their own side conversations to process the news. Lilah grabbed Shane's arm and pulled him into a corner.

"You want to do it?" she asked, already sounding more agitated than she meant to.

"You don't?"

"Of course I don't. Why would I?"

"I don't know," he said, his gaze dropping to the ground. "I thought maybe with everything . . . with us . . ."

"The show isn't *us*. We don't need it for us to exist." She ran her fingers through her hair. "This is exactly what I was worried about, that there wouldn't be enough separation."

"But wouldn't it be kind of nice, though?" His voice was pleading. "Once we get other jobs, we'll barely see each other. We'd have the same schedule for two more years. That's a fucking luxury."

She leaned against the wall, suddenly exhausted. "Or we'll break up and go through all of this shit again, except worse."

His face went slack. "You think we're gonna break up?"

"No, of course not," she said hurriedly. "But . . . no one *thinks* they're gonna break up."

Even as she said it, she realized it wasn't true. In her other relationships, she'd almost immediately been all too aware of whatever incompatibility or shortcoming would eventually drive them apart. This round with Shane had been the exception— at least until now.

"What if it was just one more season, instead of two?" She

could tell from his resigned tone that he knew it was pointless to even ask.

She exhaled. "I don't want to do one more *episode* than I already have to, Shane. I'm done. I was done four years ago. It's time to move on."

"You still hate doing it this much? Now that things are good between us again?"

"That's not what it's about. I don't hate doing it, I'm just *bored*. I don't want to keep doing the same shit I've been doing since I was twenty-two. I'm running out of time."

He scoffed. "You're not *dying*."

"I'll be an actress pushing thirty-five, I might as well be," she said dryly.

"Very funny. You know, you're not the only one who's going to be affected by this decision." She was shocked at the sudden bitterness in his tone and fought to keep her own voice even, to not let herself be baited into losing her cool.

"Fine, you wanna play that game?" She held up her hand and began ticking off her fingers. "If we say yes, Margaux and Brian are stuck being our fucking sidekicks for another two years. Natalie won't get to do her show. Raf booked that superhero thing. Most of the crew is either going to the spin-off or has another job lined up already. Keeping it going just because you're afraid *you* can't do anything else would be more selfish than ending it."

His nostrils flared. "You don't have anything lined up yet, either. You're choosing *nothing* over two years of guaranteed work?"

"What happened to 'I'm not worried about you'? What happened to 'you're going to be fine'?" She dropped her eyes to the ground, taking a deep breath, trying in vain to calm her galloping heart. "What happened to 'I'll never pressure you into anything you don't want to do'?"

He didn't say anything for a moment, but she could hear him breathing, rapid and shallow. "*You'll* be fine. I won't. I can't give this up, Lilah, it's the only thing I can fucking do. You saw me on *LNL,* I'm not cut out for anything but Harrison."

The cracked, ragged edge to his voice drew her gaze back to him, and she took in the full picture of his agitation. His red face, his disheveled hair. He looked like he was on the verge of tears.

She was shaking uncontrollably again, her whole body this time, her heart pounding faster than ever. As she swayed in place, vision swirling, a cold sweat breaking out on her forehead, she realized too late she'd barely eaten anything all day, her plummeting blood sugar finally catching up with her.

And now she was having a fucking panic attack.

She slumped harder against the wall, covering her face with her hands, gasping for breath as her chest grew tighter and tighter, her legs jelly, her lungs locked in an iron grip.

No matter what, she was trapped. She'd be miserable if she chose the show. But if she chose herself, she'd lose Shane.

She dropped her hands and looked up at him in desperation. She didn't know what she was hoping to see. He was just staring at her, frozen, his face blank. Nausea swirled in the pit of her stomach as she suddenly understood.

This was where the line was drawn. He wasn't going to choose her, either.

A spontaneous sob burst out of her, loud and ragged, humiliating her even further.

"I have to . . . I can't," she choked, peeling herself off the wall and stumbling toward the door.

29

Nine years ago

As Lilah approached the hotel bar, she wasn't sure whether she was hoping he was there or hoping he wasn't.

They'd left things ambiguous: he'd wrapped her in a hug once they'd exited the stage after *Intangible*'s presentation, murmuring "Buy you a drink later?" in her ear. But if he'd meant at the UBS after-party, they'd barely had a moment to themselves, spending the whole night swarmed, shaking a never-ending supply of hands.

When she got back to her hotel room, she considered staying there. She was exhausted, her voice withered to a rasp from shouting over the music for hours. But though she eyed her bed, she found herself touching up her makeup, dabbing perfume behind her ear, smoothing out the wrinkles in the overpriced cocktail dress she'd been wearing all day. It wasn't that late yet, a quarter after midnight. Even if he wasn't there, she might as well have a drink on her own, decompress a little after the overwhelming day she'd had.

But when she rounded the corner and spotted Shane leaning against the bar, she knew she'd been lying to herself. If he hadn't been waiting there, she would've turned around, gone back to her room, and had her heels and dress off before the door even closed behind her.

He hadn't noticed her yet. He was facing the main entrance, obviously trying to play it cool, but giving himself away by glancing up anxiously every time someone passed. She tried to ignore the fluttering in her stomach she always got when she saw him, amplified by a hundred tonight.

She was just having a drink with a co-worker, that was all. *A co-worker you're way too attracted to, after midnight, at a hotel you're both staying at,* the you-should-know-better voice in her head whispered. She pushed it away, coming up behind him, placing her hand between his shoulder blades without thinking twice about it.

He'd changed out of his tux, into jeans and a T-shirt, the cotton warm under her palm. He looked at her, not bothering to hide his grin, sending one of her own spreading across her face in response, like he'd dropped a pebble into a pond.

"I thought maybe you were sick of me already," he said.

"Not yet. Although it feels like I barely saw you all day, is that weird?"

He shook his head. "No, I know what you mean. This whole thing has been fucking crazy."

The bar wasn't especially crowded, but it was light on seating, so she stood, too, her shoulder brushing his. The bartender came to take Lilah's order, and she hesitated. She'd only had one drink at the after-party, and her buzz had already worn off. White wine felt safe enough.

Once the bartender poured her glass, Shane lifted his whiskey, and she did the same.

"So, what should we toast to?" he asked.

Lilah looked down at the bar, then back at him. "Maybe just . . . the future?"

The corners of his eyes crinkled, her gaze dipping straight to his dimple.

"To the future. It's coming for us, no matter what."

She meant to take it slow, but that first glass was gone before she knew it, buoying her to the perfect level of tipsy—not enough to be impaired, just loose-limbed and playful, everything he said somehow the funniest thing she'd ever heard.

By the time she was halfway through her second glass, they were comparing childhood scars, which was mostly a transparent excuse to touch each other. She tried not to shiver when his fingers brushed over the raised line on her forearm where she'd gotten five stitches after being thrown from her bicycle. In return, she'd lightly tilted his chin up with her fingertips, feeling the mottled spot he'd busted open trying to cannonball into his friend's pool from their roof.

There were empty chairs on either side of them now, but they ignored them. He was close enough that she could smell the faintest hint of toothpaste on his breath, beneath the whiskey. *He brushed his teeth before this.* The thought sent a giddy thrill through her.

He'd hoped they would end up this close.

"So tell me, Lilah Hunter," he drawled, his vowels long and lazy, as he leaned even closer. "You got someone waiting for you at home?"

She took a long sip before she responded.

They probably should've discussed this already, but neither of them had been eager to bring up their personal lives while shooting the pilot. Now, though, she could admit to herself that it wasn't out of professionalism. She hadn't wanted to know.

She lowered her glass and shook her head. "I just got out of a longish relationship. Two and a half years, on and off. We broke up before I moved to L.A.; I didn't want to do the long-distance thing. He lives here, though—we're actually getting breakfast tomorrow before the flight."

"Oh yeah? And you're still holding a candle for him?"

"You mean carrying a torch?"

A self-deprecating smile played at the corners of his lips. "Shit. Holding a candle is, like, no one else can compare, right?"

"Right. Yeah. But no, no flames of any size anymore. We're just friends. Sort of. I do hate him a little bit. But I don't want to give him the satisfaction of knowing that. So . . . breakfast."

His eyes glittered with amusement. "Right. Of course."

"What about you?"

"Well, I don't know him, but I'm happy to hate him, too."

She laughed, nudging his shin with the toe of her shoe. "Come on."

He shook his head, his smile still teasing. "Same as you, nothing serious since I moved to L.A. Although maybe I should've locked someone down before all this happened. Now how will I know if anyone likes me for me, or because I'm a big fancy TV star?"

"You won't. But once you're drowning in pussy you probably won't care."

He snorted. "Now *there's* an image. What a way to go."

She fought to keep a straight face. "It's true, though. You should be glad you're single. It can be tough on a relationship, when one person starts getting a lot of attention. Hard to avoid all that temptation."

"That's not really the temptation I'm worried about," he said, almost to himself, then knocked back the rest of his drink. When he glanced at her again, though, the laughter was gone from his expression.

She knew she was blushing, her reaction hopefully hidden in the low light. She felt tongue-tied and awkward for the first time all night, so she turned back toward the bar, finishing her wine, too.

"It does kinda feel like we have something here, though, doesn't it?" he asked.

She held his gaze for a long moment, trying to figure out his angle, his expression infuriatingly blank.

"With the show, you mean," she said.

He nodded. "Yeah. Seems like it might actually go somewhere." He paused, his eyes flicking over her face. "I'm glad . . . I'm glad you're with me. That we're in this together. I heard it can be lonely at the top." The side of his mouth quirked up sardonically.

"It can be lonely no matter where you are." It slipped out more melancholy than she'd expected, and she bit her lip, self-conscious.

His brow creased a little, and he shifted his weight closer. "What about here?"

She shook her head slowly, her gaze never leaving his, unsure what the answer really was. Both felt true: no matter how much she was enjoying his company, she felt a strange, desperate ache expanding inside her the longer they stood there.

She leaned in, murmuring in his ear like they were sharing a secret. "I'm glad you're with me, too."

He pressed his hand to her lower back, sending an electric current shooting up her spine, hot and cold all at once.

"What do you think? Another round, or should we call it a night?"

It felt like they were on the verge of something—a wave cresting, lifting them high; it was still unclear whether they'd be able to ride it safely to shore, or whether they'd get pulled under, thrashed, bruised, barely escaping with their lives.

It thrilled her, that unknown. The potential in it. Her heart thundered in her chest, her skin prickling with heat.

They weren't done yet. They'd hardly even begun.

"I could do one more." She glanced over at the corner, where two plush armchairs sat angled toward each other across a small table. "Should we move over there? I think I need to get off my feet."

Something unreadable flickered in his expression. "Sure."

She smiled, nodding her head in the direction of the bathroom. "I'll be right back."

As she washed her hands, she let the cool water run over the inside of her wrists for an extra moment, locking eyes with her own reflection, trying to see what he saw. Blown-out pupils, pink cheeks, a look in her eyes verging on feral.

She looked like someone about to make a big, bad decision.

When she returned, he was sitting in one of the armchairs, both drinks on the table in front of him. She came up behind him, placing a hand on his shoulder, and he jerked at the contact.

He glanced up and they locked eyes, her stomach turning molten at the expression on his face, the same one she'd just seen reflected back at her in the mirror. The next thing she knew, his arm was around her waist, pulling her smoothly into his lap, her arms circling his neck automatically, legs dangling over the arm of the chair.

She wanted to laugh, but it died in her throat at the intensity of his gaze. He didn't kiss her right away, though. He just looked at her, brow slightly furrowed, eyes tracing her face like there was a secret message printed on her skin that he could only decode up close.

She reached up and cradled his jaw in one hand, his late-night stubble rough against her palm, and pressed her thumb gently into his dimple, almost without realizing she was doing it. He smiled, the corner of his mouth rising to meet her thumb, and leaned in, closing the gap between them at last.

It was gentle at first, the way he kissed her. More tender than she'd expected. She could tell how hard he was working to hold himself back, though, from the tension thrumming through his body, his ragged breath; a delicious kind of frustration coiled low in her abdomen as his lips teased, explored, savored, his spring-loaded restraint slowly driving her out of her mind.

"Fuck, you smell amazing," he murmured. "I just want to . . ." He turned his head, teeth grazing the edge of her jaw, stopping short of a bite.

She inhaled sharply, then pulled his face back to hers, sucking his bottom lip into her mouth before kissing him deeply, unable to take it any longer. He groaned low in the back of his throat when her tongue brushed his for the first time, one arm clutching her closer, his other hand tangling in her hair.

She melted into the warmth of his body, their kisses turning feverish and demanding, his hands teasing her now, stroking her bare arms and legs, splaying over her waist, touching her everywhere except where she really wanted. Soon, she was squirming in his lap without meaning to, his breath hitching every time she shifted against the bulge in his jeans, her thighs squeezing together, desperate for relief.

She couldn't remember the last time she'd gotten this worked up from just a kiss, like she might come from the slightest brush between her legs; but then, it wasn't just a kiss. It was the wait. The anticipation. The way his eyes had swept over her when she'd shown up at the bar, when he'd first seen her in this dress, when they'd sat across from each other in that audition waiting room.

Plus, he could *really* fucking kiss.

Eventually, he pulled back, resting his forehead against hers, his voice hoarse. "Jesus Christ."

"I'm Jewish," she muttered, her brain too scrambled to come up with anything else.

"Well, so was he."

She giggled, which turned into a whimper as he buried his face in her neck, his stubble scraping the sensitive skin before his lips soothed it, tasting her racing pulse with his tongue. She clung to him helplessly, finding his mouth again, her heartbeat staggering between their shared breaths. His hair was soft between her fingers, just long enough to hang on to, so she did, tightly.

There was no other way this night could have ended, she knew now. It might not go any further than this, making out like teenagers who had nowhere else to go. But it would. It had to. Every part of him she'd lingered over with her eyes felt even better under her palms, and she was feeling selfish, greedy. She wanted more. She wanted to own him. She wanted every hair, every scar, every inch of skin and ripple of muscle to be hers— even if it was just for tonight.

Out of the corner of her eye, she caught the tail end of a

couple of scandalized glances thrown their way, cutting through the haze just in time, yanking her out of the alternate reality where she was seconds away from literally sucking on his fingers in a public bar.

"Shit," she mumbled, hiding her face in his neck, her cheeks burning. "Do you think . . . there are a lot of other people staying in this hotel, right?"

His laugh rumbled against her, his palm skating down her back. "Seems like it, yeah."

"You know what I mean. Upfronts people. UBS people. Do they know it's us? Are they looking?"

"Some of them are looking. But I don't think they recognize us. I think we're just being . . ."

"Embarrassing?"

"Are you embarrassed?" His voice was low and husky in her ear.

She raised her head, then shook it, surprising herself.

"Do you want to stop?" he asked in that same tone, his hand firm on her upper thigh, rubbing his thumb in soft circles, sending tiny sparks shooting across her skin.

That one was easy. "I really, really don't."

"Good." She thought he'd kiss her again, but instead he just studied her face, reaching up to brush a piece of hair out of her eyes. "Did you know this was gonna happen?" he asked quietly.

"I had a feeling. Did you?"

"I didn't want to get my hopes up. But I really fucking wanted it to."

She took his hands in hers, intertwining their fingers, unsure whose were shaking.

"What else did you hope would happen tonight?" she asked.

He let out a deep, unsteady breath, shaking his head. "Nothing we can do in this chair without getting arrested."

She could get addicted to the way he was looking at her, if she wasn't careful. Let herself be fooled into thinking it meant something. That it was actually about *her* and not the thrill of the chase, the excitement of the unknown, the intoxicating blend of inevitable and wrong.

The whole thing felt bigger than the two of them, the only logical next step in the surreal situation they'd been thrown into. Even if the casting had shaken out differently, even if it hadn't been Lilah, she knew without a doubt he'd be down here any-way, in this same chair, some other Kate draped across his lap.

She looked down at their hands, then back up at him. The sour turn of her thoughts must have been written all over her face, because he was studying her with concern.

"Where'd you go?" he murmured.

She shook her head, brushing it off, trying to smile. "I'm right here."

She leaned in to kiss him one more time—a slow victory lap after a pulse-pounding sprint—then eased off his lap, grateful her legs were steady enough to hold her. She tugged him to his feet, too, leading him wordlessly toward the elevator, their drinks abandoned and untouched on the table.

She wasn't going to let her brain ruin this for her. There didn't have to be anything profound about this moment, no deeper connection than lust and loneliness. It didn't matter that it wouldn't ever go anywhere.

They were probably better off if it didn't, anyway.

30

Now

RIP—Relationship in Pieces!
Supernatural sweethearts Lilah Hunter
and Shane McCarthy give up the ghost!

Less than three months after *Intangible* stars Lilah Hunter and Shane McCarthy shocked the world with public confirmation of their long-rumored relationship, the pair has officially called it quits.

"They've always had chemistry, but at the end of the day, they're just too different," says a source close to the couple. "But they're committed to keeping their working relationship civil and ending the show on a positive note." Representatives for Hunter, 32, and McCarthy, 35, declined to comment, other than to confirm the split.

Hunter and McCarthy, who previously starred together on UBS's flagship drama for five years, have had their share of ups and downs since Hunter's highly publicized return for the ninth and final season. Between a racy photo shoot cut short, guest director Jonah Dempsey quitting mid-episode amid rumors of an on-set brawl, and their spontaneous kiss during McCarthy's stint hosting *Late Night Live* in January, the pair's behind-the-scenes antics have kept *Intangible* in the headlines—and on top of the ratings. However, their breakup should effectively squash the whispers that the it-couple status of its stars meant *Intangible,* whose series finale airs May 18, might be in for a last-minute resurrection.

. . .

For the final *Intangible* wrap party, they'd booked the ballroom of the same hotel where Shane and Lilah had shot their *Reel* cover. It must have been a coincidence, but as Shane made his way through the lobby, he couldn't shake the eerie feeling of déjà vu that settled over him.

He'd come alone, of course. Dean hadn't been able to make it: though it was still under wraps to the general public, he'd just been officially cast as the first bisexual *Bachelor.* The producers had already whisked him back to Oklahoma to shoot promotional B-roll of him "at home," conveniently obscuring the fact that he'd lived in Los Angeles for almost ten years. Shane was both thrilled for his brother and extremely grateful that he wasn't in his shoes.

He could've found a date, but as he nursed his whiskey and looked out at the room, he was glad not to have a relative stranger at his side tonight. That wasn't what this was about: it was about saying goodbye. He knew it was borderline toxic to think of a workplace as a family, but as he slowly made his way through the crowd of familiar faces—most of whom he'd known for close to a decade—it was hard to get the word out of his mind. He felt like he'd talked to every person in that room over the course of the evening.

Well, every person except one.

Spirits were high: they'd just gotten the news that Rosie and Ryder's spin-off, *Invincible,* had been officially picked up for a full season a few weeks earlier. Shane bumped into Polly, congratulating her on her new showrunning gig, but she was already so drunk and giggly that he was sure she wouldn't remember a thing.

Late in the evening, he saw Walt by the bar, and he gave Shane a gruff hug—the first time Shane could ever recall hugging him. When they separated, Walt clapped him on the shoulder.

"Thank you, Shane. For all your work over the years." He raised his glass. "The end of a fucking era, right?"

"Right." Shane clinked their glasses before taking a sip. "Have you figured out what you're doing next?"

"Nothing for a while, thank god. Lance has been trying to get me to go to Peru, stay in one of those transparent pods on the side of a mountain. You heard of these? Supposed to be incredible."

Shane cracked a smile. He hadn't seen Walt look this happy the entire time he'd known him.

"No, I haven't. That sounds nice."

"What about you? Have you booked anything?"

"Actually . . ." Shane looked down into his drink. "Actually, I think I'm going to take a little break. Go back to school."

Walt blinked. "To *school*?"

"Yeah. I'm starting classes in the fall. Psychology. I'm sure they just accepted me for the novelty, but, hey, whatever it takes."

"No shit." Walt shook his head in disbelief. "The thirty-six-year-old freshman. I bet you could pitch that as a reality show, if you wanted."

Shane laughed. "I don't know about that. I think I'm ready to live my life off-camera for now. Besides, I'm doing all my gen eds online, so I won't be on campus for a while anyway."

"Oh really?"

"Yeah, in case I want to get out of L.A."

Walt raised his eyebrows. "Anywhere in mind?"

Shane shrugged. "No, just . . . in theory." He took a long swig of his beer.

Walt looked him over appraisingly. "You know, I'm happy for you. I never would've called it, but I think that might be just what you need."

"Thanks, Walt. Me, too."

It was then that he heard it: Lilah's laugh, cutting through the room, as clearly as if she were standing next to him. He couldn't stop his head from whipping around automatically, his stomach lurching when he saw her, absorbed in conversation with Margaux and Natalie.

He looked back at Walt, whose brow creased in concern. "I really was sorry to hear about you two," Walt said. "But I appreciate that you were able to keep it separate. Not bring it to set."

Shane forced himself to smile. "You mean, for once?"

Walt grinned. "You said it, not me."

Shane turned around again, only to find this time that Lilah was staring right at him. She looked away again, her expression inscrutable. "Yeah. Me and Lilah . . . we're good. It just wasn't right." He turned back to Walt. "I'm sorry about the show, though. That we couldn't continue."

Walt shrugged. "I told the network it was a bad idea to base their long-term decisions on your relationship—no offense—but all they've ever seen when they look at the two of you are dollar signs. But I'm not sure how much more we could've squeezed out of it once you were together, anyway. Kate and Harrison, I mean. Nine years is a hell of a run."

"Right." Shane sipped his beer. "Probably best to go out on top."

"I guess that's what you're doing, too, huh?"

"That's the idea."

"And who knows? Since you two are on good terms, maybe they'll get you back together for one of those recap podcasts in a few years."

Shane laughed. "Let's not get ahead of ourselves."

Walt drained his drink, setting it on a side table. "I should probably go congratulate her before I forget. I'll tell her you send your regards." Shane thought he saw a conspiratorial twinkle in Walt's eye before he excused himself to go talk to Lilah.

The news had broken between the time they'd wrapped and the party: Lilah had booked a starring role in a prestige miniseries adaptation of *Macbeth* set in the corporate world, scheduled to start shooting in New York in the fall.

He leaned against the wall, watching Walt approach her, only looking away once she caught him staring again.

When the party was down to the last stragglers, Shane slipped out, taking the elevator to the top floor. He made his way down the empty hallway, hand in his pocket, fingering the key that had been burning a hole there all night. When he reached the door to the suite at the end, he hesitated before inserting the key into the lock, glancing back over his shoulder one last time to make sure no one saw him.

"You're in trouble," he called to the empty living room, shutting the door behind him and kicking off his shoes.

Lilah appeared in the bedroom doorway, eyes wide with panic. "What? Why? Did somebody say something? Do they know?"

"Not that." He stalked toward her. Her eyelids fluttered in anticipation as he reached her, but instead of pulling her into his arms, he crouched down, wrapped his arms around her thighs, and threw her over his shoulder with a grunt. She shrieked in surprise, and he had to bite the inside of his cheek to keep from laughing as he carried her back into the bedroom.

"I'm talking about these," he said, running one hand up the seam of her stockings, past the stretch of thigh bared at the top, grabbing a rough handful of her ass. "You think it's funny to show up dressed like this, parading around in front of me all night when you know I can't do a damn thing about it? When I shouldn't even be looking at you?"

"Kinda?" He couldn't see her face, but her voice was breathy in a way he knew was half-amused, half-turned on.

He reached the bed and tossed her down with a soft thump. She grinned, stretching out like a cat, the hem of her dress riding up high enough to flash the garters clipped to the tops of her stockings. Her dress was short but loose, high at the neck, practically a tent, not revealing whatsoever—but as soon as he'd walked into the party and seen the stockings, he'd known what it meant, his mind racing all night about the possibilities of what else she might be wearing underneath it. A secret message just for him.

He felt overheated all of a sudden, stripping off his suit jacket and loosening his tie without taking his eyes off her.

He stood there for a moment, taking her in.

It wasn't so much about how she looked, though that didn't hurt. The teasing silhouette of her body under the pooled fabric of her dress, the pristine—for now—crimson slash of her lipstick, color high in her cheeks, hair spread out like a cloud behind her head.

It was how she was looking at *him*. Soft and open and tender, hungry and satisfied all at once. Better than any fantasy he ever could've conjured on his own, because she was real, she was her, and she was his.

He must have paused for too long, because she propped herself up on her elbows. "What?"

"Nothing." He shook his head. "I'm just really fucking lucky."

The corners of her mouth curled up. "It isn't luck."

"No," he said, pulling his tie off completely before unbuttoning his cuffs and rolling up his sleeves, her eyes tracking his progress. "I guess it isn't."

It may have been luck that brought them together initially—luck, fate, chance, whatever they wanted to call it—but it wasn't why they were together now.

It was the work they'd done over the past nine years to finally be ready for each other. It was waking up and choosing each other every day: facing the world as one indivisible, united front, no matter the obstacle.

It was love.

Back in San Francisco, in the greenroom after the panel, he'd come dangerously close to losing it—losing her. He wasn't proud of it. He'd been in a state of shock, fear clouding his ability to think straight. It had taken the sight of her breaking down and bolting out of the room to snap him out of it. Even months later, he was still ashamed of not getting his shit together as soon as he'd seen the look on her face after Walt had confirmed the news.

But all that mattered was that this time—*this* time—he'd gone after her.

She wasn't in the hallway, which meant she hadn't made it

far. He'd tried the door to the supply closet to his right, finding it unlocked—and Lilah huddled on the floor, sobbing, illuminated by the bare bulb swinging gently above her.

He'd pulled her to her feet and straight into his arms, the two of them clinging wordlessly to each other for a long time, Shane shedding a few tears himself before either of them was calm enough to speak.

"I'm so sorry," he'd murmured into her hair.

She hiccuped, her voice thick with tears. "No, *I'm* sorry. I'm so embarrassed, this hasn't happened to me in forever. I hate my fucking brain sometimes."

"Don't be embarrassed. I love your fucking brain all the time." She pulled away enough to look at him, her face bright red, her eyes still shining with tears, and he fought back a smile. "Glad to see you took my note about the snot for this one," he teased gently.

She barked out a surprised, genuine laugh as he offered her his sleeve to wipe her face. She blinked up at him, suddenly earnest again. "But what are we going to do about the show, though?"

He pressed his forehead to hers. "Lilah. You are the love of my life. You made me believe in the *concept* of having a love of my life. Fuck the show. All I need is you."

She'd started crying again, only stopping once his mouth found hers and stayed there. They probably would have kept hiding in that closet for hours if they hadn't nearly given an unsuspecting custodian a heart attack a few minutes later.

As it turned out, he'd been correct in ways he hadn't anticipated. It had been Lilah's idea that he go back to school, suggesting it out of the blue while she was helping him prep for yet another audition he couldn't have been less excited about. They'd tossed the sides in the recycling bin, Shane laying his head in her lap as they'd talked through his options. In a way, pursuing psychology was like an extension of the things he enjoyed the most about acting (and bartending, for that matter): listening, connecting, trying his best to understand other people, helping them understand themselves.

It was hard to predict exactly what the future would hold. For now, his schedule had enough flexibility for him to travel to wherever she was, and she could pick and choose her projects around him. But even if that changed down the line, he knew they would find a way to make it work, because there was no other choice. He'd lost her once—almost twice—and that was more than enough for one lifetime.

It had been her idea to fake the breakup, too. He'd wanted to tell the network outright that they didn't want to do it, testing out the fearless assertiveness he'd learned from her—but she'd persuaded him otherwise. This way, they'd have the added bonus of taking some of the unbearable public scrutiny off them—at least for a while.

They'd have to go public again, sooner or later. They were too old to keep sneaking around like delinquent teenagers. He wasn't worried about that, though. Now that the show was officially over, interest in them would wane soon enough. In a way, he was even looking forward to it: he could finally gloat in front of the world that, somewhere along the way, he'd done something right, to earn the love of someone so brilliant and beautiful and complicated and strange—someone he both understood completely and was surprised by every day. The woman he'd carried a torch for for almost ten years, whom no one else could hold a candle to.

But for now, he could still be selfish. Enjoy having her all to himself.

He eased himself onto the bed, one knee at a time, slowly

pushing the hem of her dress up her thighs as she reclined again. "Maybe 'grateful' is the word I'm looking for," he murmured.

" 'Blessed'?" Her voice went breathy again.

"That, too."

"Show me."

Every subsequent inch of her that he uncovered had his pulse pounding harder in his ears. But when he reached her waist, he stopped short, sitting back on his heels.

The spot on her other hip that had been bare and unmarked when he'd left her bed that morning was taped with a small square of black plastic wrap.

His jaw went slack. "Is that what I think it is?"

"Could be." She half shrugged, her coy tone at odds with the unrestrained grin spreading across her face at his reaction.

All he could do was gape at her.

"Wow, speechless already," she teased. "Guess I didn't need to bother with all of this, then." She arched her back, pulling her dress over her head, and his blood evacuated his brain so quickly that black spots danced in front of his eyes.

"Whoa, whoa, whoa. Let's not go that far," he said once he was able to, his voice an octave lower than it had been a moment ago and twice as husky. "I just didn't realize we were that serious."

She threw back her head and laughed, a laugh that started in her chest and rippled through her whole body. He would live inside that laugh if he could, sustain himself forever on it.

He brought his hands to her ankles and slowly slid them up her nylon-clad legs, her smooth skin, brushing over the plastic wrap as he made his way up her body.

"You'll have to be careful," she said quietly, and he knew she wasn't just talking about the fresh tattoo. She was talking about herself.

Her heart. Her trust. Her loyalty. Access to her softest side, to all of her. The privilege to build the rest of his life by her side, his fate permanently intertwined with hers, wherever it led. None of it easily won or given, or to be taken for granted.

He moved up the bed until his face was even with hers, bending down to kiss her.

"Always."

ACKNOWLEDGMENTS

While the writing process for *How to Fake It in Hollywood* was much, much, *much* easier than this one, it was also much lonelier. I could never have gotten this book across the finish line without the support of the following people:

Jess and Claire: Thank you for continuing to be the best partners on this journey I could ever ask for. I would be completely lost without you, in so many ways.

Shauna: Thank you for believing in this book, and for always pushing me to take it to the next level. Even though it didn't come easily, it has been a joy to watch it reach its full potential under your expert guidance.

The Ballantine team: Mae, Taylor, Melissa, Corina, Kara W., Jennifer, Kara C., Kim, Erin, Andy, Jenna, Debbie, Saige, Elena. I know I only see the tip of the iceberg of the work you do to bring each book into the world, and I am incredibly grateful for everything you've done for both of mine.

Sarah: Thank you for creating the perfect cover for Lilah and Shane's story.

I am so thankful to have found a community of writers to help navigate this bizarre industry together. Your friendship means more to me than I could ever express here. Ray: Thank you for loving Shane and LILAH from that first terrible draft through the countless rewrites and additions since. I couldn't have survived it without you. Mazey: Thank you for alternately showering me with compliments and threatening me with violence to get me through my revisions. It worked! Victoria: Thank you, as always, for your taste, insight, and brilliance. Grace: Thank you for answering all of my dumb and extremely specific questions about the minutiae of TV production, and I'm sorry for all the places I ignored it for my own convenience. Kaitlyn, Courtney, Karina, GennaRose: Thank you for being there to celebrate, commiserate, and laugh so we don't cry. Lillie, Rachel, Elena, and Sarah: Thank you for your generosity and kind words about *How to Fake It;* it truly means the world to me. (I am especially stressed about leaving anyone out of this section, but if you're an author and we've ever interacted, I'm grateful for you!)

The readers who embraced and shared their love for *How to Fake It:* Thank you, thank you, thank you. Putting anything creative into the world on such a large scale is an intensely vulnerable (and scary) experience, but it's worth it because of you.

Walker: Thank you for being the reason I write about love.

ABOUT THE AUTHOR

AVA WILDER is the author of *How to Fake It in Hollywood*. She lives in Oklahoma City with her husband and their toothless cat.

ava-wilder.com
@avawilderwrites